COMMUTER COLLECTION:
SHORT STORIES FROM THE EDGE

J.P. OSTERMAN

J.P. OSTERMAN

COMMUTER COLLECTION:
SHORT STORIES FROM THE EDGE
COPYRIGHT © 2015 J.P. OSTERMAN
All rights reserved.

This book is a work of fiction. Names, characters, places and incidents are either the product of the author's imagination or are used fictitiously and any resemblance to actual persons, living or dead, business establishments, events, or locales is entirely coincidental.

Published by: ITM Press

ISBN-10: 0692395946
ISBN-13: 978-0-692-39594-3
Completely new edition copyright © March, 2015
Second Edition copyright © October, 2015
Printed in the United States of America

Cover Photo: © pio3 | Shutterstock

ITM
Press

DEDICATION

For my granddaughter, Rachel Marie Brown,
precious in this world.

ACKNOWLEDGMENTS

I want to thank my fifth grade teacher, Sister Rose, who encouraged me at St. Joseph's Elementary School. I also want to thank the late Dr. Joanne Dempsey, Professor of English at the University of San Diego for giving me a thirst for Greek drama and Shakespearean literature. For encouraging me in Texas, I thank Ben Johnson, a friend in the Licensed Professional Counseling (LPC) program at Texas State University; and Dr. John Garcia, Professor in the LPC program at Texas State University. In Florida, I thank my fellow Space Coast Writers' Guild members, and the Brevard Scribblers. I also thank my friends Debbie Sanchez and Chaplain Marjorie Shaffer for their encouragements. Most of all, I thank Drew, Andrew, Jennifer Brown, and Keith Brown for their encouragements, *and* tolerance. Thanks, especially to Drew for formatting *all* my book covers.

CONTENTS

CORRIDORS

PART I
YOU'RE FIRED

"The electric bill, $162.53, groceries $150 a week. I have *no* job ... and we're stuck in this *dinky* apartment." After twenty more minutes of flipping checkbook pages, and seeing my name, *Rae Anne Westman*, under my husband's name, *Tim Westman*, I did some more number crunching on the calculator. Then I stopped, breathed, and began stared out the window. There had to be *something* to be grateful for because making this month's rent is gonna be tight.

For the past two days a large rare colony of monarch butterflies had been migrating from Mexico to Canada, fluttering through Carlsbad, reshaping the air to a speckled tapestry of orange and gold. I had to be thankful for this, after all, not everyone has a chance to look straight into the sky, to stand outside on a balcony with their hands in the air and say out loud without caring who hears: "God, it's great to be alive!" A butterfly danced on my fingers, and I whispered, "Please, time, stop, just once." And I breathed.

Ring, the Panasonic sang.

It's gonna wake up the baby! I raced into the kitchen. Who the heck could be calling *me*? We had just moved to Carlsbad, I had no friends, and the creditors weren't calling, yet. It had to be Tim, telling me about his day, but he wasn't supposed to call until after lunch.

"Hello?" I answered. Through the pause, I checked the caller ID. "Tim, what's going on?" The steady silence sent a rippling scare through me.

"I'm coming home. I've been fired, Rae," he said.

I tried to picture his face as his words cycled through my brain, but I was too stunned and my stomach began churning like a gurgling drain.

"What happened?!" I asked. The checkbook was right in front of me, enlarging.

"He fired me for doing my job, Rae Anne. *That's* what happened," he answered.

I tried remembering how he looked this morning before he walked out the door, but all I could recall was his face on the day we moved in here, and jokingly telling him," Tim, no matter how hard you try...even though you look like Robert Redford and could pass as his double in a movie, please *never* again try to do an imitation of him 'cause you sound so darn bad!" He laughed too! Suddenly, I saw us *never* laughing again.

I slid into a chair, but found myself on the floor between the table and the toppled canary cage. "Tim, you had to do something! No one fires someone for doing their job. That's plain crazy!"

"It *wasn't* my *fault*, Rae," he said, and then he kept talking.

But I couldn't hear him. If he were home, I think I woulda lost it: screamed, cried, drank, and then stood on the balcony rail, wanting to dive over it. But we have two children, and I have to think of them, and hold myself together. Still, we had moved—uprooted ourselves and teenage daughter—*seven* times in the last *twelve* years. We had bought homes, lost homes, went bankrupt once, and were now finally inching our way back up the financial ladder. We had high hopes for Tim at his V.P. marketing job with Riata Technology. Now dashed, like the few dead butterflies that had lost their bearings and crashed into the patio window.

"The bills! What about food, Tim?" Everything in the kitchen turned white through the spots in my eyes. "Next to being diagnosed with breast cancer three years ago, this is the worst news ever." I felt my eyes stinging through tears. "What happened?"

I heard his deep sigh of helplessness. "Remember when I talked at a meeting about selling five millions dollars of imaging sensors?" He had his voice at a whisper.

"Yeah." As always, Tim had a structured way of reiterating facts, and I tried hard to keep them all straight.

He grew even quieter. "Steve Lerrefeiht, the CEO, now says the new line of chips won't be ready until *next* year, even though he told us all they would be out of manufacturing in *two* months. I've already booked the orders!"

"My gosh! I think that's pretty good considering you've only worked there for a little over three months, Tim."

"Yeah ... *now* you're getting it." He coughs, an

3

obvious gesture to disguise his words from someone talking outside his door. "That means I have to cancel all those orders, and Steve and the others in management will have egg on their faces. So he says he needs to cut my position to make up for the lack of product and sales."

"What a scoundrel. He tells you a product's ready, you go and sell it and bring in millions, and then he fires you!" I could hear more noises in the background. Tim must have to pack up his things to leave soon.

"Steve says the orders *I* booked will put the company in the red."

"But he's canceling the order, Tim." All the logic sounded circular, like a palindrome! "It sounds like he, or maybe more people in upper management, just wanted an excuse to get rid of you. What do you think?" Silence. "This *just* doesn't make sense! Something strange, and illegal, is happening at Riata, and the big shots are keeping *whatever* they're doing a secret." I clenched the edge of the table while trying to hear and understand his *every* word.

"I think Riata has been borrowing from investors, telling them they're making a profit," he whispered quickly.

"Tim, *that's* fraud." I had every mind to speed right down the I-5 Freeway; and with the baby in tow, march into Mr. Steve Lerrefeiht's office, smack him in the face, and then give him a rage-full of my mind.

"Of course what he's doing is illegal. But I can't prove it, Rae. Besides, corporations can fire anyone they want…and any time they want. They don't need a reason." He sniffled, and I knew it wasn't because of an allergy.

"If that's what Steve's doing, it is fraud all right, Rae.

But he can do what he wants. He's the CEO." Tim never articulated much emotion, but through one breath he said what he had always said before: "I'll look for a job when I get home."

"What are we going to do, Tim? What!" He said nothing through the sounds of a door opening and closing, and people talking around him. Meanwhile, I cursed Steve Lerrefeiht as I remembered scenes from horror movies. "If I could, I'd cut *him*, and your boss Claude Filmer from limb-to-limb!" How Claude Filmer ever became V. P. of Engineering, even Tim couldn't guess! From what Tim said, Filmer never says a word at meetings, but just stares at people, analyzing them like a ferret in search of new objects to dig into and explore. "I could just *gut* Kent Smith, that other manager there…and drown Thornton Manning, that Technology guru who always boasts about his Harvard degrees! If I could have my way right now, I leave 'em all bloating, insect infested, and graying on a beach, Tim!" When another butterfly smacked against the glass door and its guts splattered, I stopped and gasped.

"Stop it, Rae," Tim yelled. "Rae, you're wasting energy on people who don't matter. You're getting depressed again. Did you take your medicine?"

I hate it when he uses that tactic on me. He's treating me like a baby. So I lied. "Yeah."

"You need to take it every day, Rae," he says, his voice low and serious. "And if this medicine isn't working, you need to see a doctor—"

"I know. And get a new medicine. I was fed up with the treatment now and sick of him changing the subject. Then I remembered a source of money. "Tim, what about the stocks Steve gave you?"

"Gone."

"No!" Another image came to mind, paralyzing me. A concrete foundation with pipes and two-by-fours. "We have sixty-five thousand dollars invested in that house! We're going to lose everything!"

"Rae. I have an idea."

A pause ensued like the one after he had asked me to marry him.

I laughed. "Remember your *last* idea?"

"Do you have to put me down constantly? Do you—"

"*You* moved us here." My heart began pounding, my face flushing with heat. "*You* promised we wouldn't have to move again. You said we'd build a house. What's going to happen *now*?" I wanted to slam the phone down, cut him off, and make him pay for the past. "This is the *fifth* job you've lost and *blamed* someone else. We've moved *seven* times! I can't take it anymore!" I wanted to say, I quit, and I'm leaving. I don't. My children's faces flash through my mind.

"Let *me* talk, Rae," he shouted. "You keep interrupting me! That's *your* problem."

A possibility crossed my mind. "How about calling a lawyer?" I see the phone book and pull it off the shelf.

"*Mmmmm*, I want to see if I can find another job first. I have two weeks' worth of severance pay. Besides, when Steve hired me, I now remember signing his *at will* termination policy. I can't sue him for just letting him go...and I don't have any evidence of fraud."

"Oh yeah," I said, sitting down, slumping in the kitchen chair, and slamming the phone book. "I remember seeing that paper among others in the contract. Damn!"

"Prosecuting him will be tough, Rae. And I won't get my job back."

"Sue him for breach of contract then." I had a

successful counterattack. "Steve promised *in writing* to pay our rent until the completion of our house. And our storage unit! He promised to pay for the move, closing costs, storing our furniture—" I feel faint, my legs numbing under me.

"Rae!" he shouts.

Wiping my eyes, I gasp through a revelation. "From the beginning, Tim, this job was too good to be true. It's as if Steve showered you with everything you wanted to hear and with every perk you asked for…only now to make you look like a rotten egg to all his customers."

Tim took more time than usual to answer. "Whatever, he let me go, and I have a lady from human resources at the door who wants in and wants to check in all my technology."

"He didn't just let you go, Tim, Steve *fired* you."

"You're right, Rae." He sounded beaten, with failure in his words. "He fired my ass! There, I said it. Gotta go."

"Bye—"

PART II
THE VOICE WITHIN

After he hung up on me, I smelled a scent I hadn't smelled before. The odor reeked under my arm pits like I'd sealed the spots on my blouse with a hot iron. I never realized I could perspire that way!

Outside, it began to drizzle. A few butterflies began dropping out of the air. Then came the hard rain. Soaked orange wings slapped against branches, and black bodies broke around twigs. Some wiggling bodies tried clinging to life in a frenzy of useless flapping. Some fell in bullets from the gray-black sky. Orange and white wings flailing against the grain of bombarding thunder and cracking lightning appeared as a scene out of a medieval manuscript where God cast out rebel angels from Heaven. Most butterflies that hadn't arrived north by now have lost their corridor of safety.

I imagined the ruin of my family, especially Carolyn and Joey. I pictured the terrible outcome. We'd lose everything, and I couldn't do a damn thing to stop it. Carolyn, fourteen, had just started middle school. This was her third school in two years. Now she was popular; and so much so, that she rushed to the car every afternoon to tell me about her day. And Joey liked Rainbow Preschool. This was *his* third school, but he was thriving.

My stomach began churning on a wheel of injustice when I realized that Steve Lerrefeiht was getting away with a sort of murder. Everyone appeared to cower in his path, but not me. Running my fingers through my hair and drinking some cold water, I remembered sessions with my doctor, and strained to recall everything he had said in our therapy session, but the words were like seeds falling on hot pavement. I did recall one word, "solution."

I stared at the phone until my eyes burned. I could phone Steve Lerrefeiht, but common sense intervened. He might not be the only executive lying to investors at Riata. "But how? How can I prove that?" I asked myself in the mirror.

I felt more defeated than ever, until I imagined me wearing a Riata pin! I could see the insignia like a bad hallucination on the lapel of my blue blazer. "Could I? Naw," I answered the shock-faced woman staring me back in the mirror. I rubbed my forehead. "Gosh, I need to wash my hair too 'cause it looks like dish-water blond paste." I turned from side to side. "And I have to start putting on a little make up. I've just let myself go here *way* too much for *way* too long o' time. I look two years older than forty! And turning forty was bad enough!" Still, the more I tried not to focus on my 'round the house stained clothes, the more I began conjuring imagines of myself dressed once more in a business suit! "If you'd change a bit ... just do three or four little things to look presentable," I told the teary-eyed woman in the mirror, "you *could* get a job at Riata."

My mind was pummeling me with negative self-talk. "No way! Are you insane to think you could pull off something as crazy as infiltrating that corporation?!"

I guzzled down some water. "I have to do something," I answered the angry sulking woman in the mirror who felt trapped, and like a mere pawn in life. "Think of what the therapist said, 'solution.' Think *solution*, Rae Anne. It's the *only* way we're ever going to discover what *really* happened to Tim. He's been laid off, actually fired, five times, but he blames *everyone* else! Do you believe him?" I waited for a reply…from myself I know, but intuition was telling me no. No, I've never believed him when he told me he'd done nothing to get himself fired, *five* times. "So let's find out the truth, instead of *him* accusing *me* of having a far-fetched imagination, and then threatening me with doctors, hospitals, or a new medication. That's bull!"

I was right. I *could* do something. I just needed courage, and encouragement … from the deepest well inside of me that I'd never really tapped into get me out of the messes I had created for myself. "I'll do it!" I said to her. "I can get a job at Riata. But the hard part will be not telling Tim. If I'm going to find out the truth, I can't count on a liar to keep my plan a secret!

I sat down and slumped in my chair. Maybe Tim was right though…maybe he didn't do anything wrong and Steve fired him to cover up what he's doing wrong at Riata Technology, Inc. Maybe all this time, Time has the type of personality that attracts ego-maniac bosses, who are constant hiring and firing people to feel secure and at the top of their game.

"Still, I could be thrown in jail if go in there impersonality someone." I tell my little yellow chirping canary that just flittered through its cage.

Again, I recounted the injustice. Steve fired Tim, on this day, April 30, four months ago to the day when he hired Tim. That meant Steve had to have been plotting Tim's demise from the start. I needed more information, in the forms of email and perhaps a computer database of clients and companies. Only Tim could give me those. Then, upon infiltrating Riata, I'd need to answer several questions—and maybe more—to show fraud and call the police. How long has Steve been defrauding investors? Are other employees involved? If clerks had compiled computer records of Riata's monetary transactions, on which computer would they be, and could I access them? Did the fraud extend beyond Riata to other companies? Was manipulating sales part of some grand, stock market scheme? Anger was spinning a cocoon of steaming emotion all through me. "I will get a job at Riata!"

When I heard the grind of an engine come to a sudden stop, I knew Tim had arrived. He stepped through the door, dropped a heavy box, flipped off his shoes, and plopped his briefcase on the table.

I wiped my eyes. "Tim, I'm so sorry—"

"Me too, Rae." He grabbed me with such fervency that I almost mistook his strong kiss and tight squeeze as some type of final farewell. I cried some more; and when I pulled back and searched his eyes, I trembled. He looked the same, but he wasn't. Steve Lerrefeiht—no Riata—had broken him.

"One day has changed everything, huh?" he said, hitting a kitchen chair next to me.

I tried to think of positive words, but couldn't, only small talk in the form of an exchange of information about Joey still sleeping, and Carolyn needing to be picked up from school in a few hours. Hell, I could barely conjure up comfort for myself! It took over an hour just to think of *one* solution. "You said you were going to call former colleagues."

He glanced beyond me to where the butterflies once caressed the sky. "Yeah, I'll call, but connections don't mean interviews, Rae."

I touched his hand and gestured at fruit on the table. "Tim, please sit down and eat something."

"I can't. Gotta get on the computer and start job hunting." He leaned down and took my face in his hands. "Rae. I love you, my Rain." He laughed a little.

I cried. He stole the nickname from my brother, Tom, who had given it to me when I was twelve. My mother had gone into a rage and beat me with her hands and a broomstick for refusing to go to the store in an Indiana blizzard. I decided to show *her*, so I ran out in the cold darkness in my black patent-leather shoes. I would have stayed there ... wondering how I could catch a train and run away ... only Tom's voice coaxed me back to the warm but violent inside of the house where we were constantly finding places to shake and hide. "Raaanne!"

The storm had now returned, in a totally different shape and size, and Tim and I were all caught up in it, frozen in its eye. He released me from his embrace, and I saw his once proud shoulders sag like ageless boughs. He was so happy the day Steve hired him. We were happy and celebrating! But now dejected had built a wall of pride so thick around Tim, that he'd rather die than give up on his dream of building a company to greatness and then retiring with plenty in the bank. When Steve had hired him, the job was a promotion for Tim. In the past, he had always been Vice President of Marketing. At Riata, he was V.P. and also responsible for the *entire* sales force. This termination was not like the others, and would leave a permanent scare.

After he fired up the computer and returned to the kitchen to make a sandwich, he said the ramifications. "If I don't find a job fast ... like in the next few days ... word of Steve letting me go will spread like gossip. I have to get on this ASAP ... and find something, fast."

Outside, the rain dissipated. I remembered what the doctor had said to me, and his words flowed through my muscles, warming them.

"Negative self-talk will only make things worse, Rae Anne."

My response at the time had been, "Well positive self-talk hasn't been helping either."

As I envision him saying those words again and again, a knot *leaped* out of my stomach, and in its place I felt a settling a ray of hope. I would never know *anything* about what happened, or really respect Tim, unless I try to infiltrate Riata, and discover the truth about what happened to Tim. And maybe, in the process, I might find a way—or a couple of ways—to get revenge.

After Tim ate his sandwich and gulped down enough water to fill up for days, he changed out of his business clothes. "I have to get on the computer, and e-mail my old contacts. If I have some luck, HR at Riata hasn't severed my webpage. I can get in there and find a few unsuspecting customers who might have some opportunities for me." Rifling through the day's mail, he added before sitting down at the long desk stacked with books and sectioned off by divides of office supplies, "Maybe I might also be able to install an automatic return in the system, so I can divert all my emails here."

"Go ahead. I'll pick up the Carolyn. At least you have a little time with Joey when he wakes up. Oh, and feed him, will ya?"

He had heard me. His fingers were speeding along the black keyboard, and other than feeding Joey, he'd never leave that computer system until midnight. That's when he was also the most tired, and vulnerable, and I could gently pry out of him answers to the questions I'd need to infiltrate Riata. I let imagination have full reign in my mind. I couldn't tell Tim my plan, but I needed to find out as much information about Riata as I could in order to fulfill my plan. Then, I felt suddenly sad and lonely. Being dishonest with him about such an important event in my life was like losing a best friend; and trying to force myself to respect him when I couldn't believe him made me feel like such a backstabber. The emptiness felt nauseating, and my arms felt hollow. Curling up in bed, I realized how unhappy I had been, and wondered whether or not Tim and I could fix our marriage.

PART III
INTERVIEW WITH TIM

That night, I took my medicine as scheduled, but my hands wouldn't stop shaking. I was determined not to call the doctor for more drugs. One is enough! I felt determined to battle "the problem."

Just before midnight, Tim slipped into bed. "I scheduled two interviews in San Jose."

"Great, Tim!"

"One is the day after tomorrow, Wednesday, and the other's Thursday afternoon. I should be home on Friday."

"Wow, fantastic!" I wanted to keep encouraging him by asking him more questions about those jobs, but I couldn't stop obsessing about Riata Technology. I wanted to know the names of Tim's enemies, and if he had any friends. I remember what an old colleague once told me, "Keep your friends close, but your enemies closer." I'd target his enemies *first thing* after arriving at Riata.

"Tim, who do you think was really behind your getting fired?"

Light from the stand blocked his body. In the darkness only his lips moved. "I think Steve's old buddy and former VP of Sales and Marketing up in San Jose, Kip Tempulous."

I remembered what Tim said about him several weeks ago, and I turned to the nightstand for a drink of water. In a draw, I also rummaged lightly and found a pen and paper. Quickly I jotted down his name. Kip Tempulous had retired from Riata; however, because Steve and Kip had been close friends for years, Kip followed Steve to

San Diego to sell Riata sensors and other products. Tim took Kip with him whenever he met with reps and distributors. "How do you think he caused Steve to fire you?" I whispered with nonchalance.

"Well," he began through a yawn, "when Kip suggested that we use a few vendors under the table rather than deal with Riata's contracted company, I refused, and told him that would be dishonest, and illegal."

"It woulda been!" I said. "If you would have done as he suggested, you might not have only been fired by now but also in jail, Tim, *whew*."

Carolyn peeked through the door, saying she had finished her homework and telling us goodnight. Joey fell asleep hours ago and wasn't due up until, hopefully, seven.

At Riata, I would find Kip. Perhaps *he* was the one who instigated the fraud.

Tim pulled the pillow from behind his back and punched it. "Those damn execs, especially Thornton Manning."

"What about him?" I turned and wrote his name down on my list of revenge.

"He's Steve's hotshot whiz man and the V.P. of Technology. He can do no wrong."

I lowered my voice. I knew that if Tim were to detect any type of anxiety, he'd question me. "Who else do you think is crooked?"

"Oh, definitely that Research and Development V.P., Kent Smith." He exhaled the name.

"That's product design and testing, right?"

"Yep."

"Does Kent Smith steal ideas do you think, or what?"

Tim's voice rose in an obvious controlled rant. "That

darn Kent Smith gave me databases and sent me emails of customers he said were tried-and-true. Most companies answered. A few didn't."

"So?"

He turned my way with Sherlockian determination. "Well, as I continued to contact those unresponsive companies, and more contacts Kent Smith sent my way, I discovered they weren't active at all, but fake."

"That's strange."

His eyes opened wide in astonishment. "Yeah, I couldn't believe it! I searched for proof of their individual existence, but couldn't find any. As a matter of fact, I was able to access my webpage at the company a few hours ago, to try and download a few of those contacts. Nothing." He sighed—an expression of failure. "Then, HR must have severed my link, 'cause my screen froze and I haven't been able to access it again."

"Did you tell anyone when you first discovered the fake companies?"

"I went to Claud Filmer and a few other people. No one had an answer." He clenched the sheets. "But I *did* find something earlier."

"It looks like you've put the facts you discovered together to form one solid picture," I said.

"I think you're right, Rae," he said through the faint bedroom light as pale shock rippled across his chiseled cheeks. "All those *fake* companies merged into one firm. I searched for financial connections and a prospectus. None. But I just *know* there *must* be foreign ties." He stared into the distance, obviously still perplexed by the puzzle but incapable of solving it.

"What's the name of it?" Finding what he missed would be my goal.

"Easy, Key Stone Investments and Dye." He sat up

and gave me suspicious glare. "Why?"

"Why what?"

"Why do you want to know all this? I mean—" He settled quickly back down. "I can't do anything about it."

"I don't know." I adjusted the sheets and turned away. "Just curious, that's all ... and like you, trying to make sense of this whole job from beginning to end."

"Good luck! I haven't even been able to do that. It'd be like seeing God and his angels if we could figure out the inner workings of that scrambled up company!" He laughed and shook his head. "Rae, I know the companies were fake." He ruffled the sheets in an obvious attempt to make himself comfortable when no amount of effort would work until he could secure another job. "What I don't know is if this had something to do with why Steve let me go. I was told it was a production thing...and a financial thing to save face for the company."

Making sure my words treaded softly over my breath, I said, "Did you *like* anyone there?"

After he thought a moment he replied, "The Executive Secretary, Mira Padeson was nice. She was pretty much in charge of customer relations, kept track all the executive schedules, and—" He laughed from his firm muscular chest. "She could tell one helluva jokes." A wash of sadness brushed across his face. "She was a nice person. When she had to monitor me while I packed up my things, I saw tears in her eyes."

"She didn't like losing you there then, Tim," I said, touching his shoulder.

Then his voice turned light and uplifting, and I found hope. "Tomorrow I catch an early flight and you just wait—" He kissed me quickly on the lips. "In no time, I'll have another job ... and I'll just commute for a while from here to there, until I pick up job security with the new company, and then search for a job down here!"

He made it sound so easy and simple. It wouldn't be. I would be a single parent from Monday to Friday! Then I turned and wrote down Mira Padeson's name on my hit-list of revenge, but I put a star next to it. She was sad to see Tim leave. And he said she had treated him with kindness. I could befriend Mira.

The next morning, Tim left, and Carolyn wept when I told her he was on the way to San Jose to look for another job. She folded across her chest proclaimed: "I'm not moving again!"

Joey watched her tantrum from his highchair, mashed his scrambled eggs into liquid, and didn't stop until the wall behind him looked like decorative paper.

"Carolyn," I told my sun-tanned skateboarding girl, "if someone hires him there, he said he'd commute for a while and we could live down here." I told her every word he'd said before he left, especially those choice phrases stipulating that we'd be fine here, and able to keep our new house, except for adding more extras onto it during the construction process we could no longer afford.

Getting them off to school was a reward. Then I stopped at Starbuck's. While sitting there, sipping coffee, and staring at the La Jolla cliffs, the urge to procrastinate curled into my thoughts. I could postpone the trip to Riata for an hour … maybe even half a day.

I began watching people at their little café tables. Many were alone too. I counted the minutes as each one left the sliding door: 9:38 a.m. That was ten minutes I added to the *sixteen* minutes that I'd been comparing them to me. Embarrassment clung to me like a wet cloth. Gulping two hard swigs of strong coffee, I realized I had two choices. I could turn back, or try something new. I couldn't decide, but I *did* manage to get back into my Sebring.

As I sat there, the morning sunshine reflected off the tops of cars as they sped along a black stretch of white-lined roads heading toward San Diego. I pulled out of the parking lot to turn back, punched on the radio, and stopped because the volume hurt my ears...only to hear the famous radio psychologist Dr. Cindy Commings on the air and answering callers' questions.

"This is Dr. Cindy, taking your calls on KYBO. I have Bea on the line. What's a career wrecker for you, Bea?"

She mentioned, "career," and I decided to listen. What a fluke!

Bea praised the doctor then continued: "I have problems with going to work, Dr. Commings. I can't seem to get out of bed. Every step I take feels leaded down. And I can't concentrate."

"How old are you, Bea?

"Fifty-three."

"Why do you think you can't get out of bed?"

As Bea clarified her problem, I began to relate. Everything Doctor Commings began telling her about burn-out and depression pertained to me as well. I was fatigued, unhappy, lonely and hollow. Most of all, I believed I had failed. I wanted to scream into the radio: "I *completely* understand. I'm barely able to drive let alone follow through with a decision!" I had to change my life, and for *once* take a risk. A stitch turned inside of me, and fight looped around my heart. If I could listen to Dr. Commings help Bea on my drive down to Riata, I could transfer the advice she was giving Bea onto me, and make the needed change to infiltrate Riata.

I picked up the cell phone and pecked out Riata's number. "You can do this," I whispered to myself, "you can make this step one!"

A receptionist answered, and transferred me to Mira.

"Mira Padeson, *yes*," I whispered while she had me on hold. I had with me important credit cards, and an old social security card, and a document containing my maiden name.

When Mira picked up my call in a gentle and confident, "This is HR, Mira Padeson. May I help you?"

Step two was complete! I had Mira on the phone, and I gently cleared my throat while thinking a little prayer for help. "Hello, Ms. Padeson. My name is Rae Anne Herschel, and I'm responding to your ad for an IT technician you have posted in the classified section of today's paper."

"We currently have *two* positions available," she said, "and I need them filled fast!" She chuckled a little, her urgency definite.

I elaborated on my employment history and educational background, and Mira said: "Then let's get you into HR for an interview, Ms. Herschel. Since you're free, how about today, at eleven thirty?"

"I'll be there, Ms. Padeson, and thanks." I quickly scratched down a code she gave me to give the security guard at the gate and then we hung up. "Yes! Step three is done!"

Then I began having strong doubts like skunk odor. As every moment passed while driving down the freeway along the pristine coastline, I grew more afraid. I would meet *many* people. They would question me in depth about my employment history. I had compiled a quick resume early in this morning, but I would have to be extremely convincing to convince someone to hire me on the spot. Things could go terribly wrong. My stomach and my throat began stinging from coffee acid, and I popped a piece of a scone in my mouth, chewed fast and washed it down with a little carton of milk.

I'd need more than just doctor's words to give me a pep talk. I needed something tangible, something to crunch in my hands to remind me of how ticked off I've been, and to push me forward on the trail of justice for Tim!

In my pocket, I suddenly touched bottom and felt something stick me. Tim's Riata pin! But how? He said he had to turn his in the last time he left the security gate. Then I remembered. "Right after he was hired, Steve gave this special pin to Tim, but he said he'd lost it. Shoot! He never did. He must have handed it to me accidentally while we were taking care of Joey in that bad emergency. I had an actual Riata pin on me all along!" I kissed it, then wanted to spit on it, but I didn't. "I think this can admit me into some special places...yes! Just what I need!

I stared at the two-inch gold pin, designed with a blue shield over which two crisscrossing lightning bolts intersected. A tiny white diamond at its center appeared to be activating with the sunlight, illuminating a white line right into the center of my face like a laser. "What the heck?!" I drop the pin back deep into my jacket pocket. Still, at some point after I'd acquire my new IT tech job, I'd have to wear one just like it, and hopefully, be able to access confidential areas in search of evidence of fraud and other illegal activities. I decided that *this* pin would become like a spur. If I'd ever felt like giving up and turning back, I'd touch it, receive a good stick, and move forward.

PART IV
STEP FOUR, INFILTRATION

I'd never seen a place like Riata's parking lot surrounded by electrified wiring. The flawless blacktop, high-tech security kiosks, and seven-floor glass building looked like an area for quarantine, not a business. I drove next to a security kiosk and stopped. A woman dressed in a starched blue uniform bent down to my window and asked my name. "Who are you visiting today?"

"I'm here for an interview with Mira Padeson," I replied nervously, giving her my old driver's license. After phoning in my information to HR, she directed me to the Administration building.

Driving past her and seeing the yellow-and-red guard rail shut in my rear view window, I began shaking. I felt as if I'd been zapped with electricity, and my inner voice began urging me, *turn back*! *I can't*, I told my drive for self-preservation. *I'm inside, and so close to step five—entering the building*!

After parking, I walked toward the busy main entrance. In every corner, cameras were tracking me as I approached a guard who greeted me and escorted me toward an entryway of interconnecting hallways. Everywhere I saw employees dressed in blue and black suits and carrying briefcases and folders. I felt swallowed up with the throng as I stepped under illuminated archways displaying pictures of Riata's products and famous clients. We stopped at a circular information kiosk at a giant roundabout, dotted with laptops and digital phones. Behind several busy receptionists were several monitors displaying multi-perspective views of the first floor. Next to those four monitors were two frameless screens depicting activities on floors two through seven. Everywhere else, the color steel-grey permeated the interior design, in peppered sprays on the marble flooring, acoustical ceiling tiles, and window shutters that appeared to close automatically in case of, perhaps a robbery or inside security breach?

Receptionist One handed me a map. "Mira Padeson's office is on the second floor." She circled the site in red. "Take the elevator down this corridor to your right and get off at the second floor and go left. Her office will be the second office on the right." The lady didn't grin once, and had an expression of fatigue from being overworked! Walking away from her and glancing at people, I noticed no one smiling, or even talking, but rubbing their eyes, or gulping down coffee, and rushing like zombies to appointments. The interlinking corridors looked like ants crossing pathways!

As I approached the long elevators with people swarming around me to the point of almost drowning in them, I saw a gallery of shiny frames containing the pictures of executives, with one missing. *That must have been where Tim's picture had hung*, I wanted to blurt out. I sipped water at the drinking fountain to stop myself from blaring out the obvious that would surely summon the guards and quash my mission. Rushing inside an elevator with the throng, I felt a pang of anger, reached into my pocket, and pinched that old Riata pin between my fingers. I kept telling myself: *keep going, just a little bit more. This is step five, getting through the door, and now we need to complete step six, getting hired.* A Claustrophobic fog filled me as I exited the elevator, lifted my briefcase straps close to my neck, and turned left toward Mira Padeson's office. Almost breathless from heat, a rush of cold air flushed through the air, and I sighed in relief as I gulped down the oxygen in large breaths.

People were passing me by, but I couldn't smell coffee or food. Several laptops struck my arms, and all I received back was a harsh stare or "watch out" shout. I felt trapped in a vacuum and rushed along in freeway traffic.

Quickly I slipped through the second sliding door on the right, and a lady sitting at a long wooden desk waved me toward her. "Are you Ms. Hershel?"

"Yes," I replied, smoothing down my blue skirt and adjusting my briefcase to my side. I noticed her tin nameplate with her name in yellow, *Tina Miller.* "I'm here to interview for the IT position with Ms. Padeson, Tina."

"She's expecting you." Tina escorted me into a chilly white conference room with tall white partitions around the perimeter. Each cubicle entrance had a small name plate, and I could hear faint chatter, dialing-and-ringing phones, and a bit of laughter from the personnel in Mira's HR department. *This place is a little more human!*

Tina stopped at a distant anteroom with opaque milk-glass sliding doors through which I could see the colors of a faint Tiffany-style lampshade, and finally smell coffee with a hint of chicken soup. "Please sit here, Ms. Hershel, and Mira will be with you shortly," she gestured for me to sit down at a small chrome table outside Mira's office.

As she left, two buff men dressed in black suits and black ties suddenly walked out of Mira's sliding door. Behind them appeared a short thin woman with a short puffy hairstyle wearing cat-eye glasses. She had on a flowered blouse and black A-lined skirt. *This must be Mira Padeson, but she looks like a diamond among funeral operators!*

"Hi, Mary," she began, shaking my hand. "May I call you Mary? I'm Mira." She chuckled warmly. "And *please* call me Mira."

I sensed such self-confidence as well as poise and sophistication as I returned her greeting. "Hi, yes, Mira, please call me Mary."

Without introducing me to the two stoic guards always standing at attention in the distance, she asked me to delve into my employment history, and I handed her my resume and references. She perused them with the eyes of a skilled chef. Then she stopped and pointed at one section on my resume. "I didn't realize you had a background in statistics," she said, suddenly doffing her glasses. Riata needs people with a background in that area. Would you be willing to take a job in our Stat department instead of IT, Mary?"

That made me happy! If I could gain access to *that* department, I could gather all the information I'd while limiting the chances of getting caught. "Yes, certainly, Mira," I said, trying hard to contain my excitement.

"Please wait a moment." She began texting on her phone. "I'm requesting different forms for you to fill out. I think you might be able to start the job in a few hours," she said, and then she cleared her throat in an expression conveying discomfort. "That is, if you don't mind rearranging your schedule. I don't mean to be presumptuous and assume that you'll, well, drop everything and start work now!" She laughed, handing me the initial paperwork.

"I can do it, Mira ... start today," I returned excitedly. Knowing she was so eager to snatch me up for Riata, I felt the spittle on my tongue dry, but then turn sour as fear rippled through me. I couldn't remember whether or not Tim had given Riata my social security number. *Uh-oh, this could be my ruin ... the end of everything.* I slumped down a little in my chair but quickly sat up.

The security guards were still peering around the room with evaluating eyes—I'm sure on the lookout for any type of abnormal body language that could be interpreted as someone leaving the building with valuable secrets. From what Tim had told me, Riata produced more Top Secret government products than chip sensors for public use. Panicking tingles spread through my body, until I remembered a visit to a local doctor's office with my insurance card. Before Riata, Tim had been self-employment. When I realized that policy had not yet expiration, and that Tim hadn't included me on his policy in order for us to save money, I sighed in relief and drank some water from a cold bottle Tina had brought to me while I waited to fill out more incoming Confidential paperwork. Then I breathed, and felt safe.

After signing the papers and stamping several sheets with Riata's special emblems and logos, Mira said: "I'm so impressed with your background, Miss Herschel. It's not every day we meet someone with an extensive background in statistics."

"Thank you." As I filled out my portions, I remembered a time before I married Tim, when I held a ten-month job at UCLA compiling statistics for several research projects. I felt like Mira was giving me a value I didn't deserve. *I'm saying anything negative and to the contrary!* I remember Tim telling me what an honest person I am. *Not now, and it's okay, isn't it?* Still, trying not to shake while writing, I signed the last paper, upon which included a temporary sticker giving me confidential status to work at Riata. My lungs filled with the chilly air of revving success, and I felt an energy trickle down to my toes that I hadn't felt in years.

Yes! I'm hired! Step six complete. My enthusiasm morphed into caution as the pin in my pocket stuck through the fabric to my skin, pricking me a bit. Could I accomplish the rest of my mission? With a flash drive in my briefcase, could I find Tim's old laptop and retrieve evidence on that fake company? Even better, can I find the culprits, and who specifically is responsible for all those inflated sales that ultimately backfired, striking Tim and getting him fired? Who had it in for him?! I kept telling myself: *I've got to find all that information.*

A pot-bellied man dressed in a shiny pin-striped suit with obviously dyed black hair, gray eye brows, and steel-rimmed glasses stepped up beside Mira. He had a thin folder tucked firmly under his arm. I craned my neck, trying to look up into his oval face dotted with dark spots on his cheeks, and I noticed his deep-set blue eyes with gray melon-shaped bags. He had to be someone who sat at a desk most times and hardly exercised. After nodding at me with a condescending expression on his pasty-dour face, he pulled Mira to the side, and they began whispering. I believed they might even be having a little spat when I saw him shoot the folder in front of her and glare at her. When he turned to approach me with the folder and the temporary Riata *Confidential Access* sticker, I spotted his large insignia pin on his lapel, unlike any other I had seen thus far, with the word, *Riata*, burning bright and emboldened in red, and accentuating the crossing white lightning bolts. A brilliant diamond was at its center, and beneath the pin, a small gold-blatted name tag: *Steve Lerrefeiht.*

He extended his hand to greet me. "From what Mira says, you're qualified, and I heed her advice, so you're hired," he said in a baritone flat voice. "Welcome to Riata, I'm Steve Lerrefeiht, the CEO."

I felt disdain as I slowly shook his hand. "Thank you, Mr. Lerrefeiht." He had to have felt my sweat! Happily, he couldn't read my mind. *This is the scummy scoundrel who had once shook Tim's hand, but then fired him. I can't wait to find evidence to take you down!*

During my internal ranting and raving, he had opened the folder and was pointing to the second page. "Do you have a problem with the salary?" His voice was sappy sick.

"How much again, Sir? I was just focused on the job description." *That's it … make him believe the company comes first in your life and nothing else.*

Another gentleman was walking toward us with taps on the bottom of his loafers, and Mira straighten up tall, and remain unmoving from her position as he tried passing in front of her, but could only approach Steve by going behind her. Some type of war was raging between them, and she appeared ready to fight. His name tag read, *Claude Filmer, V.P. Engineering.* I recognized the name! I'd also need to be sweet as honey to him as well so I could bring my enemy in close to me. As he and Steve began bandying dates and times for when I could start, I took stock of Claude Filmer. Much shorter than Steve and thinner, Claude had thin eye lids through which I could barely see his pupils, a bristly mustache, and a gray fringe of hair around his bald head. He had a sneaky weasel sort of appearance that made my stomach turn. Worse yet, whenever he concluded a sentence, he straightened his lips and dropped his shoulders, reminding me of former President Nixon.

Taking the folder from Steve, he snapped it into my hand. "Ms. Hershel, we'll start you at Step Five, with a Level 3 salary position. That's $5,725.00 a month, full benefits, and forty hours a week. That folder contains all the information you need. It's your contract, and Mr. Lerrefeiht would like you to start in our Statistics department immediately. So after someone shows you around Riata, go to lunch, read it, and then sign it … that is, if the contract lives up to your expectations." He chuckled lightly, really more of a strange eerie giggle, obviously to cover-up or compensate for whatever faults were at play deep in his psyche. "Give it to Ms. Padeson here," he gestured whimsically at her, "and she'll tell you the office to report to." Then he turned and left.

"Yes, Sir," I called to him as Mira stared at his back with angry eyes and adjusted her cat-eye glasses on her nose.

Steve puffed out his chest and said to Mira, "I believe she can just grab a cup of coffee right now and fill out all this paperwork, then tour our facility, right?"

Mira stood small next to Steve's beer-bellied body, but she exuded the impression that she had the answer to every imaginable problem occurring around Riata, while he, the unapproachable intimidating CEO, knew nothing. "Yes, Mary, you fill these out in my office—" She gestured warmly at her sliding-door office. "—or dine in the cafeteria. Lunch is in fifteen minutes anyway." Her smile glowed with sincere friendliness, and her eyes beamed with unwavering honesty. "Then I'll take you around Riata and introduce you to everyone."

For the first time since I had arrived, I felt confident my mission could succeed, until Steve came between us. "Oh—before you go, I need to give you this." He held out a small pin to me, Riata's special insignia. "You need to wear it on your person every day, and *every* employee has one. Along with a special ID badge Mira will give to you, this pin is your ticket into our golden gates!" He laughed.

That yellow-and-red little gate, golden? The guy's hallucinating!

I unclasped the back and stuck the pin on my jacket.

"Thank you, Mr. Lerrefeiht, I won't leave it on Alcatraz,"
I joked back; and he pointed at me like I'd told the
perfect joke, all the while chuckling from his rotund belly.
A dull ache nipped at my stomach and worked its way
into my brain. I needed my medicine, but I couldn't get
to my purse.

Steve walked toward the exit, stopped suddenly in a
forgetful gestured and turned around and called: "Mira,
after lunch, also introduce her to our executive team."
He then sized me up slowly from head to toe and my
head began throbbing through his lingering gazes.
"Yes…you'll do well in our Statistics Department, Miss
Herschel,"

Mira's throat reddened, and she appeared speechless as
she slammed closed the paperwork, obviously having read
something I had signed but didn't recognize as harmful or
disturbing. "Are you sure, Mr. Lerrefeiht, that Mary
needs to report everything she does to Dr. Manning, Mr.
Filmer *and* Mr. Smith?" She held all my paperwork in the
air and the sheets swished a bit.

My job seemed like a job *she* wouldn't even take!

"They're all short on help. If there's a lag in Statistics,
they might need her help." His voice flattened and
exerted authority.

"The company has seen *more* vacancies this morning,
Mr. Lerrefeiht." She re-organized all my paperwork in
delicate taps and secure pats of perfection.

I heard the innuendo. She had told him his Executive
Departments were losing valuable employees.

He waved her toward him; and with agitated body
language, pulled her by his side. There, they talked for
almost a minute—he a threatened squirrel, she a
mockingbird defending her territory.

I knew I'd have to face each all four of those strong

intimidating executives at some point, but I never thought I'd have to work for them all at the same time! I glanced at my watch. I couldn't believe that in such a short time I had progressed from IT Tech, to working for executives on their most sensitive projects. I would be correlating data and presenting results to executives! The gap seemed surreal, and I felt panicked and dry-mouthed because I had no idea what to expect, what project I'd be working on, or who exactly was my boss.

I needed my medicine to help calm me down and focus ... but my purse was *five* feet away. I had to end their private heated conversation, so I slowly walked toward them, and they both stopped their bantering when I entered their boundary zones. "I guarantee I'll do a good job wherever I wind up, Sir."

Mira moved away from him, and he pointed at me like a cowboy aiming at a target. "I'm sure you'll do just fine, Ms. Herschel." Then he left the white conference room, his shoes blending in with all the heavy tapping sounds on the long busy corridor.

Thinking about what the radio psychologist Dr. Commings had said about taking little steps to feel better, I grabbing my purse, excused myself to the bathroom down the hall, and inconspicuously gulped down the pill. On the return to Mira's office, I believed I had a safety net at Riata, Mira. When she let me into her cozy office—so out of character with the other offices I'd managed to peer into along the way, Mira looked drained. That impromptu conversation, actually heated argument, with Steve had rendered her glasses crooked and her flowery blouse a bit wrinkled.

"Is everything okay, Ms. Padeson? I hope I didn't cause any trouble—"

"Please," she breathed while straightening her cat-eye

glasses, "call me Mira." Her voice was shaky. Either she needed a friend, or she was afraid. She gestured for me to sit down at her long wooden desk with a Tiffany lamp on one corner and several iPads and other portable devices to the left of her. She had to have had fifty people working for her in HR, and they were busy, and rushing in-and-out of her sliding door, some waving hello to her, others blurting out a quick hi or hello.

"Okay, Mira." I scooted in closer to her desk, and she began glancing around her bustling office in a gesture signaling that we had only seconds.

"You'll really be working for Kent Smith," she said, her voice low and deliberate. Her eyes widened. "Watch out for him." An employee passed by, presented her with a finished project, and Mira thanked her.

"What should I watch out for, Mira?" I whispered.

She bowed her head and leaned toward me. "Watch *everything* you do. *What* you say. *Who* you talk to." With her eyes, she signaled at objects on her desk.

I had to look like a stunned kangaroo! Glancing along with her, I searched for items that might contain hidden cameras, like pencil sharpeners or erasers. I stopped when I realized I'd probably never find one, for Riata spy chips in the form of special sensors could be in anything and everywhere. Because she had disclosed that much, I almost confided in her that I could be an ally and that, at least, I knew Tim, but I couldn't. I couldn't take a chance that Dr. Thornton Manning, Claude Filmer, or Kent Smith might be eavesdropping. I couldn't afford to be apprehended when I was so close to discovering the truth. Yet I could do one thing.

I opened my briefcase, took a piece of paper, and jotted down the name of the fake company, *Key Stone Investments and Dye*, and its website. As I'd gently treat an ancient parchment, I folded the paper, stood up quickly, and slid to her the paper across her desk. She slapped ahold of the precious document, and slipped it into her drawer.

I was shaking. If someone were to be monitoring me at this point, they'd read my uneasiness and conclude that I pose a threat. Furthermore, to Mira, I've put myself waist-deep in vulnerable waters. The sharks are above me, and an army ant could be Mira. She *could* have this same information and blow the whistle on me, getting me kicked out; or she might have been looking for the information I just handed her all along, and speculate that I'm here at Riata, trying to solve a puzzle for the FBI or something.

She stood up, walked to her towering file cabinet, and motioned for me to join her. She began riffling through several files, feigning a search. "After lunch, go to the Executive Deck," she whispered, nodding upward. "It's on the sixth floor, where Steve and all the higher ups have their offices."

Yes—she's not turning me in, but using me to help her! As I sighed, she must have seen my tears of gratitude and relief.

"We call the ride up to the executive offices 'the corridor'." She leaned into me. "It's eerie knowing you're being constantly watched."

Goose bumps rippled down my arms. "Definitely!"

She picked out a file and held it up for my perusal. Nothing was inside. "When the elevator stops," she continued whispering while now-and-then looking askance, "an executive will greet you in the hallways. They always do that because they'll see you on their monitors. It's an automated system because so much Top Secret designs and blueprints are located there." Her tone of voice grew stern and she looked at me like a protective mother. "I'll have a project waiting for you." She patted a folder someone just put on her desk labeled, *Chip 500 Research*. "I need you to run the results. So just the executive who meets you that you need use the system in Room 601 to run the statistics." The expressions on her face froze. "But I have other reasons to send you to the sixth floor."

"Why?" I whispered.

"Last week," she began, "several women just quit, and Steve let go of our marketing guy." She breathed, looked to the right, and then to the left. "I don't believe all those girls just quit, and that the marketing guy was selling secrets—"

"What?!" I almost fainted. She was talking about Tim! He *never* told me about that accusation, and I know he'd never do such a thing! I thought a demon was sucking the air outta my lungs I felt that displaced and slapped by evil. Perhaps Tim was the type of person drawn to accepting jobs with sociopaths.

She handed me a folder and closed the file drawer. "There's more to their stories, and with the great background you have in statistics, and maybe even police work—" She winked, obviously believing I might be an FBI agent. "—we can catch these sons 'o bitches and gather evidence of their illegal activities." She slammed the file door; but then realizing she might have made too much noise, patted the cabinet and quickly sat down at her desk.

Suddenly she coughed hard. So hard, I thought she might have been poisoned by the tea still steaming in her cup! The thick sound resonated deep within her chest. I wondered if she had sufficient insurance and sick days. From what Tim had told me about her, she had worked at Riata long before Steve, when the company was under the early direction of Justin Bailing, the real CEO, who rumor has it, is maintaining a corporate office in Texas. No Riata employee, except perhaps for Mira, had ever seen Justin Bailing. I'd have to ask her at some time.

Composing herself, she slipped me the precious folder that I'd need upon arriving on the sixth floor. "Now, let's go to lunch."

PART V
EVIDENCE

Forty-five minutes later, after I finished eating lunch at the fourth-floor cafeteria and filling out all that exhaustive paperwork that I needed a magnifying glass to read, I gave my forms to a runner. Mira telephoned Steve to tell him she had a project for me. She rescheduled my complete tour of Riata for tomorrow. "I have a special little project for Rae Anne Hershel that requires your attention later in the afternoon, Mr. Lerrefeiht."

"Fine," I heard him through her speaker phone.

I believe I've skipped over step seven of my plan and am now on step ten! Wow, I've come this far in just—I checked my watch—*three hours!*

I just kept telling myself like cheerleader at the sideline of a race track: *You can do this...you're almost at the finish line, to clear Tim, and tasting sweet revenge.*

Now, at 1:10 p.m., the time had arrived for me to begin my ascent to the sixth floor Executive Deck, as the entire floor is named. Before my approach to the fourth-floor elevators, I stopped when I noticed the name, *Kip Tempulous*, embossed in a picture frame of a young man who could pass as Donald Trump's twin. He was among others in a gallery, all executives with Steve Lerrefeiht at the forefront. He had his arms crossed tightly across his chest, his jaw high, his eyes peering up into a heavenly distance where no besides himself could tread. "I think there's a gallery of executives on every floor," I whispered, laughing.

My gosh, these higher ups are so stuck on themselves...and always needing to promote themselves ... or just plain showing off ... so condescending ... like telling everyone else beneath them, look where I'm at but you'll never be no matter how hard you work.

Suddenly, I noticed Kip's job title: *Vice President of Marketing and Sales.*

The lettering appears fresh! I thought of Tim. *This man has Tim's job!* I then recalled what he'd told me last night. Kip Tempulous was Steve's best friend at his old company.

Anger began baking to my bones. I had solved one mystery: who exactly replaced Tim. Not enough, but worse! That a *new* picture with all *this* information was before me now, engraved on a name plaque only *two* business days after Steve fired Tim, means Steve or one of the other V.P.s had plotted Tim's termination in advance. Now, I wanted revenge more than ever! I quickly opened my purse and wrote down the name, *Kip Tempulous.*

This list is morphing into a real hit list.

I joined a rush of people and entered the elevator. Fear tingled in my fingers when I spotted a camera high in the corner. Putting my back against a wall and lowering my gaze to the floor, I folded my arms against my waist and tried covering myself with my briefcase and purse. I must have looked like a homeless person trying on clothes in a thrift shop to anyone monitoring me. I had seconds before the elevator would stop on the sixth floor, and I grew numb terrified. I could picture Steve's face, and Claude Filmer, but I had not yet met Thornton Manning, Kent Smith, or Kip Tempulous. I had no idea what I'd say or do if *they'd* be the ones meeting me at the Executive Deck, except I recalled some more advice Dr. Commings had given her listeners on the radio this morning: "Don't let fear incapacitate you."

I decided I wouldn't. The elevator slowed, and I kept flooded my mind with her words as I breathed in the stale elevator air.

The doors parted, and there stood Claude Filmer with his hands by his sides and his three-piece-suit crisp and black. With his thin-set eyes and bald head rimmed with white hair, he resembled Mr. Burns from *The Simpsons*.

"Follow me, Miss Herschel." He said, and then sniffed the air.

"Yes, Sir." I pulled the folder Mira gave me out of my briefcase. "This is what I have to work on in Room 601."

"Good, I see you're fitting in well, *hm*, and in such a short time too I might add, *hm*," he tapped his chin and sniffed again, and then waved me on, escorting me down a bright hall lined with wooden display cases containing Riata's sensor chips.

"This place isn't as busy as the other floors," I said, trying to make light conversation.

Now-and-then we passed people who quickly snapped to attention upon seeing Claude Filmer. He'd simply nod and say, "Yes, carry on."

"This is the Executive Deck, so the sixth floor isn't as busy as the floors below." He giggled and I saw his funeral parlor shoulders shrug. "Furthermore, Ms. Hershel, we monitor almost *everything* and *every* place on *this* floor."

I thought right away: *Uh-oh, I will encounter problems while searching for evidence in this place. How to get around any problems and enact a solution will be my key to succeeding in my mission!*

Beyond the wooden display cases in rooms with special key-pad entryways, I could hear the sounds of machines and automated assembly lines.

In one of those production locations could exist the evidence I need ... but how to get access to these rooms?

As we meandered down another long hallway, we

finally arrived at a line conference doors with people quietly entering. Claude's eyebrows forked, and I saw annoyance as he opened the door for me. "My meeting has just begun. I apologize, but you'll have to sit through it—"

"But I—"

"When it's done—"

He checked his watch, and I glanced at mine on my trembling wrist: 1:22 p.m.

"—which should be at one forty-five, I'll escort you to Room 601." He flicked his wrist—his power body language.

I suddenly saw his ID card dangling out of his suit pocket. As he held the door open for me, I collided with his shoulder and purposely dropped my briefcase. Pens and pencils scattered on the shiny white floor. Out toppled my flash drive—the instrument I'd soon use to back up whatever computer files I could discover throughout the next few days, but hopefully hours, so I could quit this weird place and make it home alive to my children. "Sir, I'm so sorry—"

"Fine, just let's get this all picked up."

As I bent down to gather up my things, I quickly took snapped off his ID card and shoved it into my jacket pocket. Then I stood up and gestured into the conference room as I tried hard to distract him from looking anywhere else or checking his pockets. "Thanks, Sir, and do you have water available in there?"

After pointing at several pitchers and a coffee bar along the wall, he walked me over to a tall chair in the last row, the set-up so different among all the rest. "Will you do me a favor, Ms. Hershel?" he asked, giggling as a blush flushed across his paste colored cheeks.

"Yes, of course, Sir," I coughed in discomfort.

"Please take notes for us," he whispered through his thin lips flattening into sternness.

"Yes, Mr. Filmer." He walked away.

Noticing the Power Point style, I surmised the secretary scheduled to type notes must have quit, so I hesitantly sat down, and shoved my purse and briefcase under the table. An iPad was in front of me, and Power Point opened up and ready for note taking.

I had to tell Mira. She'd be wondering where I was, and why I hadn't texted her yet from Room 601. I texted my location, with a request: *please cause some type of interruption so I can leave.*

The conference room was large and rectangular, and employees were finishing setting up their portable tablets as I eavesdropped on their conversations—mostly how boring and unnecessary this fifteen-minute presentation might be. "What can possibly be accomplished in fifteen minutes?" many exhausted people were asking. Ten executives were seated like mannequins at the head table. I recognized Steve Lerrefeiht right away as Claude Filmer sat next to a young man with dark hypnotic eyes, reminding me a bit of the actor Omar Sharif. They began whispering.

The Sharif stranger glanced at me, nodded wistfully, and began staring at me longingly, followed by a deep sigh. I felt the implication like heat from the sun in his yearning expressions: "I so wish I were near you, right now and always." He had to be a hard womanizer, because I caught him puckering at a few other women in the room, who then giggled and began primping and pruning. His eyes were deep-set intense, and he exuded attraction the opposite of a repellant. Peeking above people to see his name plate, I spotted it: *Kent Smith, VP, Research and Development.*

41

He's the one Tim said couldn't be trusted! I once learned a harsh and powerful lesson about attractive men like Kent Smith. Behind their handsome beckoning faces and illusion of power lurks the personality of a hate-filled narcissist.

The speaker took the podium and began adjusting his notes while I began taking Power Point notes. On the giant screen behind him, I saw his name, *Dr. Thornton Manning.* When he finally finished and faced the audience as the lights dimmed, I recognized him from a description Tim had given me over a month ago. Dr. Thornton Manning was young, athletic like a mountain climber, and as serious as a nerd physicist. He began displaying new chips that rocket scientists could insert inside innovative plasma rockets to propel astronauts in a new way to Uranus. He then changed the direction of his presentation. He showed a graphic simulation of subatomic, carbon-based strings that could manipulate DNA, and generate pictures of intelligent atoms that could solve neurological issues inside the brain. He concluded his presentation by wiping sweat off his brow and waited for a reaction.

Steve stood and clapped. "You've definitely been working hard, Thornton, and you always impress me."

"Thank you, Steve," Thornton said through a soft voice of humility, and then he shook Steve's hand.

Steve patted him on the shoulder, and everyone stood and began applauding.

Thornton gestured for them to sit down. "You didn't think I asked you down here for a boring slide show now, did you?" Everyone laughed as the color in his cheeks turned to eager peach. The executives sat down. Silence ensued like the stillness before an earthquake.

From under the podium, Thornton unleashed a

covered plate. "This is the most advanced sensor in existence. It's taken me the *entire* year, and millions of corporate dollars to design the prototype." He nodded at Steve who smiled at him. The world appeared on the brink of beholding a new genius; and if his experiment was a success, historians would hail him as they did Bill Gates!

He lifted off the white sheet, but the plate was bare.

Some people in the audience stood from their seats and raced for the stage.

Turning on a special screen, Thornton exclaimed, "Everyone, look up front."

There, bubbling and gurgling under thousands of degrees of magnification set Thornton's special microscopic sensor. The heat from the light initiated a gigantic spread, and the object began growing.

"It's carbon based ... and can create an *instant* wireless connection with any electromagnetic signal once it grows to an inch," he proclaimed. "And my Mega-quantum sensor can be grown anywhere and by anyone, even on Mars!"

Then, an abnormal bright-green light and golden smoke began encircling the atomic particle...until it exploded like a magician's trick on the plate.

I fell back in astonishment, and stood up to leave as fire alarms blared, and ceiling extinguishers activated, spraying everyone like a mister watering greenhouse plants.

Steve coughed for his life and dashed back, far away. Some executives plopped down in their chairs in obvious shock. Others waved in disgust at Thornton Manning and then dashed quickly and inconspicuously out the door. I felt sorry for him, standing in front of the presentation table with defeat in his eyes, his shoulders sagging as if he might break down and cry, and his face reddening in shame. His experiment was a speck inside a smoldering crucible on the floor. I predicted Steve would fire him the minute they stepped out of the room. But that would be like cutting off his right hand to save his left hand because Thornton had so many other successful experiments he had developed for Riata.

Funny how people take one failure and transfer it to everything else and then stamp the person forever with disappointment so the person never forgets it!

Then I noticed Kent Smith smirking, and Claude Filmer giggling. They were exchanged smirks and whispers, and then began texting on their iPhones. Who were they communicating with and why? Most of all, how rude!

However, their actions began piecing together my large puzzle. As I watched those two give devious and mocking expression Thornton Manning's way, I surmised Thornton Manning had to be innocent of any type of corporate fraud. Through his high-tech advances, he was helping Riata, not destroying it. And as angry as I was at Steve Lerrefeiht, he too might be innocent, for he stomped out of the conference room, obviously angry that Thornton's experiment failure. Although he might be at least be guilty of nepotism—wanting to work with his friend Kip so badly that he fired Tim and gave Kip the job. The suspects committing fraud were narrowing down to Kent Smith, Claude Filmer, and perhaps Kip Tempulous.

Seeing this as the time to conduct some sleuthing to find evidence, I left the cacophony in the conference room, sifted through a throng of confused employees outside the door, and wandered toward the corridor where I heard so many automated machines. When I spotted Claude Filmer's officer, I stopped, took his ID badge out of my purses as inconspicuously as possible, and swiped it through his key-pad entryway. Walking in, I quickly illuminated the lights. The place looked like a homey den, neat, and with books on several shelves arranged in order of height. Under a giant window, someone had stacked organizers and several file cabinets. Strange though, Claude Filmer's outside view was of the distant ocean, so calm, blue, and inviting. If Claude Filmer was exposed as a criminal, he'd lose everything!

Then I saw three PCUs under his redwood desks. Their monitors were displaying green icons of various companies and projects. Tiptoeing toward them, I also kept looking back. This had to be the best time to search for that fake company Tim believed was fraudulent, a cover for perhaps underworld activities, or a type of black-market Silk Road: *Key Stone Investments and Dye.*

Filmer and Smith must still be preoccupied with Thornton Manning's failed experiment, and making the best out of his bad failure by making *him* look small and them appear magnificent. But why?

I clicked on a few icons, and files appeared like envelopes in a mirror. Clicking one open, I saw several miniature folders. "One contains Riata's business plan," I began in a whisper, trying to sooth my trembles and shakes, "another is written in a foreign language. Why?"

Voices outside interrupted my search, and the pressure to discover information fast was raising inside of me like a covered boiling kettle. I could only stare at the screen, my hands frozen on the keyboard.

The words, "Jail," "hospitalization," and "federal prison" flashed through my mind, but the foreign file kept my eyes fixed on the screen. Quickly I pulled my flash drive out of my purse and inserted it into the driver.

"Translate," I said. "How do I translate?"

A voice-activated system ignited, and English words flooded the screen. At the bottom flashed the company, *Key Stone Investments and Dye*, but without the address. I remembered it though its website address: KeyStoneInvestmentsDye-dot-com. My heartbeat rose to my throat! *This is it!*

Another double click yielded a special file cabinet icon: 4-902, Drawer 4, File 902. I ran to the file cabinets stacked under Filmer's window. Cabinet four was the fourth one to the left, and I began rifling through files...902. Picking it out, I saw the name, *Key Stone Investments and Dye* with several sensors surrounded by special casings deep inside the file. Taking them out, I saw a date and time written on each one, the most recent being *May 3, 2014*, with the words, *Russia bound*, written in someone's handwriting.

Claude Filmer must be selling these chips to the highest bidder...and in light of what happened to Thornton Manning's experiment, sabotaging corporate products.

I stuffed the folder and the sensor chips in my purse. "Match this handwriting to the person's handwriting, and you've discovered the criminal!"

I felt so frightened at this point that my arms and legs were numb, and my neck and shoulders were aching like I'd just finished a marathon.

Then I heard more chatter, but this time right outside the door! People were incoming, and fast. I couldn't leave. *Ah-ah, ah-ah* I breathed as I downloaded several files on Claude's desktop computer into my flash drive. I thought my breath was being sucked out by a succubus I was that terrified! I kept repeating: "I've worked so hard ... I've come so far ... I can do this ... I'm almost there…."

Then, my fingers numbed. I flexed them, and got more movement into the muscles. Then, like a sprinter dashing toward the finish line and picking up her last wind, I began downloading information so quickly, and typing so fast, that I thought energizing lightning was flowing through me.

After downloading into my flash drive, I clicked on what I had copied to make sure I had downloaded everything. There was the file, *Key Stone Investments and Dye*, and another file that I clicked open, wherein I discovered a database filled with foreign companies, chip distribution sites, phone numbers and emails.

When I heard an ID slicing through the outside keypad, I knew I had trouble. Someone was angry because the ID wasn't working. I ran on tiptoe to the door on the opposite side of the room, opened it, and slammed it shut.

"What was that?" someone asked from outside in a whisper.

"It was coming from our adjoining room," his companion replied.

Then they stopped trying to open Claude's door. I recognized the voice. It was Claude Filmer, but I couldn't recognize his companion in crime's voice. All I was hoping for is that I could gain enough time to hide my flash drive, close the files I'd opened, and find a way to escape.

The knob to the adjacent room turned and jostled. I had locked it, but they were about to bust the door down, and discover me. As I closed all of Claude's computer files, I heard Filmer's voice, stashed my flash drive behind a book at the center of a bookcase, and raced to put my back against the wall behind the door. It opened with a fright, and I grabbed the door knob before it could knock me in my gut.

"What's this? Someone's been in here!" Claude Filmer exclaimed.

"Our computers ... the file cabinet's been opened!" shouted another man. It had to be Kent Smith, but I wasn't sure. I was still behind the door and couldn't see them.

"Did *you* take anything out since we parted ways an hour ago?"

"Never!" Claude replied.

I heard ruffling and papers shuffling; then silence. "*Sh*, I think the person's still in here," his accomplish said.

"Out—where ever you are," Claude said coaxingly.

"I'm gonna kill the intruder!" his accomplice yelled.

Silence ensued; but when I heard their voices lower as if they were hunting for me in a distant place, I bolted around the corner and ran toward the door. My heart beat fast, and I was gagging on my breath to make it out of this kill zone fast. When I believed I had arrived at the door safely, one of them grabbed me by the waist.

"Ahh!" I screamed.

He turned me around.

Kent Smith! Womanizer Kent Smith!

He put his hand over my mouth and dragged me to the center of Claude's office. "I'll teach *you* for breaking and entering and stealing things!"

My heartbeat pounded in my head as everything around me faded to blinding white. *I'm facing Death ... and gonna die.*

All the while Claude Filmer was patting his thin lips and looking like a stunned possum in the corner. Kent Smith had his tie off, and he wound it around my lips, gagging me, and then tied the knot so taut I thought my neck might snap.

Black and bold, Kent's eyes held my frightened gaze. I felt like a lamb stricken down by wolves. "Give me what you stole," he said coldly.

Solutions raced through my mind. *I can use the flash drive as a poker chip to play for my life.* I nodded yes, and he took off the gag. But when I opened my mouth to speak, I couldn't talk...my lips felt numb and swollen.

Smith extended his hand. "I'll take whatever you stole, now, Ms. Hershel, if that's even your name."

"No, *ah ah*, I want to make sure you let me leave this office alive," I said slowly as if anesthetized.

Claude walked toward me and grabbed my shoulder. "Just do as he asks, Ms. Hershel. Hand over what you took now. We won't hurt you. You have my word."

My vision was like an oscillation scope, their images waving in and out of existence. "How can I believe you?"

"You can't," Kent said firmly, now rifling through the filing cabinet. "The gun's in here somewhere..."

"No!" I shouted.

Then another stranger walked in while reading texts on his iPhone.

I read his badge, Kip Tempulous. *He's Tim's replacement, and Steve's old friend from Silicon Valley!* He was a tall thin man, a Tin Man of sorts. "You're—you're all—all in this together? Stealing—"

"Not stealing, Ms. Hershel, just reclaiming what corporations have been stealing from *us* all along," Kip said. "We're taking what's owed us ... millions."

I had to keep stalling for time, and leading them on. "Mira Padeson knows I'm here, so you better just let me go and turn everything over to Riata." When I swallowed and exhaled, I felt light headed, and felt the remaining seconds of my life slip away…in vivid images of my children, and Tim, flowing through my mind as a life scroll showing me my sins and accomplishments. *But I don't wanna die,* I prayed. *I can't die … too much to do … and the kids!*

"Who the hell *is* this lady?" Kent Smith asked, finally pulling the gun out of the file cabinet. "The FBI? And *you* hired her, Claude?" He turned off the safety and gestured angrily at Claude.

"Yes, but everything about her resume appeared solid and useful…including her statistics background," Claude replied.

Kent moaned. "What were you thinking? That we could use her expertise? Idiot!"

I had to stall for time in the hope that Mira was looking for me. I spit in Kent Smith's direction. "You sabotaged Dr. Manning's experiment." Then I gave Claude Filmer the dirtiest look I could imagine. "You're stealing Steve Lerrefeiht's company."

Kent grinned and then laughed.

As he pointed the gun to fire between my eyes, I shouted at Kip Tempulous, "You destroyed my husband! Go to hell."

"Her husband?" Kip asked.

"Who's he?" Kent added. "I've never heard of any Hershel." They stood statue still, like men waiting for a light bulb moment that would never arrive.

Meanwhile, the hallway noise had stilled.

"They're out there … Mira and everyone … right now," I said, panting wildly. "Really!"

If I can get them to open the door, perhaps someone will come in at least to be nosey, and see what's going on in a confidential office setting. Please, someone, be out there, and want to come in here…

None of my captors moved as they listened with their

breaths that appeared stalled inside their chests. For seconds, I believed time had freeze, and God's angels were helping, me.

Then the outside key-pad exploded and the door began rattling, but Tip Tempulous was there, trying to keep it shut as Claude Filmer ran out the adjacent door to escape.

"Open up! We know there's a problem in there!"

"Mira! Help!" I shouted.

Kent ran to the door, ready to fire his weapon at her. I lifted a heavy trophy off the bookcase and heaved it at him with every ounce of my strength. It stuck him in the back, and he dropped to the floor writhing in agony.

First, I saw a foot through a crack in the door, then a skirt, followed by several feet. "We have police! Open up!"

The door broke open, guards entered, and Tip Tempulous and Kent Smith surrendered to a line of armed police officers.

Rushing over to the bookcase, I retrieved the flash drive, but dropped it, watching it tumble to the carpet in slow motion. My mind wasn't working ... felt like a glitch ... no stall in my brain. "Evidence, here, Mira," I said.

She handed me a bottle of water and led me to safety on an office chair. "I've got it, Rae Anne," she said gently, showing me the flash drive in her fingers. "Here just drink this." Through her cat-eye glasses, I could see her teary green eyes wide with shock. She looked just as shaken up as me through all the corporate commotion. "Wow, I can't believe what you've done...what you've found. You're amazing, Rae Anne." She put her hand over her heart and swooned like I'd accomplished a James Bond maneuver!

In the minutes following, the sixth floor turned into a maze of madness as Steve appeared, police detectives materialized, and guards began running in-and-out of various offices to hunt down and apprehend Claude Filmer.

"I know he escaped through that adjacent room, Mira," I said, patting some of the cold water on my neck and face.

"Got him!" The words come through an officer's speaker phone. "We found him hidin' in the assembly room down the hall. He's in custody."

"Whew, thank God," I said, almost passing out in relief.

"I want every crime you've charged them with to stick," a woman's voice resounded from behind a line of officers.

"Who's that, Mira?" I asked, feeling a bit more recovered and my shaking subsiding.

Mira smiled and her eyes rounded as her mouth opened in amazement. "Get ready, Rae Anne...here comes the *real* boss." She gripped my forearm and began staring at the door as if she was expecting the President.

A refined woman stepped into the room, noticed Mira, glanced at me in wonder, and began walking regally towards us. Dressed in the nicest most expensive suit I'd ever seen, she could not only pass as a middle-aged model, but also an intelligent sophisticated college professor.

"Who's the person I need to thank?" She knew. She just wanted to make me say it.

I couldn't, but Mira did. "Rae Anne Hershel," Mira said.

"Well, thanks to you, Ms. Hershel," the woman began, "we've been able to finally nab the people responsible for skimming millions of dollars off our books, and for committing fraud. We've been trying to capture them for years, but a few bad lawyers in our company, and even investors, have been keen on hiding them and their illegal activities in that fake company you managed to find—"

"Key Stone Investments and Dye," I said. Then, as she kept talking about their criminal activities, fear replaced my wonderful moment in the spot light. *I'm not Rae Anne Hershel ... I'm Rae Anne Westman. When should I tell them? Shoot! I could get thrown in jail along with all those criminals I just help capture! What do I do?*

On one of Claude Filmer's office screens, the police had activated a Skype connection and were assembling the three criminals in a lineup at the station. Their faces were angry and red-flushed, and their appearances disheveled beyond recognition.

"I'm pressing charges of fraud, and I accuse you of theft and absconding with company funds," the elegant woman exclaimed with authority.

The police officer began reading the three criminals their rights, but Kent Smith interrupted him. "You have no legal say in this matter. Only Justin Bailing. And Justin Bailing died years ago. So Steve—"

"*I* am Justina Bailing, Chief Executive Officer of Riata Technology," she returned, her head held high and proud.

The police officers on their end appeared to sway in the announcement, and every person in Claude's office and in the hallways stopped their conversations with even the cosmos respecting her position in the universe.

Steve Lerrefeiht walked up behind the magnanimous woman without saying a word. He appeared stunned, as when he had wide-eyed observed Thornton Manning's technological innovations.

Part VI
Upheaval

From articles in various magazines and newspapers, the public believed the multi-billion-dollar business tycoon was a recluse, a man, or perhaps dead. They were so wrong!

As the Riata Telecommunication's Department transmitted the entire arrest on screen in Claude Filmer's tossed office, and in every room throughout the company, employees learned the truth. Justin Bailing was not a recluse, or dead, but a woman who had retreated into shadowy vistas to assume a false identity to satisfy her investors. She told those investors she would go public *only* when she believed the corporate world would embrace a female executive magnate, or if the company were to encounter grave obstacles and face bankruptcy. This was Justina Bailing's shining moment!

Now, the paparazzi and TV stations were networking around Riata with crab-like tenacity, eager to get a review with her, and making her a public figure as if she had risen from the grave. Reporters and photographers appeared to be bending the security gates to get a good view of her, take pictures, and talk to any of her acquaintances.

After police took the arrested three criminals off screen to their holding cells as TV reporters continued their narrations of current events, I began debriefing with Mira and Dr. Bailing. "I have a confession," I said, my stomach in knots. After telling another Riata employee to turn down the volume on the monitor, I breathed and exhaled, "My name is not Rae Anne Hershel."

"I knew it!" Mira said. "Are you in the FBI?" She

leaned in a little closer to me, to whisper. "CIA? Or maybe British Intelligence?" She appeared ready to write a thriller!

As Justina waited alongside with intrigue in her green eyes, I was fidgeting. "No, I'm not with the FBI, Mira. My name is Rae Anne Westman—"

"Westman? As in Tim Westman?!"

I nodded with an expression of embarrassment. "I'm his wife."

Justina quickly broke away to hand a detective her formal paperwork pressing charges against Filmer, Tempulous, and Smith. Then she returned. "What brought you're here to Riata? And *who* is Tim Westman? As head of HR, Mira, you seem to know him."

I broke down in tears, no longer able to contain my pent up emotions. Furthermore, I'd just had a gun pointed in my face, and my life almost lost, so my head and heart were flowing with weird energy that I was beginning to come down from as if I'd been drugged and recovering. Justina sat down beside me with Mira on my right.

"Tell me what's going on, Rae Anne, so I can help you, because you've certainly helped me today," Justina said, patting my arm gently.

"Well," I began, drinking a sip of water, "Steve fired my husband, accusing him of booking too many orders that would basically hurt the company next year."

"Ridiculous!" Mira said.

"That's been proven false by what we've discovered," Justina added, turned away briefly, obviously summoning Steve Lerrefeiht to report to her. "Go on, Rae Anne."

I inhaled and dried my eyes. Having the two of them like sisters being so supportive of me—especially Justina who could help me *big* time!—I began to feel safe, secure and stronger. But really, I had accomplished something tremendous, all on my own. I had saved an entire corporation in just one day, with the clock now at 2:57 p.m. Did I really need *anyone* to affirm my worth? My self-esteem? *I—me!—Rae Anne Hershel Westman blew the whistle on criminals, and probably saved a lot of jobs, and helped people.*

Meanwhile, Mira had Tim's employment folder in her hands, had opened it, and was showing Justina its contents. "He didn't deserve this, *uh-uh*, not at all," Justina said with anger in her eyes. "I need him on the phone, ASAP. I intend to fix this *now*," she told her assistant.

I took my cell phone out of my purse and gave her Tim's new number. "He's job hunting in San Jose, Ms. Bailing—"

"Call me Justina," she corrected.

I laughed, "Okay, but I just know he'll talk to you. He'll be shocked, because he thought you've been, well, dead, so I know Tim will be mighty surprised!"

She grinned, and her smooth Dianna Sawyer complexion exuded a calm collectivity. "He'll be even more surprised when I offer him my private jet to fly here right away!"

"Wow!" Mira exclaimed, taking off her cat-eye glasses and cleaning them with her skirt, obviously her way of compensating for her utter amazement at being in Justina's presence again, especially knowing she was alive and reassuming her rightful ownership of Riata.

"I don't think Tim will say no to that, Justina," I said.

Somewhere during our talk about why I had infiltrated Riata, and showing Justina all my fake IDs, I realized I was a knowledgeable and articulate person, as well as, *okay*, a risk-taking sneaky whistleblower. Still, I'm capable of doing *big* things, and helping people, if I just had the chance. I'm just like everyone else navigating this good-n-bad world: trying to find a purpose, a job I can do well, stay put, make some hard cash, and not be dictated by fears.

"Rae Anne…." Justina said emphasizing my name. She appeared ready to pronounce a heavy sentence on me.

I gasped. *My eyes have to be elephant-sized!* "Yes, Justina?" Then I sat up tall and swallowed down my rancid smothering fear. *I can take this…I'll get a good lawyer if need be. My life's not over.* My imagination was rolling like a paver over a street.

"How would you like to work at Riata permanently?"

I coughed, and gasped again, and Mira handed me some more water as a police officer told me he would be keeping my fake IDs and *not* pressing charges. "Yes, yes of course I'd like a job here at Riata, Justina. That'll be great!" In between the details of various jobs and their descriptions, an FBI agent interrupted us.

"Ms. Bailing," the burly man with holstered weapons began, "Claude Filmer cut a deal."

"Really?!" she exclaimed. "What kind of deal?" She gave him a retaliatory glare.

"Don't worry … he's gonna pay for what he's done," he said, taking out his notepad and briefly flashing us his long list. "In exchange for turning on his partners in crime, he'll get twenty-five years in federal prison, without parole, and we're able to learn the *entire* scope of their illegal activities and operation."

"He's done horrible damage, Sir…and they're hardened criminals who must pay," Justina said.

"Oh they will … they all will, Ms. Bailing because in the end, every dirty deed they've done is gonna bite 'em all in the ass," Agent Dan Morris said.

Mira and I shivered when we saw his head shake with anger and his stunned expression indelible on his list.

"Because of their executive positions in your company, Ms. Bailing," he began, "Claude Filmer and his companions were able to incorporate *five* fake companies."

"Five?!"

"Yes. Key Stone Investments and Dye was just a front for four more fake companies that we're now raiding and shutting down. We're using our best hackers, because their dark net connections were so astute at laundering money and pushing untested products…even a few prototypes from your R and D department." He checked a few more pages in his notes and compared them to an incoming text message from the FBI. "They've managed to collect electronic payments of over *twenty* million dollars. We found their hidden accounts—"

"Let me guess, in Swiss banks?" Justina asked.

"I bet some posh Caribbean island," Mira added.

He laughed, "All those." Then he sighed and continued. "We discovered pages of top-secret chip designs and government projects, thanks to what Ms. Hershel managed to download," he nodded at me in complimentarily.

"Yeah, well, I'm grateful I'm alive," I added.

"I'll get to *that* in a minute," he said, shooting me an eager glance.

What more could he be referring to? I wondered.

Agent Morris flipped a page in his notebook. "We discovered Kent Smith had stolen several designs from your R and D department, and was negotiating with the Chinese for a sizeable payment. We also were able to get the names of a few Russian spies with whom they were networking."

"Dr. Manning will be furious!" Justina said.

"But thanks to the deal Claude Filmer cut, we can interrupt all those illegal negotiations," he said. "And the CIA is on the way to discuss the foreign implications that might boomerang on Riata."

"Whew," Justina began, "thank goodness we can nip all these illegal transactions and networks in the bud, because if we can't, investors will surely sue my company, and I'll go bankrupt." Still she kept her cool calm demeanor as she asked her assistant to contact Thornton Manning.

After Agent Morris finished reading from his extensive list of their criminal activities, he was about to leave but then stopped and gave me a congratulatory expression. "Oh—there's a reward the government offers in cases such as these…where we've been hunting down some of the most nefarious spies, but then a civilian steps in and leads us to their arrest and imprisonment, Ms. Westman."

"That means a big sum of money for you I bet, Rae Anne," Mira exclaimed.

"Wow, go on, Agent Morris," I said, as Justina continued putting together her final touches on an employment package for me.

"I can't give you an exact amount … but I can tell you we've paid out a few hundred thousand dollars in reward money," he said, closing his notebook and shoving it in his Columbo-style overcoat.

It might have been raining outside, but I felt the heat of the sun pumping excitement through me. "We're having a house built, so maybe the reward money can pay for the entire thing!" I almost wanted to faint with gratitude. "Thank you, Sir."

He laughed. "My pleasure, Mrs. Westman."

As Justina finished talking business with him, and what she could expect to happen to her legally, Mira opened my employment folder. "You won't be needing Rae Anne Hershel's information," she laughed, throwing my fake employment history in the trash.

"I think I'll like the Statistics position, Mira," I said when she offered me two *job* positions. "I can work with Dr. Manning then, that is, after a few days when he'll finish with his conniption fit…'cause you know he's gonna have one when he discovers those criminals sabotaged his experiment and stole all his designs."

We paused as if praying, and Mira lowered her head in empathy. "Yes, he'll definitely be upset, but he likes Riata, and he lives close by. So I'm sure, like all of us, he'll recover after some time passes, and move forward with more of his world-changing ideas."

"And I'll have the job of my life, being a researcher alongside him!" I thought nothing else could make my day, until…

Tim showed up, at 5:30 p.m. with Carolyn and Joey. After Agent Dan Morris left minutes ago, we walked to the sixth-floor conference room, where Justina had already spoken with Thornton Manning to negotiate new employment terms and cool down his smoldering anger.

Joey ran up to the stunned athletic genius, tugging on his pant leg, and pointed to a little robot Thornton had stationed in the corner. "What's *that*? Where'd ya buy *that*? Can I have one?"

"Oh that's one of my little-but-great machines," he replied to Joey.

He had a sweet attentive face, his round-blue eyes like sponges absorbed every bit of Dr. Thornton Manning's knowledge and expertise.

"What's its name did ya say?" Joey asked.

He walked over the three-foot, steel-shiny robot and said to it, "Operation on, Rain;" and the robot's eyes flared red, its arms extended, and its clanging body joints began moving as if the robot was preparing to march in a parade. "Its name is Rain, Joey."

"Ah!" Joey cried, running to Tim and me.

"What did you say your robot's name is, Dr. Manning?" I asked.

"Rain," he replied, and then he shut Rain down so Joey could approach it and touch it.

Tim hugged me. "He said 'Rain,' right?"

We laughed.

"What's so funny?" Justina asked as Mira handed paperwork for Tim to resume his old V.P. of Marketing and Sales job at Riata.

"That's the nickname I gave her a long time ago," he replied.

I stretched up until my lips reached his earlobe. "Who woulda thought that such a hard time in my life could end up so differently, and now in the name of a world-changing robot for Pete's sake?" Again we laughed as we rounded up the children to head home to Carlsbad.

"Take the day off tomorrow Justina says," Mira called to me as I gathered my briefcase and purse to leave.

"Thanks, we need it," I said, "and I'll see you Thursday then, at 9 a.m. sharp."

On our way down the elevator to the parking lot, we passed changed people, happy people.

"I heard Steve Lerrefeiht's been fired," someone said, pushing the button to the first floor.

"Yippee!" another person said.

"I'll never believe he wasn't in cahoots with those other criminals," another added.

"This place feels like it's been fumigated and now has

fresh air flowing through it, thanks to Dr. Bailing taking over," a man said.

Eavesdropping on more conversations on our way to the exit, I could hear their concern for their jobs and families. Several workers might have lost *everything* if not for the "mysterious spy and whistleblower" employee who had exposed so much fraud and saved Riata.

Tim appeared altered too. Tired and worn, he looked like Colossus carrying our burdens of survival on his shoulders for so long. I bet he was also a bit angry with me, that I had pulled such a risky stunt that could have backfired and landed me in jail. *Anything* can occur that can change a person's life and alter it on another direction, at any second, for good or for bad.

"I'm sorry, Tim," I said as Carolyn and Joey ran to the car in the chilly drizzle.

He sighed and gave me a quick hug. "Apology accepted. I'm just glad I'm picking you up here and not at a police station," he laughed.

I shrugged and pulled my collar against my neck. "Well, at least you have your job back."

"Yes—because the interview I had this morning in San Jose really bombed," he said. "And with all the changes, this place is going to be great place to work at from now on."

I didn't want to tell him what I had really learned, because that would mean our marriage might be over. I believed he was a liar, and I almost called him a liar to his face. Wow, had I been wrong, and I feel red-faced ashamed of myself. I guess the saying is true: work on yourself first, because only then can you start inspecting everyone else around you. I'm realizing I'll be in self-analysis and self-improvement mode all my life! Tim had been telling me the truth all along. And from now on, I'd have to start being honest with him, no matter what. I'd have to start telling him *why* I had been sad for so many years. I correct myself: *depressed* for so many years.

"I really want to work, Tim. I just can't stay home all the time. And I don't want to keep moving. I just can't take moving again." I began crying. "I don't think I've *ever* lived in one place for more than four years…in my entire lifetime. I know it's not your fault—"

"It's not *anyone's* fault, Rae, it's just called life," he said, holding my hand.

I felt his warmth flow through me. *I have his hand to hold!*

"Yes, I know moving has been hard on you and the kids, Rae, and I'm sorry the jobs have been so, well, darned awful." He held the car door open for me, and we stared longingly at each other through a wordless exchange of love and commitment.

He was always so nice and gentlemanly, and I had always admired his drive to provide for us, and his desire to be a good husband. Heavens knows I'd been working hard to be a good wife to him!

"I can't wait to get you home, and well, make the best romantic dinner I can conjure up with fish sticks and tartar sauce gravy."

He laughed and winced at me. "I guess this is gonna be some kinda romantic night we're gonna have, Rae. I can't wait!"

Homeless Man

I wake up and remember ... it's Halloween. I pour my usual cup of coffee; and because the weather's cooled down, I walk outside on my back patio and breathe the crisp air. The morning sun is blazing bright over my neighbor's rooftop, and when I look south into the pine trees behind the back fence, I see a hanging body, swaying under a giant branch. Coughing, I almost drop my coffee! Is *that* a real person? Naw, can't be. It's probably a scarecrow someone hauled up there as a Halloween stunt. But the body is at the center of a preserve, a no traffic area.

I dash to the fence and push apart several pepper tree branches that are backlashing whips. Looking up, I see sharp sunrays ... and then nearly blinding light illuminating a dangling limp body. It's dead center from my back yard at about thirty feet behind my wooden plank fence. This is not some scarecrow someone stuffed with hay. I notice a beard and hear a crow cawing and flies buzzing. He's *definitely* a man. Then I hear rocking creaking noises ... the dead man's heavyweight and his strangulation rope sawing away at the branch.

I run into the house. "Ben—wake up. Someone's dead out in the back!"

He groggily pops up, half-awake on the side of the bed. "What? In our backyard?"

"Yes, Ben, someone's dead, and the body's hanging on a tree in the preserve. Get up!" I tug his white t-shirt. "Come on, now!" I must look like I see invading aliens. "Whata we do?"

He yawns and staggers to the bathroom. "Call the cops, Francine. I'm coming."

"Just hurry!" Calling 911, I relay what I see outside my patio door that's spooking me. I believe a dead person's soul haunts people until the body's removed from the place where the person died and is buried. *This* wandering soul must have double-whammy spooking abilities because homeless man didn't have a peaceful death. *Anything* can happen! It's Halloween.

When the police descend on my family like we're harboring terrorists, neighbors begin huddling on the curb and whispering on the sidewalks ... in front of *my* house. They're all pointing at the pine tree, and the dead man's body swaying with his neck cocked sideways on a frayed manila rope. Some people vomit, some are crying, and a few wave in disgust and leave. The wind's picking up, so the dead man's drooping arms are swaying at his sides like they're rubber.

"How did he die like *that*?" someone asks.

"How did he even get up there?" another shouts.

"It *looks* like suicide, but could he have been murdered?" another whispers.

"Doubt that," a man answers. "There isn't a light back there anywhere ... or electricity for that matter, for someone to maneuver through that dense forest."

"Suicide then," the woman moans.

"What the heck was going through his mind to do something like that with so many kids wandering around in the area," a woman says with her fingers quivering over her lips.

More snowballing questions pop through the air like uncontrollable gunfire.

Then, I burst out crying. Ben hugs me. Then I noticed our son Stevie recording the scene on his iPhone for YouTube. I almost knock his out of his hand. "Stop it! Have some respect."

"But everyone's doing it," Stevie replies, shuffling his feet in a bit of shame.

Five people slowly lower their devices while also ensuring their videotapes of death are saved. Stevie is right, but capturing the dangling body, ambulances, and cop cars for worldwide viewing and thumbs-up emoticon approval doesn't make the viral spread of someone's private death moment ethically or morally acceptable. Something feels so disturbing, to my very core.

Meanwhile, I'm overhearing important conversations: "Who he is?" "Anyone ever see him around here?" "His clothes look so ragged!" "A policeman just said the man is *definitely* homeless." "God why in *our* neighborhood?"

One neighbor says: "This is gonna be one helluva Halloween for sure. Maybe we'll even see a ghost!" He taps his camera enthusiastically until he sees me scowl a bit and wipe away my tears.

"Oo, yeah cool," someone yells.

In between frenzied moments of police sirens blaring up-and-down the street and detectives canvassing my back yard, anxiety like the odor of pungent gas spreading from a broken pipe is trickling through the entire neighborhood. I wonder if some people are thinking the same things I am. Six years ago during the bad economic downturn, *we* might have been forced to hunker down in an uncultivated land. We lost everything. Thank God social security hit our bank account 'cause that money saved us from homelessness. Not everyone gets saved.

Two doors down, orange Halloween lights are wavering in a brisk breeze. Five doors west of me, carved pumpkins on an acorn-sprinkled lawn have hallowed out smiles. The corner house has a mailbox flying a plastic bat flag. Meanwhile, behind my backyard, firemen are high up on cranes and close to capturing the hanging man with a long steel cane and ropes.

Suddenly, their cables *snap*.

Homeless man drops.

His body hits the ground kicking up pine needles. Beneath his body could be anything, from turtle eggs to acorn shards, pine cones, and raccoon droppings. Feeling sick again, but also angry as heck, I peek over the fence and watch firemen and the police cordon off the area with yellow tape. A large black SUV appears, and people dressed in white HazMat suits and CSI jackets begin processing the area. Where they gonna take Homeless man? Dumb question. You've seen the shows ... to a slab, in a morgue ... probably for quite some time he'll remain unburied for quite some time.

Suddenly, a face pops up in front of me. The detective starts asking me questions. "Did you know him? Did you see anything out of the ordinary? Did you hear anything last night?"

"No."

Ben and Stevie answer the same. Then she begins what appears to be her usual routine, questioning those who haven't scattered like ants.

I feel so squeamish. The sun is rising high and shining hot and hard. In a few hours, it'll be right over that blasted pine tree like a beacon. Then reality sets in. For as long as I live here, I'll have that pine tree in my sight and Hangman's body in my memory. Never to be forgotten.

"Uh-oh," Ben begins a he points to several places behind our fence. "People are startin' to throw flowers behind there."

"That's just what we need from now on," I groan.

The little area where Hangman died is becoming his final resting place.

"Can you throw these over when you have time, please?" a little girl asks me, handing me a small wildflower bouquet to toss over my fence as a memorial.

"Okay, but this is enough, no more, please," I tell her. Then she cautiously runs across the street and disappears behind a throng of neighbors.

Two hours after the firemen, police, and coroner leave, I start breakfast. I cook sausage and toast every day. I have food, and a home, *every* day. Suddenly, I realize all my things and my home could shatter, like crystal breaking on the floor. I try not to mix my tears with the butter I'm slathering on the toast. And the sizzling sausage smells like dog food.

Then, the doorbell rings and I answer it. There are two small children dressed in rags with holes in their tennis shoes. "Trick or treat!" Their high little voices are music.

I'm startled. Who'd send their kids trick-or-treating before noon? "It's a bit early for trick-or-treating." I show them my watch. "It's only eleven in the morning." I glance behind them. "Where are your parents?"

They look sad as one child gestures over his shoulder. I peek out and see a scratched, white dirty van with a missing bumper idling down the street. Oh, they're homeless. I see something deeper in their round innocent eyes. They don't appear to know their homeless situation, and Halloween is the perfect day for people to store up food for winter.

The dangling dead man pops into my brain. "What do I do?" I only use debit cards and never carry cash. What's to give? I have an idea. Last night, I bought two giant bags of peanut butter cups to hand out to trick-or-treaters. "Wait just a second," I tell them. I find one bag, rip it open, and pour out a river of peanut butter cups into their plastic Walmart shopping bags. They have shocked eyes, and then they smile like they'll be eating dinner for days. Then they run away, their skinny legs carrying them on the wind to the next house. I *should* feel good, like I did something positive and helpful. I don't.

My son Stevie is in school, and Ben just finished breakfast. I grab the car keys. "We need a wheelbarrow full of candy, Ben. Come on, trick-or-treaters are coming."

"Yeah, fine, okay, Francine."

I have an idea! "When we're done picking out candy, we can buy a lot of toiletries. We can put them in Glad wrap bags with McDonald's gift cards and give them to homeless people holding signs on the streets."

"What?" He scratches his head.

"We can hand them out to homeless people instead of money," I reply. "Well?"

He shrugs and nods approvingly. "That's better than doin' nothin'."

Gratitude for Blue

"Should I take the Sebring ... or the Volvo?" I asked one early sunny January morning while basking in the tropical breeze outside my Makakilo, Hawaiian home. Usually, I could trace at least one brilliant rainbow in the sky. However, this morning felt different from the breezy, balmy best days, as I counted two ... and then *three* rainbows popping out of a giant cloud. In the distance, curving shrub-covered mountains appeared to descend like a drift diver to the blue shimmering ocean. Wanting to watch more of the rare event but running out of time, I realized I had to make a thirty-minute drive east to town for a doctor's appointment.

Now there's really only one town on the island of Oahu, so people just call Honolulu, "town."

This day was turning out to be a bit chilly, so I kept vacillating: "The convertible, or the Midnight Blue Volvo?" I usually drive the convertible. Who wouldn't when you live in perfect Hawaii? But my husband Drew and our children Jenny and Andrew were on the mainland. That's what Hawaiians call the contiguous United States. They had flown to California after Christmas for a brief visit with relatives, so I was all alone at our house overlooking Barber's Point Harbor and the Pacific Ocean. If I'd decide to take the Volvo, at least it has a moon roof, which is a mini version of a convertible, right?

I can't explain my decision, but I decided to drive Blue into town. That's what I called "the Volvo." While taking in the spectacular rainbow site for the last time, a still voice inside of me kept drawing me to Blue, coaxing me to avoid the shining green Sebring as if snakes were slithering in the front seat. "Okay—I'll take Blue!"

The drive east on the H-1 Freeway was stop-and-go in spite of the open Zipper lane flowing with cars in the far-left lane to accommodate rush hour traffic. *The Zipper* is about a three-foot tall, movable, concrete-brick lane divider. In the evening, the opposite occurs. A giant contraption that looks like a yellow glass cocoon called a Barrier Transfer Machine, slowly crawls along the Zipper lane, repositioning the linking barrier blocks for a free-flowing western commute. Let me tell you, free-flowing never happens, and there are always wrecks, and stalls, and people who like to race.

On my drive home from the doctor, I had just transition to the H-1 west from Honolulu—

Smack!

My head struck the left side of the headrest, I couldn't steer, and at 55 miles-an-hour, missile-flying Blue launched at the white zipper blocks.

Bump—bang!

Colliding cars were all around me; and that white Zipper—with glowing halos popping up all over it—that white wall and I were going to hit. I'm going to die!

I'd always read what happens to people when they're confronted with a life-threatening situation. Flight or fight. I couldn't do either, except step on the brakes—pushing the pedal to the floor hard!—my last chance to stop Blue and save my life. But I was in the center lane and—

Crunch! Another strike.

Screeeech— screech— People were stepping on their brakes all around me.

Pop! The right airbag deployed, and I heard—

Thud—crack—thud!

I bounced. Blue's top collapsed two inches, the top

liner flapping like a fan on my head.

Scrape—scraaaape ...

I was a punching bag being pounded on by cars crashing into Blue.

Thump! *Bang—hit*!

Blue soared forward!

Did I get struck on my left again?

Blue shimmied back-n-forth. Did she just make a quick one-eighty?

Wham! Again we scratched the Zipper! *Scraaape* ...

From behind, again, someone rammed the bumper! I flew forward, my rubber band of a seatbelt snapping me back. Blue jolts, then suddenly stops—

Chomp!

I felt the whiplash as my front airbag *finally* deploys. Another car struck Blue at the front end, and the left bumper pinged the Zipper.

When the micro-collisions around me finally stopped, I noticed smoke ... from my front end ... and heard hissing ... and smelled a strong ion scent that had to be radiator juices ... and burning rubber ... then, silence.

Someone once talked about a calmness that descends around people after a storm. I couldn't feel a darn thing, only raspy noises from my lungs. Did I make it? Survive?

Blue suddenly exhaled, and the front end dropped, tilting left.

"Ah!" I screamed, reaching for the bent steering wheel. The left front tire had completely deflated, leaving me catawampus as if stuck at the top of a malfunctioning carnival ride. Breathing fast and shaking, I looked through the glass-spawning windshield and saw a giant black truck about two yards in front of me. "It's on top of the Zipper barrier! Rocking like a seesaw! How could a truck *land* on the Zipper?"

Breathe—blink—focus. My heart rate felt a hundred and twenty-five! I could hardly see anything over the slowly deflating airbag.

"Lady, are you alright?" a short Hawaiian man asked me through Blue's shattered windshield that looked smashed by a knight's ball and chain. Glass was everywhere ... but none had sliced me, at least I couldn't see blood. I began fighting the airbag to see my fingers and legs. *Whew*, no blood—*whew*! The man hopped on Blue's crinkled hood and was cautiously inspecting the inside peeling headliner. Between him and me was a little swinging spinning crystal ball on a fishing line, churning bright rainbows.

"I—what—what happened?" I could hear a rattle in my voice and a sudden spurting of the engine—Blue giving up her ghost. If I could open the left window to the scrunched door, I could lick the concrete zipper. "What did I—"

"You didn't do anything," he replied as a firetruck pulled alongside Blue. "That red truck over there—" He pointed at a large smoking truck in the right lane. "Hit you on the right, and then that truck there—" He pointed at the black truck rocking on top of the Zipper. "Drove right over you. You're lucky to be alive."

The truck's rear tires were still lightly spinning from when it had collided with Blue's bumper and drove over her, caving in her roof. Thank God I had the moon roof closed! For seconds, I thought my heart left my body. Did I cause this? Was this *my* fault? I began crying. "I—wasn't—I didn't speed or anything." I tried moving my shoulders. I couldn't. My neck felt stiff. Was it broke? Strange how body parts feel either extra sensitive or totally numb when they're circulating adrenaline. My mind felt in a fog ... and I felt disconnected from my legs and toes. My ears were ringing, and all I could hear was Blue, hissing, and now-and-then creaking. Soon she'd been giving up her tires to the hot flat pavement.

"Like I said," the Hawaiian man began as firemen and paramedics raced toward me and the two trucks that had crashed into me, "you didn't do anything. I'll tell 'em that."

Yes!—thank God this wasn't my fault! Relief came as a whistling wind and slant of sunlight through my scraped left door. "Thank you! Thanks! God bless you!" He slid off Blue, and a police officer waved him to his car while firemen revved their jaws of life and began cutting through Blue's right door support bar. "Ma'am, don't move," one fireman ordered, unfastening my seatbelt.

"Move? I can't feel my lips when I talk!" I said as a man dressed in white checked my pulse and gave me a quick physical. "She's okay. You can take 'er," he ordered.

The Hawaiian man shouted, "Lady, you're lucky to be alive!" Then he was gone.

A line of rubberneckers took his place as cars slowly sputtered by me. Those drivers had a *real* case of shock eye. They were gazing from me to the truck that was still tilting like a seesaw in the wind on top of the concrete Zipper.

I grabbed a fireman's study hands, scooted cautiously under the crushed moon roof, and fell into the arms of four medics who lifted me onto a gurney. Then the ambulance whisked me to the hospital where emergency room nurses strapped me to another gurney for *two* hours. They called it *observation*. "Don't move your neck, Mrs. Osterman until we get your X-ray results."

I called the two-hour time constraint "regaining my balance" and re-adjusting to normal. But it also gave me some serious time to think, time to feel, and time to cry. The Good Samaritan man had told me, "You're lucky to be alive." Those words repeated in a happy song in my brain, along with, "God—I coulda died!"

I didn't. "I'm alive! *Wow*—yes—I'm alive!" Gratitude began pouring through my mind, in between my calls to the nurse for water. She wouldn't give me a drop. Several times I asked her 'cause I couldn't feel my tongue or scratch my itching nose!

"Again, Ms. Osterman, we have to wait for the doctor's okay."

"*Erg*," is all I said. Before the accident, I would have yelled at her for not understanding me. Now, I could only look up into the square white ceiling tiles. At least they didn't put me under one of those bright blinding lights that you have to sit under at the dentist's office. Gratitude! I began to appreciate even the tiniest little things in life.

Better yet, I felt grateful for life itself. For breaths of air moving in and out of my lungs, 'cause I'd heard that the man who hit me had a broken rib and a few broken bones. He was in an exam room down the hall. Every now-and-then I could hear him calling out for someone. What I wouldn't have given to pry myself out of my neck restraints and straight-jacket hold to give him a piece of my mind for racing on the freeway!

Suddenly, a calmness settled over me in a secure cradling blanket. Life's too short ... too precious ... let it go ... his insurance will pay for what he did.

Life has a tendency to give back to us in the long run what we dish out to others. Karma is what I think they call it. I even felt grateful for Karma!

Then, I began contemplating my own deeds and actions. With this new lease on life and gratitude directing my next moves, I had the chance to make up for some things I didn't do that I shoulda done, and to say the simplest of words that I didn't say that I shoulda said, like *I love you* and *I'm sorry*. Strange how quickly my micro-neglects made me want to fight neck whiplash, hop off the gurney, grab a phone, and dial everyone on my call list to tell them *everything* I'd always wanted to say but didn't. I really *wanted* to be different, 'because I'd almost died! I *had* no other choice but to change, because I felt grateful to be alive.

Two days later, Drew returned from his trip. With my neck in a brace, we went to the scrap yard to see Blue. Driving down the H-1, I spotted the place in the opposite direction where the racing trucks had rammed me. A cold shudder rippled through me, even though the Hawaiian air felt silk smooth on my arms. The hills were lush and rolling, with clouds huddling the peaked mountains beyond Aiea. And little ocean crests were frothing on the Pacific as sailboats skimmed the tricky rip-current waters. I jumped in my seat— "ah!"—almost every time Drew sped up and changed lanes.

"It's okay, I'll slow down." He has a tendency to speed. But now, it looks like he too swallowed a spoon full of gratitude and is doing some changing.

Dangers lurk everywhere, but having an attitude of gratitude makes me focus on hope, not sink into a self-protection mode, and not let this accident turn me into an amaxophobic.

Sniffling now-and-then from crying, Drew touched my arm several times. "At your follow-up appointment yesterday, the doctor told me, that in his notes, someone had written, *it's amazing she lived through that crash.* He kissed my hand, but I couldn't turn to talk to him because of my cumbersome neck brace. The doctor had me commit to wearing the bulky white collar for a week! I felt the humdrums settle again into my bones, but then gratitude kicked in like a smack from an angel, fixing my thoughts on appreciating life. "Drew, I forgot to tell you, the insurance agent, Frank Dickson, representing the man who hit me called this morning."

"What did he say?"

"The company is allowing me ten massage visits," I said, turning a bit and smiling. "Ouch!" Even my shoulders hurt. "And more massage therapy if I need 'em." I imagined lying on a luxurious massage table at the Marriot in Ko Olina. That bubble burst fast. Those kinds of high-end treatments I'm sure wouldn't count. Darn it. Still, I felt grateful again to be alive. I'd heard the drivers who were racing their trucks and then struck Blue were in bad shape and would need a whole lot more tender care than just massage therapy. Gratitude comes in all sized packages.

At the salvage yard, really a car graveyard, I couldn't hold back tears—and Drew had to hold me up! We finally meandered the dirty lanes through tall piles of rusted-out cars and scrap-heaped auto parts to discover scrunched up Volvo Blue. She was sitting on the sidelines of stacked crushed cars, her shiny midnight-blue skin half-shaved off her body, her tires flat, her rims gashed and dented. Around her in the dirt, oil stains had settled as spilled perfume. There she set completely broken and dilapidated in the dirt, her final resting place.

"She looks like two open sardine cans!" I shouted, fighting against whiplash to race to her.

Drew had his hand over his mouth in shock. "And look at those brown tire marks from that truck that drove over you!" He pointed at crisscrossing indelible tracks no polish could remove. "The weight of that thing crushed the top *and* the front end!"

Panting and my heart pounding, I couldn't touch her, and my neck cracked as I turned away in tears. "I think I was an inch away from being squished beans in a can." I quickly imagined me with a broken neck, and dead, and I nearly threw up. Feeling grateful to be alive, again, I stepped closer to Blue and mustered up the courage to peek inside the shrunken cage that used to be the driver's seat. Blue appeared to have suffered so much to protect me. Still, I had to reach the shattered passenger window with her key, open the glovebox, and grab our things, because Frank Dickson had diagnosed Blue's condition— completely totaled. I touched her hot bubbled paint now baking in the Hawaiian heat of the afternoon. I'd always parked her in the garage. I ran my fingers over a midnight-blue patch of her skin. "Thanks, Blue." I looked up into a parting cloud in a sky-blue current. Somewhere, there's a rainbow, and I quickly grabbed the dangling crystal ball off the rear view mirror, holding it tightly in my hand, a remembrance of Blue. "Thank you, God."

"Your Volvo *is* totaled, Mr. and Mrs. Osterman," the manager of John's Recycle Center said, shaking our hands and then giving Drew some paperwork. "There's no putting it back together as you can see." He then gave Drew a little box, our items from the center console.

I sighed in relief. "Thanks, Sir, 'cause there's no way I'm going inside that tight precarious space again!" I walked around Blue ... the same way I walked around her to size her up before buying her. I got a headache in the dissonance! She had flat peeling tires, and her doors were missing most of her midnight-indigo skin. She was bare sheet metal, veins of wiring, and steel rod bones. What was left were accordion doors, and her once shiny trim was scratched, dented, or missing altogether, perhaps pinging somewhere along the H-1, or being pulverized by the Zipper contraption. I cried. "She's gone ... *dead*, damn it!" With trembling hands, I gave the manager Blue's car key, my heart.

Wearing gray-stained overalls, he walked up close to me. "But you're alive, Mrs. Osterman," he began, shaking his head in amazement. "If you'da been drivin' in any other car, you'da either been dead or paralyzed." He kept talking while I kept crying, and Drew stretched his arm tenderly over my shaking shoulders.

Then, a powerful Hawaiian gust of air slipped around me as from the Hawaiian goddess Kapo who saved Pele from the evil god Kama-pua'a. Inhaling the scent of sweet Plumeria, I and saw beyond all the junk, stacked tin, and salvage items that had once meant so much to people. The smallest and rustiest parts were being prepared for re-purposing, to be re-created into something new for *new* ownership. I guess it's like our bodies after burial. After hundreds of years, our elements seep into the water table, drift back into the ocean, and evaporate into the clouds to rain down on the earth and create something breathtaking and new. In billions of years ... we'll unite with ... the stars.

Again, gratitude filled my soul with an appreciation for my life. My inner voice said: If I had driven the Chrysler Sebring convertible two days ago, I *would* be dead ... right now, really *dead*.

Was this the same inner voice that had directed me— no, guided me—to the Blue?

Hm, wow! Again, tears of gratitude stung my cheeks: gratitude for life, living, and my feet touching the earth, at *this* moment.

Now is all we've got.

Suddenly, blue appeared everywhere and in everything. Blue in the sky, ocean, rainbows, shirts, tennis shoes, the manager's eyes, and the blue whale mosaic on the side of a tall Honolulu office building a few blocks in the distance.

Gratitude began coursing through me in shock waves! I started remembering moments that changed me, moments of missed opportunities, and moments where I'd grabbed opportunities that have molded me into the person I am today. We are *who* we are, in *this* moment. And in all circumstances, I decided right then and there, that I'd make sure gratitude would rule my life and not sadness over all my losses.

Since then, I haven't had the opportunity to buy a Volvo again because the insurance company didn't reimburse me for half of Blue's value. I could have been bitter and fought harder, but bitterness and cynicism deplete a person, and I'm tired of arguing and fighting. I bought a Mercury Cougar instead. But I'll always remember Blue, and I keep a few pictures of her around that I took before they dissected her into pieces of scrap. Where's she now? Hopefully, a company has molded her into more special forms, and she's giving people care and protection, people who I hope will be grateful for what they've got.

Gratitude has the same tendency to melt away distress and replace negativity with hope, and an appreciation for what we have and not to linger or lament over what we don't have and want. 'Bye, Blue!

AT THE EDGE!
SOME SLICES OF CHILDHOOD LIFE

EARLIEST MEMORY

Scream!

I wake up. It's mommy. I've never heard her like this before!

Shout!

That's Daddy. Something's wrong!

Scream ... shout....

I'm really scared now. In the corner is my nightlight, but it's dark. I feel sick. My heart is beating on my lips. Find Mommy and Daddy. Get up. Up! But my toes are cold. I can't see my feet. Start walking down the hall.

I can't go *there*...I'm so scared. Go on. *Step*. Go on. *Step, step....* Still, I'm so scared! *Step*. I'm more scared! Blackness everywhere...and wood under my feet. Blackness is going to eat me up!

Light!

There's their room. *Whew* ... breathe. More light! *Whew*. Run to it....

Tommy's standing in his crib against the wall. His fingers are white like they're going to pop. He's crying so hard his face is bright red! I can't reach him...can't pick him up like Mommy and Daddy.

There's Mommy in the doorway, by the bathroom. Her head is shaking...her hair's all messed up. Why's she shaking?

Daddy's in the bathroom ... yelling at her. She's going to hit him ... duck!

I can't feel my arms. I can't feel my legs. My stomach's growling. It's going to bleed out. Oh-oh...I peed. Oh no! She's going to slap me for that! Just walk over there...walk, now try and say something. But they don't see me.

Mommy just threw something at Daddy! Now, he's

shouting at her again!

Sting ... my eyes hurt ... burn. The light's so bright. Stand behind Mommy ... no ... in the corner! There, now the light doesn't hurt.

But she's so mad, moving around the room now, shouting and yelling at Daddy. The light keeps stinging me like stickers in my socks. Tommy's still crying.

I walk up and put my fingers through the bars. He calms down, just a little bit and starts sucking his fingers.

Daddy doesn't know I'm here. I can't see him in the bathroom. Did mommy make him go away? Disappear?

My lips won't move ... I can't talk ... they don't see me ... maybe I disappeared! I can't feel anything right now. Am I gone?

I'm only eyes ... looking all around. I'm lost!

Mom

She would have turned seventy-eight this April 25, but she died February 1, 2003, my mom.

I never really knew her, although I do know one thing about her: she never got mad.

She just raged....

The humungous snowstorm of 1965 walloped Hammond, Indiana that winter. I was in second grade and my brother in kindergarten when Mom ordered us: "Go to the little store and buy a gallon of milk. Take the sled."

"But mom, the storm! We can't," I said.

I peeked outside at the snow drifts covering the next door neighbor's windows. No way could my brother and I even find the walkways and street! And the snow plows had shoveled mounds of brown salty peaks into everyone's front yard. The entire block was the abominable snowman's arctic home!

Her black pupils rolled up so I could only see the whites of her eyes. "Damn it! Damn you!" She picked up my brother and threw him against the white steel radiator. "You *will* go!"

My brother bounced off the radiator and landed at my feet. I saw his ashen pained face and shaking body. I'll never forget his haunting plea without words, *Help me*.

I couldn't. I was about to threw up! "Come on, we gotta go," I whispered to him as he limped over to the closet where we put on our coats.

Pulling a red sled, we wound up walking that long trek to the little corner store. I couldn't feel my feet, face or cold-gloved fingers. I remember paying the cashier. My whole body was numb. My hands wouldn't stop shaking...always shaking.

Living on Spruce Street and Warren Street with my mom and stepdad for many years, we could always hear shouts and screams at end of the block. What a monster house.

Many years later, I returned to that fright zone on Spruce Street. I wanted to walk that entire round-trip distance from the house to the store as an adult.

When I was seven, the trip felt like ten miles. Strange how objects change in size the older one gets. In reality, it was twenty blocks round trip. Yet on a blizzardy January day when everyone's snowed in and school is closed, I guess walking ten blocks with the wind-chill factor at minus ten degrees below zero feels like God froze hell.

Strange is the moment when a person learns that most things that happen in life you have no control over, and we're helpless to stop them. At least we know we're not alone in the good-n-bad battling it out on Earth. Still, I keep getting goose bumps while trying to swat away that black-haired raging ghost who keeps invading my life, still trying to poison everything for me.

Nothing goes to the grave permanently.

DAD, THE BASKETBALL PLAYER

Tonight the Florida Gators are playing the Connecticut Huskies. I'm remembering a time when my Dad and I were close, for at least once …

His last wife had just died in January of 2012, and I returned to visit him after her funeral to help him rearrange things. He never asked for my help, but I wanted to be the best daughter, and clean the house, clean that back office room she had filled half to the ceiling, and help him transition from married life to bachelorhood. He was eighty-six at the time, and I don't think he'd ever lived alone.

Day after day, I hauled bag after bag out of the back room. ["Mom" was a bit of a hoarder, oh well. This is one of those family secrets, so please don't tell!] Then he asked me to clean out her "things." We're talking about three closets worth o' things! That's okay though.

While I worked, I felt my dirty hands…they touched every object of hers; and I believed she didn't deserve to be let go of so quickly, so abruptly. At times, I cried, but I never let him, Dad, know. I just kept on goin', movin' my hands, and cleanin' every room.

After dropping off all her things at the local Goodwill—that usually happened at around 4:30 every day—I went to MacDonald's and had one of those delicious Shamrock Shakes, the small one. It was the beginning of March, and St. Patrick's Day was just around the corner. While sitting and eating at the fast-food restaurant, I couldn't stop thinking about my real mother.

She was Irish. She 'da loved Shamrock shakes! I wonder if she ever had one? I wished I could have one with her because I have rounds of questions to ask her. Too bad she and I never connected. She had some *serious* problems. I wonder what plagued her all her life? I wonder why Dad never stopped her?

That's what I kept thinking about while sippin' that shake.

There's a literary device in literature called an *epiphany*, I believed invented by Irish author James Joyce. An epiphany is a moment when you suddenly see or understand something in a new, clear crisp way. Usually that moment changes you, evolves you to a higher level of consciousness and navigating in the world that's so difficult at times and confusing. I had one right then and there in Mac's:

Have you ever noticed that so much conversation you should be having with the important significant people in your life, you're only having in your head? No wonder some people turn out the way they do. *Ahhh...*

Then I'd return to Dad's house, back to all that hard cleaning up.

At nights, my Dad and I had super, usually left overs, but they were the best leftovers I ate while visiting him—sausage with sauerkraut, and peaches, and beets, and three-bean salad, the latter being "mom's" favorite.

Thereafter, I'd washed dishes the old-fashioned way, 'cause with only Dad and me in the house, dirty dishes were scarce. I wanted that kitchen looking immaculate, the refrigerator squeaky clean. I couldn't predict when I'd return again, or if I'd ever return.

In the evenings, Dad would settle down in his rocking chair, on the left of me who liked sitting and reading on the couch, and we'd watch basketball. He liked the Lakers, and Clippers, and Blake Griffin, who had a car commercial at the time. "The Griff," my Dad and I would call him. But the guy had troubles making the free shots!

I kept telling Dad, "If they can't make the baskets, they can't win."

It's true! The winning team in basketball is the team who makes the majority of baskets; and in football, catches the bullet ball and steps over the goal line.

The winners are always the happiest when the game's over.

Living with my dad and stepmom for a short time, I used to think life was about winning or losing, black-and-white. Nope. Not *one* person I ever met is void of problems, but I've always been able to discern a winning blessing in their lives as they work through their difficulties, and endure ... to the ultimate end.

AUNT LIZ

Somewhere between bubbly Mary Poppins and savvy Martha Stewart is my Aunt Liz. The first child of my immigrant Hungarian grandparents, she was the oldest, the responsible one. She told me two years ago that she like playing baseball when she was a teenager—to the chagrin of her parents because she was a girl. She also liked fishing, cooking, hunting, and family gatherings. She once told me she could take squawking live chickens, pluck 'em, boil 'em, and bake them for supper. She could make the best chicken noodle soup! She could also make homemade sausage, pickled pigs' feet, and the tastiest, fluffiest apricot-buttermilk Jell-O. Aunt Liz could even fix electrical wiring and plumbing problems! She wowed people. Two weeks ago, she died in hospice; but she's still so alive and vibrant in my mind.

I have been entertaining a habit lately. Usually people think habits are bad; but believe me, some habits can be good for your health! I work in the same office with my husband most of the day, and my sixteen-year-old son has ADHD and Asperger syndrome. They can be demanding and draining:

"Mom—I need help with the oven!"

I help him make a casserole.

"Mom—I need you right now! Come 'ere!"

I take the serving plate before he drops it while he peels off the two frozen hamburger patties he wants to cook on the hot smoking grill.

Then, later on he asks, "Mom—where's my shirt?!"

"In the drawer," I reply, and then two minutes later he wants me to go to Taco Bell and buy him a $5 Quesarito box. Off I go! By 5:30, I'm tired. I need a break from all the writing and taking care of everyone. My habit begins!

Every day for about ten minutes, I like to go to the backyard, sit at the edge of the pool and swirl my legs knee-high in the water. Memories of Aunt Liz flood my mind. My brother and I used to do the same things with her when we'd go fishing with her at her cottages at Lake Monitou in Rochester, Indiana. In the early evenings, as the sky rolled with bright orange, with water lapping on the shore, the row boat lightly thumping against the wooden peer, the lily pads undulating at the center of the bay, and sounds of boat motors rumbling as fish enthusiasts made their way to open water for night fishing, we'd talk and laugh with Aunt Liz.

"What's the biggest fish you ever caught?" I asked her. I was about eleven.

She pushed up her glasses and swirled her strong legs through the murky water. She had blond, frizzy, naturally curly hair and warm green eyes. She also had a peculiar way of pursing her lips that made her nose lightly twitch. "We used to go fishing in Minnesota during the summer," she began. "We'd rent a cabin, and then return with all kinds of sun fish and blue gills and cat fish." Then she glanced into the setting sun. For a moment, she appeared lost there. "But we also caught some pretty big muskies!"

"Is that fish you have over your fireplace?" my brother asked.

"That's it!" she replied, again swirling her feet in the water.

"We never had to stock up on food 'cause we could eat fish every night," she said with a proud strong expression.

I could catch fish, kill 'em, skin 'em, and fry 'em up in butter. Aunt Liz taught me. I could fish from the peer, fish from the rowboat, and fly fish. She even showed Tom and me where to find the juiciest and plumpest worms. She knew every perfect location to fish on Lake Manitou, and my dad knew the best baits and most popular lures on which the fish liked to bite. I've seen expert fly fishermen ... but no people more graceful and exact than my dad and Aunt Liz. If they were competing in the sport today, I just know they could win first place.

"Were you afraid of holding catfish though, Aunt Liz?" I was! They have barbels, and I was always afraid they'd sting me. I was terrified of their wiggling bodies.

"Nope," she replied. "I just hit 'em over the head with a hammer. They're dead by then, so they're easy to take off the hook."

Tom and I laughed, and then she pursed her lips and squinted. It had to be a hard memory. "What happened after that?" I was always afraid she was remembering Uncle Steve. He was with her on all those adventures, but died when I was nine. Every day, I know she missed him.

Then she told us about the ticks that landed on their heads and arms on the way back to their vacation cottage. "They were everywhere on us!" she said, her voice high-pitched.

"How'd ya get 'em off ya?" my brother asked.

"With hot matches!" she replied, trembling.

"So that's why you always wear a hat whenever ya go outside," I said. She often tried to shove one of her hats on top of my head, but I'd push them away. "I won't go under any trees. Or if I do, I'll run fast so the ticks won't bite me!"

She'd let me go. "Oh ... *okay*."

Several years later, I saw a shelf of hats—straw to broad-rimmed lace hats—in her coat closet. That was after she sold the cottages, sold her rowboat and pontoon boat, and sold most of her fishing equipment. She always kept a few poles and a little tackle box though. And in all the family pictures taken at her house in Munster, Indiana, that giant taxidermy fish she and Uncle Steve caught in Minnesota is in every snapshot—sometimes stuck between peoples' head, always a reminder of her and him.

Well, my break is over. I gotta go back inside, and back to fixing dinner and washing dishes. Actually, only Aunt Liz washed dishes! I have a dishwasher. "Aunt Liz … you always did help me see the brighter side of things … the best of the world! Thanks. One day, I just know we'll see each other again, and go fishing."

Aunt Mary

My Aunt Mary is almost ninety-three years old, but I remember her from her younger days….

My brother and I always looked forward to visiting Aunt Mary, my Dad's sister. Of the three girls my grandpa and grandma had, she was the middle child. A daughter later, my grandma had my dad and then my dad's brother, Uncle Joe.

My Aunt Mary had black hair, brown eyes, and a *Leave it to Beaver* motherly quality. During the time I grew up, she also worked full-time at the Goldblatt's department store in Hammond, Indiana. Sometimes, my brother and I would walk there to visit her, and she'd always give us a few quarters. He and I would then buy candy, or a coloring book and crayons.

When we would visit her at her house, sometimes on weekends because my dad had visitation, my Aunt Mary's house always smelled of Hungarian pastries and spices, like walnut nut rolls and paprika. Upon entering the screen door and hopping up a short set of stairs to the kitchen, she'd always ask us if we wanted pop to drink and a snack. I think she baked every morning besides working all day, wow!

Then my brother and I would sit down in the living room and watch TV. Sometimes her husband, Uncle George would pull out his eight-millimeter camera projector and show us their vacation movies from when they traveled to Colorado and toured the Ponderosa and ate real cowboy food at western rodeo shows. Sometimes, we'd fall asleep toward the end of the show; after all, Uncle George sure did like telling *loooong* stories. But what I wouldn't give now to sneak some coffee, stay awake, and hear him one last time. It's like that play, *Our*

Town. If you could have one day to relive, *where* would *you* go?

During our visits, my brother and I always tried to remain so well behaved, polite, and nice.

"Please," "Thank you," and, "Can I help with something?" were always in our vocabulary when visiting Aunt Mary and Uncle George. Another favorite part for me was tagging behind my cousin, Linda. As a teenager in the 1960s, she had the most beautiful dresses, perfume, and records. There was always something to do at Aunt Mary's house, even in the basement, where cousin Georgie used to run the newest and best cars on his little miniature toy tracks.

We always wanted to come back! And I never once remember Aunt Mary having to scold us, which wasn't the case with our grandparents...*ouch*! My grandpa had one helluva mean razor strap! And wow, could my brother and I get into some tussles and fights, like most brothers and sisters.

Of all the favorite times to visit, Easter was the best time at Aunt Mary house. The meals were giant...the portions of ham, potato salad, baked beans, sweet potatoes and cakes grand. All day long, family would come out of the woodwork, *visiting*. That's what we used to call spending time with the aunts and uncles during those lingering afternoons and happy evenings: visiting...

"Let's go visit ... Aunt Mary!"

"Let's go visit ... Aunt Liz!"

"Let's go visit ... Aunt Tess, Uncle Bob, and Johnny in Lakeside, Michigan!"

Those years are long gone like rain water now mingling with the Mediterranean, I'm sure. Aunt Mary's home, and her family are now stories, memories and in pictures. But it's not the same leafing through snapshots in an album.

Still, I have a little silver bracelet containing three charms tucked away in a special jewelry box Aunt Mary gave me after returning from one of her trips out west. One day, I'll pass it on to my grandchildren, and tell them of those treasured times I spent with Aunt Mary.

A BIKE RIDE IN THE RAIN

I was seventeen, a junior in high school, in 1975 when Ron K. rode up to my house and asked me to take a bike ride with him. He was a tall skinny kid, and he had a bike with wide handle bars and a banana seat. What a style back then!

I didn't notice the clouds at the time, but they were about to burst open at the base with thunder and lightning! We rode down Sunnyside Avenue and then to Manor Avenue. We rode past Beverly to Belden, where there was an under pass beneath railroad tracks.

Suddenly, the thunderstorm hit. Lightening cracked through the sky, and thunder rolled over the shaking treetops. We rode to a park, but became stranded under a tunnel, in a huge drain pipe. Rain began pummeling the pavement around us. I remember laughing, but I should have felt a bit terrified at being trapped inside a huge drain pipe! Still, the drops felt soothing to my face. Ron's face looked locked in intensity. He was a person of few words, but I believe so many thoughts were rushing through his mind. For some reason, we never talked. I wish I would have said, "What are you thinking about?" or, "Why did you show up at my house?"

Actually, I should have said, "How did you know where I live?"

The air was warm but refreshing. The rain fell in giant drops. No way could we peddle back to my house. We just waited out the storm, together. We sat together in that giant drainage tunnel. Anyone would have been terrified and afraid of being inundated by a deluge. I felt secure and safe with Ron K. next to me. I never forgot him....

After over thirty years, I unpacked a middle school

year book. Inside the signature page, I saw a signature. Someone had written: Ron K. likes you. I see the words, right now. That was 1971 when I was 13. Where is Ron K. now? I wonder. Imagine ... someone liked me but I barely knew he existed. All I remember was that warm summer rain storm, when I rode with him on his bike before our senior year.

ACHIEVEMENT

I'm so proud of my little brother. He's achieved the highest level of his profession. Considering where and how we grew up, he should be honored as being the finest example of someone overcoming grave and overwhelming obstacles....

Back in the 1960s, we used to walk to and from St. Joseph's school in Hammond, Indiana. We lived on Warren Street...a quaint tree-lined place swarming with beauteous fire flies in the summer and long crystal-lickin' good icicles in the winter. Making the long round-trip trek to school, we'd talk about how we were going to live with our dad one day.

"One day, Dad'll pick us up and we'll never have to go back to that place." That place was our Mom's house. Sometimes, talking about dreams of moving and a different better future was our *entire* conversation! We'd imagine the good food we'd one day eat, like steak and shrimp, meals our mom would cook while he and I had Saturday visitations with our dad. And we'd talk about the great things we'd do, like fishing at Aunt Liz's cottages, Saturdays at Aunt Mary's house, and no more getting slapped or hit with objects.

"Just wait," I'd tell him like a concluding stanza, "one day we'll *finally* get to live with dad! And it'll be like eating all the chocolate cake and ice cream we can stuff down our throats in one evening!"

You see, our mother had a temper, and would take it out more on him than me. And she had a one-legged husband who *also* had a temper, and who often displayed anger at being number 2 instead of number 1 in her life. Yeah, my mom hit me many times with that left hand of hers, and the broom, and her teeth. Many times, I saw her thick, shiny gold wedding ring before it cracked my lip or wacked my cheek; but my brother was younger, more helpless, thinner, and gray-faced pale. He got thrown....

But he always bounced back! How the heck he managed to bounce back for the rest of his life has always amazed me!

Me? I always felt guilty I couldn't help him way back then. Strange how being young often makes a person not know how to respond to shocking situations, like a gold ring taking permanent residence in my dreams, or the whites of her eyes before her rages.

Where's my brother now? He's a pilot!

See, this has an inspiring and uplifting ending.

He flies for a prestigious airline that has an innovative boss. His boss sponsors inventors and risk-takers, like Steve Fosset, who died so tragically when his experimental plane vanished without a trace. Yet, Steve lived life because he worked hard and had encouraging people backing him.

Isn't it wonderful that people who are totally unrelated to one another can see the brilliance and talent in a stranger, and inspire them? Sometimes, you just need a break ... a chance ... or someone who sees a spark inside of you and gives you a chance, to shine in your own unique way.

I have no idea how my brother ever evolved beyond our past to excel so profoundly. All I can say, is that I'm proud of him. Furthermore, he made good choices...and he doesn't talk about the past.

A CALIFORNIA STORY

RUTH

Out of an old box, I unearthed an inscription inside a splintered green wooden frame. Wiping off a few webs, I read the phrase that triggered a rush of memories:

Don't hurry~
Don't worry~
And don't forget to smell the flowers.

I found the weathered green plaque after moving into a rental house in Glendora, California in March of 1998. The house had just been sold and bought by a *new* owner. Unfortunately, the *old* owners hadn't completely moved out. Two days after moving into *her* house, I met Ruth by surprise when the doorbell rang.

"Hi!" I answered through a crack, fighting a blustering March spring air.

"Hello, I'm Ruth Eisler," she exhaled in a delicate voice through a weary sad expression. She had on opaque sunglasses and quickly doffed them in the sunlight streaming through rafters in the large atrium entryway. She appeared haloed through the lifting wind tinting her gray hair white and her high boney cheekbones rose-rouge. "I hope you don't mind—" She pushed her faux fur collar around her neck. She looked half my size even in her coat! "But I've come to ask you if I can arrange a time when I can collect some of my things I left in the garage." She sniffled a little and the tip of her long nose reddened. "I used to live here." She appeared ready to cry! "My beautiful treasured home," she laughed in an obvious attempt to trivialize her intense emotions. Clutching her purse, she straightened her thin shoulders, using the oversized antique handbag as a shield over her starched white-and-yellow tailored suit. She had on a flowered daisy blouse that made her look like an elderly but stately Nancy Reagan. Still, Ruth appeared so lost, and forlorn.

I became concerned. "Come in," I offered; and Ruth stepped slowly like a queen into *her* home, entering the living room. "I'm Joy, may I take your coat?"

After handing it to me, she stepped through the entryway, her slender shiny black shoes tapping on the tile like an elegant dancer. Right away, I noticed our surroundings re-awaken old memories for her, except for the different furniture—*my* dining room and living room sets. She kept stopping in several spots, encountering her ghosts of moments' past but falling short of talking to them, only lost with them. Obviously, she hadn't yet let go of the place, and accepted the sale of her home—a 1960s retro-style house with yellow shag carpet, gold-toned kitchen linoleum, and art deco curtain rod covers over all the thick sunflower drapes. "Would you like some tea, Ruth? I was about to make some because I just put my baby to sleep." I gestured at tea service on my sideboard.

Her eyes filled with shock and watering gratitude. "Oh, yes, that would be nice, thank you, Joy." I led her into the living room where we spent a few uncomfortable minutes talking about the weather, my family, and an incoming storm; until she finally exhaled, and sat back comfortably in an armchair. With a story-telling expression, she folded her gloved hands. "My husband Nathan Eisler died unexpectedly eight months ago."

"Oh, I'm so sorry, Ruth," I said.

She coughed lightly and put her trembling finger against her orange tinted lips, her tears disappearing inside her wide blue eyes. "Thank you, I called him

Nate," she continued, one more time giving the house an once-over glance of a refined art dealer. "I just sold this place a few weeks ago, and moved into a one-bedroom condo in Claremont, California." She giggled and blushed, her child-like embarrassment moving me to instant empathy.

Well, at least she isn't starving...or penniless, and Claremont is a nice area. But what's she doing here?

With the mannerism of someone who had once possessed so much but lost youth and opportunity, she tenderly pushed back some gray stray strands of her bangs, set her hands delicately on her lap, and lifted her head high. "My husband had once been a prestigious executive at Santa Anita Park," she said proudly.

"You mean, the horse racing track in Arcadia, California?"

"Yes," she replied with the sophistication of a southern landowner's wife.

"Wow!" I returned. She reiterated much of how they spent their lives together at the track. Racing seasons were filled with happy moments of sipping bubbly Champaign, eating expensive entrées, and meeting-and-greeting prominent social luminaries. I was in the presence of a queen!

"We also hosted *so* many pool parties here," she said, peering around and waving at selects spots in the living room, especially the one leading out the patio to the large pool

That's when I noticed something peculiar. She hadn't taken off her gloves. Did she always wear them? If so, why? Does she have some type of skin infection? I began worrying about my newborn son and husband who'd be sitting in that chair after her!

She read my concern. "Oh, I just always wear these

whenever I go out of the house. You never know what you might touch that might kill you," she whispered.

"Oh, yeah, right," I said, looking down at my own hands. Now, I didn't even want to touch the armrests!

Setting down her delicate rose tea cup on its babies-breath rimmed saucer, she suddenly trembled, and appeared corner like a caged canary as she craned her neck at the stained window on the front door. Had someone followed her here? Was someone waiting for her outside in her car? She quickly scooted to the far-side of the high-back chair.

"What's wrong, Ruth?" I stood up, walked over to the double-door windows, and glanced outside. All I could see was her brown polished Oldsmobile in the driveway, and eucalyptus branches bending like whips their leaves Cellophane rustling in the ghostly sounding wind. "No one's out here."

When I returned to sit down on the couch and pour myself some more tea, she leaned into me with her deep-set blue eyes wide in fright. "Someone keeps breaking into my house and taking things! It's happened twice this month."

"Oh my gosh!" I gasped, my heart beat racing. "Did you call the police?" Some people take advantage of the elderly, and I felt like Grandma Ruth sitting here in front of me had been victimized.

"Oh yes, the police investigated, but say they can't find any evidence of a break in." She sipped some more tea— her thin bony fingers shaking under her tight white gloves.

I sighed deeply while watching her tremble in my off-white chair in *her* living room. The familiar atmosphere seemed calming to her though, in spite of all the different furniture. Always, her hands were shaking, and her match-stick legs were crossed tightly with her old antique handbag nuzzled next to her like a yellow cat. *She sure likes yellow* I couldn't help notice, again. "What did the burglars take, Ruth? Do you have any pictures so you can show them proof that the items have been stolen?" I was determined to conjure up every angle of help I could give her. I bombarded her with question after question— prompts that would help her with the Claremont police.

"They took several coin sets...so valuable—worth *thousands*! Damn thieves." She had tears in her eyes as she punched the air in retaliation and revenge. "And last night, when I went to the store, they snuck in and stole my set of silverware...and a few trophies belonging to my wonderful late husband Nate."

We took a pause so she could compose her heavy emotions and speak. "Could the thieves know you since they stole your husband's trophies?" I poured her more tea.

After a few spasmodic reactions, she began taking intermittent sips. "Oh, I *know* who they are," she replied with certainty.

"Who?!"

"Maids I hired years ago when we lived in Arcadia."

"Maids? But how do they know where you live now?"

"They keep following me," she whispered, glancing askance suspiciously around the living room as if searching for spy equipment.

"No one's here, Ruth, I guarantee," I laughed.

She glanced down, brooding at the yellow shag carpet. "Uh-huh, if you say."

I had to pull her out of what was obviously some type of manifesting paranoia. "What did the police say about these maids?"

She nearly spilled her tea, but caught the cup! "I don't know their specific whereabouts so I can give them the information, because they keep moving ... but they *are thieves*," she said with snarly vindictiveness. "But they *definitely* know how to bypass *all* my alarms. They know my comings and goings so they know when I'm gone so they can break in and enter my condo and rob me of everything!" Gasping, she put her fingers over her mouth and began peered around the room; then she paused, staring intently at the hallway leading to the bedroom. Was she expecting her husband to talk to her and console her?

I had to return her to the calmer moments of our cookie-and-tea discussion. "Did the police question any of your neighbors or dust for prints?"

"Dust?"

"Yeah, you know ... did the police bring in a forensics team to your condo and scour it for evidence? There had to be proof of a robbery somewhere, right?"

"Nooo," she replied, deep in thought, sipping her tea, her hands slightly trembling. I offered her more tea. "Oh, I have a question for you, Joy!" she smiled, her expression suddenly positive, her frightened mood evaporated.

Startled because she'd changed the subject so quickly, I believed Ruth felt afraid I might start gesturing her out of the house because she had dumped so many of her problems on me so unexpectedly. But I didn't like seeing her squirm.

She said she was near penniless, and the man who bought her house—the place we were sitting in so comfortably—got it for a steal-of-a-deal off of her. She was forced to sell.

I wondered why, since her dead husband Nate had

been such an influential figure in the community. I was trying so hard to make her feel comfortable in an obviously difficult emotional time. I then realized *my* feeling: guilt. I had *her* house ... *her* home ... *her* memories all around me. I was paying $1,200.00 a month to someone who had bought the place that she and her dead husband had owned for over twenty-five years.

Every ticking second in this place with me, Ruth must have also been traveling back in time: from school days with her son Peter to swimming pool parties in the immaculately hedged back yard with a view of the winding freeway and city. They shared laughs and had fights. They were like Drew and me.

Suddenly, I filled an anxiety like electricity flowing through my body. *She might be me one day ... wow! This is a ride no one wants to take ... yet a discovery everyone makes at some point in his or her lifetime.* I calmed down even though I thought I was seeing stars all around her.

"What can I do for you, Ruth?" Discomfort was showing in her blinking blue eyes as she jerkily swept back the few bad strands of thin feather-gray bangs that just wouldn't stick to her sprayed hair.

"Can Peter come over tomorrow, and pick up a few boxes he left in the garage?" She asked quickly and softly with protective voice of a doting mother. "He's thirty-five, and he's in such a *bad* situation with the woman he's living with right now." Then, her emotional damn cracked open, and she began reiterating more information about Peter that I knew, if he'd be sitting here, he'd wallop her to make her stop talking.

Ruth hadn't left *any* of those items stacked along the garage wall. Peter had, and she was still his caretaker ... at the adult age of thirty-five? I wonder what happened there, and who *is* this guy really?

"Can he come tomorrow to pick up his— his— things, please?"

I think she's on the verge of a full blown panic attack. Something more has to be wrong. "Sure, no problem!" I quickly replied. Feeling intrigued, I finished my tea, glancing at the black ominous leaves swirling on the bottom. "Anytime tomorrow afternoon is fine for him to come over and get his things." She drank the rest of her tea, telling me a little bit more about her fascinating life and current precarious living situation. Then, like a wind blowing through the house, Ruth left, her brown Olds blowing curls of smoke as it sped out of the driveway. She had to arrive at her condo well before dark so she could plan another stake out and nab the thieving maids.

The rest of the day, I continued unpacking boxes. I had a three-month-old baby, and he was becoming more active since birth, and a handful. All the while, I kept thinking about Ruth and her disheartening situation. She was alone. Her husband had died less than a year ago. She had a son, Peter, around my age, forty. Peter and her husband had been the focus of her entire life, in *this* house; and Peter had never married and didn't have any children. Ruth didn't have *anyone* living on after her. Worst yet, Peter didn't appear available to help her.

I felt ticked off. Shouldn't he, her only son, be at her side tonight, with phone in hand, ready to dial the cops in case of another break-in? I recalled what Ruth had said about him: Peter hadn't worked in months; and when he did manage to secure a job, he could never hold it down for more than a year. Now, he was living with a troubled girlfriend and they were not getting along. He was Ruth's only child, and she and her dead husband had always managed to cough up enough capital to invest in one of Peter's many wild business ventures. They all failed. I found out more about Pete than I ever discovered about Ruth!

I wondered: why didn't any of those deals pay off for Peter after she had given him what seemed to be thousands and thousands of dollars? My angry was bubbling rising lava. Peter Eisler, what a thankless thoughtless son! If *I* had a mother like Ruth, I would have kissed the ground she walked on, made sure I had a job, and provided for her, because she had always placed *me* first in her life! I decided what I'd do. Tomorrow, when Peter would come to retrieve his things, I would give him a teaspoon—no, tablespoon!—of *my* medicine, and let him know about his distraught, victimized, penniless mother!

At 2:43 p.m. the next afternoon, the doorbell rang just as I tucked my button-nosed sleeping son into his cradle. Slowly, I opened the door, and three-feet beyond the brass threshold stood shoulder-length, brown haired Peter wearing washed-out jeans and a stretched out tie-died t-shirt. *Is he homeless?* I looked deeper into his narrow blue pink-tinged eyes as he sniffled a few times. Then I smelled a powerful sweet scent. Not cologne. *He looks high on something!* I cleared my throat and backed away a bit. "I'm Joy, you must be Peter."

"Yeah, Peter Eisler, Ruth's son," he said. "How's it goin?"

"Fine," I whispered, and I wanted him quickly to know I wasn't home alone. "We have to talk softly, my son's sleeping."

Then he sniffled through his long red nose. "My ma said you'd let me pick up some o' my things? I got some records inside the garage … and maybe some tools."

"Yes, I think I saw them in there, but I'm not sure. Let me think…."

The garage had a touch keypad, and we hadn't changed the code yet, so this was the chance to discover what Peter still knew about the house so I could keep him out permanently after this moving venture was over. Peering past him to my driveway, I spotted his yellow polished muscle-car Camaro that someone had to have been babying since 1966. Perhaps his father left it to him in his will, because the man-boy Peter in front of me couldn't *possibly* have bought such an expensive car. And from what Ruth told me, he hadn't ever held a solid job! He kept coughing lightly, hunching over and shrugging. If he wouldn't stop his bad hunching habit, he was certain to develop osteoporosis.

A chasm of difference expanded between us as I gestured down the long sidewalk toward the garage. "I'll be there in a minute to open the door. I just have to check on my son."

"Thanks, I won't be long," he said with a boyish grin. Then he turned and began walking down the sidewalk while glancing around the atrium adorned with yellow-and-red hibiscus bushes, verdant large ferns, and chopped down roses, the latter obviously his mother's choicest. He stopped all of a sudden, appearing to have lost something in the dark corner dirt. With the face of a sad child, he stared hypnotized by a large fan palm, its base rimmed with frothy algae.

"You okay?" I asked, wondering if he'd asked his distraught mother that question lately.

"Oh yeah—I'm fine," he coughed, quickly wiping his cheeks with his shaking hands.

He might bust out crying! What do I do then? I didn't have Ruth's phone number or address.

He pointed at the high palm tree with its green plushness dulled by the corner's afternoon cloud-covered gloom, still its throne of survival. "I remember when my dad and mom planted that." He chuckled a little and brushed back his long hair. "I was about fifteen when the other plant there died. Gosh, that poinsettia was about as tall as me when some type of awful disease turned it into a skeleton," he huffed. "But in the beginning, that corner was the first location they planted that Christmas poinsettia after they built this house and moved in right before New Year's Day of nineteen sixty-three."

"Wow, I'm sorry," I said, feeling guilty, again, of usurping a home so valuable in someone else's world. Through the waiting and watching, as funeral guests paying our last respects, he suddenly perked up, walked out of the atrium, and disappeared around the corner.

Exhaling the chilly air filled with tingling invisible drops of rain, I believed I had become embroiled in a snowballing drama. *I have a sleeping child inside, I don't really know if this grief-stricken person is dangerous, and I have to sweep the pool before it rains! Do I really have time to help Peter move out his things…which if I recall, are all lined up and stacked in rows along the garage wall? What have I gotten myself into? Yesterday a confused grieving widow shows up at my door, and now her drugged up son who could be dangerous.*

I recalled the time after my grandparents died. Feeling like zombies, we were all meandering around the house after everyone had paid their condolences that none of us really heard because we were still in shock and dismay. Most times, mourning only begins long after the ceremony ends. I was witnessing what had happened to me years ago, and tears stung my eyes and my throat burned to stop them while holding myself together long enough to help Peter and then get rid of him, for good.

When I walked to the garage, I couldn't open the door with the code my husband texted me.

Peter was sitting in his Camaro with the door open and inhaling the dregs on his cigarette. "Try 5918," he called, flicking the smoldering butt into the street.

I punched the numbers, and the door creaked and lifted. "Got it!" *I'll be changing this code tonight.*

"That's my dad's birthday," he said, spitting on the driveway.

As I walked to the wall and began inspecting his things, all the while listening for my son to wake up, Ruth entered my mind. These precious seconds I was spending with *my* son would be lost to time; and in the future, we would resemble Peter and Ruth. The future...who knows what it'll bring? Noticing at a few scraggly boxes near the opening, I pick up one that contained records. "Those must be real old," I said, trying to make small conversation so I could bring up a much bigger topic—his unattended, lonely mother.

He had already begun loading boxes into his back seat and trunk. "The Creedence Clearwater and Led Zeppelin albums are old, but the rest aren't."

"Oh, those were my favorites too," I said, and then coughed as I tried hard not to gag on dust. Here was my chance to talk about Ruth. "Your mom's so nice."

"Yeah ... she's *that* for sure," he said.

His apathy ticked me off! "I'm sad to hear about your dad passing away, and she's taken it pretty hard it seems." I lift the record box, walk it to his open trunk, and set it gently inside.

He stopped and breathed through his exertion. "Everything that happened—" He motioned around the garage. "Losing him and then losing this place changed her all right." His eyelids were pinching back tears as he gestured at the splintered, weathered work bench enshrined with a few rusty tools and vices in front of the kitchen door. "Dad and I didn't spend much time together during the past few years, but we did construct a few fun things in this place." He had a reservoir of caring for his father as he began lifting and loading boxes with the momentum of three movers, packing them to perfection and neatness in his car. One more box and he'd be gone. Watching him work, I couldn't help but wonder: Who is Peter Eisler? I'm seeing *two* different people in one!

"Do you have children?" I knew the answer.

"Nope," he replied, rearranging some items in the last box.

"You're mom sure is such a nice person," I began. "I really enjoyed talking to her yesterday."

He laughed with a flippant expression. "Yeah, she's a kick." He sounded like he hated her.

"I'm so sorry to hear that her condo has been robbed a few times by maids who used to work for her. How terrible and frightening for her."

He stopped with a jaw-dropping shocked expression.

I held my breath, waiting for his explanation.

"She's got the cops there all the time, and they think she's kerplunkin' *nuts*," he said. The last box thudded as he dropped it in his trunk, the back end of Camaro bouncing in the weight, and then he slammed the trunk shut. "No one's broken into her condo at all, not even maids. We haven't had maids for over *five* years, Lady—"

"Joy is my name."

"Okay, *Joy* ... *no* one's broken into her condo." Then his posture shifted in a retaliatory expression. "If so, the alarm woulda gone off, and the alarm company would have called the cops." He took out a cigarette and lighter. "She called the cops." He opened and flicked the silver lighter like a switch blade in his angry fingers.

As I listened through the silence for crying noises, Peter lit his cigarette, reached inside his car for his tumbler, and then took a drink. I began searching the garage floor to make sure he'd taken everything. "She says burglars stole several of her coin collections, ones your dad had been collecting for years. So sad."

"Ha!" he scoffed, walking back inside to the tool bench still peppered with his father's things. He appeared angry, at me! "She sold everything…coins, silverware, and even her Hummel menagerie she had been collecting since before I was born." He grabbed an old beaten up satchel off a two-by-four on the wall and began sifting through clattering tools and pinging bolts, nuts, and nails. "She just doesn't remember, but I was with her when she *sold* everything. It took us two weeks … that was a few months ago."

I had believed *he* might be Ruth's thief, until I saw hurt on his defensive face as he perused the bench with the eyes of eagle, touching several grooves. Those were the marks he and his father Nate had left indelible over the years, but now he was leaving behind as he commenced on a new journey. Both he and Ruth were dealing with layers of loss, and trying to reclaim their lives in new surroundings. Still, leaving a home and all its familiar settings, like the inches set in lead on a doorframe and raw notches in a workbench, as the sun and moon cycled 'round the same spots every day must feel like losing yourself in open water and drifting with only a flimsy life preserver.

"Look, Joy," he said firmly, turning to me askance with a threatening snap of his thin body.

Before I would have run inside and demanded he leave. *No, Peter's really all cigarette smoke and no fire.* "Yes?" I asked calmly.

"When I take those tools off this bench—" He swept a few nuts and bolts like bread crumbs into the bulging satchel. "You and I will *never* see each other again." As I watched him pick off a few choice woodscrews, I realized I had been too judgmental about the loser who was had so much deep understanding about life. Then he walked out the garage door, slid inside his Camaro, hoisted the satchel into his back seat, and then slammed the door shut. "Bye! Adios!"

"Bye, nice to—"

The muscle car's engine revved, Peter shoved it into reverse, and the chrome bumper lightly nipped the street as he sped off with smoking tires like the Road Runner. I'd never see him again. *He's right about that part of life. All the time we pass people whom we never see again, but they're doing the best they can day-in-and-day-out, like Peter, and Ruth. Everyone's wearing life preservers of one kind or another.*

I don't know if it was the after-baby blues or a bit of postpartum depression, but I sat down at the kitchen chair with Ruth's 1960 bumpy yellow linoleum under my bare feet, looked out the window at the open-air atrium with dark clouds bursting hard rain, and cried. Later that day after feeding my son, I threw an unpacked box into the garage but stopped when I saw something green sticking out behind the empty workbench. I began prying it out of its tight spot, adding another everlasting notch to Ulysses table. "Ruth or Peter must have forgotten it was here," I said to the stubborn green picture frame. "Or Peter saw it and didn't care."

Finally my fingers yanked out the green plaque, and I took it to the kitchen table, cleaned it off gently with a Q-tip, and set it on the windowsill. Outside to the right was Peter's green lonely tree. *I'll never see him again, but I'll see that rare fan palm every day.*

That was March. On Thanksgiving Day, I invited Ruth over to a new house that my husband and I had bought in San Dimas. I felt better there, more relaxed because we owned the place and weren't renting. It was *our* home, and we felt such hope for our future. Ruth appeared shaky but not as distraught, although she told me she still had to call the police at least once a month because "the maids" had broken into her *new* condo in Azusa. I can't imagine how many more times she'd have to move to outrun imaginary intruders. "She has dementia I'm sure," I told my husband.

I had my dad and step-mother over that day, the latter telling me suddenly in the kitchen while whispering that she wanted back a sewing machine she'd given me as a gift years ago. A few other friends also showed up for dinner. We snapped pictures and took videos as Ruth sat happily across the table from me, telling about how she had new locks and a new alarm system. Of course, she let me in on Pete's new life with his new girlfriend. I recalled Peter's assessment of her: "She's nuts. She's lost it!" She didn't appear crazy to me, so I just listened to her. Perhaps, if Ruth had someone to tell her fears and worries to, the disclosure might make her difficulties and burdens easier to bear.

Hope, isn't that what everyone needs now and then?

A year thereafter, I moved to Carlsbad, then to Hawaii, then years later to Camarillo, then years later to Texas, and finally to Florida. I lost track of Ruth Eisler somewhere between moving from a rental house in Waianae and our new house in Makakilo while snorkeling and just trying to make sense out of a new language, culture, and street signs.

Ruth is probably gone by now. And I never did see Peter again. He was right! Most people we pass by we never *ever* see again. You ever see dandelions shed their white pods and float off in the wind? We always see people, but *never* know their lives, their loves, their losses, their hopes, their dreams, their failures, their successes, their demons, or their angels.

Still, whenever I visit my dad in Glendora, I wonder about Peter, and whatever happened to the angry, abandoned little boy inhabiting a man's body. And I'll always remember Ruth. I still have the little plaque she left at her house but that I found so many years ago that's now setting on my bookshelf. I try not to hurry, I try not to worry, and I do like smelling the flowers. Thanks, Ruth.

The Pregnancy

There isn't a time more special, wonderful, and mysterious as having a baby. That is, until my own daughter excitedly announced, "I'm pregnant!" Thank goodness for Facebook, email, cell phone, and now Skype. I've been able to keep track of all her changes and the awe she's been experiencing. Then last week, she paid us a visit.

"How was the airplane flight?" I asked after waiting for over an hour at baggage claim at the Orlando Airport.

"Fine," she replied, gently rubbing the top of her belly.

"How's the baby?"

"Fine."

"We have an app that tells us all the changes the baby is going through every week," Keith our son-in-law said, showing us his newest iPhone version.

I wanted so badly to touch her round tummy. *My little girl, pregnant...really expecting a baby ... in three months ... in three months I'll be a grandma!* I felt tongue tied. "Did you eat?"

"Yeah," she said, her round hazel eyes brimming with confidence. "We ate snacks on the plane."

"Oh that's right, you packed food," I said, and then I thought of how she used to snack: chips, dip, and pop. "Have you had milk?"

She gave me a sly glance. I know that expression! She's trying to conjure a lie. "Well...."

"The baby needs calcium," I said, pasting myself between her and that contraption of a baggage carrier. I pictured the moving baggage mover chomping down on a piece of her flowing maternity blouse and pulling her right onto it. "Do you know which suitcase is yours?" I asked. She launched into a diatribe of every food she'd eaten in the past three days containing calcium.

Her husband Keith walked up beside me. "We have a green ribbon on the handle."

I remembered putting that ribbon on that suitcase when she was in college and she had it there when she went to study in Israel for a semester. "Oh good." By then, he had the luggage heaved off the conveyor belt and the handle out and ready for departure!

Walking to the car, we began what I call *our family conversational juggling act.*

"Andy," I told my son, "Sit behind your dad." Drew has long legs and a robust frame. He positions the car seat as far back in the Magnum as it'll go. Andy is sixteen. He can handle cramped quarters for the hour-long drive home.

"Awww!" Andy retorts, moans, and grumbles.

"Jenny, you sit in the front seat," I say.

"But I wanna sit by Keith," she returns.

That means Keith, Jenny, *and* Andy will sit in the back, and I in the front. No. That won't work. I'll feel too guilty with that set up.

After we arrive at the parked car, musical chairs continues:

"Dad, can I sit in the back in the middle … between Keith and Jenny?" Andy asks. He's been like a jumping bean with a lit fuse for days, waiting for the arrival of his sister and "brother." Little does he know, things have changed!

Drew's tired. He's been driving…and driving. "No, Andy. Jenny and Keith want to sit together."

"But why?"

"Because they're married … and they want to split food and share their water," Drew replied, handing Jenny a cold bottle of water that I had wrapped in tin foil to keep cold on the way to the airport.

I had enough. "Andy, you sit behind Dad, and I'll sit in the middle, and Keith will sit in the front seat, and Jenny can sit behind Keith so she can stretch her legs. Heaven knows she's had to scrunch up like a Rollie Pollie on those airplane seats!" We play musical chairs for five minutes, trying to figure out the best seating arrangement. This is worse than arranging seats for a wedding reception!

Finally, Jenny sits down comfortably in the back seat, and I'm next to her. Andy, of course, looks like a squished bug next to me—also nudging me in the ribs until I stick my bulky purse between us. "Andy, you could use a pacifier to suck on until we get home," I said when Andy whined, again.

Jenny laughed, Drew laughed, Keith hugged Jenny, Andy scowled, and I felt like a mama crow scouting for her baby bird who had too soon sprung from the nest.

The drive home was like a rickety-rackety stagecoach ride: "You have enough room, Jenny?" "You want some more water?" I bought grapes … ya want some?" "Ya want some more?"

"Mom!" she finally said. "You're acting crazy!"

I felt hurt. "No … crazy is screaming and shouting and thinking I'm seeing things that I'm not. I'm *not* acting crazy," I said in a low calm voice. "I'm just concerned that's all." Whew!

"Okay, but you're being *overly* concerned," she said softly.

All right. She's right.

I remembered my pregnancies. I never received a call from my dad asking me how the baby was doing or how I was feeling. Not a call from my mom asking me how the baby was doing or how I was feeling. Shoot … I don't even believe I ever heard: "Congratulations! I'm so happy for you!" I was an anchor on their backs, or that dead albatross in *The Rhyme of the Ancient Mariner*.

At home, I offered Jenny some yogurt—Greek yogurt's the best. The amount of protein in one serving is almost twice as much as regular yogurt. But how do I force her to eat some and not appear overly concerned? I snuck out, went to the store, and spent fifteen minutes sifting through all the pancake mixes, trying to find the best organic pancake mix on the market. I never go that store! Too expensive, but it sells organic … just what my daughter needs for her growing baby girl—my grandchild. Gosh, I'm *brimming* over with excitement.

The next morning, I made pancakes; and I added yogurt, an organic egg, and Borden's two-percent milk. She ate a few. "Chewy," was her comment. That's all right … I can handle that thankless complaint.

Oh well … at least I got my way, and she got half the dose of her daily calcium. And the baby probably grew just a teeny bit because of my overly concerned disposition. Hopefully, one day, when my daughter's girl finds herself expecting a baby, I can tell her the story about me, her mom, and my games of protective mother hen.

Further in the future, she might also be in my shoes, and the children after her, and the children after her, or him. All our actions extend so far beyond us.

JENNY'S FIRST BABY

"Mom, you don't need to think I'm going into labor all the time," Jenny texted me after the last I phoned her because she didn't call me back. She's three weeks away from her due date, and I'm a second away from making an emergency plane reservation to California!

Hey, I can't stop being concerned no matter how many birthdays she'll have. I'm her mom! I was worried sick. I hadn't heard from her after I phoned twice and texted four times! She's always tried being so independent, but whenever she had to have her braces adjusted at the orthodontist's office or had to get a booster shot at the doctor's office, she had to have *me* with her in the room. She might *say* she's a stoic trooper, but I know different.

My granddaughter's due in three weeks, but Jenny says she's been experiencing minor "labor pains," off-and-on for over a week, and her doctor says the baby—my granddaughter!—has dropped two centimeters. I can just picture Jenny dealing with pregnancy alone, with me now living in Florida and she in California. Yeah, she's married, and her husband is great, but I've always been there for her throughout her life, trying hard always to be a good mom, even though I've had my weaknesses and I'm sure shed some of those onto her. Sorry 'bout that, Jen.

I want to tell her, that when I had her at age thirty, I had her at home, and not in the hospital as she and her husband have planned for their birthing experience. I guess, thank goodness the year is 2014, and obstetric and anesthetics have advanced in magnificent ways, thank you Dr. of the Epidural.

Meanwhile, as I try patiently to wait for her call, I

think: Just wait. *One* day, *you'll* be in *my* shoes with the baby *you're* now expecting ... and feeling like *you're* in hard drive over what to do next. Just wait...'cause that time will be here faster than you know it. So, have just a *little* compassion on me, the new grandma, will ya, Jen?

MAY 12, 12,015 A.D.

I'm torn between living now and appreciating the moment, and wanting to be alive ten thousand years from now. My imagination keeps me wondering, and sometimes keeps me awake to the point where I wonder if I'm sane or crazy.

Ten thousand years from now....

I believe the Earth will be overheated, but we'll combine our resources to solve our "overwarming" issues. We'll become a global government, that is if religious beliefs don't kill us all first! We're strong. Humanity's tough. The ability for us to care outweighs our capacity to dominate. But, will we evolve to another species, especially if people colonize Mars? Atmospheric conditions and gravity are so different there. We'd have to adapt, and we'd surely slowly begin to change in appearance and brain capacity. Will God still love us? In Zechariah 8:7, He says: "I will save my people from lands east and west." So yeah, He'll always love us!

Now back to my desire: that I'd like to live ten thousand years from now. I'm thinking about the technological advancements. Everything from TV to telecommunications will have changed. I'd like to live in a world comprised of holographic technology, where we have no more computer monitors, PCUs and screens. You want to write a book? "Talk" or "speak" your book creation. You want to make a movie? Just talk to your quantum-computer system that has every type of graphics program and capability built into "her" or "him."

Around the Earth, satellites will be innumerable, and appear as stars trekking across the sky. We'll be able to access them individually. Our apps will be holographic, and our world will be sensory augmented to include intense experiential events. Want to attend the president's inaugural speech but can't? Just superimpose yourself in the president's crowd via holographic social media, and you'll be there virtually. We will live in a virtual world driven by augmented technology capable of exuding sensory experiences to us, personally and uniquely.

Even our DNA will be mapped out for doctors, thus allowing experts to view our mutating cells, diagnosing a disease, and then prescribe a cure. We'll even have nanotechnology capable of repairing problems in our brains.

What about Mars and planetary exploration? We'll be able to view exoplanets, but not necessarily arrive at them. Mars will be colonized, and perhaps several of Jupiter's moons. We'll find a way to dispose of all our trash on asteroids, make the moon a transition station, and launch our garbage into space. What will be our priority?

To save and preserve Earth, no matter the cost.

As for now, I'm watching a full moon. It's beautiful in the Florida night. I suggest you do the same. We're all running out of time.

METEORITE GIRL

PART I
THE EXPERIMENT

As a child, I watched reruns of *Star Trek*. I used to pretend I was part of Captain Kirk's crew when I'd talk to my dolls at the plastic kitchenette in the basement. We'd travel around stars and scale magnificent galaxies in warp drive. We'd eat alien food, well, really warm Jell-O I'd mix with frozen fruit cocktail and peas. And I'd dress up in flashy futuristic outfit, well, really old Halloween costumes I'd rip apart and staple back together to create a 2350 C.E. body suit. When my mom was smacking me with the yellow broom or whacking me with the back of her hand over the little things, I was a green-bodied dancing alien, or steering the *Enterprise* alongside Spock, or one of Bones' assistants, scanning my sick doll with the cracked porcelain eye. What was more spectacular? I found an experiment to conduct in every episode!

Now?

I'm a person of a certain age. Let's say, over thirty. Okay, okay, I'm over forty, but so what? Hey, I put in several years of serious time as a chemistry and biology teacher. And after taking a sabbatical, I've come to the existential realization that I'm *really* going to die one day. I guess a lot of time on my hands yielded thinking time. Drats, for trying to having a bit of fun. Still, I realize I want something of me to live on in the universe. Doesn't everyone?

Last night, while inhaling trans-fat potato chips and sipping a fructose-filled Slurpee 'cause I'm gonna kick the bucket anyway so who gives a hoot, I watched *Meteorite Men*. The host made a revolutionary hypothesis: "Meteorites are everywhere in the atmosphere as fine grains. Their particles disperse in the rain and wind, and fall everywhere. Those particles, some microscopic, are even on your roof!" He stirred a small magnet around the inside of a desert rain gutter and showed the camera little particles on the ends of the magnet.

I sit up straight like a fire cracker popped outside. "Wow—I can conduct the same experiment! Last week, a handyman went up on my roof and sprayed out my rain gutters. He said there were little vines growing in the residue. And last, night it rained; so I must have some pretty fertile meteorite compounds collecting around the downspouts that I can gather up with a magnet and show people. I can even make a YouTube video to go viral 'round the world."

"Liz, who ya talkin' to?" my husband Len calls out from the bedroom.

I want what *this* adventure to remain a secret. "No one, Len. I'll be in bed soon!"

The next morning after breakfast while Len works in the computer room, I speed down to the local Knowledge Exchange and buy a six-inch magnet. I think of some more things I can do after duplicating Meteorite Man's experiment. If I can collect a substantial amount of the small cosmic-wonderful particles, maybe I can melt them down into one rock and sell it so Derrick, my eighteen-year-old son, can buy a car for school. Maybe ... if the specks are *real* rare, I can sell the rock and have some hard cash, *ka-ching*, yes!

After arriving home and unwrapping the black-and-red magnet like it's Christmas, I run to my shaded backyard. Where do I begin my experiment? The gutters. That's where rain runs off from the roof that must contain meteorites. Following the gutters, I end up looking under two curved downspouts and notice glittering particles. Over the summer months, the run off must have been substantial 'cause when I clump the particles together, I can almost cup them in my hand. Maybe this entire neighborhood is a little meteorite field, most likely from the abnormally intense Perseid meteor shower in August.

I blink when I see a few glowing speckles as if they're reacting weirdly with the air and my having stirred them up. No way. But maybe *these* particles originated from a beyond the Oort Cloud. Wow, maybe they're remnants of an ancient star!

Looking up at the clear blue sky, I wonder how long exactly it takes for those elements to drift down and wash down from so high up in the atmosphere. *Anything* from the cosmos can be up there right now...and even change at first contact with radiation and ions in the unprotected thermosphere. Looking down and poking around in the solid glitter soup with a little stick, I can't see anything dangerous, just dirt and glistening silver-and-gold speckles, like fool's gold. Nothing like kryptonite or goopy rocks that might morph into organic creatures at a human's touch!

I stir the magnet among the shimmering glistening residue under both spouts, all the while remembering reading *Macbeth* and the three witches brewing a potion in a caldron. When I lift up the magnet several times into the strong morning sunlight, I see tiny, glowing, gold-and-silver flecks. Wow—these could be ancient elements in existence since the beginning of time! And I have them right in my fingertips! I touch them gently. Let some drizzle into my palm. I smell them cautiously like inhaling the scent of a beautiful red rose. Then I gently down the special residue in a glass and collect some more. In a half-an-hour, I have over a tablespoon of speckled iron-ore deposits. The other shiny speckles had to have been just worn out deteriorating roof shingles.

Going into the house, I wonder what *else* will happen if I mix these particles with things around the house. Water is the first solvent. I know they've been exposed to rain, but not sugar and salt. I'm gonna try a bit of everything with these meteorites.

I take the glass holding the ancient silver-and-gold elements, trickle in some water, and stir. The solution glows light blue and yellow as if everything mixing together made a flash run through the visible spectrum. Then the particles disappear like the solute salt! "What? I know I saw iron-ore and touched solid particles. What happened? A failed experiment, that's what happened, darn!"

"Liz, did something happen to ya in there?" Len calls in a frantic voice from the computer room.

"*Nooo*, I'm just disappointed that's all."

"We need detergent?"

"Disappointed!" He needs hearing aids.

"A ham sandwich with those pickles I like would be nice right about now...please?"

"Sure fine ... in a sec," I call back, staring into the glass of clear water in search of at least a few pebbles. "It looks like something inside this mixture mysterious dissolved everything!" I tell the uncooperative invisible variable. Oh, well. I thought I had touched something big and worth some money. Everyone's dream, right?

As I make his sandwich, Len hears me sigh and groan some more, but I tell him I'm not sick, just feeling dump and stupid. Then I hear the engine of a lawn mower outside, and notice my neighbor working in a flower bed.

Oh my gosh. "Len, our grass is almost ankle high. Your sandwich is on the table. I'm going out to mow the lawn."

After my long mowing adventure in the humid Florida sun, I'm hot, sweating, and dry-mouth thirsty. Running to the kitchen, I gulp down a glass of water on the counter.

Uh-oh, oh no! It's the glass containing my failed experiment! "Shoot—what have I done?" I stomp. I burp, and burp again, and then run to the bathroom and swirl out my mouth with Listerine. Trying not to panic because I know the water is void of any particles, I don't feel sick…and I don't feel any different. "I'm fine," I tell the universe. "Right?" After I wash my face and brush my teeth, I squint at myself in the mirror. I check my tonsils, "*Ahhh.*" I'm fine. Not telling Len or our son Derrick anything about the experiment and what I did, I eat some lunch and take my pulse and temperature. "I'm fine. Nothing weird is happening," I keep whispering as I finish my housework. I pass the rest of the day watching TV, doing a little typing, and fixing dinner. "But gosh, it's 7 p.m., and I feel so tired," I say to my reflection in a white plate I take out of the dishwasher. "Weird!" I go to bed early.

The next morning, I wake up, take my thyroid pill, and put Len's pill into the palm of his hand. Yawning, I walk away to go back to bed.

He grabs my arm and pulls me back. "Liz! What the hell kinda makeup did you put on your face? When the heck did ya buy *that?*"

I touch my nose and lips. "What are ya talking about?"

He squints at me like he sees measles. "*What* did you *do* to your *face!*"

I rub my stinging eyes, trying to dissolve the gritty stubborn sleepers. "I didn't do anything." He sees *me* as disgusting? Huh! *He's* the one with the beer belly and straw whiskers. I walk to the bathroom sink, turn on the light, and look in the mirror.

"What the...." My face almost hits the glass!

I brighten the lights, and see silver patches on my forehead and cheeks. Did a poltergeist visit me during the night and paint four silver nickels on my face? I touch all four of them, tap them several times, and then pinch them to see if they're just odd pimples. Nope. There's one on each cheek and two on my forehead.

"No way!"

I try picking them off. Len's next to me now, shouting for me to stop. I see blood under my nails, and when I check my reflection again, there's a speck of shiny silver on my chin. The more I try removing them, the more they're growing, and multiplying.

"They're not coming off, Len!" Pulling away from him, I rub a silver spot until my fingertips numb, until he grabs my wrists, forcing me to stop. "Some more are here, Len! Look at my darn face! I look like I belong in a carnival show. Shoot! What do I do?!"

"Try this." While filling the sink with water, he hands me his hard Lava soap. I lather up my face and then drown it in the sink. Meanwhile, he's been lifting up my nightgown, inspecting my legs and back. "There's one here too," he keeps poking, "and another here...*oo*, wow. I don't know. I just don't know, Liz." As I dry my face, he gives up, exhales, and backs away from me. I've seen him reel a little when I frosted my face with the newest healing mud, but nothing like the disgust and fear I see now. "Liz, something bad's happening to ya. What did you do?" With another towel pinched between his fingers, he glances at the closet where he can lock himself in and me out.

"Well, I definitely don't remember touching anyone who looked like this!" I reply, drying myself off while trying to crane my neck at some more spots he's pointing out on my back and side. I pat the nickel-sized silver spots on my cheeks with alcohol. When I'm done, I see a line of silver under both my eyes. "Damn! This is insane!" Every muscle in me feels numb as I gulp down some water he shoved into my shaking hands. "They *won't* come off, Len. They're changing my skin...all over my body!"

By now, Derrick has heard the commotion, and he's at the bathroom door. When he sees me, he gasps and jumps back. "Mom!" He leans toward me, but I waved him away. "Mom—what happened?"

Repeating those words like they're on replay isn't helping anyone calm down. "Hurry up and get dressed, Derrick," I tell him.

"Go now! We're taking your mom to the doctor." Len adds.

As Derrick leaves like he's racing for a gun, I try scratching off a silver shiny patch on my chin. No use. It's definitely my skin. "What could be happening?!" I throw a bloody washcloth on the floor; but realizing it might be contaminated, I flush it. Then I shake the bottle of alcohol around and swab the floor with a towel. That should disinfect the place, and I tell Len not to touch me until we discover what's wrong."

"Get dressed and let's go," he shouts.

After a few hurried minutes, we leave for Doctor Rias' office. He's my G.P. and part of a huge medical center. Urgent Care opens at 9 a.m.

"What's wrong with me, Len? What's happening to

me?!" I'm in a cold navigational fog, and numb, and scared out of my wits.

"Well," Derrick begins, "what did you do yesterday, or the day before that?" He hasn't cried in a long while, but I see tears and his white shocked eyes

Speeding around several cars, I tell them about the meteorite experiment I tried duplicating yesterday. Len and Derrick keep giving me nasty looks like I drank bathtub water.

"Mom, you and your experiments ... now you're in *real* trouble," Derrick says. Then he sinks down into his back seat. "What about us? Maybe *we* can catch it!"

"No," Len corrects him. "She drank it ... and we haven't touched her ... but I'll disinfect everything she touched with Clorox *right* when we get home."

Feeling like a leper, I know what happened to me isn't my fault. "I drank the mixture by accident," I tell them, again. Then I remember what my dad told me so many times: "Liz, you never think before you do things. Think first. *Use* your brain!" I always heard, *stupid*. Am I? Or am I just overly inquisitive about things? Well, look where my imagination and experimentation have taken me now!

The brakes squeal when Len parks the car at the Urgent Care Center.

"What did you drink that weird stuff for, Mom?" Derrick keeps repeating.

I grab my purse and hold it close to my chest. "I *said* I drank it by accident. I was thirsty after mowing the lawn and I reached for the wrong glass." I'm suddenly so thirsty, and guzzle down all of Len's water.

He shivers a bit. "Are ya turning into a fish? That's the second full glass o' water you've downed, Liz."

"No!"

"Well, that's one helluva thirst ya have then." He takes a sip of yesterday's coffee and bites off a chunk of his cereal bar while glancing at me as if I might evolve fins in front of my ears.

After another round of *why'd ya drink that* from Derrick, I tell him, "Why don't *you* mow the lawn then once in a while, Pecksniffian."

"What's that?" he grimaces.

Molten anger is pumping through my veins. "It means you're criticizing me! Please stop it." When I see a silver spot on my knuckle, I turn serious. "What if you two don't have me around anymore?"

After a second's sigh, he says, "Sorry," as he sinks down into the back seat.

I shouldn't have said that and scared them that way because I see their pale frightened faces and shaking hands. But I'm *more* terrified and confused.

Then I open the door to leave—*snap*—the handle comes off in my hand!

Len looks as if his heart might stop and he pats his chest. "What the heck! What the blazin' heck?!"

"I don't know! I don't get this either!" With a strength rolling through my body like a lightning strike, I force the door open with my shoulder. Derrick throws me his hoodie out the window. "Mom, put this on. People are gonna be terrified when they see you."

After I don the jacket, I run through the parking lot toward the sliding glass doors. Trying not to bump into people, I see them jump out of my way like I'm a bowling ball.

All the while, I can't stop wondering: What am I turning into? Can Doctor Rias stop it?

PART II
METAMORPHOSIS AND INTERVENTION

When I meet the receptionist at Dr. Rias' office, I notice her name tag and feel knee knocked. It occurs to me that maybe soon, I might not *have* a name! Whatever is happening to me ... I could die.

"Cindy, *ah*, is, *uh*, Dr. Rias in?" I whisper, bending a little over the counter. Trying not to draw attention, I quickly push the hood off my head and show her my face. Then I cover up again. Several seated patients squint at me but then return to their magazines.

Like a grenade dropped, Cindy scoots back from her desk. "I—uh—I—uh..." She glances around, searching for a disinfectant spray or intercom. She's a young girl who obviously just completed her brief term as a medical reception. "Doctor!"

I have my hands deep down in my pockets. "Cindy, don't panic, please. I know this looks bad, but—"

"Doctor—help!" she cries. Patients like scattering flies leave the waiting area, and two nurses run out from the back with two doctors trailing behind them. One is Doctor Rias. A tall man with short black hair and black rimmed glasses, I would have taken him for a researcher, not a physician.

"Oh my, we need her chart, right now," he orders Cindy. "What's your name and birth date?" he asks me.

"Elizabeth Miller, September 21, 1970."

While Cindy starts chart hunting, Doctor Rias ushers me through three hallways to a distant cold room. I don't think the place has seen human breath for years! After covering the exam table with extra absorption padding, he gestures for me to sit down. Leaning into my face with his little flashlight skimming over my eyes and face, he begins inspecting the silver patches on my skin. "*Hm, hm.*" Then he stands up, scratching his neck in a confusing gesture. "How did this happen, Elizabeth?"

I tell him the experiment I tried yesterday after watching *Meteorite Men.* "I accidentally drank some of the water I mixed with those particles I collected from around my downspouts."

"What kind of metallic dust? Where did you say it came from?" he asks skeptically.

"I believe the particles that dissolved in that glass of water came from meteorites. You know, outer space," I reply.

He coughs, like he's gagging in disbelief. "Elizabeth." He crosses his arms. "I don't know any kind of meteorite that can cause *this* type of change in a person's body, especially this fast, since yesterday." He takes out his iPhone, snaps several pictures of my skin, and then sends them to someone. "Go on, tell me more of what happened," he coaches, whipping off his stethoscope and listening to my heart. "Just breathe normally."

Yeah, right! Breathe normally? Could you in my situation? I think. Exhaling, I begin: "Well, I understand meteorites in the form of dust and particles fall through the atmosphere all the time. They land everywhere around us, but most collect in substantial quantities on rooftops and flat surfaces. I bet if you look right now, you could sweep some up along this street." I show him my right shoulder where I remember seeing another silver patch of changed skin, and he starts taking my blood pressure. "I wanted to see some of those particles for myself, and touch some, 'cause they must be ancient, so I conducted an experiment with a magnet and a tablespoon of particles I collected from my gutters." He rubbed his chin in doubting gestures as he scribbled in my chart. "Honestly, Doctor Rias, it was an innocent water-type experiment." I felt like crying, and I did. He handed me a Kleenex, and I blew my nose. Inside the Kleenex, I see a few glittering particles! I remember inhaling some yesterday? Oh my Gosh! I didn't just drink the solution … I also inhaled some of the meteorites … even touched my eyes while I mowed the lawn. Quickly, I roll up the Kleenex—now hard evidence—and thrust it in my pocket. If I'd show him, he's surely going say I've been poisoned, or I'm contagious to the rest of humanity, I just *know* it. No, I'm going to wait for a diagnosis first. I need some time to think of what to do should he, or other important people in power, decide to quarantine me. After a few seconds of watching fear and unbelief play in his eyes, I asked, "Well?" I sniffle, patting a few tears off my cheeks.

"What happened when you touched these silver patches on your skin?" he asks, putting on gloves.

"I think they spread." Seeing my reflection in a mirror over a sink, I point at two curved silver lines under my eyes. "I tried washing the spots off my forehead and cheeks, but then these two rings appeared." I point at a few more places on my arms and neck, and then pinched a few of the silver-spotted patches on my neck. "I can't tell which ones are new, or which popped up on me overnight."

"*Hm*," he keeps saying, looking askance and exhaling. Then he slides over to a drawer and takes out a syringe and tubes to collect blood. I extend my arm, and he taps it for a vein. "I need a sample so I can rush this to our lab and get some results." As my blood eddies into the barrel, I think the texture looks a bit thick; but just as I'm about to mention that, he asked, "Did you apply anything to these silver scales?" After taking my blood, he rolls his chair over to the door and calls Cindy to rush it to the lab.

I answered his question. "I tried washing them off my face with soap twice, and then I used alcohol." I shrug and massage my stiff neck. I'm so thirst...again! I gotta drink, and I run to the faucet and suck down some water. Meanwhile, I hear commotion outside. Len and Derrick are at the door, but Cindy is stopping them from entering the room. I'm sure I'll be able to see them soon, I hope, unless Dr. Rias diagnoses a contagion. That thought makes me panic, and I gulp down some more water.

"Stay here, Elizabeth." He sloughs off his sterile gloves. "I need to do some research from the pictures I took while we wait for your blood results and some more specialists."

As he leaves, I shout through the closing door: "Len! Derrick! I'm sure I'll be able to see you soon!"

Len calls back, "I love ya, Liz! We're here, and we won't leave until we get some answers!"

Feeling more confused and frightened, I hop back up on the exam table and stare at my reflection. Looking a little more closely at my eyes, I notice another change. I dash to the mirror. Opening my eyes as wide as I can, I see a sliver of a silver ring around my black pupils. "My God! Whatever I have is spreading, making my eyes look cat-like! Yuck!" I feel on the verge of hyperventilating, so I suck down some more water and splash a handful over my face.

"What did ya say, Liz?" Len shouts.

"Mom, you all right?" Derrick asks through the door. I see the handle jiggle. It's locked! After drying my face on my sleeves, I try opening it. The handle won't budge.

"I'm locked in!" I shout, trying to open the door again.

Then I noticed three hinges attached to special key pads and motion sensors. "This door's high-tech, Len," I gasp, cold air drying my throat. "Doctor Rias is obviously confining me here until he can discover some answers. He must think something serious is wrong with me. We gotta wait." As I hear Len and Derrick groan in anger, I remember how I forced open the car door. Can I do repeat that right now? I bend down like a sprinter at a start line. Then, I change my mind. Busting out won't help me or my family but only make the situation worse, and most likely result in a police chase.

Len pounds on the door. "Damn!" He tries jostling the handle again.

"Len, just wait," I tell him. I hear a frustrating sigh, and then he exhales in resignation. Then I notice Derrick, crying. "It'll be all right, Derrick," I say slowly, trying to control my shaking voice. "I just know I'll be all right. You'll see. Doctor Rias just needs some time to figure out what's wrong." Then I have another thought that makes me shudder and stop dead still. If there are special locks on the door, chances are they're watching me. With my back against the door, I cry. I feel so isolated, disoriented, and scared ... *chilled* like a dark-cold January day is sweeping through this high-tech sterile room.

"They better figure out what's wrong soon or I'm callin' the cops," Len says. "We have rights!"

"I don't think so," I mumble so he can't hear me. I'm sure the government has special provisions for people like me who might pose a threat to humanity. I'm sure they have some secret site where they inspect strange things they don't understand. Then I hear Cindy and Dr. Rias mumbling to Len and Derrick. I have a little ringing in my ears now-and-then, but I can make out their words. I can also see a little bright outline of their bodies behind the door! My vision's changing. What else is next?!

Cindy and Dr. Rias are asking Len and Derrick to wait outside in the waiting area until Dr. Rias can come up with a diagnosis. Len is arguing with him, but I know fighting is useless. The only way I'm getting outta this cold, white monitored room is when Dr. Rias, or someone else higher up, lets me out. As I drink more water, I feel downright terror stricken. Under some silvery patches on my hand, I see tiny veins under my shaking fingers. I know I'm changing as time ticks on in seconds. Changing into what or who? And what will the experts do? I can only wait, pray for a sure-fire remedy, and hope.

Doctor Rias suddenly appears on an LED screen on the wall in front of me. His round face is Zeus-sized compared to the scurrying lab assistants and telephoning nurses behind him. They've been hailing experts, most likely medical specialists and powerful officials like the CDC, and I'm definitely trapped under their high-tech magnifying eyes. Glancing around while trying to stay calm, I see more than just an advanced LED system on the wall. There are two, small, red-flashing corner cameras that have definitely been recording my every move. This *must* be a room they've prepared to contain an outbreak; and until they clear me, *I'm* patient zero. I scoot back on the table, but the lights are intense, and I cover my face. I feel a few more little silver patches pop up on my hands and face. "God—what's happening to me?!" I cover my face with the little cotton pillow.

"Liz," Dr. Rias begins, "we've notice that the lighting is making the breakout worse."

"Really?" I glance at my arms. A few more spots have *definitely* appeared, and I can't help but to run to the sink and gulp down some more water.

"Yes, Liz." He now has a life-or-death rhyme to his voice. "So we're changing the illumination from full-spectrum to soft white. We're hoping the alteration stops whatever you have from spreading."

"Me too," I tell him. "So what's next?"

"We wait for your lab results." He calls Len and Derrick over to the screen. When I see their faces, I feel a calm reassurance spread through my body.

"We're here, Hun," Len says, wiping away tears, almost choking on 'em. He rarely cries. So what's wrong with me *must* be bad, and dangerous, 'cause he's not holding back *any* of his raw emotions.

"You'll be better soon, Mom," Derrick adds, with curious squinting eyes. He keeps trying to bump Len out of the way so he can get a clear view of my face.

"Let's hope so," I say, hopping back up on the exam table.

Part III
Trapped and Fighting to Survive

Two hours later that feel like a dragging day, a woman dressed in a yellow hazmat suit with a helmet and thick mask enters the exam room. She looks ready to treat me for Ebola as she stops starry-eyed with her back against the door. She *is* scared to death. Someone's forcing her to deal with me, and she is not a nurse.

So many thoughts scamper through my mind. Should I make a break for the door? What do I do if they discover something bad and alien going on inside of me? What's going to happen to Len and Derrick, and my mom and dad? How do I tell *them* that their daughter could end up a carnival act, in a dungeon somewhere, or dead?

I see a handle at the edge of the exam table. I've never been a violent person, but I need to make a dash for the door. As the woman with the bright blue eyes behind the mask approaches me, I jiggle the handle, trying to break it off. No use. Whatever strength I had in the car was just temporary.

Then I look down past the handle to the gray-and-white laminate floor. I see brown clumps of hair. *My* hair! And it's all over me and the table. "My hair's falling out!" I scream. Again I look at my reflection over the sink. "All my hair is gone!" I gasp. "I look like a shiny silver mutant out of an *X-Man* movie! What the hell is happening to me?" I can't stop repeating that, and crying, and heaving in the cold clinical air while running my hands over my scalp and picking up all my hair that I'm trying to savor between my fingertips, 'cause maybe this head 'o mine might have to embrace permanent baldness. All the while, the woman in the hazmat suit is saying calming words, but they're just high-speed waves flowing in one ear and out the other. Strands of my short brown hair are sticking to my arms hands. I try wiping them off, until the hazmat woman hands me a basin of warm water so I can wash. Now, even my fingers and hands are covered in silver, just like the sterling tableware in my credenza.

"Ma'am," the woman begins, her wavering voice sounding serious, "we have your blood results. Your DNA has changed." Speaking through her mask and hazmat suit, she sounds as if she's talking through an underwater microphone. "I can see this mysterious change is so hard on you. But hundreds of people are working right now to find a solution. Just stay calm." After a few seconds, she adds, "We need to run a more comprehensive analysis, so we have to move you from this facility. But you'll be okay. And you're safe."

"Move me?" The word *move* keeps resonating like *remove*, and I stand up to retaliate. "Move me where? What about my family?" I'm also hungry…having a craving for apples, pears, peanuts in the shell, and water melon. Watermelon? I sound like I'm expecting a baby and need pickles!

After telling her I haven't eaten breakfast and would like those foods 'cause I'm feeling sick and squeamish, she says, "I'll get them right away, but in the meantime, call me Selina." She has a humming wand the likes I've never seen before in her white-gloved hands, a green-flashing scanner thicker than a laser pen that's reading my vitals and sending them to an outside source. "There's a special room we're preparing for you at Patrick Air Force

Base."

I hear a helicopter; and looking up, I can see a silvery outline of one coming this way in the distance. "Is that for me, Selina?"

She checks her wrist device. "Yes, but how did you know?" She steps back, obviously startled and scared.

"I can see it through the roof, although it's just a faint outline, that's how I know," I reply. After she types my response, I say, "I have a gut feeling I'm not leaving your sight until that copter lands and whisks me off."

In the meantime, someone's delivered a food cart. I see a red apple, a little bowl of peanuts, slices of watermelon, and two pears. I start gobbling them down, until I remember a scene from a *Batman* movie where the Penguin tears apart the catch of the day and gnashes the slimy critters between his teeth. I just lost my appetite, and push away the tray. All the while, Selina has continued scanning me and sending the results.

Then I remembered Len and Derrick, and an idea occurs to me! "Selina, have you sent someone to my house? I told Dr. Rias about the experiment I conducted with particles around the downspouts. Maybe one of the experts can find an answer to this genetic ailment that seems to be changing me into a shiny silver candlestick." I laugh, but then I start crying, again.

Handing me a Kleenex, Selina receives a reply from someone on the iPhone that's strapped to her forearm. "There are officials from Washington, D.C., the CDC, and the Space Agency all over your house taking samples, Elizabeth."

Whew! That's the first time I've heard her call me by my name. It makes me still feel human even though my physiology appears to be morphing into a different species. But what kind of species, and from where? And am I alone?

I slouch in helplessness. "I bet the neighbors think I'm a terrorist or something, right Selina?" I dry my eyes with a smooth cloth she gives me which she then encases in an evidence bag obviously destined for more testing. "I probably can't go home again ever if people find out about me." Again I cry.

She exhales through soft blue eyes that remind me of my grandmother's eyes before she died. I can't help but trust Dr. Salina Hayes. And she's staying with me in spite of her fear, and she even touched my scaly hand a few times, even if she did have on gloves. "We have to move *now*, Elizabeth," she suddenly says, walking to the far end of the room. The wall behind her begins opening to an artificially-lit hallway. At the end of the corridor must be an outdoor exit. Squinting there, I can see through several layers...to an alley lined with black SUVs and an ambulance. I can't see beyond them; but from the sounds I'm hearing, I believe there's an extensive police escort. Gosh, I have enhanced sight *and* hearing!

After leaving this place, I know I'll be stepping to an unpredictable future, and might never see Melbourne, Florida again. I gasp in panic. "What about my Len and Derrick, Selina? When can I see them to say goodbye ... for a while?" As I hop off the exam table, I feel an afternoon coolness brush over my face and arms—a brisk off-shore wind flowing into the exam room from the alley. So many people are out there to take me, and they're prepared to face me and whatever virus, genetic ailment, or contagion they suspect I might have. To them, and most likely everyone around the world who might find out about me—that is if the experts who are about to apprehend me inform the world about me— people will see me as either as a danger, or a wonderful invention with helpful qualities. But first, I have to discover some positive qualities or useful capabilities myself. I just hope the people who are about to take me away from home and family won't throw me into a satellite docking bay at the Cape and launch me into the sun!

When I finally arrive at the alley, I spot a gauntlet of SUVs. I was right. I also surmise they have firepower too, so I better just obey them and not run for my life. Four masked men and women wave me toward a long ambulance.

"I'm here with you, Elizabeth," Selina says. "I'll ride with you all the way to your final destination."

I thought she said Patrick Air Force Base! Did something change? I can't imagine anyone committing such an outright conspiracy—to be so bold as to kidnap me without telling Len and Derrick where they're taking me and forcing me to stay. Walking slowly toward the masked crew, I inhale the sweet air deep into my lungs. On the pavement are tiny pools of rain water and little clouds reflecting in large puddles. As two sand cranes fly high overhead, little sparrows soaring alongside them are chirping, their tweets inaudible to everyone but me. With my every step, I want to absorb the sun's warmth, and feel the heat permeate every inch of my smooth silvery arms and face. It takes centuries for a photon of light to travel from the center of the sun to Earth. I never want to stop remembering how luxurious the ancient newness feels 'cause I may never feel the light of day again.

Then, an ocean breeze rushes in, caressing me like a balm. As I walk toward another woman directing me into the ambulance with tinted windows, I see a line of yellow-and-red hibiscus flowers tossing like a troupe of Flamenco dancers. Will I ever touch a flower again? Up high on the metal roof, the sun's bright reflection is blinding, and I almost drop to the ground until Salina lifts me up. Then someone drapes a white drop cloth over me. "Hey! Get this off me!" I fight, kicking and screaming. "I want my husband and my son, now. I have my rights! I want to speak to Len Miller—"

Suddenly, a spray hits my face, and I collapse into yellow hazmat covered arms. I'm not unconscious, just like a rag doll. I remember seeing someone stunned by this type of an incapacitating agent, like GHB or ketamine that can induce a state of paralysis while enabling a victim to remain aware of his or her surroundings.

"Mrs. Miller," the man in the yellow suit begins, "Len and Derrick can't return home right now, and you can't either. We're taking you where you can move around more freely until we have a diagnosis and counteragent."

I can't speak, but I know that what they're doing has to be illegal, isn't it? Kidnapping me and forcing me into exile? I suddenly remember I book I read, *Stranger in a Strange Land.* I wasn't born on Mars or raised by Martians, but how people are treating me seems inhumane. I must have rights ... even though I did conduct a weird experiment that left me quite changed, and is evolving me into something different from human. Into what? I can't even begin to guess with all this silver material popping up over my body, replacing my smooth skin!

Minutes later, I find myself inside a large white building with a cold concrete floor resembling an airplane hangar. It's not, because I see thick shiny acoustical walls as in a movie theater and a few skylights high in the ceiling. Someone has made the place habitable because a large plush couch is situated in a corner, and in front of it, the latest 4K Ultra HD TV. Along the wall I notice a stainless steel fridge, kitchenette set, and shelves of food.

The man greeting me—or should I say my limp body—asks Selina to carry me to the couch. "Asap," he shouts, "then leave, fast. She'll sleep for a while now."

Before dozing off, more medical experts surround me and begin prodding and poking me, scanning and testing me with all sort of equipment, but the phlebotomist is having trouble inserting the needle into my veins. "A few more hours and we won't be able to extract any blood," she says. Before they all leave, a man dressed in uniform blue pats my shoulder. "Mrs. Miller, we're getting closer to an answer. But we need a little more time, and one last genomic study." He gestures to another side of the room. I can see beyond the walls...outlines of several buildings as my super-vision appears to be getting stronger, and my hearing more fine-tuned so I can hear little animal sounds outside this facility.

After some time, I wake up and begin to regain some feeling. At least now I can wiggle my toes and fingers! I hear people talk beyond this sanctuary hangar. Then I notice the high curved ceiling with several round lights covered with a strange shiny fabric like cellophane. Are they afraid I might break the lights and hurt someone? They must know more about me and what's going on inside of me than what they're telling me. Dirty criminals! Keeping me here against my will!

"I waaant to seeee my huzzband," I say. "Nouw." My cheeks are analgesic numb, and I can't feel my tongue yet.

The yellow-clad guard watching over me by the kitchenette backs away as if he's afraid I'll regain consciousness and strength. "I think your husband and son can Skype with you in just a while, Mrs. Miller. We're putting them up in another safe place while we search your house to find the microbial agent that infected you."

That's the first news I've heard of that! And *who* exactly are *you*? I wonder. The guy's got bedside manners the size of a hen's brain. "Wh*aaa*t biologic*aaa*l a*jjj*ent?" I managed to force out of my cotton-dry mouth now starting to regain sensation from the effects of their drugs.

He dashes to the door beyond the kitchenette. "Turn on the monitors! She's waking up!" he calls to people monitoring me. Now I see beyond the outside walls more clearly as I sit up and drink a glass of water someone left for me on the coffee table. I've been to Patrick Air Force Base. It's by the ocean, by Cape Canaveral where satellites launch. I smell the air. It's musty, and I see dust particles swirling in the light streaming in from the two high skylights. There isn't a cloud in sight! I'm *not* in Florida. In my stupor, the ride to this place must have taken hours. Squinting to see past the outside walls, I can make out flat land with heat waves beating off hot sand. The sun appears as a fiery gold nugget above the western horizon, and a sidewinding snake is slithering into a hole in the sand-slanted hard ground. I see undulations of a wild breeze whipping up the sand in streaks of diamond dust. Then nothing except beating heat.

"You're at Homey Airport, Mrs. Miller," a voice says. It's coming from the large-screen high-tech TV. "I'm Agent Stockard, your liaison with the military personnel here. You're fine, Mrs. Miller. You're safe. Just rest and regain your strength."

"I don't feel fine *or* safe," I counter, standing up after experiencing a long stay in groggy land. I plop back down on the couch, reach for a glass of water on the steel-legged coffee table, and splash some over my face. Before I set it back down, I notice my reflection in the clear liquid. I'm completely silver ... *and* bald! The only thing the same is my shape and green eyes, except for the little silver rings around the pupils. I drop the glass. "My God ... *all* this happened to me in just a *day*!" Several robotic cleaners dart out of an entryway in the distance. With suction arms, they're vacuuming the white cold floor. These are not your average iRobot vacuums on sale at Amazon. These metal critters are special...and there's gotta be more somewhere. But I've never heard of the place, Homey Airport, that Agent Stockard just mentioned. "Where's Homey Airport?"

Agent Stockard is talking to me from the sixty-inch crystal-clear TV. His resolution is so exquisite; I think I can touch his middle-aged chiseled face and the lines of medals on his Air Force uniform. He obviously fought hard in a war and received honors. When I touch the screen, the reception fizzles out and then hisses back on. I jump back. "What the heck was that?!" Then I look up at those covered bright lights. I must have a special capability they've already realized in order for them to take such a protective measure.

After another attempt to calm me down, Agent Stockard replies, "Tomorrow, after you rest, we have some people you need to meet. You'll be able to relate to them. You're not alone, Elizabeth."

I've had enough! "Okay...that's it!" I pick up and smash a glass of water on the floor and then sweep up one of the iRobots. I wanna pull out its flailing, little claw arms then crunch its aluminum-plastic body under my feet. I wave iRobot into the TV screen threateningly. "I wanna know where I'm at, what you're gonna do with me, and who I'm meeting tomorrow who I can relate to. 'Cause unless you've got someone like me stashed somewhere around here, I don't see me relating to anyone!"

With iBot squirming, hissing, and bleeping in my face, I begin feeling guilty. His mechanical eyes appear drooping sad. The government might be hurting and trapping me, but I can't harm humming, hissing squeaking quirky iBot. It has oval glowing binoculars for eyelids that blink over bright-blue optic eyeballs as if it's an AI in the process of becoming more aware each time it *beep-bops* in my hands. I can't become hurtful and violent even though people have injured me.

"Okay, I won't hurt you and become like them," I whisper to iBot and then set it down gently on the white cold floor. "I never could hurt anything." Once stable, iBot ejects its roller ball feet, rotates, and then returns back to sucking up all my mess.

Plopping down on the couch, I cringe when I see a large, armored robot enter the furnished hangar. Wow! This one looks half-Terminator and half-android! It's carrying a tray of fruits, vegetables, and an assortment of nuts. This special robot has steely-flat fingers, a wired barrel of a torso, and Terminator's shiny face, arms, and legs. I scoot back as far away as I can from the tower of steel with blazing red eyes.

"Here you are, Mrs. Miller. I'm Evan. Enjoy." He has the voice of a seven-year-old boy and sets the tray on the table. The thing's hulking but a helpless child!

"Thanks," I tell it. Evan has socket-swinging hip joints, elbows, and knees. I think it's a special military experiment because Evan appears impervious to weapons fire. As the giant AI leaves, its round titanium knee joints squeak while its rigid forearms pump on its ball-jointed elbows.

Now, I'm more confused now than ever. Now, I have to not only deal with all *my* changes but also this wild, weird, wacky place! "Agent Stockard, what's this place called again?" I'm here, at least for a while, until they can figure out a solution for me. I guess I can't blame them for feeling terrified of me. They're mission is containment, and they believe I could infect and change the entire population. Although, Agent Stockard *did* say he had people around here with whom I can relate. Where could *they* be? Using my special sight to the outside world, I can't see anything move beyond these two buildings. Where they're housing them, I haven't a clue. But I'm sure I'll meet them soon.

"You're at Area 51, Mrs. Miller," Agent Stockard says through the moving TV monitor that turns to face me wherever I move. He's Skyping from a large facility with comfortable chairs and long shiny wooden tables around which other blue-suited officials and medical personnel are conversing. They're consulting people on transparent monitors and exchanging information on laptops and other portable devices. Agent Stockard must be in a top-secret area because I can't see one door or window. And the walls, like this place, look thick and lead protected. Maybe that's why I can't discern much beyond my hangar.

"Area 51?" I recall some history. Area 51 is where government officials supposedly took aliens who crashed landed in the desert. Realizing that, I feel scared for my life! I touch my arms. Are they gonna experiment on me after they discover the problem? Over my dead body! With my hands on my hips, I march over to the large screen and give Agent Stockard what I think is the meanest grimace I've ever given anyone 'cause even my teeth hurt!

"I don't know what you intend to do to me, Agent Stockard, but I'll never let you conduct an experiment on me, you—you…"

I can't help it. I collapse back down on the couch, and fall asleep!

PART IV
ACCEPTANCE AND PURPOSE

The next day, I wake up with half my body hanging off the soft beige couch. Yawning and sitting up, I see the time: 8:30 a.m. on the giant screen TV, and then I hear gnashing, clanking, and suction sounds. The ten-inch octopus-shaped iBot is under my feet, sucking popcorn off the floor with its vacuum paws, and siphoning potato chip into suction-cup multi-purpose fingers.

"What happened…'cause this place looks like a tornado spun through it?" My memory is foggy, and I feel like I have one humdinger of hangover! But how? I didn't drink one beer!

Then, like a sudden cold snap chilling me to the bone, I remember what happened to me yesterday and how I wound up in a hanger facility in the middle of the Nevada desert, Area 51, Agent Stockard told me. Could the alien microbe acting on my physiology be playing Scrabble with my human mind? "Oh God…help me!" I cover my eyes and cry as little iBot's mechanical finger spins itself into a claw and hands me a wad of Kleenex off the floor.

"Thanks." I blow my nose and wipe my eyes. "You're becoming my best friend around here," I tell it through a few sniffles as iBot's claw spins into a rickety finger and pats my knee in a consoling movement.

There's a feeling worse than loneliness, and I'm reminded of what happened ten years ago in Hawaii. While swimming a ways from shore on an abandoned Waianae beach, the surf surged. A bomb wave rose up out the deceptively calm ocean and came crashing down on me, almost drowning me if not for the deep gasp I inhaled before spiraling to the churning bottom. That titan curl must have had it in for me 'cause it began dragging me to the open sea, but I kept kicking against the current while crawling through grains of sand to the shore. Where's north, south, east, west? Confusion filled my mind like the watery darkness smoothing me. I forgot about hunger and thirst. I just needed a pocket of air, one bob into the light so I could see the shoreline and sun-yellow sand.

Breathing deeply while watching iBot vacuum up the mess, I realize that life-saving feat out of that cold, lonely thick depth *has* to remain in the forefront of my reality. Now, and every minute if I'm going to keep my sanity, begin to adjust to my evolving self, and accept my new life, whatever my future looks like in spite of the terror I'm feeling. I notice my hands. I can barely stop shaking! How am I ever going to make it through the day? Making matters worse, the changes occurring in my brain might reverse me into simpleton hunter-gatherer, like Rhodesian man who lived over 125,000 years ago, or evolve me into a superhuman! My thoughts begin spinning in a whirling dance!

I ask iBot, "Ya got any aspirin for my one helluva headache?"

It bobs up in an obvious excited move, twirls around, and rolls over to a low shelf at the food storage site. After meeting iBot half way with a strange plastic cup of water in my hand, a sliding door in the distance opens, and Terminator Evan steps into the room with its two titanium feet clanking on the shiny concrete floor.

Swallowing the aspirin, I notice Evan about to trip on an area rug under the kitchen table. "Stop. If you fall, you'll crack the floor and topple everything off the shelves!"

Halting, Evan says through red-flaring eyes, "Thank you for the warning, Mrs. Miller."

I think, *Oo—that boyish voice again*, as I wince and scratch my nose to hide my laugh. "Whoever approved your vocal modulation, Evan, should be thrown out there in the desert with the snakes!" I whisper to him.

Evan's hulking shoulders *whirr* as the steel clavicles lift on their balled rotator cuff in a shrug. "Mrs. Miller, I brought you breakfast."

I wince at the dissonance but wave him toward me. After carefully stepping over the edge of the rug, Evan, the towering titanium robot with the torso-barrel circuitry sets a tray of fresh fruits, vegetables, and nuts on the table. "Agent Stockard thought you might like this instead of the popcorn and potato chips you demanded last night." Again, I flinch at that high-pitch boyish voice that sounds like a cartoon character. Oh well, the voice *does* make Evan appear less threatening. Evan glances at iBot, and then at several messed up spots on the floor, his red-flaring eyes blinking as if analyzing how much more work needs to be done in order to finish cleaning up. Then Evan begins staring at *me*…with those thin-steel eye lids pinging over red-flaring eyeballs.

Feeling suddenly guilty, I back up and sit down on the couch. Oh-oh…*I* caused the grand mess on the floor…and the reeking wet root beer spots on the couch…and squished hamburger meat in between the cushions. Then I hear more little squeaks and creaks behind me as if people are squeegeeing a window. Peeking over the sofa, I see miniature robots moving over the wall in perfect crisscrossing symmetry. They're cleaning it and pulling out dents out of the wall covering.

"What the heck did I do in here?" I rub my eyes and drink water from another weird plastic cup that Evan just handed me. "Thanks, Evan, but can you *please* tell me what happened?"

Having mopped up some more mess and obviously finishing its last task, little iBot backs away from the sofa, reels in his octopi-suction arms, turns 180°, and rolls off to a little opening that appears dented as if a large dog had tried squeezing through it but failed to escape.

"This doesn't look good for me," I tell Evan, as Evan's bright red eyeballs pan side-to-side. *I* had tossed the room like an angry protester demanding justice. I bet big trouble is about to head my way, any second. That's probably why Evan's still hanging around the kitchen table between me and the sliding door. Did I regain my super strength? I can't remember! I try lifting the sofa. Nothing. I'm stumped! What did I do last night?!

Then Agent Stockard walks through the hissing sliding door with a pile of clothes in his arms. I'm dressed in what I wore when I arrived here; but my shorts smell of French fry oil, and my t-shirt's mottled with ketchup and mustard. With my skin morphing into some type of new silver biology, I must look like a hand-painted silver Christmas ornament. But I can't locate a mirror. Have I changed from yesterday? If so, how much?

"Can I have a mirror so I can *see* my face, *please?*" I should have asked Agent Stockard why he wasn't wearing a hazmat suit as they all had on yesterday when people were scared out of their wits, and poking and testing me. But locating a mirror takes priority right now, 'cause I need an answer to one question: Am I still human? I also want the results of all my tests!

As Agent Stockard walks past Evan while Evan maintains a red-line of optical sight on his trajectory, Agent Stockard replies, "No mirrors for now, Elizabeth." Dressed in a starched blue uniform with lines of colorful shining metals over his heart, he has a distinguished walk and a confident expression on his slightly wrinkled face; and there's kindness and gentleness in his hazel eyes. I would guess he had at *least* served in the Gulf War.

"Why can't I have a mirror?" Frustrated, I show him my hands and walk into the little kitchen. "If you changed like this, wouldn't you want to see yourself too, 'cause maybe you might never change back!" Trying not to feel too disgusted at my appearance, I notice my fingers are the same shiny silver as yesterday. I touch the back of my left hand. My epidermis appears tougher and smoother as if I'm evolving a complete metallic coating! Gasping and then quickly steadying my breathing, I think of what could be happening to my heart. I can't imagine how those tiny meteorites and DNA-altering alien microbial could *still* be working on my insides! But I'm eating food, so my internal organs can't be *that* altered. And I *do* have a memory of using the bathroom…at some point during the night…if only I can remember when exactly.

Evan steps toward me and opens a sliding compartment on his chest. Wow—Evan's not only a military titan but also an instructor they must use to train soldiers! A show begins playing on his small chest screen, and I sit down on a kitchen chair and force myself to eat a little food while watching what happened last night.

At 9:30 p.m., I saw my reflection in a glass of ice water. Dropping the tumbler, I then went into a rage, shouting and screaming. I pulled dishes out of the small cabinet next to the tiny sink and threw them like bullets around the room. I smashed glasses. I even hurled one at Evan.

The show plays on, but I can't look at it, except into Evan's blinking red-flaring processor eyes. Oh my—what dejection I see! Walking slowly toward the AI gargantuan, I stop when Evan clanks back from me. He's afraid *I'm* going to *hurt* him! Wow, I just called Evan, *he*. Maybe, there's hope that people will still see *me* as a human being at some point in the future and not some silver alien frightening entity.

Then I notice a tiny crack in Evan's little screen. I had attacked him. Regret, in knots, wind through my stomach. "I'm so sorry, Evan." Crying, I sit down on a kitchen chair. "I'm so sorry. That's not like me, honest! Please, forgive me?"

Evan touches my shoulder with the gentle tenderness of friend. "It's okay, Mrs. Miller." His quirky childish voice isn't irritating anymore. "I had to take away all the drinking glasses though and replace them with plastic Sippy cups to make it harder for you to see your reflection."

I glance at the coffee table and see *three* Sippy cups, the kind toddlers drink out of to keep from spilling. Perhaps in the middle of the night, someone had to make a helicopter run to a distant 7-11. "Seeing my reflection made me do all this damage? Wow!"

Handing me a crushed box of Kleenex, Agent Stockard slides up a chair and sits down close to me. While I wipe my eyes, he explains: "We finally realized that whenever you see your reflection, in a mirror or water, you experience an avalanche of anxiety followed by an outburst of rage."

"Oh, wow, oh gosh." I'm so embarrassed, and clench my fists in self-degradation, but he's a calm sea of kindness.

"So, to help you, Elizabeth, until you get used to your appearance, it's best you just stay away from all mirrors or anything reflective for a while. You need time to adjust to all your biological changes." He opens his lips to say more, but then suddenly stops as if realizing he must keep some facts secret.

I gasp and notice my surroundings that are making me feel claustrophobic. "I understand." I want to argue but I bite my lip.

I need to remain calm and collected. So I continue to mirror Agent Stockard's easy-going manner—folding my arms and crossing my legs. After all, I'm an outdoor person. I *need* some fresh air and sunshine, but I know I have to convince *him* and his bosses that I won't explode into a rage or throw a tantrum over being forced to reside at Area 51. Still, I guess life could get worse. They could confine me to one of their underground facilities or labs!

"I'm used to myself now, Agent Stockard, really I am." So, I tell a little white lie. Then I remember what he told me yesterday, and I perk up. "Hey, you said there are people you want me to meet." I quickly walk over to the coffee table and begin picking out clothes from the pile he brought in for me. I like the long, light-blue flowered blouse and white leggings. I think they'll match best with my silver skin that I'm trying so hard not to look at 'cause I know I'll have another conniption fit and psychic break! I can't do that, if I ever wanna get outta here. The phrase, *stay calm and cooperate,* flash through my mind as I glance at an assortment of colorful Sippy cups on a shelf below one that Evan just finished hanging.

As I dash behind a curtained partition in the corner, a changing area, I notice all the fixer-upper robots that had been repairing the walls scuttle toward the exit, and I begin changing. This little four-by-four space is probably the only niche where I have some privacy. Then I remember the other thing I need to ask him. "Agent Stockard, what exactly is wrong with me? By now, you all must know." I peek around the curtain into the hardness of his cheek muscles. The news must not be good. He's hesitating with his answer.

Finally he huffs. "It's a biological agent that's attached and altered your DNA. We know the results of the genomics test, but cannot reverse the effects of the microbial agent without damaging your entire body." I wanna cry...again! "We know what happened to you," he continues, "because we have other samples with which to compare *your* blood sample. Theirs are slightly different though because the method of exposure is different."

Another bout of dizzy disorientation hits me, and I nearly drop to the floor until I prop myself back up and catch my breath. "You mean there are other people here? People who *look* like *me*?!" I quickly button my flowered blouse and inch the white leggings up around my hips. I almost knock down my entire little dressing niche I feel so thrilled! "Who are they? Where are they? When can I—"

"Just a moment," he interrupts.

Needing an instant answer, I jump out of the changing area. Agent Stockard's been consulting with someone on his wrist device, but then quickly and stealthily shuts off the connection when he sees me.

"We think you're ready to know more," he begins, gesturing at the opaque sliding door. "Come on, Elizabeth, follow me." As he walks toward the exit of freedom, I'm behind him like a rolling snowball, and Evan catches up as we leave the hangar. When the door closes behind us, I imbibe—right down deep into my lungs—the warm dry air that's undulating like a sidewinding snake along the whipped desert landscape. In front of us is a long walkway lined with red pointer sensors. Surely they'll emit a *powerful* sting and blaring sound if anyone steps off the illuminated path.

"Yep, they'll sound an alarm, Elizabeth," Agent Stockard confirms, obviously reading my body language and surmising I was about to test the technology.

Lined up in teams on both sides of us, white-clad medics, military personnel dressed in camouflaged uniforms, and men and women in black suits and black ties are monitoring our every move. The latter people must be agents on the hunt for UFOs and aliens. What in the world is going on, I wonder, inside the giant warehouse in front of us? Hardly feeling my legs and arms, I step as quickly as I can to keep up with Agent Stockard who's calling guards to stand down from the thick opaque double-door entryway.

Something bothers me as I observe all these people and military personnel. I thought they'd be scared to death, ready to shoot-to-kill me, or haul me off to an Area 51 jail. But they appear comfortable and only prepared to chase me and capture me if I attempt to escape because I see a few nets with harpoons in the background. They must be used to seeing someone the likes of shiny silver me!

As we approach the looming white warehouse, my pulse begins *beat*-beating faster. "Who's inside?" I ask Agent Stockard. "How long have they been here? If there are people are like me, has anyone ever changed back to normal?" I'm firing off questions like a rambling idiot! But I'm so nervous and worried, like I'm heading to school for the first time. Waiting behind Agent Stockard while he inputs his eye signature and handprint into a security screen, I spot a distant snow-covered mountain range on my right. The long line of high white peaks and brown sunlit slopes look like reclining bodies after Thanksgiving turkey. What I wouldn't give right now to be camping there, or disappearing in some pine scented forest to live off the land with bears and maybe Big Foot, given what I know now about Area 51.

Leaving the desert-dry outside world, we step into an unending high-tech lab with four fun zones at the forefront. They appear to function as a greeting area or information booths. Amidst all the distant chattering and droning equipment, I notice tall transparent monitors positioned above and around small hard drives all along the walls as far as the eye can see. In front of us, the four fun zones are showing holographic scenes over sections of high-advanced computerized flooring. Feeling astounded, I lean in and tell Agent Stockard, "This must be where we're heading in broadcasting and watching TV." People must have been gaming on them, because I see four, different holographic nature settings. And they appear so real and inviting! I keep wondering: *Who* developed all these experimental prototypes? Will *I* be able to test them? I can't imagine every even thinking such a thing, but I continue marveling at each new technological invention and thinking, I can't wait!

I tell Agent Stockard, "*Nothing*—nothing!—around here and inside this place is even on the market! Who created all this technology—from iBot and Evan, to holographic gaming capability?"

He laughs a bit and gestures at the fun zones. "Go on over and take a look. They're awesome. You'll see." He coaxes me forward as if suggested I'll never want to return home after experiencing such a wonderful world of virtual-reality.

Walking over to the zone on my far right, I stop at a little raised platform that looks like the bottom of a tread mill. Agent Stockard tells me it's a multi-purpose platform, an activation site that can generate any virtual landscape.

Agent Stockard calls, "Activate ski function."

Virtual skis appear under my feet. Then 3D ski poles shoot up out of the sheen flooring. Then snow appears under my feet—looking so real and shimmering that I can almost touch the chill! Obviously, someone's been skiing in the Alps that suddenly materialize all around me. The display setting launched, and a 3D swishing ski run appears right in front of me! Now, if you didn't pinch me, I'd tell ya I was right smack center of a ski resort, in the friggin' Alps, and about ready to lose my life on a downhill ski run! Furthermore, the sound system is so unlike *any* Bose I've ever heard.

"Yikes! Stop!" I shout, not at all prepared to launch down the ski run.

Agent Stockard shrinks the setting, and I return back to reality.

Feeling relieved, I shiver. "*Brr*, it sure feels cold! Participating in *these* games will be like stepping into the actual place!" He laughs as I smell so many fragrancies in the air around me. "Wow, the woodsy scent *must* be emanating from those Alpine trees in the distance…and I smell hot cocoa brewing in the Hotel Firefly…and I hear people talking alongside a kindling fireplace that must be in the hospitality center." Now I feel a craving for chocolate and whipped cream…right now! But no hostess is going to step out of this fake world and offer me some. If one did, that would *really* blow me away! "Every experimental device is programmed with augmented capabilities, Agent Stockard. Is this entire place like a magical Oz or what?" I back off the platform, and the scene reverts to empty space with only a prompt on the front of the platform: *call on to initialize*.

"If you tell our virtual-reality system, MARKY we call it, where you'd like to visit," Agent Stockard begins, "MARKY will activate a full-body reality experience, just for you, out of all its saved images."

I keep walking backwards until my derriere hits the sliding door. A computer system? That can *know* me?! Maybe even read my brain waves and generate images from my memory? No, no…I am *not* ready for this! I don't *want* this MARKY system. I want to see Len and Derrick, now. "I don't—"

"Over there in Zone-1," he interrupts, "you can surf. And all the beach scenes are Zone-2. In Zone-3, you can activate *any* tourist destination or natural wonder in the world."

I'm getting angry because he acts like I'm living here permanently. No, no—uh-uh! "Agent Stockard, I have a home. And a family. I want leave and go home." I know they won't let me, but I'm gonna try. "At least I want to talk to them. Come on! They must be worried out of their minds about me!" Then, again, I begin crying, and Evan reaches over and hands me a strange cloth that looks like a special eye glass cleaner…most likely his titanium polishing cloth!

"You'll talk to them, Elizabeth, in just a bit, I promise," Agent Stockard says softly. We just have a few more things to do; then you can Skype with your Len and Derrick." He speaks their names as if he's come to know them personally. Most likely, throughout this entire catastrophic ordeal, he and many other experts have become extremely close to Len and Derrick.

Still, Skyping isn't *seeing* them personally, but at least the government's compromising. Suddenly, Agent Stockard steps out my line of vision, and I see a bustling area beyond the four gaming zones that's a great room with technicians tinkering with robotics, assembling android parts, and coding. Three of the technicians I notice *can't* be human! They walk from the high-tech room through Zone 3 that automatically activates a dune scene with dune buggies racing to a finish line. Then the three people step out of Zone 3 and walk right toward me!

"Who are they 'cause they look like X-Men characters or a *Marvel Comic* creation?" Terrified, I grab Agent Stockard's sleeve.

"He's still makin' ya call 'im Agent Stockard?" one of them asks, in a female voice. Dressed in a white dress, she has shiny orange-metallic skin that looks like brass, and short black hair and green eyes. If she'd have wings, she could be a Monarch butterfly! That's what I'll call her, Monarch Lady.

The two people behind her, also shaped like women, have on white dresses as well, except the woman on Monarch's Lady's left has shimmering green skin like a perfect emerald, and the woman on her right has shining black skin with little white patches on her face. Are the white dresses they're wearing uniforms? So far, I don't see them carrying one for me. But I do notice the four of us have *two* things in common. We're shiny metallic, and we're women.

Whatever has transmuted our DNA *must* have something to do with our extra X-pair of chromosomes. The two women behind Monarch lady are whispering and laughing while keeping their distance. They must sense I'm about to freak out and want to skedaddle fast, so they're letting Monarch Lady take the lead, speak first and break the ice.

"Well?" Monarch Lady asks Agent Stockard again in an exasperated tone of voice.

Agent Stockard's cheeks redden. "Okay, call me Bill, Elizabeth," he says, facing me apologetically.

"Did you tell her the positive thing about our condition?" Monarch Lady asks him softly.

"Not yet, Mary," Bill replies.

So that's Monarch Lady's name, Mattie, that must be short for Madeline, I surmise. Still, she's Monarch Lady to me. Yet, I wonder what *they're* calling me?

Crossing her arms, Green Emerald Lady begins, "We've already lost one of us, Myrtle the Beetle." She looks up into the air and begins talking to someone invisible but present. "Show her what Myrtle looked like, MARKY." I quickly learn from Bill that MARKY is a super-cloud processor, its name an acronym: Multi-Arched Reality Cartography, and responsible for powering and sustaining *all* of Area 51!

"Yes, Daniella, a computerized voice resounds.

So Emerald Lady's name is Daniella, I surmise.

In Zone-4, where I was about to embark on a ski lift adventure, another image appears of a women with shiny red skin dressed in a flesh-colored body suit.

"She—we called her Myrtle the Beetle, was our friend," Green-Emerald Daniella says. "But she left us a few weeks ago."

Monarch Lady has a sad face as well. "Myrtle changed back to normal, and they—" She gestures to workers in the high-tech great room. "Released her to go home."

Black-and-White Lady steps forward a bit. "That was after four years of being beet red and mutated like us!"

I gasp in relief and about jump for joy! "So I can change back too…and go home?"

Monarch Lady's straight orange lips curl into a grin. "Yeah, ya could, but your change back to normal will be just as difficult as the microbe that changed you into meteorite girl." Then she giggles.

I'm offended! "I'm *not* meteorite girl."

"Meteorite Girl," Black-and-White Patch Lady says, snickering through the joke.

"Stop calling me that!" I fist up and begin walking toward her to punch her, but Bill pulls me back.

"Mary and Daniella still have chips on their shoulders," he whispers. "Forgive them, Elizabeth. Really, they're nice...and they're good people...you'll see."

Mary is Monarch Lady, and Daniella has smooth emerald-green skin; so I can easily match their colors to their names and remember them. Then I recall the last twenty-four hours of my trauma-induced life. Of course I understand how angry and resentful they feel! The alien microbe and meteorite particles that transmuted our DNA, making us into freaks of nature, are so unfair!

"Yeah, we all are experiencing the same alien condition, or disorder, depending on how ya look at the change," Monarch Mary begins. "So after some time of experimenting with our new changes and abilities, we discovered we can take a negative and turn it into a positive by working here at Area 51, for the government, and jet-setting 'round the world as spies with our combined reflective powers."

"Wow—reflective powers?" I ask, glancing at each of them. Then, I remember an art lesson from college. I look like a polished silver spoon, Mary appears to have 24 karat skin, Daniella is brilliant emerald, and Black-and-White Patch Lady, whose name I still don't know, all appear to blend in like perfect symmetry in nature ... like the mini-robots I could hardly hear when they were repairing dents on the wall. Colors can refract and reflect in perfect ways to create a specialized invisibility cloak ...

wow.

"You'll see soon," Black-and-White Lady says while remaining at a distance behind Mary and Daniella.

I could always read people pretty well and respond appropriately, but Black-and-White Lady's body language never changes, and her tone of voice is always flat.

"We fly all over the world and help the government with various projects while now-and-then visiting our families in secret," Mary says. "We *do* get a lot of perks for combining our four forces into a powerful reflective power though. We seek out the enemy and plant tracking devices for special ops units who then seek out the enemy, infiltrate 'em, and then take 'em all down." She appeared satisfied with her special role.

Still, reflective powers? How does *that* happen? I wonder.

They have to see my confusion, because all three women step together and form a line. They appear ready to demonstrate an awesome combined capability! I slide behind Bill as a cold fear trickles into my gut.

The woman with metallic black skin and white patches unleashes a portable device out of a pouch she's carrying by her side. "I hear your name is Elizabeth." She has watery brown eyes and shows me an image of herself before she changed. Her shape is the same; but with no hair, no eyelashes, and shimmering skin now, I can't match her old face to her new alien body. "Yes, that's my name, Elizabeth." Trying to sear the memory of the last time I saw my normal face in the mirror so as to never forget it, I grab Bill's sleeve for protection, but he pats my arm in a comforting gesture. Still, I think they're gonna hurt me even though I know intellectually they won't. Heck, I'm barely getting accustomed to my own changes let alone *theirs*.

"It's all right," Bill whispers aside to me. "They're harmless, and they're trying to be your friend. They've been where you're at and know what you're going through. Let them prove themselves."

Sighing, I give in. "Okay, I'll try. Besides, I don't really have a choice, and there's no way out except right between the three of them," I laugh.

"I'm Selina," the woman with shiny black skin and white patches on her face finally tells me. "I've been here for two years, working with Mary and Daniella. But when Myrtle left, all our reflective powers that made us invisible and undetectable on radar fizzled away."

Monarch Mary put her hands in her dress pockets. "It seems, and Bill you might want to test my hypothesis—"

Uh-oh—another hypothesis! I did that yesterday and I never want to conjure up another one again!

"It seems," Monarch Mary continues, "that when one of us kind changes back to normal and returns home, someone new comes along out of the blue and takes her place."

"I'm the next one who's slowly changing back to normal," Selina says, in a Hispanic accent. "I started turning shiny black like a polished black Cadillac after my car tumbled into a ditch in Sonora, Mexico. They flew me here right away, poked-and-prodded me, and finally concluded that a microbial altered my DNA, just like what happened to you," she nods at me. "But the good news is ... the microbial *does* wear off."

When Selina touches a little patch of *real* skin under her ear and smiles in elation, I about jumped for joy! "Yes! At least I won't stay shiny silver forever! At some point, *I will* change back to my former self!" Then the years ... the number of exact years ... didn't stick in my brain. "How long precisely will I be this silver candlestick color?"

"For about four years," Bill replies, turning away, trying hard not to laugh but instead coughs through what he obviously perceives as funny.

I used to believe he was my only contact with reality, except for iBot and Evan, who are still situated well behind me at the sliding door. I have to stay patient, and calm, and listen closely for more information.

Selina continues, "In a few months, I should be normal again, and able to go back home." She begins crying tears of relief; but then a sorrowful expression appears on her face, and she lowers her gaze to the floor. Obviously, she's grown accustomed to her colleagues and is feeling uneasy about leaving them and Area 51. She seems ready to say, "I'll miss you all," but stops when Monarch Mary clears her throat and rubs premature tears out of her eyes.

"I changed into what I am, this emerald color, because of a water shower," Daniella says, her shoulders lowering in an expression of half-dejection and half-acceptance. "A car doused me with rain and mud in San Jose, California when I was on my way back to work at Ace Metrix." She gestures with her hands over her torso. "I've never been the same since."

Monarch Mary appears mad as she glances at me and then Bill. "Have you told Meteorite Girl what she's gotta do if she decides to stay with us and join our team?"

"You mean there's somewhere else I could go?" I ask, expecting the answer will be either jail or a subterranean chamber until I reverted back to normal. If those are the choices, I'll take working with *these* three long shiny ornaments any day instead of *that* kinda cooped up existence!

Bill folds his arms and groans. "No, not yet. I want

Elizabeth to meet you first, and then I thought you could try connecting with her and see what happens...what capabilities you all might now have. Then I can explain other options to her, and give her a choice."

"If we can all manage to *stay* connected," Monarch Mary said.

"What do you mean?" I ask.

Suddenly, she clasps my hand. "You'll see!" Her grip is firm and energizing! "Come on, everybody! Let's see if we can create a perfect optical chain!"

Emerald Daniella grabs her hand, and Selina clasps Daniella's hand.

With her shiny black fingers extending my way on my right, Selina shouts, "Come on! Your hand, Elizabeth! Now!" She looks like a girl I knew in kindergarten who's begging me to join in on, "Ring Around the Rosie."

When I take her hand while staring into her enthusiastic eyes, I also take hold of Mary's hand on my left. I feel a wild wind whipping energy swirling around me like I'm at the center of a hurricane! Yet I see everything as plain as day beyond our circle, including Bill, who appears in a calm zone, and obviously expecting the whirlwind result. What is happening between us? Our DNA must be interacting through an invisible alien connection!

As Bill steps back, everything outside our four-person circle alters into a prism of rainbows around us.

"What just happened?" I think I died, and am in limbo between light and heaven!

Bill is glowing with happiness. "You did it! I can't see *a thing* in front of me. This is perfect, Ladies ... even better than before." By now we've generated a large audience, every person clapping, shouting praises, and recording our experiment.

Monarch Mary says: "Keep holding hands while they analyze and test our invisibility shield. But I believe we're bending light in perfect transformational optics."

Daniella adds, "We haven't been able to produce a cloak of invisibility since Myrtle left." Her green-hued lips sulk in sadness. "But now, Liz can help, at least until Selina leaves."

"Sorry I'm changing back," Selina says apologetically.

Wow, I *never* thought I'd *ever* hear of any of them express regret over returning back to normal and leaving Area 51. I suddenly let go of Mary's hand, and then unclasp Daniella's hand. There's a *swooshing-whizzing*, energizing sound when the air around me turns back to normal.

Whatever is happening in our DNA *has* to be meant for some type of alien presence among humanity. Whatever the aliens intended to occur on Earth, maybe the best experiment ever, had obviously failed, but instead unleashed a partial manifestation to humanity. Still, no matter what happens, I'll always wonder, why me?

Bill and several medical specialists are now around us, conducting comprehensive scans. As I listen to them and my three comrades talk excitedly about the best transformational optics performance they've ever witnessed, I realize I'm a part of something big ... more than just an experiment. I suddenly feel humble while trying to wrap my brain around so much power we four possess when we link together. But how our gift can help humanity and possibly stop war and evil dictators? I don't know yet; however, for once throughout the existence of Homo sapiens, we *could* have real peace! Now, that's one heck-of-a-way a simple science teacher like me can have a purpose in this world.

Smiling happily over our powers of invisibility, Bill

approaches me and begins telling me the history behind the alien microbial. "For the past thirty years, since the appearance of Halley's Comet in 1986, four women at a time have been a part of our Area 51 program. But this is the *best* we've ever seen a team! Before, we could only accomplish small mini-missions. But now, if tests yield the type of results we just witnessed, and we can extend the amount of time you all remain invisible, we perform more stealth maneuvers. I believe we can really make a difference in the world." He pats me on the shoulder.

Wow! Someone's actually happy with me.

Emerald Daniella approaches me. "We help people by infiltrating difficult and dangerous places and extracting them." Her green emerald skin is blinding to Bill and the other personnel who have on special lenses in order to observe us now and scan us. But the four of us have no problem at all with our sight and hearing, that is proving to be superhuman as well as our invisibility powers.

"Meteorite girl," Black-and-White Selina begins, "I'm gonna leave ya'll soon. But someone new 'll take my place. And ya gotta stick with us…help us find terrorists, criminals, and people who need rescuing from those oppressors. Can ya do that? For only four years? Until ya turn back to your old self and old way of life?"

I feel as if I'm circling on a merry-go-round as I glanced at each of their faces that appear suspended in animation as they wait for my answer. Len's face flashes through my mind; then Derrick's sad lost blue eyes. What'll they do without me? I do *everything*. Maybe that's a problem. People need a dose of self-sufficiency once-in-a-while; otherwise, too much dependency stifles people, makes loved ones feel smothered, incompetent, and incapable of pursuing and accomplishing *their* dreams. Thinking back over the years, I've been doing that.

Derrick will *never* learn how to live alone in the world successfully if *I* keep doing everything for him. It's sad...but true. Maybe this change *in me* is for the best, for *everyone*! Len and Derrick will be just fine without me for a measly four years. So, yeah, I'll miss 'em; but if forty-eight months away from home means saving people and helping the downtrodden in war-ravaged countries, I don't mind at all being part of a special alien group.

"Okay," I finally say, patting Monarch Mary's orange shiny arm. "I'll be one of you." They clap, until I hold my hand up in a cautious expression. "But *only* if I can at least talk to my husband and son now-and-then."

Agent Bill Stockard has jubilant eyes. "Of course, you can talk to your family, Elizabeth. We just need you to live here under the radar until you change back—uh-uh—which should be in four years."

"You hope!" Daniella says. "I've been emerald green for over four years...but I'm hoping a change will happen to me soon, so I can return to San Jose."

As they continue to tell me more about how they each became meteorite girls like me—infected with an alien microbial like me—I unbutton the top of my flowered blouse and inhaled a draught of fresh oxygen into my lungs. I wonder about my unpredictable future with these multicolored women, living in the confines of Area 51, and the fantastic spy journeys we're going to embark upon around the world. Who woulda dreamed?!

I guess no one can predict what life has to offer, and what changes might occur when one *really* decides to pursue a dream, like I pursued mine when I tried duplicating that *Meteorite Men* experiment. All I know now is ... I'm Meteorite Girl. No first name. No last name.

I can't stand the name! But that's what the three of

them are calling me. So, I guess I gotta get used to it.

And until I do, I'll be meeting a lot of brilliant scientists, trekking around the world, making friends with robots, saving people, and participating in fantastic, full-body virtual-reality experiences. I can't imagine saying this, but maybe, just maybe … I might not wanna go back home to Melbourne, Florida.

THE MAN NEXT TO ME

"Mind if I sit here? It's a long ride to Albuquerque, and I sure could use this aisle seat," George Gibson said to a young man in the window seat. He glanced at his watch and checked the time on his pocket watch: 1:30 p.m. The bus would be departing for Albuquerque in fifteen minutes. *I made it just in time!*

Pulling his briefcase next to his leg, the young man shrugged. "I don't care."

The Greyhound was crowded with people settling down in their plush blue seats while greeting their temporary neighbors. There were a few seats left in the back and one at the front, but with the luggage racks crammed with carry-ons and the long narrow aisle peppered with feet, George chose the aisle seat. Sitting in the window seat was a young man dressed in a business suit.

Ducking before sitting down, he missed hitting his head on a lopsided duffle bag that looked ready to topple down. He didn't want that! As a man over eighty, he had survived a few skirmishes against the Japanese in the Pacific, and he wasn't about to let some insignificant bag snap his neck when he had one last mission left in the world to accomplish. Covering his shiny bald head, he shoved back the black carry-on, and then plopped down in the blue cushioned seat next to the young man. "I'm breathin' like a tired old bear in a forest," he laughed, and then sank comfortably into his seat and while repeating his important goal: *I gotta locate Donny and my grandchildren ... somewhere in Albuquerque.* At his last doctor's appointment in Santa Monica, his longtime friend Dr. Berkley put his caring hand on George's shoulder and told him: "George, you are getting too old to be living by yourself. You should move closer to your family, both so they can help you when you need some help, but also so you can enjoy your senior years with the family I know you miss."

The bus's brakes hissed, the old diesel engine growled, and the folding doors sealed shut. The street outside the depot looked like a raceway of zigzagging cars with several busses leaving the station. Closing his eyes, George felt his laboring breath *wheeze* in his chest like an accordion as he slowly unbuttoned his coat, took a white handkerchief out of his coat pocket, and with shaking fingers dabbed his sweaty forehead. He began listening to other chattering passengers as they tried to talk above the outside noises of honking horns and clutch-heavy truck drivers merging onto the freeway clover-leaf. Slowly the Greyhound slid into the right lane and established a humming rhythm of accelerating motion in a vague direction toward Albuquerque. The trip would take a little over nineteen hours, with the first rest stop slated for a small station in San Bernardino in a few hours.

The clashing sounds of suitcases, food wrappers, peanuts pouring out of Cellophane, and clanking drinks triggered old memories. As he listened, his brain flooded with long forgotten old memories: racing through a hallway to get to class in sixth grade ... and then charging through enemy lines on a tropical island with his bolt-action U.S. M1903 Springfield rifle ... and then a couple years after the war, sitting high on the seat of his green John Deere cultivating rich black earth ... and then, that sad fall of 1960—maybe this exact date—after a horrible summer drought struck his farm and he was forced to leave his family in search of work. He felt the old sorrows in aches and twinges of pain in his chest—really grief he had suppressed and never wanted to experience again. He leaned over and moaned, holding the area over his chest while trying to conceal his pain. *I can't have 'em all lookin' and makin' me get off the bus now when I've been tryin' hard to take care o' myself, get on this here bus, and find Donny...just gotta find him!* He jostled his coat and stacked a few magazines, rearranging everything quickly and with jagged movements when they weren't all blurring in front of him. Several times, he stopped, trying to distract himself with all the vivid memories that were flooding his mind as if a man had burst in his brain. *By gosh! What's happenin' to me? I've never been hit with so many memories like this. Is God tryin' to tell me somethin'?*

Then he felt his heartbeat race in his chest and quickly settling back to a steady pace. He looked at the young man sitting in the window seat. He appeared submerged in his own memories, or maybe day dreaming about someone he left behind, or thinking about someone in Albuquerque.

Ya never know the insides o' people, but I do know one thing. This young feller sittin' next to me looks educated. And thank goodness he has a cell phone, 'cause I might need him to make a call for me to Albuquerque Information to find Donny. I just gotta find Donny... I gotta!

Lifting a tiny blue cooler that felt like a weight when it plopped on his lap, he took out a bottle of water and chugged some down. Then he poured some drops shakily into his handkerchief and rubbed his stubble face with the backs of his hands. He wanted to stop the flow of flooding memories, but couldn't. *Quiet down! That's enough! I'm gonna spook people if I start talkin' back to all voices comin' at me from inside my head!*

No self-talk command worked, until he glanced again at the young man in the window seat and noticed the afternoon sunlight streaming in on him like a fine midsummer's day. In reality, they were in the throng of a wind-whipping fall!

The young man appeared to be basking in the warm rays of sunshine, his vision following shaking tree branches, stucco barriers, and greenery-disguised cell phone towers transmitting message of limitless opportunities.

"So many opportunities are ahead for him, but I've lost all mine," George whispered, dabbing sweat off his forehead. He almost leaned over his right armchair to tell the man how time flies by and with no do-overs, except the young man appeared absorbed in his own deep rehearsal. Wiggling in his seat and pushing the backs of his arms into the cushion to adjust for comfort, he finally said to the young man: "Thank ya kindly, young fella. I guess ya got somethin' mighty important you're preparin' for in Albuquerque huh, 'cause ya seem to be thinkin' pretty hard," he chuckled jokingly.

"What?" the young man jumped, startled that George had struck up a conversation and suspicious of his motives. Wearing a charcoal-grey business suit and expensive cashmere coat, the young man had slicked black hair and a bold face void of wrinkles. "Oh, yeah, I have a convention to attend in Albuquerque," he said, taking off his cashmere coat and folding it with perfection. George noticed the young man's scruffy shoes, obviously traveling shoes, and then his stripped white and blue socks! Next to his briefcase he had a large thermos with Super Mario pictures. The young man noticed George's attention to the details and gestured in embarrassment. "I was just strategizing about the best way to sell my product to the type of buyers who will be there." The young man wasn't muscular like Superman, but with his crisp white shirt and faint scent of expensive aftershave, George believed he was a salesman. That meant they had something in common!

"The name's George. George Gibson." Coughing up a storm while gesturing to the man to wait a second, he pulled out his hankie and covered his mouth. Then he breathed and recovered.

"That's some cold you have!" the man said, flinching from him and inching his side against the opaque window an inch away from his right cup-holder armrest.

George didn't want him believing he was ill and contagious, or worse, to have him leave and talk secretly to the bus driver who might call and ambulance and have him removed from the bus. *I can't have that...gotta find Donny!* "Oh, this is just allergies," he began, waving in nonchalance while sticking his hankie back in his coat pocket. "It's nothing, really," he said. After the young man sighed in relief, George scooted as close to the aisle as he could get while remaining comfortable in his chair; and the young man settled back into his seat, and indication he was satisfied with the explanation. "What's yer name again?" He tapped his ear. "I can't afford the fancy hearing aids they have these days, so I have to keep askin' people to speak up." Chuckling, he knew he hadn't asked the young man his name, but he *did* know how to strike up a conversation and extract information. *Make the other person feel special. That's the key to sales, and always yielding to the customer 'cause the customer is always right.* The last company he worked for, Hoover, had named him salesman of the year in 1965 and 1967 because he could re-open closed doors after people slammed them in his face. He extended his hand for the young man to shake it. "Like I said, my name's George Gibson."

The young man had a perturbed glare in his green eyes

as if implying, *I'll tell you one thing but then leave me alone.* "Pete's my name." He quickly shook George's hand; then turning aside, he took out a little bottle of sanitizer from his coat pocket, squirted a dollop into his hand, and then rubbed them clean. "Pete Turner." He slid his black briefcase gently under the window, and patted it as a parent would tuck in a child. With a cold shoulder, he turned away from George and continued staring out the window.

The overhead air vents finally flushed in cool fresh air as passengers grew quiet and craned to see out the long windows. The bus had vibrated in a blustery vortex as it transitioned into another lane. In front of him, the rows of bobbing heads reminded him of the long cafeteria lines he had to wait through in elementary school ... then the cafeteria lines he'd push through when he was in the Army ... then the long endless line he had to endure to check out his rifle during World War II ... and finally, the rows of lines at the back of an LCVP boat landing on a small island in the Philippines. He was part of ten teams of buddies who had charged a beach to kill the enemy.

When he glanced at Pete to strike up another conversation, George's memories began appearing like a TV show of his life in the opaque window behind Pete. Like the wind venting its strength of storm on the glass, he felt about ready to hyperventilate! He was about to open his mouth and order all those visions: Leave me alone! *But if I say that and start tellin' 'em off, Pete'll think I'm nuts, in need of urgent care, and stop the bus. I can't have that! I haveta make it to Albuquerque, and find Donny!*

Relief wafted through him when the bus driver pulled his microphone down from the ceiling console and clicked it on to make his first speech of the trip. A burly man in his mid-fifties, he touched his travel cup and turned down the air vent to make himself heard above the outside encroaching storm and winds, jostling the bus now-and-then. "Good afternoon folks. I'm Daryl Grainger, and I want to welcome you aboard Bus 1442 to Albuquerque. We at Greyhound know you have several travel options, so I'd like to personally thank you for choosing Greyhound."

"His voice sounds like a disc jockey on a radio station," George chuckled to Pete.

Pete gave him a sour glance. "Huh? Oh, uh, I suppose." Then he returned to staring out the window.

Daryl the Driver continued with his introduction. "Our first fifteen-minute rest stop will be at a transit station in San Bernardino. We should arrive there approximately 3:45 p.m. Meanwhile..."

He kept talking facts about San Bernardino, their final destination at Albuquerque, and protocols in case of an emergency. George had tuned him out. He was seeing his life play out in colorful patches on the window behind Pete. *I'm gonna haveta fight real hard to make these damn visions go away, and try 'n control my temper at 'em, or Daryl up front's gonna get me an ambulance!* He put his hands on his temples and pressed real hard. *Stop it! Stop it ya hear me?* When he opened his eyes, he saw a scene of himself sitting in a little wooden desk in third grade and snickering at the teacher who smacked him with a ruler. *No! Stop it! Get outta my head! What're ya tryin' to do to me...steal my soul?* He felt guilt at bullying someone back on the playground who two minutes before had called him a sissy and spit at him. *I know what's happenin'...God or the devil usin' my emotions as weapons against me! Damn! Every darn thing I've ever seems to be poppin' up on that dark window?! Damn! I can't get rid of 'em! So how am I gonna live like this until I make it to Albuquerque without going nuts?!*

As he opened his mouth to hush a memory of the time when he was sixteen and sipping a milkshake at a soda fountain booth, another memory welled up and appeared on the window: The dejected expression on his wife's face back in 1960 when he left her standing at a Greyhound station in Chicago. He was gone for two years to take a job as a door-to-door salesman in Denver. "What was that date, Sue Lynn?" he whispered, snapping his arthritic fingers while squinting hard at her apparition to remember. "Come on, you can jostle my memory. Ya always had a knack for doing that, Sue Lynn...always made me feel better when things were down." When Sue Lynn and their past together began appearing in the scroll down of his life, he couldn't stop her image that enlarged to the entire length of the window!

"What did you say?" Pete replied, jumping a bit with a puzzled expression on his smooth young face. "Sorry, I almost fell asleep. It's been a long morning." He held up his cell phone that snapped George back to reality with the time: 1:35. "We still have about two hours before we stop in San Bernardino." He yawned and settled back down lazily. "Tomorrow, I've got one helluva schedule...one big long day," he lamented.

George tapped his finger on his bottom lip as his cheeks pinched with wrinkles of frustration. "Oh, I'm just trying to remember a date, that's all, Pete. Sorry to have woke ya up."

Pete sighed, opened his Super Mario thermos, poured himself some coffee, and took a hesitant sip. "I thought you might be asking me about the convention in Albuquerque."

"Oh *ah*, no, sorry."

Pete leaned away from George in a move conveying a need for silence and for real distance. Then he gave

George a brief nod and a straight smile before turning to look out the window. George smelled the aroma of his strong coffee, and he sank back into his seat as the scent conjured up one of the dates he was trying to forget. It was October 7, 1960, the day he left Sue Lynn, Donny, and their farm. Looking up, he saw the scene playing in brilliance on the window behind Pete.

He was sitting on a paint-chipped bench next to Sue Lynn while Donny was playing jacks on the sidewalk. The Chicago bus depot had the radio on, blaring through the depot, playing "Lonely City." He had to leave and catch the bus. As the driver called out the last hail, he stood up, put his arms around Sue Lynn, and kissed their son, Donny, a Little League pitcher, goodbye. Donny was a feisty toe-haired boy of seven at the time.

"That Chicago depot had almost the same type of roof shingles as the one we just left in L.A.," he whispered. He reached to his sides and felt the seats, their roughness abrasive on his fingertips. *They were covered in the same type of coarse fabric, and even the people looked the same...except for their clothes.* Then he heard a light snore coming from across the aisle, and he noticed the sleeping woman with short sandy hair. *She's dressed like a young surfer but she looks forty!* He heard Pete slurp more of his hot-steaming coffee. When he turned to imbibe the inviting smell, the show with Sue Lynn at the Chicago station resumed on the window, and he filled with sadness and regret as he saw the sadness on her face and anger in her watering eyes. A dry coughing spell overtook him as he saw what he had told her: "I'll be back in a few weeks." She was crying. He couldn't fool her. He'd be gone quite a bit longer than a month, probably more than six months. *Funny how words can tell a lie but faces don't.*

"After that long goodbye, I didn't see Donny again

until he was ten," George said, hitting the air as Sue Lynn's spirit disappeared in the opaque window. "Gosh I hated havin' to leave like that, and her thinkin' 'o me as a failure!" For a moment, he believed Sue Lynn was standing in the aisle.

"What did you say, Sir?" Pete gave him a surprised expression and peeked over a few passengers. "Is there someone you want to sit with? I'd be glad to exchange seats." With eager eyes, he began glancing around in search of another seat.

George felt embarrassed for failing to control himself, scolding the apparitions from his past. He guzzled down some cold water which snapped him back to reality, and then waved Pete back down to his seat. "Nope, thanks anyway, Pete, but no one *I* know is on this bus. I—I just need—needed a bit of fresh air." He slowly reached up and cranked the vent open to full blast as beads of sweat began bubbling up on his forehead, as images from his mind were appearing behind Pete. A sudden burst of coldness struck his face from the ceiling vent, and he inhaled huge draughts of air. *I'm fine ... I'm okay ... I can do this ... make it to Donny's place ... wherever that is.*

Pete pulled out a tin of mints. "You want one? Maybe a little sugar might help." He popped a mint in his mouth and began sucking. "Sugar always gives me a little energy whenever I need to concentrate."

"Thanks, Pete." George shakily picked one up and set it on his tongue. As the chill of mint trickled down his throat, he gestured in fatigue and scratched behind his ear. "I was just remembering a time I said goodbye to my family, that's all." He looked down at his stiff hurting knees and began rubbing them while re-living the lyrics of "Lonely City." Nice ta meetcha, Pete. I don't think I said that before," he then said, breathing Pete's coffee-scented air now mixed with spearmint. "That coffee sure smells good."

The strong roasted scent ignited memories of another past event in the window behind Pete. Sue Lynn had materialized as his young wife, scurrying around to make breakfast in their little farm kitchen. With her hooped rose-flower patterned skirt, she looked like a dancer from the 1950s show *American Bandstand.* After breakfast as usual, their son Donny would grab his lunch off the chrome table, hug George goodbye, kiss Sue Lynn, and then race out the screen door that banged behind him to catch the school bus. He remembered thinking at the time that *every* household was playing out that same wonderful scene. It was inconceivable that all those people could be having *anything* bad happening to them inside their four walls ... like falling on hard times, their crops failing, and being forced to leave home-and-land to hunt for work and beg for a job, like he had to do at that time.

"It was me. *I* caused my family to die!" George suddenly blurted out while rocking gently. He moaned, and then wiped his face with his shaking wrinkled hands.

Looking over seats in front of him, Pete flinched and appeared anxious as if he might flag down Daryl to stop the bus.

George took several deep breaths, laughed a bit, and motioned for him not to worry. "*Eh*, sorry there," he breathed. "I was just thinkin' about dying plants, and a time when my farm experienced a drought, and most o' the crops died. No need to worry. I didn't kill anybody." Through Pete's reddening and frightened expression, he added, "Do I look like a killer to ya?"

Pete's lips straightened in an expression of deep thought. "No, well ... okay." He settled slowly back down into his seat with an overly cautious glare on his clear youthful face.

He looks like someone hit 'im when he was a kid. Maybe I can make him feel better. "You sure do look like that race car driver Tony Stewart, Pete," he said, breaking their tautness, heavy in the air.

"Really? You think so?" Pete peered at his reflection in the shiny rim around the tray table, and then shrugged and scratched his scalp through his thin, black-slicked hair. "Maybe, a little."

George dabbed tears out of his eyes. *I better start controllin' myself better when I see these past illusions playin' out my life stories, or people might think I'm some kinda nut-job or criminal and call the cops! We could have squad cars tryin' to stop us, and then I'll never find Donny for sure!* His outburst clearly wasn't intentional, but it certainly caused Pete to stop in his tracks and gasp in fright. George felt like he was fighting for his life, with mysterious abnormal spirits; and he was getting firecracker mad at the pictures in the opaque window that seemed to be enticing him to challenge everything bad he had ever done.

Stop it ... and quit it ... and leave me alone! He kept countering them as each new scene emerged in the window behind Pete. Those defensive commands weren't working, and he was becoming dizzy with confusion. *Why...why now is all this happening? I can't afford to expend all this energy fightin' to keep my sanity. I need to find Donny! These phantom visions are drainin' me!*

He couldn't understand why, except he believed the haunting memories would subside after he got some sleep on the long ride to Albuquerque. He coughed, sniffled, and then leaned in Pete's direction in an apologetic move, to distract him from questioning him about his deteriorating physical and mental condition. *Just change the subject.* "*Ahhh,* all those luggage trunks o' mine in the cargo hold, and that carry-on up there in the rack were sure heavy gettin' to LA .. .and then on this darn bus, Pete," he chuckled. *I've been haulin' 'em around for years ... ever since I was a kid!*

"Yeah, I guess they would be heavy," Pete said, glancing at the overhead rack that lightly rattled as the bus dipped on the freeway.

Sitting up and clearing his throat, George pointed at the bottom of the bus. "Everything I own is in two trunks down there." Then he laughed. "Two small trunks." He became lost in thought at the details of packing everything to perfection so they'd fit nice and neat in those treasure-chest style trunks. "That's it. That's all I got left in life, Pete." He beamed with pride, until he thought about everything he had owned over the past fifty years: a farm when he was in his mid-twenties, a home in his mid-thirties, five cars total, three tractors, and six business suits. The latter were the most important, but he had to leave them behind at his Santa Monica room-and-board. He just didn't have room enough for them and the gifts he needed for Donny and his grandchildren. "Everything's gone now," he mumbled, staring at a stain on the carpet. "I sure hope someone who really needs a good suit has one of 'em I owned by now." They were old and a little worn, but he had maintained them and even given them names! *Surely now those suits might be helpin' someone.* Maybe he *had* left something positive behind for the human race.

Pete's eyebrows arched in an expression of wincing pain. "Don't you have a place to live? A home to go back to?" Adjusting his left armrest, he was obviously trying to get comfortable while still managing to talk to George at a safe distance. Then he crossed his legs. He looked like an executive sitting high at the head of a knightly conference table.

From all of Pete's jerky movements and cautious responses, George gleaned he had a reserved personality, which was puzzling because Pete appeared so outgoing and observant—qualities of an archetypal salesman. Part of him felt like cutting off the conversation too; but Pete's immaculately tailored suit and hallmark expensive briefcase reminded him of himself over fifty years ago, back in 1960, when he had left Sue Lynn and Donny as he hunted for work and transitioned from farmer to traveling salesman. Back then, he was full of big dreams of becoming rich and buying a city home for Sue Lynn and Donny. All those dreams faded fast, while on the road. He was successful at times, but never reached the financial bar he needed to grasp the American dream.

Then he noticed something astounding about Pete! Squinting at him harder through the bright light of his overhead bulb, he noticed details on Pete's face that looked like his son Donny! The last he'd heard about Donny, over ten years ago, he was working as a city official for the city of Albuquerque. *By now, Donny might be working for the Mayor!* With the resemblances multiplying, George began talking up a storm, even as he kept telling himself to shut up because his conversation had to be boring Pete to death!

"Where did you say you live?" Pete asked, his voice cracking in a bit of irritation.

Peering with confusion at him, George felt suddenly shaken. "*Ah*, lemme think a sec, Pete." Recollections of his former residences in Santa Monica jumbled with the insides of the B-and-B he'd stayed at in San Gabriel, and the cheap hotel room he'd rented ten months ago. He fell back into his seat. "I had a room in a house I shared with a couple 'o guys a few weeks ago." Groaning, he reached into the pocket in front of him to look for a magazine. "But I decided to take my doctor's advice and move closer to my family, so I packed up, and now I'm headin' to Albuquerque." He smiled and returned to taking in deep breaths of air after he found nothing in the pocket to entertain him. "Darn, I shoulda bought a newspaper to read…somethin' to keep me occupied," he laughed.

"Oh, here, take mine," Pete said, offering him a few crumpled sections from the *LA Times*. "I'm done with it."

"Thank ya, Pete." After taking the paper as if exchanging silk, George grabbed the arm rests as the bus came to an abrupt stop in bumper-to-bumper traffic. "Gosh—I hope Daryl up there knows another way 'round all this congestion 'cause we gotta make it to Albuquerque!"

Pete waved off the outside lines of cars that appeared to extend to the eastern horizon. "This is nothing. In a few minutes, we'll be back on schedule."

"Let's hope!" George said.

"Life's not going to end if we're a few minutes off schedule," Pete huffed.

Wishing his water was scotch, George took another hard gulp. "Sure, right." He felt his arms tingle and another sharp pain strike like lightning through his chest. Talking might stop it. "Say, where ya from again, Pete?" He knew Pete hadn't told him anything beyond his name and his next job, all superficial. *Most people in life are superficial … hell I am … and now, how can I expect anything else?*

Pete scratched his thin black sideburn. "Hollywood." He sipped his coffee and his chest rose and fell in movements of discomfort at having to reveal personal information. George sat straight up energized. He wanted to make Pete feel more at ease, and stop the pesky invading spirits and the noises in his mind. "You said you're from Hollywood, so ya been in any films there?"

"Uh-uh," Pete replied, shaking his head no and shrugging coldly. Then he adjusted his little air vent, nestled into his chair, and began looking sternly at the seat in front of him. Folding his arms, he burrowed his shoulders into a comfortable niche in the cushion and inhaled deeply, his exhale reminiscent of someone relaxing at the beach.

George noticed his irritation and brush off, but he had sold encyclopedias in Hollywood twenty-five years ago. "That's a mighty big city, Hollywood."

"It sure is," he began, "but I don't live there anymore. I was born there and went to school there. That's all. That's it."

"Oh," George said, the H-O-L-L-Y-W-O-O-D sign on the hill flashing through his mind. That city was a beacon for small town people trying to fulfill their dreams of becoming a movie or TV star. Most encountered failure. What was Pete searching for? "You don't look like you come from a big city though, Pete."

"What about you?" he snapped back. "You mumbled something about leaving your family. Where are they? Where did *you* come from?"

Feeling confronted by Pete, George stumbled for words. He didn't know whether he was trying to get to know him better, or change the subject and alter the focus. Pete was now riveted to his seat, and fighting some type of emotional pain. *Something bad must have happened to him in Hollywood.* At several points throughout his life, George had walked in Pete's exact sorrowful situation, so he decided to follow Pete's line of questioning, hoping later on to learn more about the young man next to him. "Well, I don't know about where you started from or have been, but I've been *all* over the good ol' U.S. of A."

Pete grew less tense and slid an inch toward him. "Oh yeah? Where, exactly? I like traveling and selling too. It's the *only* way to go! That way, I can always escape a place when I want to." He winked. He obviously liked the ladies and always exuded a noncommittal attitude to them.

Leaning back after glancing at the disheveled lady sleeping across the aisle from to him, George adjusted his water bottle in his cup holder as the bus unraveled from traffic and picked up speed toward its first scheduled stop in San Bernardino. "I started my life on a little farm in Indiana, called Hannah. It's about a-hunnert-and-fifty miles southeast o' Chicago. Since ya travel, ya mighta heard of it."

"Nope," Pete replied.

George let out a little laugh as he reached up and turned down the brightness on his overhead light. But he couldn't see any difference in brightness between Pete and the window that was still God's screen, or the devil's screen, showing his past as if vying for his soul. More disturbing now, unexpected rainbows in halos were surrounding the little lights below the luggage racks. So unusual! *Are those angels eavesdropping on me?*

Afternoon sunlight was streaming harshly through the window, inflaming the pictures from his soul with vibrant colors: Sue Lynn's shiny banana curls vying for space on her delicate shoulders, her gentle blue eyes, long pale piano-playing arms, and her tender dessert cakes, nut rolls, and apricot-filled cookies, all stretched out to him with beckoning gestures; and his son Donny's happy call *'Dad'*; and finally his farm's gentle rolling hills with crops ready for harvest—that suddenly changed to snapping sticks in the drought.   Outside the bus alongside the freeway, violent shadows from whipping eucalyptus trees were fanning the apparitions, now appearing like angry switches in the window as the bus increased in speed.   He almost stood up and ran, if not for the little calming rainbows now high in the air, soaking up the images immediately after he saw them.   At times, he felt suspended between Pete and the world that was rushing by outside.   *Strange...so strange. I want to fall asleep like I have that sleeping sickness disease! Falling ... so sleepy I can't....*

"George, hey ... George!"   Pete's calls and wide eyes finally reeled George back to reality.   "You were talking about a place called Hannah, Indiana.   Then you looked like you passed out.   You all right?"

George remembered their conversation and looked away from the images of his past playing on the opaque window.   *If I just keep my eyes off of 'em, they gotta go away. Just keep talkin' to Pete.*   "Oh, yes, I can't blame ya for not recognizing the name o' the city, young fella.   Most people haven't heard of Hannah either."   He laughed again, and glanced in the window.   A tiny show began playing there, his memory of the small town and those days when he walked through tall wheat, playing baseball with Donny in the fenced yard, and picking corn.   Those olden days were showing so vividly behind Pete, he could smell the cornfields!   He could taste the steamed, buttery, first-picked corn-on-the-cob!   Then the show stopped. Just a blur of trees outside the window now.   *I've been wishing 'em away, but now I want more!*   Then he recalled a Christmas card he received after several forwarding attempts two years ago. "Last I heard about Hannah, it ain't farm country anymore."

"What happened to it?" Pete asked.

"Well, about fifteen years ago, most independent farmers sold their land to large agricultural corporations that bulldozed much 'o the town to build a mall."

"That's called expansion and capitalism," Pete laughed, showing George the cover of the latest LA downtown magazine.

George tapped it in distaste. "Ya, and look at that smog. Who wants to breath yellow-brown air that burns your eyes on a bad day?" He sat back and returned to his hometown memories. "Yep, everything about Hannah has changed all right, everything from Schererville to Wannatah. It's all 'modern' now...hip they call it." He chuckled and turned sad. "Much 'o the old downtown is now office buildings for lawyers, and a few restaurants." *I'd hate to see the place, now lost to commerce.*

Pete had a puzzled expression. "Indiana is so far from Los Angeles. How did you end up in LA?"

George folded his arms and settled down for storytelling. "Well, after my parents died, I took over the farm after the war." Again a memory appeared in the window behind Pete, so real as if he could step into it. "Then in 1960, when times were awful, and the economy was in recession, I had to quit farming and become a traveling salesman. Finally, a few years back I retired."

"So you *must* have been a pretty *good* salesman!" Pete said, sitting at attention.

"Sure was...for years." George choked up with a bad cough, and a sudden pain pierced his chest. After patting the area over his heart and sipping some more water, he asked Pete, "What are *you* sellin'? Dressed like ya are—" He gave him a solid once-over inspection. "I can spot a travelin' salesman, one o' my own kind, and near-n-dear to my heart" He patted his chest, another strong pain piercing through to his lungs. It felt like he had an elephant siting on his chest as he turned away to recover his breath.

Pete brushed lint from his suit coat. To cool of a little, he pulled open his coat, thinking about the long the drive to Albuquerque. "I sell mannequins, all around the country." He reached in his pocket, pulled out one of his brochures and handed it to George. "I'm on my way to Albuquerque for our yearly convention." Motivation sparkled in his dark brown eyes. "I'm due to meet-up with a couple of my regular customers there and if I can book just a few more orders, I'll win a week's vacation in Vegas. God, I can't wait 'cause I've sure as hell earned it!"

George had opened the brochure and strained to read the print. "My, yes, this sure is a mighty fine brochure, Pete." He felt sentimental as one image stood out to him, and another memory appeared on the window behind Pete. "I knew a lady once who looked like this mannequin right here … and a beautiful thing *she* was." He pointed at one at the center of the brochure dressed in a 1950s hoop skirt.

"Oh yeah?" Pete perked up. "She might have been the model for this mannequin."

"I doubt that, if you look close at the fine print at the bottom of the page, where it gives the details for this mannequin, it says the cast date was 2013," George laughed, but then turned suddenly sad and serious. "She's gone now," he whispered. "Sue Lynn's gone."

"Oh *she* must be the person you were talking about so angrily … I mean, whispered about a little while ago."

As minutes of conversation ticked by, George noticed

an increase in Pete's curiosity. "Oh, I wasn't angry at my family ... just myself. After all, parents take a part in how their children turn out when they're grown up ya know, Pete," he said softly, taking a chance with his words because he had learned to treat Pete's sensitivity to divulging information with caution.

Pete had his glance transfixed to the back of the silver tray in front of him where his deep brown eyes had to be playing out past memories of his own. "Yeah, I guess you're right."

The bus suddenly swayed from a wind gust as it picked up more speed. Daryl came on the mic, "Sorry for the interruption folks," he began, "but I'll keep our speed right at the limit, that way we should be able to make up for the time we lost when we got stuck in traffic. The wind is picking up as we transition to more open spaces, so for your own safety please keep your seatbelts buckled, and stay in your seats as much as possible. Unless we run into further delays, we should have no problem reaching our first rest stop on schedule." People listened attentively, and then returned to reading, sleeping, eating and discussing their lives with fellow passengers.

Trying hard to recall the exact words he'd said to Pete about his family, angry words at that, he couldn't remember telling him anything about Sue Lynn or Donny; but if Pete said he did, he must have. He grew suddenly confused and anxious while working hard to keep up a portrait of wellness for Pete and the other passengers. "I have a son who lives around twenty-five miles outside of Albuquerque."

"That's great, George," he exhaled in a gesture of relief.

"He has three children, and I *might* have a few great-grandchildren by now too!" Again he coughed, but this time, into his handkerchief. Pulling it away, he noticed blood, and he quickly wadded it up and stuck it back into his jacket pocket so Pete wouldn't notice. "Maybe, just maybe, if I show up at Donny's place with all the gifts I bought for 'em ... maybe, I *hope*, just maybe I can make it up to them."

"Make what up?" Pete asked, tucking his cashmere coat gently behind his legs.

"Well," George felt his throat dry as he tried to swallow back tear. "Maybe I can make up for not bein' there for 'em all when they needed me. And if they'll accept my apologies ... just maybe one o' the kids might squeeze me into their family." With shaking hands, he turned away and wiped tears out of the corners of his eyes, but he couldn't get rid of the burdensome guilt he'd been carrying for abandoning Donny when he was so young and finances took a turn for worse on the farm. *Years ago, Donny abandoned me in return. Well, I can't blame him, 'cause he's livin' what he learned!* "I made a big mistake leavin' 'em all for so long and travelin' on the road," he whispered, turning away from Pete. But leaving Donny and Sue Lynn to hunt for work didn't compare to the pain he felt for not being next to Sue Lynn in her last months of life. As that scene appeared behind Pete, another sharp pain pierced his chest, and he began patting the area over his heart. "And if one of 'em can't find room for me, and forgive me, well, I'll just buy me one of those little mobile homes in one of those fancy trailer parks." He settled back down at the warming thought of a possible happy future. "It'll have a pool, and lots of lantern lights, and a little space out in the back where I can plant some seeds I brought with me, right here in my pocket." He tapped his weather-worn pants and then returned to patting his chest. "I'll grow a few ears-o-corn and some radishes. And if that sand ain't too hard in Albuquerque, maybe I might even try my luck at growin' tomatoes."

"That sounds like a plan for longevity," Pete agreed, "a real good plan."

George scratched his head in a gesture of contemplation. "I don't know though. Tomatoes are delicate things to grow. Worse than roses! Bugs love 'em and worms eat 'em right up." He felt a nasty taste in his mouth. "Lousy worms!"

"You make them sound like they're locusts," Pete joked.

"Well, they are!" George returned. "One year those lousy worms almost destroyed an entire crop of my soybeans. That's the year before the drought, and I nearly went bankrupt!" He wiped his eyes and drank some water that Pete had given him. "I walked down every row 'o soybeans and sprayed *every* plant by hand with pesticides to stop those nutrient sucking worms." He breathed and then coughed through strings of phlegm clogging his throat. "It took me two weeks to make it through that field." Looking past Pete, he believed that same field was in the distance outside the window. "But ya know what?"

"What?" Now fully engaged in George's story, Pete leaned more toward him.

"I got rid of those vampire worms." He pointed sternly at the half-dead field as if he'd won a successful fight against unrelenting Nature. "Yes, sir, I walloped 'em good!"

"It sounds like you beat Mother Nature and solved your problem with a lot of hard work," Pete commented softly. "So why did you nearly go bankrupt?"

George exhaled as he took out another white hankie—

a flag of surrender. "The rains came the day after I finished spraying each plant, and washed away everything I'd just done into the ground."

"Oh, wow! Sorry about that, George," he said through an expression of compassion. "To me farming sounds impossible!" Then he swept back his black bangs in a stilted move showing uneasiness in handling other peoples' painful emotions.

"I'm not lying, believe you me!" George said firmly.

"I didn't say—"

"I'd *never* lie about somethin' as serious as that, Pete," he whispered loudly, but then patted Pete's arm in a display of tender calmness. "People in my generation generally tell the truth, 'cause we're honest."

Pete reached up and turned off his overhead light. "I definitely heard that." He appeared scolded, his cheeks blotchy red. "I hope, well, I can learn to be that way." He was showing his vulnerability.

"Well, Pete, maybe what ya need is a little hardship entering in yer life."

Pete reeled. "No—no thanks, George, I'll take a pass on that one—"

"Lemme tell ya something," he interrupted, bending closer to him across their double-side armrest. "When ya' live through hard times, like I did during that 1960 recession, ya' learn to make friends and *be* a friend. You learn to barter, and be truthful with people." Now, George's mind was creating apparitions of those past acquaintances in the opaque window behind Pete. "When ya promise Jim Frakes or Pat Harner you'll lend 'em twenty dollars to treat a sick cow or fix a broken combine, ya' keep your word. Ya' never ask for anything back, but ya' know you'll get back whatchya give. You know they'll come through for ya' when the going gets tough."

He remembered they had tried to help him and Sue Lynn before he lost his farm and had to go on the road to find work, but people can only help so much. Ultimately, every well of friendship, outreach, and church assistance runs dry. He never snubbed them or retaliated when Pat, Jim, and the rest of their community gradually left his circle of friendship. "Yes, those were the days, Pete. They were far from perfect, but they aren't *anything* like today. No, Siree."

He felt himself suddenly transported back in time to a scene playing in the hallucination behind Pete. He was shaking hands with old Jim Frakes in his gray-and-white overalls, and then met Pat Harner at the corner coffee shop for coffee and donuts. Almost every morning— except for winters, sowing time, plowing and harvesting—he'd meet bald Pat and greet Jim who always wore the same-old, stained, blue jeans. "I think they're all dead." He felt his eyes suddenly heavy, and his body numb.

"George—hey!" Pete brought him back to reality by snapping his fingers in his face and giving him and an urgent drink of water.

"I'm okay, now, thanks, Pete," George breathed, trying hard to avoid the unstoppable events transfixing behind Pete. "Kids your age don't know the ways of the old world." He shook his head in disappointment. "It's too bad, 'cause all you young folks are missin' out on *real* friendship, and doin' what's right in the world." He saw a new image in the window: month-after-month of mailing checks to Sue Lynn and Donny. *But I didn't do what was really important...bein' there for 'em all. Now, I'm sick, alone, and payin' for what I didn't do—just bein' there—what did I do, just mail paychecks to 'em. Yep, come to think of it, I've been just*

*a paycheck most o' my life. Didn't havta be that way. I surely loved
Sue Lynn and Donny, but I made the stupid mistake of stayin' on
the road and never goin' back for more than a day or two.*

"*Hm,*" Pete exhaled, engrossed in thought as he sat
back in his seat, "I never heard my parents talk about, or
frankly say anything about those times."

George shrugged. He couldn't make Pete understand
the community-based closeness he experienced with his
fellow neighbors if Pete hadn't ever experienced such
relationships himself, even with his own parents. "Well,
Jim's gone now. And Pat Harner died right after I took
to the road to make ends meet."

Pete had returned to his previous state of absorption
in George's life. "Where's your wife Sue Lynn now? You
mentioned earlier she was gone. What do you mean?"

A memory of Sue Lynn wearing a 1950s hoop dress
appeared in the window behind Pete. "Well, thank ya for
asking." Concentrating on steadying his shaking hand
and aching fingers, he quickly poured some water in a
plastic cup full with ice that someone from the front had
sent back to him. He then drank some and set it in the
cup holder. "Well, Sue Lynn and I were married a long
time ago. She passed on over fifteen years ago now."

"Oh," Pete said, "how did she die?"

"Cancer." He felt the bitter taste of the word in his
mouth as Pete offered him a cup of coffee from his
thermos. "*Ahh*, thanks, Pete," he said after taking a sip
with his trembling hands. "This is so much better than
just plain ole water," he chuckled. The warm soothing
liquid conjured up visions of his beautiful Sue Lynn, and
he reclined a bit in his seat. "We had a son. I mean, *have*
a son 'cause I'm sure he's still alive."

"What's his name again?" Pete asked.

"Donny, but I haven't seen 'im in at least ten years."

He exhaled as he recalled several gifts he had for Donny and his grandchildren that were wrapped with tender perfection in his giant luggage trunks. "I brought him, Andy, Fletch and Sue Beth some presents I've got tucked away nice-n-neat in the cargo hold."

"Who are Andy, Fletch and Sue Beth?" asked Pete.

"My grandkids." George reached for his wallet but remembered he didn't have one photograph. He was hoping they'd recognize him from pictures their father might have shown them; but first, he'd have to make it to Albuquerque and hope they'd recognize him when they'd see him. "I hope they like what I'm bringin' 'em."

"What's that?" Pete asked.

"I have a Barbie doll for Sue Beth." George replied as Daryl the Driver announced their imminent stop in San Bernardino in thirty minutes. "The doll is a collector's edition. It says it right on the box!" Then he began coughing...the gagging culminating in a horrible fit. It woke up the sleeping woman across the aisle from him who quickly handed him layers of Kleenex. When he finally managed to stop coughing, he noticed...*more blood...lots 'o blood! Where's it comin' from?* He recalled his doctor's words. *Looks like the Doctor was right. I need to find Donny. I just hope he will forgive me and help me out while I'm sick!*

However, the sharp pains in his left arm and the heavy weight on his chest weren't subsiding. Wanting to motivate himself to keep on going even though common sense was telling him he'd be better off asking Daryl to call him an ambulance, he began repeating his goal. *I just have to make it to Albuquerque! I have to lay my eyes on Donny and my grandchildren!* Even though he had no idea *where* in Albuquerque they were living let alone *what* they looked like. After he collected himself and drank some water he continued to tell Pete about his grandchildren. "I once heard Andy really likes baseball cards, so I'm givin' him my special Topps 1963 Pete Rose RC#537 Rookie card. It's worth some big bucks!"

Pete found a thin blue blanket in the overhead, unfolded it, and handed it to George who draped himself in comfort. "What about Fletch?" Pete asked, quickly sitting back down. "You must have brought him something too?" Pete was obviously trying to distract George out of his pain by keeping him talking until they reached San Bernardino for their break.

George replied through shaking discomfort in his chest and lungs, "Fletch is my youngest grandchild." He breathed, but thought he might pass out until he saw Sue Lynn's beautiful presence in the opaque window behind Pete. "Fletch must be twenty-five right about now." He reached into his coat pocket and gently slid out a shiny gold pocket watch. "I bought this on a JC Penny special over ten years ago, Pete. It's the big surprise I have for Fletch, including the gift I wrapped for him."

"Wow, that's nice!" Pete marveled as a gold spot on the watch sparkled in the reflective gleam of his ceiling light. "I wish I had, well, a dad who'd given me something—" He paused, damning up his emotions in a heaving inhale. "But I don't."

"Thanks," George began proudly, and then patted Pete's shaking hand. "I spent my *last* dime on 'em all. I hope they like what I'm bringing 'em." He gently tucked the watch back into his pocket.

Pete drank some more of his coffee. "I don't see why they wouldn't like your gifts. And that pocket watch you've been saving for him—" He appeared choked up with emotion and a longing expression until he regained his usual controlled composure. "Well, no one ever gave *me* anything like that." He set his coffee cup in the holder and then leaned on the arm rest as he listened to George. "Tell me more about your son Donny."

George believed he could see Donny's image as a teenager in the window behind Pete, but Donny wasn't aging along with the rest of the memories of his son. He grew tense, and once again persisted through another coughing episode. He quickly regained control over his unsteady breath, but controlling the uncontrollable was becoming impossible. He remembered the prescription cough syrup he had in his cooler, pulled out the brown bottle, opened it, and gulped down what he thought was a tablespoon.

"Wow, George, if that's booze you'll be drunk in seconds!" Pete exclaimed.

George laughed. "Naw, it's just cough medicine. I've been takin' it for … for a while I guess."

"I hope it helps, you look red in the face…and your fingers look, well, blue." He grimaced and pointed at them. "Are you sure you're okay? You don't look okay."

"I'm fine, Pete!" he replied firmly. "Really!" George wanted to get back to his story about Donny so he could distract Pete from his coughing fit.

Pete watched George intently as he replaced his syrup in his cooler. "All right George, tell me more about Donny."

George finally remembered where they left off in their conversation. "Well, I believe Donny's fifty-something now. I used to call him Dig as a nickname, but he hates that."

Pete laughed in an expression of disbelief as the outside lights reflected on his strong smooth face. They were getting close to the San Bernardino station. "How did Donny get a nickname like that?"

Daryl's loud voice cut quickly cut through all the chatter and noise on the bus to announce their arrival at the small depot. "In ten minutes we will arrive at the San Bernardino Transit station, so take this time to gather your things and put them away before we arrive." People began standing up in the aisles and taking down their carry-ons.

George coughed and exhaled deeply, trying to focus his thoughts on Donny's nickname. Suddenly, he saw stars everywhere around them...then darkness.

"George! Wake up. George!" Pete shouted, poking George's shoulders.

When he finally came-to, the sandy-haired woman across the aisle from him slipped Pete a bottle of water, and a few passengers turned attentively around to respond to the sudden and unusual commotion.

"I'm fine," George coughed, waving them down. "Really I'm fine, but thanks. You can go back to doin' what you're doin'!" After taking a bite of a protein bar that the woman unwrapped and put into his hand, George continued to tell Pete how he had nicknamed Donny, Dig. "Well, when Donny was a boy, a filly got mad when Donny saddled her up for a ride. Tess was her name. When Donny jumped on the saddle, Tess bucked him off, and Donny flew screamin' and hollerin' into the air, landin' right on his butt."

Pete grimaced. "He must have been really hurt!"

"You bet, but it coulda been worse if not for the rope he caught when I threw it to him. Donny diggin' his heels into the dirt and rode Tess for a spell like he was water skiing." He laughed, until he saw the painful shadowy scene begin on the window behind Pete—just another memory appearing in a scroll of his life that he thought wasn't supposed to happen until death. *What's this all mean for me?*

"You laughed though, George," Pete said slowly with a hint of sadness in his low voice. "But I don't think that accident was very funny." He turned somber as he looked at the seat in front of him and began picking at the tray as if trying to make it smudge free and perfectly shiny. "And that *Dig* nickname must still be haunting Donny, where ever he is, even now."

George felt an avalanche of regret. "Yeah, I shouldn't have called him that. And I'm sorry I ever did, but I can't take it all back."

"Nope, words aren't like sticks you throw to a dog," Pete added. "My dad used to say some, well, harsh—I mean downright *ugly* things to me and my sister Kimberley." His voice grew quieter. "Kimberley's still a mess because of his alcoholic tirades."

"What about you?" George asked, fixing his gaze on the seat in front of him. If he'd look Pete in the eye, Pete might stop talking, and he might be forced to see how he shouted at Donny and Sue Lynn after a few of his own late-night drinking bouts at the Hannah bar.

"I travel, that's what I do," Pete replied, "and never go home."

George coughed through another painful ache in his chest. "Well, I can't turn back the clock." He almost said: *that's probably why Donny cut off our relationship.* But he knew the nickname incident wasn't the only reason why Donny no longer wanted to see him. He wiped more tears out of his eyes onto his sleeves. *I wasn't there at Sue Lynn's side to say goodbye when she exhaled her last breath and died in the hospital from cancer.* "Sorry for laughin' at ya, Donny," George whispered into his wet hands. "Sorry 'bout callin' ya Dig, and bein' a jerk." He glanced at the window, replaying the event manifesting from his mind.

"I shoulda been more serious…not always jokin' about everything. And I shoulda been there for yer ma."

"George?" Pete asked as the sandy-haired woman sitting across from George set more Kleenex on George's lap. The woman was gesturing for Pete to stop upsetting him.

"Ma'am, I have nothing to do with this!"

George was slumped down a bit, his shoulders rising and falling in slow soft breathing motions. "I'm sorry. Forgive me for *everything.*"

"This old man's been talking up a storm since he plopped down next to me," Pete stood up and whispered loudly over George. "He's been off-loading his life's dark secrets and venting his emotions. No matter *what* I do, look away, or try stuffing him with coffee, water, and peanuts, he just keeps dumping on me."

"Well," she grimaced, sweeping up a scruffy worn-out handbag from the floor, "just tell him to get ready 'cause we're almost at the rest stop."

"I tried that, but he's completely focused on getting everything that's bothering him out of his system for some reason."

"*Humph.*" Snapping back in her seat, she curled up in her blanket like a cat sleeping off the aftermath of a dog attack. It was apparent that something bad had happened to her as well before boarding the bus.

"George, sorry if you're upset, or if I did anything to upset you, but you have to wake up and tell that lady——" He pointed firmly at her. "——that you're fine, and well, that *I'm* not to blame because you're so upset. I have to admit though, I'm worried about you," Pete whispered as he raised and then lowered his armrest that kept sticking between them.

George didn't respond, but let out a frothy sound

from his congested lungs.

"George?!" He patted George's left arm, and then tapped it as he called louder: "George!" Some passengers in the row in from them peered over their seats with concerned expressions.

"Huh—what?" George suddenly gasped. "God, I think I felt—*cough cough*—" He sat up straight, and began wheezing and panting his way back to consciousness. "I'm fine," he waved for people to sit down.

"You passed out again, George," Pete said, peeking over the seats behind him, and then he gave two passengers the A-Okay signal. He sat down and handed George more water and offered him another mint. "I was trying to apologize to you, but now, I think I better let Daryl know you're not doing too well, it would be best if he had an ambulance waiting for you at the rest stop." He checked his watch. "We should be there in about five minutes."

As Pete began flagging down Daryl, George gently slapped down his hands. "No, Pete," he breathed, several times, like a skin diver coming up for air. "I gotta make it to Albuquerque, Pete. I just gotta." He coughed, and his vision suddenly tunneled into the overhead light that appeared welcoming and glowing; and the window behind Pete was now like a bright stage playing every memory, good and bad. "No!" he cried, covering his face. "I'm not ready! Not yet, God! Not now! Please don't take me!"

"George, what's wrong?" Pete stood up, and several passengers turned and gasped as George collapsed in his seat, his arms and neck drooping like a doll.

The woman across the aisle released George's recline mechanism on his seat and put his dangling arms next to his side. "Did he ... is he—"

The motion of the mechanism lifting him up made him inhale back to life, but he couldn't move. "I'm just...just awful tired now, Donny," he told Pete.

As the bus slowed to exit the freeway and bounced over a speed bump toward the San Bernardino rest stop, Pete shouted, "Call an ambulance, now!"

The woman across the aisle from George was already on her cell phone. "They're on their way." She had tears streaming down her eyes and fear exuding from her shaking hands. Then she began patting George's clammy forehead with Kleenex and cool water.

"Thank ya, kindly for takin' care o' me all those years, Sue Lynn," he whispered to her, licking his dry lips.

"But, Sir, my name is Sandy Walston. I'm not—"

He turned away from her looking towards the window. It was beaming with a bright white light, and Sue Lynn appeared in white angelic form. Her banana curls were shimmering, her red lips glistening, and her arms white with welcoming grandeur. "I'm comin' Sue Lynn." She was motioning for him to join her, waving him inside the window. "I'm just gettin' too tired— *breathe breathe*—to keep on fightin' to—*wheeze wheeze*—to keep the farm, Sue Lynn," he said, knowing he was now between life and death. *I'm not ever gonna make it to Albuquerque to find Donny... or Sue Beth ... or Fletch ... or Andy.* Slowly and with trembling hands, he reached up and tapped his coat pocket, the place where he had tucked Fletch's special pocket watch.

"Just rest, George," Pete began, "and take it easy so we can make it to the station, make a few phone calls, and locate your son Donny."

"I sure could use some rest, Donny," George said, now believing he was staring right into Donny's brown eyes. "I love ya, son ... and—*moan*—I love ya. I never told ya that a lot … but I do."

"He asked if he can come home," Sandy Walston repeated from across the aisle. "I thought Albuquerque was his home."

Pete shook his head no. "I think he lives in Santa Monica."

A stranger peeked over his seat and interrupted them. "When we were walking back from the restroom a while ago, I thought I overheard him say he was living in LA."

"No, he was living in Indiana I believe," a teenager behind Pete said, and then he quickly sat back down and covered up with a blanket. Obviously, he didn't want any part of the debate or to really get involved with their problem.

"It sure is strange, Donny," George said with faint words. "I always thought Albuquerque was hotter 'n hell, and I don't know *why* ya picked livin' there. It's desert."

"It *is* desert all right," Sandy said in between speaking to the paramedics who had her relaying information about George over the phone.

"But at night, when you look down on that city, it sparkles like a patch of stars," George said longingly, now seeing Sue Lynn's angelic form waving for him to leave his seat and join her. But he couldn't even move a finger, and his legs and arms felt cold next to him— oxygen deprived and tingling. "Yep, wherever we're goin' it'll be a fine place to plant our feet 'n settle down, Sue Lynn." He felt his soul slipping out of his body to join Sue Lynn's haloed-white body in the energizing bright-white light outside the window…until Pete's face transfixed between them.

"George!" He put a glass of water up George's blue lips. "Here! Drink this! And hold on … we're almost there to get you help."

Groaning loudly, George couldn't move to clutch his chest as the massive heart-attack pain shot through his heart and chest, cutting off all circulation.

"You'll know when ya we make it Albuquerque," George moaned as the bus slowed to a stop. "You'll see diamond lights in the sky ... a runway to heaven."

"Don't talk like this, George," Pete said, jumping over him into the aisle. "Open the door! Fast! This guy George is dying!" he called to Daryl,

After one last energetic plea—*God! Ya gotta give me just one more minute to ask Pete to do something for me!*—he weakly touched Pete's sleeve and motioned him closer. "Give Donny and my grandkids all my gifts, will ya, Pete?"

"What?" he exclaimed, reeling from him. "But George—"

"Please, Pete, just find Donny, in Albuquerque, and give 'em my gifts." Now Sue Lynn was hovering in the light beyond Pete like a white yearning angel with outstretched arms. He gasped again, feeling his last breath in life as an oxygen lump in his throat. He had only a few ticking seconds to beg Pete for help. "Please, Pete?" He felt tears on his cheeks, cold watery tears like icicles.

Pete had a restless tremor and terrified round eyes. "George, I don't know—"

"Just say yes to the old guy," Sandy Walston exclaimed. "He won't be the wiser if you don't." Her eyes shone the knowledge of pending death as she stared down at George's failing body.

George heard her lies. "No!" He motioned for Pete to move away from her, and she shamefully stepped back. Then he glanced wide-eyed at Pete. "Just do this *one* thing for me, Pete. Can ya? Can ya, Pete? I won't ever ask ya for anything else." The child in him was pleading with Pete, the kindred spirit buried deep inside everyone to help a fellow human being in agony.

Then Daryl the driver came charging through the aisle. "Everyone—off the bus and make room for the paramedics," he kept repeating.

All the while, George wouldn't let go of Pete's sleeve as the two medics with life-saving equipment hopped over seats toward George.

"I feel tired now … *so* tired," George said, "but you keep lookin' for those Albuquerque lights, Pete, and give everything to Donny."

"Fine! Okay, George," Pete huffed, rubbing his forehead in an expression of agitation and resignation. "I will."

"Thanks, Pete—*breathe wheeze*—you're a good boy … and I'll be watchin' ya, Pete … and seein' ya giving 'em all their gifts."

"Oh gosh! You mean you'll be watching me? Like a walking spirit?!" Pete's face changed to spooky white.

"One day, *cough*, you'll be at death's door too, Pete," George worked every ounce of energy God gave him to lift his arm and give Pete a last touch. He made it! Barely touching Pete's finger. "You'll see." But he couldn't sit up to meet Sue Lynn's angelic beckoning hand. "Gotta' make it. Gotta—"

Then George groaned in pain, and fell lifelessly into the carpeted aisle peppered with stains and mud tracks.

Nudging Pete out of the way, paramedics began their diligent attempt to resuscitate him. They tore open his buttoned shirt and engaged the defibrillator.

But all Pete heard was the resounding a shrill *beeeeep* flat-line echo on George's heart monitor. He ran off the bus into the chilly air, the wind blowing leaves scratching the sidewalks with sap and rust orange. He began pacing the loading zone with Daryl. "I don't think he made it," he kept repeating.

"I've seen people come back from the dead fifteen minutes after someone proclaims 'em DOA," Daryl said, smoking a cigarette and coughing.

Five minutes later, a paramedic disembarked with his head lowered to the ground and slowly approached them with bad news. "We pronounced him dead." Activating his official paramedic event watch, he called into a recorder, "TOD is 3:25 p.m. The Medical Examiner is on the way."

Pete gagged, holding back vomit as he held onto a large metal trash can in front of a bench. "Damn—I can't believe this just happened … a guy dying right next to me!" he lamented just as Sandy Walston handed him a cup of coffee and his expensive cashmere overcoat. He had dropped it as he rushed to leave when the medics told him to go. And none too soon as a chilling wind whipped around them. "I can't believe he died, Sandy. That's your name, right," he said, puffing on another cigarette.

"Yes," she replied softly.

"Thank God someone gave me one of these," he said, holding out the cigarette smoking up the air, "or I'd be a basket case right now." He felt shaking and careened in regret. "Damn! I told myself I'd never start smoking again."

Sandy laughed. "I've said that myself quite a few times. But when stress hits, well, people revert back to bad habits."

He threw down the half-smoked cigarette, spit, and then rubbed his hands for warmth. "I keep thinking I'll see George just get off the bus." He sniffled, the cold cutting him to the bone. "He sure liked coffee, and drank mine like he hadn't had any for years," he chuckled, the frigid air sticking on the roof of his mouth in choked back tears. "George was so looking forward to buying a cup at in the station." Gesturing at the bustling entryway that looked like a giant rest stop for inquisitive tourists, he laughed and patted his coat pocket, a long-forgotten automatic gesture. "I stopped smoking a few years ago, but I could use a pack right now!"

"Sorry, I don't smoke … but I drink," Sandy laughed and then turned sullen. "You wanna go inside and see if the place sells beer?"

The pole lights and rustling trees with their shedding leaves appeared as spinning sticks through his confusion and disbelief. "That sounds good to me, just give me a couple of minutes." He glanced around her to see what the medics were doing. "I never in my life believed *anything* like this could happen." He plopped down on a bench, contemplating what to do next.

Sandy sat down next to him and pulled her collar around her neck. Her nose was red from the cold wind, and her cheeks were flushed with a burnt-orange blush of fall dryness as her sandy-streaked hair blew across her square dimpled jaw. "Well, are you going to do what George asked you to do?"

Her words never registered with Pete. He was too distracted by the event, and the wavy disorienting sunlight playing Scrabble with all the clouds, trees, fellow passengers and even a few pedestrians stopping to assess the urgent scene. His senses felt numb; his direction distorted. *Maybe this is how babies experience their world right after birth.* He scratched his head, his prickling fingers bringing him back to the harsh reality of life speeding past them like the whirling red lights on the ambulance. "Do

215

what did you ask me?"

She slumped down in obvious frustration. "Are you going find George's family, and give them those gifts he kept talking about?" Someone had handed her a cup of steaming hot tea for Pete. When he took the cup, felt the heat rising over the Styrofoam, and smelled the tea's bitter scent, he knew he was sane and thanked God that he was still in the world of the living. He had never liked tea, but now he wasn't complaining. "Thanks, Sandy."

"You're welcome," she said shyly as he sipped some more.

"That Japanese tourist at the back of our bus told me to give this to you," she whispered. Then she asked him the question again, but this time softly as the Medical Examiner's wagon pulled up alongside the ambulance. "Well? Will you take George's things to Albuquerque like he asked you?"

Staring into the tea's bitterness, he drank some more tea, considering if the tart flavor was really a forewarning of consequences to come should he decide to abandon his promise to George. He sipped a little more and then quickly threw it into the trash can. "I'll try to contact George's family, *after* I finish my job at the sales convention in Albuquerque." He saw Daryl about ready to leave the paramedics and hand the keys over to a Greyhound manager wearing a long blue coat. "But first, I'll have to talk to Daryl and get some information about him. Really, I know nothing except what George told me about the contents of his luggage," he chuckled, the laugh interrupted by the crisp air striking his face. He quickly pulled his collar up around his ears. *I could die in this changing weather!* He remembered how desperately George wanted to change for his family, but it was too late. *But if George could change ... I can try too.* "I can't deliver *anything* to *anyone* until I have names and a location. So, maybe I will, and maybe I can't," he told Sandy as he stuffed his hands in his pockets for warmth.

"Well if you believe in ghosts or angels or even George himself could be watching you," she whispered in a fearful shivering tone, "I recommend you fulfill George's last request, or they might pursue you until you do!"

Pete exhaled in resignation. "Yeah, even though I don't believe in Ghosts, I guess I'll search for Donny and George's grandchildren then." He stood up to walk to the café inside the small station. He noticed the roof had a sharp slatted appearance. Sounds, sensations, tastes, and images were flowing through his mind with an acuteness he had never before experienced. Sandy was walking in front of him, still chattering about spirits and angels, but he stopped. He couldn't leave George. He had to talk to Daryl. "See you inside in a little bit, Sandy, and I'll take you up on that beer you offered," he shouted through a breezy wave.

"Okay," she said before leaving. "I'll getcha one."

He motioned at the baggage carriers unloading luggage. "I guess we'll be here a while anyway until they find us another bus." As she left for the station, he thought of George's words describing Albuquerque as the City of Never Ending Heat in the middle of the desert. Perhaps George and his beloved Sue Lynn were already there in spirit, searching for Donny and his grandchildren.

Then Sandy's words came to mind, and he winced and shuddered in the snapping wind that struck his socks under his pant legs. The thought of George's spirit, his ghost, or angels coming after him made him more determined than ever to make Daryl help him find out the necessary information about George's destination and the contents of his huge trunks so he could locate Donny and the rest of his estranged family. *This is gonna take some hard work 'cause George didn't even know where Donny lives.* Slowly, with his insides shaking and cold, he approached Daryl and the coroner gliding George's white draped body out of the bus. Stepping back, Pete believed he could smell pastries baking in the bus-stop café and hear the hissing sounds of an espresso machine. They were his usual enticing tangible favorites, making him want to find a way to leave and take the fast way out of the uncomfortable situation.

When he saw teary-eyed Daryl move toward him with George's possessions in a little black bag, he couldn't move. *That gold pocket watch for George's grandson Andy, who George had never met, is inside that black bag. It was so important to George, to give everything to them that he'd worked so hard to buy for them, most likely from his worn-out farm savings account.*

As the Greyhound manager also approached Pete to take his statement, Pete stood up straight and tall and determined. *I don't want George's spirit attached to me for the rest of my life, so I better hunker down, as George would say, do the right thing, and find Donny.*

Sandy had warned him not to ignore the promise.

Pete bit his lip and pulled his coat tight around his chest, and jumped when a bus honked behind him. *I'll take these trunks to Albuquerque, and I'll find you soon Donny. Your Dad loved you and wanted you to have these special gifts. You need to know that.*

But now it's time for that beer.

JESSE'S CHRISTMAS STAR

Gasping for air and coughing, I begin picking off shredded roof tiles and splintered dry wall while kicking my way out from under our oak table. "Stan! Stan where are you?" I cough again, feeling smothered by cascading grime. "You all right?" A cold draft of frosty midnight air blows through our collapsing house, sending attic dust around me, but I'm finally at least able to breathe!

"I'm over here, Marian!" he calls from inside the pantry, the place he vaulted into when the last beam of alien light shot through the south end of our roof. "I'm fine, but you just stay put until I can get to ya and help ya!" He's pushing on the accordion door, but piles of wood and crisscrossing metal are prison bars. All I can make out through a few cracks are the dangling florescent kitchen light that's sparking and popping. And as another cold breeze shoots through our kitchen, I hear the pans on the swinging pot holder clattering and pinging.

"Okay, Stan I'm staying put, but I wonder if the cops or military have seen what's happened? They have to by now, wouldn't ya think?" Feeling colder and scooting against some creaking boards for warmth, I still can't hear any sirens coming from the frost-bitten fields or icy roads beyond the barns. I wanna cry. Everything we own—house and goods—appear gone, like a cyclone sped through our house. But that's *not* what happened!

"Where's the star now, Marian? Ya see it?" Stan asks in a whisper, his hot breath bleeding through the accordion door.

"I'll check, but I'm not wandering *too* far outta here until I make sure all those lights are gone!" The last thing I saw was the star lighting up like the center of a nuclear reactor before I dove under the table. "Peeking out of a crack that used to be our aluminum siding, I inhale another burst of the nippy air from our shot-out kitchen window while slapping dust off my clothes. Not seeing any blinding light, but still terrified to crawl out and search for the star, or what's left of it, I recall *every* second since I spotted a glowing object in the sky two hours ago...

Hannah, Indiana where we live isn't that far southeast from the Windy City and all its night lights. In spite of the night glare, when the moon is new, the stars are sparkling diamonds, salt crystals, and red-and-orange quartz on black velvet; and the Milky Way is a white speckled feather splitting apart at the seam. Every orbiting object is visible, from satellites to the ISS.

It's Christmas Eve, just one tick away from Christmas Day, at least Central Standard Time when I finish pouring pumpkin pie filling into two more deep dishes and then set them out to cool on our enclosed back porch. Looking up into the crisp-clear night sky while saying a little prayer for our son Jesse, now resting in peace with the angels in Heaven, I spot a glowing round light at the center of the murky Milky Way. I rub my eyes and take another look, then a third double take. The cosmic object is growing...and glowing, and rounding like a bright orange cinder in a fireplace. I can even see a halo of red behind the object, as if it launched straight out a sea of nebulas! Stan's been watching a recorded football game, really snoring, but I don't care, *this time*, about interrupting him. Since Jesse died to this day in 2010 in the Iraqi War, nobody better interrupt Stan and his beer-guzzling football frenzies on Christmas Eve or you'll pay the price with his ripping temper! Then again, I bake pies like they're drops in Niagara Falls and give 'em to our church for the needy. Anything to cope 'cause we've never been the same since Jesse lost his life for our country.

But seeing the enlarging, round glowing object in the sky that looks about ready to crash land or open up over our farm, I'll risk waking up Stan so we can quickly swipe up a few of our precious pictures, clothes, and skedaddle off the farm!

Running into the living room, I jostle Stan. "Wake up! We're—we're about to be hit by something falling from the sky!" I grab his flannel shirt and shake him until he unleashes off his reclining chair. "Come on…to the porch!" I peek through the living room curtains to an outside bright-yellow glowing light. "See?! Come on!" I keep waving him to the kitchen.

"What the heck?" He runs and joins me on the back porch, and we open the windows for a clear view to the cold outside.

I show him the incoming bright object and where I saw it originate in the not-so-clear cosmic background. "You think it's a meteor? An alien invasion? You better go call the cops!"

Before he makes it to the landline while I keep my eyes on the incoming blazing yellow object, the ground suddenly shakes, followed by a thundering vibrating *boom*, rattling me to the floor. Then a blast of hot air and wind flow through the porch windows as if we're in the middle of an August heat wave.

After Stan stumbles in shock back to me, we hold each other like these moments might be our last. "Stan, whatever that bright thing is, it's landed in our corn field." I point to the center of the stalk-scraggly place that's now a shimmering yellow crucible. "I wonder what's in that large spot?" I throw on my flannel coat with the brown fur collar.

"You think we should check out that alien thing?" He

slides back cautiously toward the kitchen door.

"You bet! This is *our* land…and I'm not givin' it up to *any* alien critter or object."

While I push up my boots, I see frost on the barn roof and iced-over bales of hay that look like reclining hibernating bodies on the field. Beyond them, the shining-yellow object.

Stan is standing dumbfounded with the black phone in his hand. "I can't even get a dial tone! Whatever's out there is blocking everything." He gestures back at the TV, hissing static.

"Maybe it's some type of jamming device…from a government experiment gone wrong," I say, trying to draw our fears *away* from a *real* alien invasion on early Christmas morning.

"Shouldn't we just go? Get in the car and leave? Go rattle awake the cops?" He's pale and almost breathless, but now has on his thick coat and boots.

"Nope, I'm goin' out there, into the field," I tell him, and he sighs in resignation as I clasp the top of my collar. I'm gonna do what needs to be done, so he might as well get with the program and help me 'cause I'm ready for exploring, and fighting for our land, if need be. I Ready, I breathe. "Now, Stan, let's get our sunglasses and head for that thing!"

After we retrieve our sunglasses out of the car in the red barn, I almost fall as the ground gently rumbles; but I grab Stan's hand, and we walk quickly toward the smoking area that's emitting a bright yellow light in the black scraggly corn field. The cold air hurts my lungs along the way, and as we close in on the shimmering anomaly, we begin wadding through melting snow and gooey mud.

"Just a bit more, Marianne, and we're there," he says,

coughs, and then offers me water from a thermal Christmas glass he bought last week.

I'm worried about him now. All that drinkin', tractor ridin', and TV sports watchin' since Jesse died have left him *way* outta shape. And this frosty bumpy land is no place for him, let alone *me* in my late sixties. Still I keep wondering: What *is* in our field? The ticking seconds and the object's intensifying glow are frightened us out of our wits, especially now. We stop when we hear a low humming sound! "Is that music?" we both ask, together.

"I don't know ... but it sounds like music, in a way," Stan shrugs. "Let's go find out!"

Holding his hand, I can hardly feel my feet as we whip our scarves around our faces and run like it's the end of the world to the shimmering bright crucible.

When we arrive at a large smoking hole in the ground, Stan pulls me back before I can peek over the edge. The area is so bright-white, we need our sunglasses, and we quickly don them while unbuttoning our coats. I feel as if I'm behind a shield in a nuclear reactor!

"Marian," he begins, looking into the sky and breathing, "maybe we outta go back to the house, wait until mornin', and direct the government to this spot after we call 'em. Some satellite's *gotta* be seein' all this, and some mighty powerful experts *haveta* be on their way to our farm soon!" Through pinching wrinkles of fear around his eyes and lips, he starts nudging me away from the smoking edge.

Quitting ticks me off! With my hands on my hips, I'm arguing with him. "*No* way am *I* giving away *anything* that *we* discover to *anyone*. This is *our* land. And any aliens we meet, or outer space technology we find is *ours* for the taking and keeping. So there." I think about sunken treasure and add: "Hey, when people find money under trees and in the ocean, don't they get to keep it? Don't *they* get a piece of the riches?" I watch him scratch his stubbly chin, obviously reconsidering. "I'm not looking for wealth, but it *would* be nice if we could *at least* take a cruise after all the years we've been grieving, right?"

After a few deep sighs and shrugs, he replies: "Yeah, I guess so. But I just hope we're not bein' exposed to harmful radiation here, 'cause *that's* what's *gotta* be comin' from outer space."

Slowly, I inch toward the edge of the hole and peek into the bright glowing light of the crucible.

"Well—well?" Stan asks.

Pushing the glasses the ophthalmologist gave me close to my eyes, I can make out several glowing objects. After Stan joins me, I describe what I'm seeing. "These shining pieces look like fragments of some kind of puzzle."

Stan grabs a chunk of my coat. "Whatever is here must have broken apart upon impact."

I've always liked puzzles, and now I want to put the pieces together. "Maybe there's a message on this thing, Stan." I remember the *Voyager* probe and Stan tells me the year that NASA launched it. "Maybe aliens just replied to us. Wow! And on Christmas Day!"

Gathering corn stalks, we use them as added protection over our leather gloves while we carefully pick up each glowing fragment and cart them slowly back to the house in the red wheelbarrow Stan had left along the fence after picking wild asparagus last summer. Half way back to our white farm house, I'm shocked we haven't heard *one* cop car, ambulance siren, or powerful government engine speeding our way. Shouldn't they have *seen* or at least detected the falling object that just blew a hole in our cornfield? Stan is as stumped as me!

At the house, we quickly spill the glowing pieces on

the floor and use barbecue tongs to begin piecing them together. "I feel like we're stoking a fire … or combining clumps of fire-hot sand to make a special ornament." Stan says the pieces must be hot, but I can't feel a thing, only calmness now, as if this wonderful two-foot multi-pronged object is whispering peaceful intentions into my mind.

As we almost finish putting together the glowing puzzle, the last pieces slowly begin attracting, and melting together to form one solid object. "They're reacting on a positive and negative field, Marian!" Stan says, motioning for me to back away.

"It looks like—" As the edges triangulate, I suddenly recognize the shape. "It's a large brass star!" I'm almost at the kitchen table when the cast iron pot flies off the stove into the glowing star that absorbs it and then increases in size.

"What the heck?!" Stan runs to the side of the fridge. "Get back, Marian, 'cause next the knives 'll come flyin' off the counter!"

In daylight, I can't begin to image how this alien Christmas star might outshine even the sun! "I believe this object is a remnant of some ancient race of beings," I shout. Maybe I can capture a picture and send out a call for help!" Ducking several flying iron objects, I quickly retrieve our laptop. After several attempts to get an internet connection, I final do; and I Google, *outer space star*, and receive an answer: *wish for peace*. Then, the screen background reverts to shuffling Jesse's pictures. I can't help but wonder what *he* might say and do if he were with us during this *real* alien manifestation.

Stan appears teary eyed as we both, for seconds, ignore the star that's flaring in intensity behind us. Everything suddenly becomes quiet as if a dampening curtain has surrounded our entire house, except I can still hear the northeaster licking the aluminum siding, and a pine bough spanking the gutter. "What would ya wish for right now, Marian?" Stan asks softly.

The star is smoldering warm, and its glow, calming. "Not money."

"Not more land," Stan laughs, tapping the checker board linoleum.

"Jesse can't come back to life either," I tell him, wiping tears off my cheeks. "He's gone. And with God now."

All our lights suddenly extinguish. The circuit breaker *click*s.

Stan grabs my hand, and we turn around and watch the brilliant alien star bulge and undulate as if waiting for a verbal cue to alter into something different.

"I guess, if I could wish for anything," I begin in a whisper, "I wish *every* bullet-firing weapon would disappear off the face of the Earth. Then, just maybe, proof of aliens will motivate people to stop fighting and eliminate all war."

After I said those words, the ground began shaking, again; and Stan and I dropped to the floor. The bright star doubled in size, its glow intensifying ten-fold! Scooting away from it until my back hit the leg of the kitchen table, I remember that old movie, *Journey to the Center of the Earth*, when James Mason and Pat Boone escaped death by a lava flow propelling them through a volcano. But now, there's not much between Stan, me, and the shining, humming alien star! From under the table, I see Stan jump into the pantry and shut the door.

Then I hear crackling sounds, and I peek into the living room where I see hot white lines of lights emanating from our melting gun cabinet. Oh my!

They're Stan's hunting guns! And they're melting, and changing into a different compound like airplane contrails. I tell Stan everything I'm seeing. "And your white liquid guns are breaking through the popcorn ceiling, tearing apart the roof, and streaking high into the sky!" I think I hear Stan crying, or toppling down cans of food to shield himself. "Everywhere on the planet, the same process must be happening, Stan." Then I turn speechless when I notice the blinding-white star is at the center of our living room and spinning like a pinwheel on fire! Each tip of the five-sided star begins shining a perfect ray of light through our roof into the night sky. Through all the crashing debris and dust, the upper atmosphere appears like a field of streaking lightning! To where all the changed weapons are launching...I have no idea. And I can't see any alien ship or portal amassing all the outbound energy.

"Stan! Ya see what's happening?" I cry to him while ducking under the table and covering my head, all the while hoping and praying that the alien star won't disintegrate us like one of those gamma-ray guns on the old alien movies.

Stan is huffing and now-and-then screeching from behind the pantry door. "Just say put, Marian! I think your wish just came through, and every war and gang shooting has stopped!"

I sit cross-legged under the kitchen table as each star beam shoots through our roof and makes my wish come true. *Every* bullet-firing weapon should *now* be removed from the face of the Earth, and people around the world *will* experience a real Christmas gift of peace on Earth, just like in World War I when "Silent Night" played and armies stopped fighting.

A blinding ray of starlight is the last thing I remember

before almost losing consciousness under the kitchen table.

Now, as I finally find the courage to kick out and break out, all I see are four shattered walls and a laptop with our son Jesse's pictures still scrolling down. That's all that's left of our house, and a smoldering hole under the place where the brilliant Christmas Star spun out of control at the mention of my wish to change the world.

Stan just busted out of the accordion partition that used to be our pantry. "Wow, that's one helluva wish you asked for, Marian," he laughs, and then coughs, and then swats away dry-wall dust out of his face as he sneezes. He looks changed and energized, as if he's ready to begin again somewhere new. Then, while helping him clean off his face, in his eyes I see a strange reflection, and we hold each other tightly and look through the pine-tree windbreak that's been shielding our place from disastrous winter storms since 1974. There's a strange, yellow glowing light blending with the horizon. I believe it's the Christmas Star, still disintegrating every weapon of war around the world for a true Peace on Earth.

"Merry Christmas, Stan," I tell him, and kiss him on the cheek.

He kicks a pile of wood in our frost-biting coldness, finds two blue curtains I sewed in 1977, and wraps us up tightly. "I love 'ya, Marian...and Jesse." He's crying again. That's okay, 'cause that's really life...a lot of shedding tears with Christmas happiness now and then.

As we glance into the white-diamond sky, I feel Jesse through an angel's whisper over our shoulders. War is such a venomous killer, but tonight, an alien touched Earth, and is spreading Peace on Earth ... hopefully, peace for good.

Stan just found the car keys in his pocket. "Come on,

let's hit the road and get to the sheriff's office."

I kick some planks out of the way, grab the laptop, and kiss Jesse's picture before I close the cover. "At least now we'll get a brand new door with the insurance money," I laugh, all the while looking into the night sky at all the hot-bright altered metals that are disappearing in space. "This is gonna cause a lot 'o commotion 'round the world, Stan. But *I'm* not tellin' anyone what I did."

"No need to," he says, pulling the curtain over his ears as a brisk wind whips around us. "Just say this is the best Christmas ever … and let's savor it!.

Winter Retrieval

Our Milky Way galaxy is full of dust, visible light and radio waves. We are in the Orion Spur where Earth is beginning to mingle with a small satellite galaxy or clump of invisible dark matter that's leaving behind unexpected echoes....

I brush snowflakes away from my eyes and gaze up at the Christmas tree on 3rd Street. My name is Linda Grayson, and right now I'm cold, chilled to the bone, *burrr*! This tree lighting ceremony makes no sense at all: a 6:30 p.m. outdoor (*outdoor*!) party with about three hundred shivering people. If this place hadn't sprung back from ghost town status during the oil boom of 2010, there wouldn't be a party here at all. Town square would be Wild West buildings buried in ice and snow! So most people who decided to burrow into their coats and tiptoe out into tonight's dance of winter are like me and my family: new to Aldridge, Montana and rebuilding the city ruins. But *wild* doesn't come close to how this place looks right now.

This weather and the night sky *sure* are abnormal. When clouds, part we see shimmering meteorites in the atmosphere, and bright red-and-green northern lights. People are shouting against the wind, saying some type of new phenomenon is happening. Leslie Staple, the Mayor, just sent out a mass text message, asking if we want to cancel tonight's ceremony. Thank goodness for social media so we can communicate! Most everyone votes to watch this spectacular cosmic show unfold and switch on the tree lights.

As people clap and O *Christmas Tree* begins blaring out of a loud speaker, Leslie calls: "Light the tree!"

An arc of energy springs in a *bang* from two wires to a transformer, startling people and blowing the loud speaker.

Leslie says the surge is harmless, that arcs have occurred at rare times in Aldridge's past. "Nothing to worry about everybody," she shouts, texts and tweets.

As people decide to stay and not flee, I say under my breath: "I haven't seen *any* electrical surge like *that* since I've lived here. This is some *weird* town. What strange thing's gonna happen next?" The few people who hear me move away.

Then I hear that warning from the past again circulating through the crowds:

A few months ago, on September 22, the autumnal equinox, an old retired couple said they'd seen a sign of something terrible about to occur. I remembered the day because at 107°F it broke the old record of 105°F. They told our local newspaper reporter that they had spotted four eagles abandoning their nests and flying south early. "A *baaad* omen," the husband said. "Last night, we saw strange northern lights. Long streaks of red and bright blue...*completely* abnormal. A hole is opening up, letting something into the atmosphere, and we're not stickin' 'round here to find out what!"

His wife added, "We're hightailin' it to Florida!" They packed up their Chevy van and left with a full trailer behind them. Before they crossed the town line, they yelled out their windows: "Something terrible is coming. It's up there and scarin' even the raptors! Get out! Leave while you can!"

Townsfolk scoffed at them. "What the heck are those old coots rambling on about now?"

As I shopped at various places over the three months since then, I heard talk about their strange prediction; but people waved it off as an outburst of dementia. Yet, no one ever really forgot what they'd said.

Until about an hour ago, when townsfolk started reminding one another of the omen after the whipping arctic wind and gold-green-red atmospheric illuminations began sweeping down on our party. Minutes ago, our town's electrician switched on the Christmas tree lights with no problem, but now the aurora borealis appears to be interacting with the bulbs. Some of the boughs are vibrating...and a few light poles in front of the shops look as though they're crawling with electricity! Their bases are smoking, so guys are dousing them with snow.

People are sending photos of the strange sights on their portable devices, asking several questions along with their attachments: "Check out this sky and send me some answers!" and "Have you ever seen anything like this?" and "What could be happening with the electricity?"

Now and then, our devices stall...so frustrating when we're trying to communicate to the outside world to figure out why these strange occurrences appear to be defying physics. This certainly was not in the weatherman's forecast for tonight.

On the evening news last night, the weatherman predicted a minor storm in most of the northern states, the onset of a mild nor'easter for the east coast and for us, just the usual winter snowstorm. However, this snowfall is morphing into a snow-blowing titan; and until we know for certain what's happening we're sticking together. I believe everyone from Aldridge is here right now. Something big is on the way, we don't know what, but we need to feel connected. When someone suggests we go home, I see terror and a dread of being alone on their faces. Odd, because most people have basements, and there's even an old nuclear bomb shelter somewhere in town. I don't remember ever noticing a sign indicating a shelter though. This is certainly turning into one of the oddball electric blizzards. When a few of the new residents suggest we find the old shelter and go there if conditions worsen, those who've lived here for generations shout, "No;" and, "no way!" They sound spooked. I'm not gonna argue with 'em! Still, it makes no sense that we're all standing out here in the freezing cold for a tree lighting ceremony. The only explanation I can give is that I feel grounded here, like a strong magnet is under my boots. No way am I gonna say that because people'll call me crazy just like they did that old couple. Looking around the crowd, people appear grounded too...and if everyone else wasn't seeing what I'm seeing right now, I'd call myself nuts.

Beyond the town square, I notice the tops of evergreen trees are bending, fighting against this biting wind that's blowing into a snow squall. Yet we can see right through it all...into the meteor-filled sky! Some kind of light energy is definitely affecting the atmosphere as Mayor Leslie's professor friend Dr. Dempsey is texting. She came to Aldridge for winter break to visit Leslie and has her iPhone and iPad interfaced to her research facility sensors.

People are shouting: "I've never seen an aurora flow so spectacular;" and, "Look, another meteor shower!" Everywhere around the tree, people are aiming their phone cameras at the snow, wild lights, and bright colorful rippling sky.

Strange as it seems, lights from the aurora appear to be feeding on the camera flashes. Every time someone snaps a picture, there's a sort-of backlash that makes the person's face glow. Mayor Leslie orders everyone to hold back on the picture taking. I smell a little ionization in the air as after a heavy rain--a real molecular charge.

The Christmas tree appears to be taking the brunt of the effects of this intensifying energy show. Green-and-gold light dancing all around it! Its hot bulbs are vaporizing the snow into sizzling water that's trickling down the pine needles, creating instant icicles. Children are breaking them off low at the boughs and sucking on them. "Fresh water popsicles!"

"Don't drink that!" their parents are hollering, pulling them away.

For us adults, the colorful tree lights are psychological triggers, warming our bodies. It's the only warm thing besides the tepid hot chocolate the PTA committee is serving at the covered kiosk fifty-feet away from the Greyhound station.

Looking at the covered loading-zone platform a bit more closely...either I'm going nuts or the luminous snow is playing tricks with my vision...I see tall thin shadows that look like people...a long line of them forming at the platform. Even though I'm reluctant to call Leslie's private number (my husband gave it to me as an emergency back-up), I rattle out a text, really a litany of angst-filled questions to her: "Are those people at the loading platform waiting for a bus? I heard on the news that the highways are closed. The platform is glowing yellow. From what? Please tell me you see this too! Is there another entrance to another building around the station? Something's wrong somewhere on the street next to the station."

It seemed like only seconds later, Mayor Leslie begins a Skype broadcast call to everyone in the contact list on her city mobile phone. Those who don't have her number are crowding around those who do so they can hear the news. Half her face is covered with a thick plaid scarf. She has on a Soviet ushanka hat with strands of her brown hair whipping her rose-red cheeks. She begins: "A couple of announcements to answer some of your questions. Number one: There are two old boarded-up entrances beyond the Greyhound platform. Number answer: I'm looking for more info to determine what in the world is causing that bright glowing light. And number three: If anyone in town has any knowledge to share, please let me know. One entrance, as most people in town know, is to the station," she continues. "There is also an entrance to a tunnel to the right of the station after the fork in the walkway. At the end of the tunnel beneath the boarded up old saloon is the 1950s nuclear shelter. So far, that's all I've been able to get out of our Aldridge old timers. When I asked them about the tunnel and the shelter, they become extremely anxious. Every one of them is warning me not to open up the tunnel." She's about to end her fuzzy Skype connection. "I and the other City Council members are trying to decide if their fear is enough to deter us from opening the place up. It sure looks like we might need it! Meanwhile, stay in your small groups. I'll get back with you when I know more."

She had seen it too! I wasn't nuts! While I'm still frustrated, I feel relieved, and trying hard to keep track of my teenage daughter Jenny who is making friends with the picture-snapping crowd. Bundled up next to me is Mark, my three-year-old son. All the while, the words, *why'd we have to move here*, keep reeling through my brain. Even Nature seems to be attacking Aldridge, making my bad attitude worse. I haven't made things better by voicing my opinions of the place. The renovated ghost town buildings around the square look like somebody slapped blocks and stucco over 'em. Hideous! And I let people know it. They haven't liked me much either.

Why have I stayed? I want a home. We've moved sixteen times in fifteen years and I've never had a *real* home. I gave up several careers too. I love my children, but I've been purposeless and numb. I'm tired of Mark clinging to my knees, and Jenny's continuous complaining is like rancid milk: "Why'd we have to leave California? It's hell here without beaches! I hate winter and I hate *you*!" Shouting as she runs away, crying.

As usual, I apologize: "Sorry, Jenny, but your Dad is a geologist with the oil company and we have to go where his job takes him." I don't scold her for the disrespect though. I just let her have her outbursts, hoping that one day we'll return to our close mother-daughter relationship. She does have a point: this place *is* desolate. She keeps calling Aldridge and its ghost town shops: "Dead End, Montana."

This mysterious little dot of pepper on the map is where we've just begun to spring back from the terrible meltdown of 2008 when we lost our home and abandoned almost everything we owned inside it, just for this job. Today, I should be forgetting those grim things 'cause it's my birthday, December 21. Wow, phenomena for a surprise party!

As a small choir of children begin belting out a half-flat round of *Jingle Bells*, a few more lights on the Christmas tree pop. Three streetlights launch into the sky and explode like firecrackers. People drop to the snow covered ground, dodging glass.

My cell phone chimes back to life. A chorus of devices begins pinging!

Dr. Dempsey sends out a text: "Electricity and light are interacting in astonishing new ways. A few of my colleagues are researching our situation. They say we're *not* in danger. We have a magnetic field event also in play from the polar regions." As I watch the static-filled video of one of her expert friends spout encouraging words, he didn't make me feel at ease *at all*. In fact, with the little knowledge I have about quantum physics, I feel worse!

From what I'm seeing, I know more lights are going to explode. I lasso Jenny and Mark. When we turn to dodge flying glass, to my surprise I slip and fall right into my husband Hugh's arms. Our family and everyone near the tree run. A few minutes later, we reassemble at the north end of the town square.

As people continue to watch the popping tree lights, street lights, and even a few smoking cameras, Hugh says: "I thought I'd get off early from work and surprise you. What a night, huh?"

Everywhere I look, people are marveling at the meteorites, the transparent glowing snow, and the radiating aurora borealis--lights sucking the energy out of everything electrical. All I see is weird change.

Mayor Leslie tweets about her visiting friend, and I read her messages to Hugh. "Dr. Joanna Dempsey is a tenured physics professor at Montana Technical University." It was founded in 1900 as the Montana State School of Mines with a focus on mining engineering and electrical engineering. A trusting peace fills me. "She's researching what's going on with these currents of electricity and magnetism and their volatile interactions with the northern lights."

"If our devices ever stay connected to the internet long enough for her to get answers," Hugh says in a frustrating tone, rubbing smears of ice off his phone's shimmering face. As we wait, he hands me a small present.

I cup his gift to my heart. "Thanks!" I kiss him.

"You remembered my birthday!" I was just about to say, "The kids forgot."

"They remember," he says. "They have presents and cards waiting for you at home." As he sweeps up Mark to hold him, I stash the little pink-wrapped box into my coat pocket. Then he presses rose-cheeked Jenny into his thick down jacket and hugs her. Stretching my arms as wide as I can, I try to hold them all.

"Happy birthday, Mom," Jenny and Mark say.

For the first time in a *long* time, we're a family; and the chaos slips away...

Suddenly, the sky begins glowing with an iridescent green...then red...then blue. The atmosphere appears to be peeling away to the core of something round and brilliant.

People begin huddling; children *oohing*-and-*aahing*.

Thick rippling northern lights surround us, the town square and the Greyhound platform.

"It looks like we're slowly being surrounded by a protective wall," I shout. While marveling at the meteor shower directed at one point high over Aldridge, Hugh and most people agree with me. The news of the wall spreads.

"This is some kind of attack," Chuck, our local auto mechanic and strong-man body builder says.

"An alien invasion most likely," several people add.

We crouch down and gather in our small groups, continuing to try and re-establish cell phone connections.

"Maybe it's a blessing," I say to terrified people around me. Even Jenny and Hugh doubt me. I realize that a blessing is just *my* perspective, and trying to convince panicking people that we could be experiencing something positive rather than negative is useless.

More bright colors materialize above us, forming what

look like curving roads into space.

Someone calls out, "Maybe it's the Air Force searching for a landing strip."

"That's *not* any government agency!" another replies. "I'm a Vietnam vet, and those lights that look like roads into space *aren't* from our military."

A transparent wall of light is shining above us, its bright gilded edges descending.

"You call *that* a blessing, lady?" a man calls over the crowd, obviously at me.

Leslie shouts, "Everyone, stick together in your groups 'til we get feedback on the atmosphere."

Hugh and some of his co-workers, all logical engineers, are chasing down several panicking people who disagreed with Mayor Leslie and attempted to race through the transparent wall.

As they calm down from their revolt, Hugh returns to our larger group of townsfolk and says in his usual reassuring manner: "I believe that this entire spectacle is only Mother Nature protecting us from harmful radiation. I'm a geologist, and I know a little about atmosphere conditions as well. We just need to remain calm, like Leslie is ordering, and wait for experts to explain this unusual aurora…this wall."

"This looks like a *real* alien invasion," a woman in our group cries. We're comforting one another the best we can inside this wall that appears to be completely isolating the center of Aldridge.

Mark has a smile on his face. "Angels!"

"No, spirits of dead people are all around us," Jenny whispers. Some of her teenage friends are snapping pictures and tagging their videos *alien invaders* that they're trying to up-load onto YouTube.

Catching them, Mayor Leslie says: "Put 'em away or I

take 'em. If people believe your videos are real, you could trigger panic around the world."

Suddenly, a rumble resounds, shaking the town.

Everyone pauses.

The reverberation stops.

"What the hell is that!?" people shout, testing the ground with their boots.

All our cell phones begin ringing....

It's the Flathead Avalanche Center transmitting an Emergency Alert. A powder snow avalanche is coming, the largest and most turbulent kind. With the news of the impending disaster, Leslie rounds everyone up as close as we can get to her. She explains: "These powerful snow slides can exceed speeds of 150 mph and masses of 10,000,000 tons. Their flows can travel long distances along flat valley bottoms and even uphill for short distances. Aldridge is directly in its path."

The wife of the man who owns the grocery store around the corner says: "You mean that avalanche could ram Aldridge *now*?!" She faints and her husband catches her.

People dart out of our massive circle. Individuals make frantic calls and peck out wild SOS messages. The nearest town is over seventy miles away, and the people there are hunkered down for a hammering snowstorm. We're unreachable, until tomorrow. The Center gives us one order: "Find a central location and take cover."

"Which building should we go to?" several people ask, pointing at dark shops.

Snow drifts had made their doorways almost imperceptible.

"Kick our way inside!" others cry.

"Break windows if ya have to," the owner of a small clothing store says.

When that small crowd tried digging through a snowdrift, they gave up and returned to the rest of us. As more people reassemble, I direct the small children to hold hands and stay close to the adults. Hugh is gathering disoriented individuals to congregate with him, and Jenny is rallying for her teenage friends to join Hugh.

"Pray," a woman shouts.

"Pray harder," others cry.

Through chants of various litanies, mild crunching sounds begin emanating from the direction of the forest roughly ten miles outside of town. The incoming torrent of snow! Around town square, snow drifts have doubled in the streets. Even before the avalanche, roofs are collapsing and walls buckling. People are clinging together with their children.

The pastor returns breathless from his church. "I can't get into the sanctuary. It's snowed in. *Everything* appears to be snowed in!"

"We're left out here to suffocate covered in fifty feet o' snow!" a woman shrieks.

"There's no time to dig to find doors and windows," a parishioner says after someone suggested that we break off tree branches and start using them as shovels.

"My house is around the corner," someone proposes.

"I already checked my place," his next door neighbor says. "Drifts are piled half way to the roof. We can't get inside in time."

"The roof of the school is gone too," screamed the principal of Aldridge Elementary.

Everyone looked like shivering Eskimos in the white snow.

Then I notice that Greyhound loading platform and that yellow light increasing in intensity. "Look at the station!"

Mayor Leslie, Dr. Dempsey and a few calm City Council members gather the rest of the townsfolk and begin assessing the bright spot.

Meanwhile, the perplexing transparent wall is settling and firming around us. The snow inside the wall is at a trickle, the wind silent. While we're being sheltered inside a massive transparent curtain; a huge drift is building outside along its edge.

"Wow--snow and wind have stopped *everywhere* inside this thing!" someone shouts.

"What is it?" another asks.

"Where'd this towering barrier come from?" people shout.

A few of them are crying in relief while some children are screaming in response to their parents' shrieks.

Above us, the rays of light that looked like take-off lights into space have merged into one super-highway, touching down at the glowing Greyhound platform.

"We *must* be under an attack of some type!" someone yells.

"I'm telling ya it's an alien invasion," another shouts.

Mayor Leslie whistles; everyone listens. "We've got an avalanche barreling down on us! There's no time for talk about aliens. Let's get movin'!" She orders Council members to line people up and prepare to lead them onto the illuminated platform. "That's the only refuge even remotely useful, even if it *is* glowing like the dawn. Past it is the tunnel that leads to the bomb shelter. Ten minutes, and we'll all be safe." As people line up, everyone suddenly stops.

The platform has altered. Something or someone, inside or outside, our mysterious protective wall had begun extracting massive quantities of a glowing material that looked like bright gold dust streaming over the platform. The rising particles are coalescing high in the sky, forming a shimmering transparent highway. Mark calls out, "It's the yellow brick road!" At its ending point was not Oz but a bright-white circle in space.

"What are they taking?" "Who are they?" "*Where* are they?" A flood of questions.

Everything inside our protective shield is calm; outside, trees are thrashing, and electrical currents are popping and arcing. Dr. Dempsey passes the word: "My guess is that the thick transparent walls are being energized by the town's electricity, the aurora, the wind, magnetism, and even oxygen."

People are kneeling. "It's a miracle, thank you God for this wall."

"Even if this thing *is* a miracle, we can't count on it lasting," Mayor Leslie yells. "Our protective shield could leave at any time." She points at the illuminated loading zone. "It looks like the old underground bunker is the *only* safe place we have left that can protect us all from the massive wave of snow. We have *no* choice but to make a run for it under those flying particles, break open the barricaded tunnel, and seek protection in the old bomb shelter." The town's patriarchs begin arguing with her-- the old timers who know secrets.

She keeps waving them toward a special line while directing the rest of us toward the illuminated platform. A few people are crying. That platform *does* look frightening with all the glowing particles streaming over it and into the sky. Several are afraid to even go near it, saying they'll take their chances standing outside, hoping the glowing barrier will outlast the snowstorm. They believe the forest and buildings will probably stop the avalanche before it arrives here.

"The forest is slowing it, but not for long." Leslie

begins. "You won't survive out here if this miracle dissipates."

The yellow glowing platform and flow of energized dust particles are intensifying.

"Whoever is taking the particles needs 'em," a crew chief of one of our oil wells says.

Glowing metallic specks are lifting out of the entrance to the Greyhound walkway like bats at dusk in whooshing and high-pitch whisperings unlike anything anyone's ever heard. At the end of the glistening road is a white-twirling hurricane in space. The glowing particles are forming at its vortex—some type of doorway.

"The particles aren't coming out of the station, but the barricaded tunnel," one of Mayor Leslie's scouts shouts after he joins her at the front of the line.

Dr. Dempsey believes several atomic numbers are combining to form these particles. "It looks like they are a new element, creating a new form of energy, and what we *are* witnessing above is some kind of doorway." She looks directly at us with serious eyes.

An engineer says: "Energy is used to power machines. There must be some kind of craft up there in space."

Just then, sounds of the avalanche rumble the white-covered ground.

Leslie orders: "Go! Run for it!"

"Someone's gotta break into that tunnel so we can get in," Chuck the mechanic says. "I'll do it!" He yells for his friends to follow him, and they scramble for the platform.

The glowing particles appear to be flowing at their peak above their heads. The bright highway into space and the white cycling doorway appear ready for use.

Last in line, I can hear serious banging and kicking followed by thuds of wood smacking concrete. Seconds later, word comes down the line, "The husky scouts have kicked a hole large enough to let people enter."

With brilliant yellow particles streaking high above her, Leslie drops like a sprinter. "Ruuun, RUN fast!" People are reluctant as they begin slowly walking to the platform until she and Council members grab them and push them down the walkway toward the tunnel.

"Everyone, move it," Hugh screams, dashing to help her.

Mysterious tall figures have gathered at the front of the platform in a V-line formation. I mistook them as real people. They weren't; but *whoever* they are, they seem to be guiding the new elements, and watching *us*.

Several screaming people stop several feet in front of the platform and began arguing with Leslie. "*No way* are we going near these shadowy things. They not human!"

"There's nothing left in town that can protect you," Hugh argues. "You'll be committing suicide!" He grabs the holdouts by their coats and shoves them to others who have passed through the V-line formation. By now, most people had passed the particle part of the journey. At the end of the loading platform, Council members are directing townsfolk into the tunnel.

"I don't wanna be swallowed up by aliens!" an old man cries, cocoon-like at the V-line formation of entities.

"Just close your eyes and go," Hugh orders. "We haven't died and we're not gonna die. I have kids and a wife."

"I'm walking the children on the platform now," Leslie calls, leading them quickly through the V-line shape of shadowy figures.

Mark is in front of me. "Mommy, I see Indians, the kind we're studying in school."

I push him ahead, assuring him that no harm will

come to him since they hadn't touched anyone thus far. "I can't see their faces." The few people ahead of me agree, saying only the children claim they can see the entities' faces. They say the mysterious figures are *real.* Mark wants to touch one of them. "No way," I tell him.

At the end of the Greyhound walkway in the distance, I see people racing into the tunnel with glimmering particles streaking over their heads. Last in line, I hear sharp cracking noises behind me, lightning snaps above ground. I glance back and see a wall of snow topple our Christmas tree two blocks away. Worse yet, the transparent shield is losing its colorful intensity, and is shrinking!

I yell, "We've got seconds!" I lift Mark over old rotten boards and rusty nails that are dangerous darts along the tunnel threshold. "Go to Daddy, Mark, run!" Hugh is coaxing him toward his strong arms. Then Mark is gone and I'm alone. I look back and up at the transparent yellow road and steady stream of glowing gold particles. The flow of shimmering elements appears to be at a trickle, nearly exhausted, which could signal the end of our protective wall.

As I'm about to step inside the tunnel, two beams collapse and block the threshold. I jump back. I can't move! A tall shining body materializes between me and the entryway. The figure appears holographic, like engravings on a driver's license. Her face becomes clear...the regal appearance of a Queen!

I hear people way inside the tunnel. *They're* safely inside the bunker.

"Mom!" It's Jenny's voice. "Hurry, Mom!"

"I've got Mark right here Linda," Hugh yells. "Run— NOW, Linda!"

I can't. The Queen, or this new atmosphere, or both,

have me frozen in place. If the glowing bronze Queen won't let me pass, soon I'll be dead. I look into her shining green eyes. They have no pupils, but glimmer in rapid undulations. Wherever these beings are from, their eyes are processing differently than ours, and her body can't be flesh and bones--at least what *I* would call flesh, never mind she doesn't seem one bit concerned about the pending avalanche. I look over my shoulder. Maybe I can divert her attention to the incoming disaster. Nope, that doesn't work because she's inspecting *me*. I can only peer up to the bright transparent highway in the sky onto which I suspect she and her shadowy comrades will launch off-Earth. Fear of being buried alive is ripping through me.

I try speaking, "Let me pass!" I can't hear my words; my lips feel rubbery. These beings are not only manipulating light and electricity but also sound, and I'm caught up in their shift in space or reality, their extraterrestrial zone. Now I'm trapped, and can see their world: mountainous land with dipping green valleys and trenches, rippling auroras, a white-sparkling swirling sky, and luminescent blue lakes. It's beautiful, but I feel dread at leaving Earth and my family.

My eyes sting; the atmosphere is dry. I can't blink. A strange pure smell wafts through the air. Am I supposed to die? "Riiiight noooww diiiie?" My words echo back in hot belts bouncing off an indigo barrier between her and me. *Why are you stopping me? Did I do something wrong?* Maybe the brilliant Queen who looks more like a cartoon character than flesh and bones wants to take me!

"Yeah right, me," I want to say if I could speak. *You want Dr. Dempsey who's down there in that tunnel, not me!"*

Her head turned. Body language.

Did you understand me?

Is she telepathic, capable of discerning the kind of person I am? Uh-oh, not too nice a person lately. Maybe she believes the world would be better without me. My God ... I really haven't been living right.

I hadn't cared much about the people of Aldridge. I'd been walkin' around with a brick on my shoulder, and sarcastic. I'd been on an emotional landslide since we lost everything, and blaming everybody.

Tonight, I began to feel differently. I'm part of a community now and I don't want Aldridge and innocent people snuffed out by an avalanche.

Memories of Hugh, Jenny and Mark are flooding my mind, and I feel prickly tears on my cheeks. The light gravity of their world is making my tears and skin feel silken but tingly. The Queen is watching them, now touching them! I still can't move. Clothed in what looks like pure liquid gold, she has the presence of a powerful leader. The faces of her shadowy companions are directed at her, appearing to be waiting for orders. She's stretching out her hand at me.

What do you want?

The shadowy figures are lining up, hovering on both sides of her. They're reaching out to me as well.

You want to take me with you? With every bit of energy I can muster, I blurt out, "Nooo waaay!" My eyes have to be terror-stricken. I can feel electricity playing on my skin in pricks and pinches. Soon I'd either be engulfed by their world or the arriving avalanche.

I want to stay alive. I can't live like this much longer!

Then I see a human hand next to the Queen's luminous body. Hugh! He grabs me, pulling me into the tunnel. Falling down on wet bricks, I look back. The gift he gave me is now in her glowing hands. It must have tumbled out of my pocket.

She's holding the glowing pink-wrapped box next to her heart while nodding at me. *Wow,* she's saying, "thank you."

She must have observed *me* holding it to *my* heart! I breathe, "You're welcome."

The Queen and her companions transform into colorful bright lines, flying from the platform. But I'm too far inside the tunnel to see what happens to their golden highway into the heavens. All I see is a bright white flash. They're gone.

Unleashing its powerful snow keg, the avalanche engulfs the town square. Hugh and I sprint down the tunnel, gravity and momentum propelling us.

Behind us, the raging snow is smashing buildings, demolishing every sign and sculpture in our little town. The entryway to the station rumbles and reverberates with clouds of dust, falling rock and crashing boards.

I'm safe ... out of breath and my heart's pounding, but safe.

"What *happened* up there?" Hugh asks after we enter the bunker. Someone gives me a cool drink of water. I'm in a state of shock with everything around me spinning. People start congregating around me as the spinning finally stops. I hear several say they're hearing strange noises and feeling terrified that some of that mysterious new element is around us. My children are calling, "Mom," but they can't get through to me.

"Give her some room and let her catch her breath," Hugh says, rubbing warmth and feeling into my shoulders. Jenny and Mark finally break through and grab onto me like they'll never let go. Hugh takes my coat.

I'm sweating! I put my back against the cool wall and dab my face with a damp cloth. My lips still feel like someone's punched me, but at least now I can move them. "It's gone, Hugh." I drink some more. "The gift you gave me is gone. What was in it? *That's* what she took...what the alien Queen wanted!"

"What happened to ya up there?" an old-timer asks. Several others ask: "*Alien Queen?*"

I tell them the short-story version of what happened from the time the tunnel support beams collapsed to the time Hugh rescued me. "What the alien Queen wanted was that box ... my birthday present."

Hugh brushes some ice off his collar. "It was just an arrowhead. I bought it at the badlands Makoshika State Park where we saw those fossils and relics last summer."

Water is sitting in little pools over the concrete floor. Florescent lights are zapping, and the jagged walls and long slick ceiling are shimmering. There are dark cracks and blocked passageways, leading to other tunnels and mine shafts. This is no ordinary place! I stop leaning on the wall, walk fast to the center of the bunker and sit down on a crate that someone had overturned for me.

"What made you want the arrowhead, Mrs. Grayson?" Mayor Leslie asks.

My thoughts reorganize. "I liked all the shiny speckles. It looked like ancient American Indians had fashioned it out of a unique iron mineral."

"A rock from outer space maybe, like that meteor shower tonight," Jenny says.

Hugh grabs a folding chair and sits down next to me. "Linda, *you* were the one who wanted to buy it at the gift shop. As a geologist, I appreciated its unique appearance and intended to analyze the arrowhead after you opened the present." His face shone disappointment.

I remember the arrowhead's exact location. "It was on the bottom shelf, in the back, next to a mirror. When

I saw its reflection, the arrowhead looked holographic. I believed I was seeing things." I felt faint at the time, but also drawn to the arrowhead. "Then the sales lady put on white gloves like it was something special and handed it to me."

"Yeah, she was wearing gloves when she boxed it up as well." Hugh handed me a protein bar. "Obviously, she knows something about that arrowhead that no one else knows, and probably wanted to get rid of it."

"I believe the alien Queen wanted that arrowhead because it's probably the last of its kind."

"*Real* alien life," some people exclaim.

"They have to be ancient beings eons beyond us," Dr. Dempsey says.

With urgency in her eyes, Mayor Leslie quiets everyone. "I finally connected with the County Recorder. This bunker *is* a former excavation site."

Stillness creeps through the crowd, and people begin peering at the walls and ceilings. They pull up their collars and close their coats.

Little whispers and undulating wind sounds are seemingly white-washing spirits everywhere in our huge bunker.

I thought Leslie would have quit trying to research our old ghost town--considering the events of the evening; but I can see she's the persistent type. We might need that quality when outsiders start flooding Aldridge.

I catch up with Dr. Dempsey to tell her more about my experiences because I really want find a safe clinic where a doctor could test me for any unusual changes. With wild-wide blue eyes, she pauses from her scrutiny of the ceiling and walls. "Our universe is complex and full of surprises. The most astounding secrets are often hidden in plain sight. It may be that in our search for alien intelligence we have been looking in the wrong direction." People begin listening to her like eager students. "From what you described, Mrs. Grayson, I believe the aliens were manipulating all frequencies of the electromagnetic spectrum, playing on it like a musical instrument...even some sound frequencies that are beyond human hearing. They used these energized particles they extracted from our old mine to initiate some kind of propulsion or transport window to launch to their destination. They also used Earth's magnetic field like a pole vault into the cosmos."

"Special rocket fuel," Jenny says, treating me like a hero, hugging me. I have Hugh snap a picture of that.

"While they were here, Doctor, where and how did they live?" Mayor Leslie asks.

"Obviously obscured and camouflaged by manipulating light," she replies.

"If some of that powerful golden mineral is *still* inside this ancient site, who knows *what* new technological understanding we could attain," I say.

Dr. Dempsey had asked us earlier: "Ever want to have a 'life do over,' teleport, time travel, have your computer work at lightning speed, or be guaranteed of no turbulence on your next flight?" People had puzzling looks on their faces, but I imagined life on Earth changing in a flash if what she said were to come to fruition. She continued, "Make no mistake, discovery of the new element and energy source *will* change our lives."

"Aldridge could become a bustling city," Mayor Leslie said. Her cheeks turn a bit pale. "We'll certainly have busloads of engineers and scientists from Silicon Valley, Cal Tech, and every other institute and government agency flooding here...and experimenting." She looked down, her body lightly shaking. That idea appeared to scare her and some others.

I said through the sad stillness, "I guess that old couple was right about change coming."

Mark just sat up from his slumber. "Did the angels stop the snowstorm, Mommy? Can we go home?" His soft innocence touches me, and I don't have the heart to tell him that most likely home is no more.

Dr. Dempsey is continuing to expound on what she believes could be a new direction for humanity. While attempting to download information, she's astounded to find an extra-fast connection. She guesses it's because of the remaining particles in the air, this new element and the highly-charged energy output. I walk over to a walled off section that has a long fissure as wide as my thumb. Several people have their ears pressed next to it ... listening.

"Crackling sounds and whispers ... hear 'em?" they ask.

I can hear the sounds up close to my ear even though they seem to be emanating from deep within the earth. "The aurora penetrated this entire structure. This place *could* be part of some kind of communications conduit." People back away.

Suddenly, we're interrupted by the sounds of tumbling wood and shattering glass above us, remnants of the snow slide that's tossing everything into a scrap heap.

I have an alarming thought, gasp and clutch Hugh's arm. Startled people look at me, and I say, "I think that arrowhead saved us, not necessarily the alien Queen. If I wouldn't have had the arrowhead, she couldn't have retrieved it, and we'd all be dead."

Gulping down coffee, Hugh set down his cup. He pulled me close to him, his comforting warmth soothing my anxiety.

Everyone hears my comment, and people begin asking me questions: "What's your name again?" and "Where'd you live before you moved to Aldridge?"

Too frazzled to answer every detail, I'm still caught up in the memory of the Queen nodding thanks. "That arrowhead had to be precious to her, and everything worked together in unison, providence some people are saying, to save us."

There are things I can't tell them because I don't know any words to describe the experience. I stood in *two* universes. Should I be worried that I haven't felt the true effects of the Queen's alien planet? It's like getting a shot that takes a while for the immune system to fight the flu. Now, I'm noticing colorful strings on the rocks. *Is something on a molecular level changing me? Just me?* When I inspect the rocks and strings up close, they morph into glittering golden gems. I'm sure not going to be the first person to say that I'm seeing miniature 3D string creatures. People will call me crazy, or maybe, the long-lost daughter of the alien Queen.

BACK TO CHILDHOOD....
I WISH I WAS TWIGGY

I was in second grade, seven years old, when I woke up after I was supposed to be fast asleep and walked into the living room. The TV was on, playing the *Miss America Pageant*. I saw Twiggy walking gracefully and elegantly down the runway. People were standing up in the aisles and clapping for her. Twiggy was beautiful with her perfect cheekbones, sultry eyes and red lips! She had on a glittering dress, the newest fashion hemmed half way up her skinny thighs, and she had on sparkling expensive jewels! She was a gorgeous thin model with a stick figure, and people were applauding her. The crowd adored her! To have people love you that much?

I looked down at my body. I was a bit chubby, and the awareness of my shape compared to hers disgusted me. I wanted to throw up! I wanted to slough off all my fat like a snake and become someone better, someone prettier, someone brighter, someone more intelligent, someone ... *hm*.

I was no Twiggy, at all! I remember feeling sad that I couldn't look like her although I wished to Heaven I could. Whose fault was it? Who made me so horrible looking, like a turtle's face under a shell? At that moment, I hated being born ... hated everything from my round reflection in my bedroom mirror to my chunky reflection in the bathroom mirror. I started hating even taking a bath ... I looked and felt so ashamed and disgusted about myself, and my body.

Twiggy ... she had the perfect figure and short blond hair. She was tall and had the perfect beautiful brown eyes. She was everything *every* magazine and movie producer wanted to make the world worship. Why couldn't I have been born a Twiggy?

My mom caught me watching the late-night beauty pageant. "Joycie, go back to bed."

"But I wanna see who wins!"

"Go, now before I crack ya!" She punched off the TV, turned off the lights, and left the living room. It was the same room I watched *Star Trek* and *The Outer Limits*.

Mom was so opposite Twiggy. She had short black hair, dark brown eyes that looked entirely black, especially when she went into a rage, and she had a full robust and rotund figure. She had three children, and she'd go on to pop out a few more she couldn't take care of. I heard her threaten me from her distant bedroom. "Get to bed, *now!*"

I hated her at that moment. Not because she wouldn't let me watch Twiggy, and the rest of the perfect models, but because I looked like her, only blond. I saw myself becoming her one day, and I began boiling with disgust and the drive to change. "Okay...I'm going."

I went back to bed. Thereafter, I'd never been satisfied with the way I looked. Not because I didn't look like Twiggy, but because I looked like an overstuffed teddy bear, and had to go on a perpetual diet. No beauty contest for me! After all, men love Twiggy. I'd became conditioned much later, that if you ever want a guy and to keep a guy, you better always be Twiggy.

SHADES OF PINK

I remember springtime in Hammond, Indiana when I was a little girl. My favorite flowers were lilacs. They bloomed in white, shades of pink and gentle purples. Coming home from school, I used to pick them by the vase full and then give some to my grandma.

Grandma Anne Conneely was from the City of Kilkerrin, in County Galway, Ireland. She had a strong Irish brogue and liked to tell me my future by reading tea leaves at the bottom of our tea cups during snake time. Of course, at the center of her coffee table were the lilacs. The whole house filled with their perfume!

"Joice," she'd begin, "you're gonna have a bright future…and go to college…and make lots o' money."

"Really, Grandma? You think I can be a teacher, like Sister Rose?"

Sister Rose was my fifty grade teacher and my favorite! Every day, we'd sing for a half-an-hour, read aloud our geography lessons, and learn a little French. Before the final bell rang, she'd ask me to clean to blackboard. The only thing I didn't like was that she made me sit in the back because I was tall, like the tall boys, and could read the board from a distance. Still, I hated the back row! Then again, when we had to progress in those colored reading charts, I could sneak the higher levels and cheat. Guess what? I learned later on in life, that I only cheated myself.

After tea time with Grandma Anne, came play time, and I'd go outside and pick some more lilacs. I wanted to make sure I could capture a different color and see if I could find one that might stand out among all the rest. It's like searching for one of those mutant four-leaf clovers. I never could find one, although I searched along the foundation of the house, cracks in the side walk, and around swing-set poles…nothing, only *three* leaf clovers. Grandma said those were good too though, because the three-leaf clover is the symbol for the Holy Trinity.

After searching some more, but finding no deep blue lilacs, I'd return home, with sagging blossoms in my hands. I'd quickly give them to Grandpa McCarten though, 'cause he was home by then from his painting job. He'd smell them, and set them in his shaving cup with some water. Then he'd gently push me towards the staircase, because upstairs is where I lived, and that's where I had to eat supper.

Still, before I'd leave for upstairs, from around the corner I'd watch Grandma set my flowers at the center of her table, followed by Ketchup for Grandpa's fried potatoes. Everything smelled so delicious and inviting on the first level of the Warren house. Upstairs, the nightmare would ensue. I had no choice. Shaking and trembling as if I might lose my life every night by way of my mother's erratic behavior and combustible temper, I'd slowly walk up the stair…like I was walking down death row…all the while crying a bit because I really wanted to stay with my Grandma Anne and Grandpa Harold.

"Even dogs shouldn't live like this," I told myself all the time.

After dinner, the competition for the TV began like a horse race! You wanted to leave that giant oak table fast or else mom might slug ya, or wallop ya with the back of her hand, or whack ya with the broom stick. *Go! Leave! Fast!*

Whoever made it to the sofa first, after the news, could choose which show to watch. Fights broke out, but we all generally agreed to watch funny shows:

Bewitched, *The Munsters*, and *Gilligan's Island* were our favorites.

In later years when my dad finally rescued me, I liked *Happy Days*, until I wandered off from home.

Honu Means Sea Turtle

I was forty-seven, living in Hawaii, and had a life crisis. My mom had just died, my job went south, my kids kept whining and complaining, and my husband wasn't lifting a finger with any of the chores. And he was coming home, yelling at me, like Freudian man kicking the dog instead of blasting his jerk CEO boss. So what did I do?

Go scuba diving! Here's what happened one day in the deep blue world, on this particular dive at Fantasy Reef...

We had just left Captain Joe's boat, the Nori Z, for a drift dive around the Sea Tiger at about 85 feet underwater off the coast of Oahu. I had taken the usual precautionary measures: hooked my rope gear to my buoyancy compensator (BC) and had a clean slate hooked to my BC so I could communicate in writing.

When you dive, you have to have a partner, but when I spotted a giant sea turtle trapped in a massive cage at about thirty feet below water, I left that man and headed straight for the trapped turtle! I had to act fast...she appeared so lifeless, like a glob of dying hovering fungus!

Hawaiians call the green sea turtle, Honu, and the species is endangered. You're not allowed to *touch* these sacred creatures *at all*. Still, I was kicking my blue fins and pushing against the rushing current to get to her.

The Honu symbolizes a navigator, who can find her way home time after time.

Have you ever felt lost? Disoriented by life? Felt like a needle on a compass cycling wildly, trying to stabilize one direction? I have, so saving this Honu began to mean *everything* to me.

Flapping my legs and straightening my arms, I felt like a bullet launching to her, swimming as fast as I could through the crystal blue water with colorful coral below me, and parrot and angel fish darting all around me. I felt an instant connection to the distant trapped Honu hovering listlessly in the cage, even though I was still yards away. I thought my Nitrox might run dry in my tank I was inhaling and exhaling so fast to try and reach her!

Honu will swim hundreds of miles to lay its eggs, migrating home to its place of birth.

Where do I belong? Where do I fit in? Why do I feel so discombobulated and out of sync with the universe? Saving Honu might answer those questions for me.

There are other Honu myths as well as the navigator story. Some Hawaiian legends say the Honu guided the first Polynesians to the Hawaiian Islands. Another story tells of the green turtle being part of the legend of Kailua, a turtle who can take the form of a girl at will. In her human form, she looks after the children playing on Punalu'u beach.

You ever need saving?

I do, I kept thinking feet below sea level...with the cold tingling my arms and legs as I swam steadfast toward Honu. *If I can just rescue her, I might just keep on going...disappearing into everything blue and living in the sea. What matters? What's everything all about?* You'd figure I'd have solved that by age forty-seven! I hadn't, which means, something's terribly wrong...and how am I going to make it? *Just swim to her...save her*, I kept repeating in my Nitrox swooning mind.

But what angered me to my core is *who* would put such a giant death trap there, obviously intending to kill Honu?!

Frantically, I waved for our entire party to join me. I couldn't crush and crunch the death trap alone.

In the ocean, you cannot be a loner, because if you

find yourself anywhere isolated—as I did once on the deck of a sunken boat with eels attacking a school of flounder—and unobserved, you *could* die.

The giant turtle was almost inanimate, near death, floating inside the cage.

Quickly, I grabbed the steel-netted cage, and began twisting, turning, and pulling on the door.

Open! Open!

The turtle's body appeared to be slowly depleting of energy, her oxygen reserve almost used up, her thick heavy flippers lightly swaying to lifeless death. This sacred Honu had to have been fighting for quite some time against unforgiving odds to free herself for hours!

Finally, the door unclasped and opened!

My diving comrades were all around the perimeter, pounding and ripping apart the netted steel cage with all the energy they could muster.

Delicately and gently, I glided inside, beneath the Honu, and gently put my right hand on her hard underbelly. Lifting hard, knowing I was touching sacredness, I guided her out of that constricting cage. Outside the cage, that everyone was stomping on and crushing to a flat pancake, I swam with Honu face up, maintaining neutral buoyance while mesmerized by her beautiful ascent…waiting in the deep blue current for resiliency to spread through her life force with fresh surface air.

Then I rose toward the rippling waters along with her. I had to make sure she reached air, while respecting her sanctity and not touching her.

Finally, her face broke through the solid blue to the surface! Breathing with her, next to her, I felt the sun warm and vibrant all around us, but haloing her like an angel. I spit out my mouth piece. "You made it! Thank

God! We made it! We're alive!"

Then, she dove underwater, and disappeared in a distant crashing of waves along the shore.

They say there's a Honu, who navigates all the turbulent waters, who sees children in distress, maybe about to die, even though they are oblivious to her, and she rescues them and helps them breathe.

When I dove back down to that menacing cage, everyone had it rolled up into a mangled mesh and were continuing to pummel it with their flippers. After seconds, we all gathered around the contorted netting and kicked it into the disappearing deep.

Why was it there? Who put it there?

My answer I speculated...turtle soup or some rich person's collection.

Was I ticked off! When we all surfaced on the boat after the dive, we couldn't stop talking about the cruelty and thoughtlessness of illegal trappers and traffickers in exotic and endangered species.

Years have passed since that 2006 adventure. But in times when I believe I haven't made a difference in the world, and in seconds when I cannot breathe, or in the ticking of the clock that's rendering me lifeless and broken and disoriented...

I remember Honu.

I bet she's had children since we've met. Have you ever seen a turtle hatchling?

Neither have I, but they're everywhere in and around tropical oceans...waiting to rescue you too should you find yourself lost. All you need to do is meet them between ocean bottom and surface air.

I bet Honu is still alive in that wonderful magical world of ocean blue. She's gliding with her pals, and can leave decades more in search of other lost souls to rescue.

Frogs

A few weeks ago, I found a frog in my pool. He (or she) was gliding through the water, like someone doing the breast stroke at a swimming meet. I have to tell you…I don't much like frogs. They're not comparable to snakes, but they look greasy, grimy, and warty. Who would want to touch one o' those things? Not me, even though I remember eating frog legs once or twice when I lived in Indiana (*cough, cough*). But, when they're in my pool, and nearly drowning, I have no other choice but to save them. How?

With the pool pole and net, that's how! So when I saw that little critter struggling to find a way out of my pool, I grabbed the long pool pole and scooped her out. Quickly, I ran to the screen door and opened it. Turning the net inside out, I flicked the pole—trying hard to dislodge that little critter out of the sticky net. Boy, do frogs like to hold onto white pool nets! That little thing just wouldn't let go! I had to jostle that pool pole several times; until finally, the tired frog let go of her hold on the net. She landed white belly up and spindly legs pointed stiffly to the sky. Trouble still! She wasn't breathing! "Oh no, you're not gonna die on me!" I told her.

However, I was *not* going to perform mouth-to-mouth on a frog. Taking the pole and delicately pumping her pinkie-sized white underbelly with it, I finally resuscitated her. She jumped, flipped over, and hopped away—all the while unaware of her dance with death. I knew different. Death had encroaching on her. She probably had only seconds to live *if* she had remained in my pool.

Wow … I saved a frog. Who'd have thought of that? A frog … a *teensy-weensy* frog.

Sometimes, do you ever wonder what you're living

for? What life means? Why you're here? I do, and today
... *today*, I rescued *two* more frogs from drowning. Two
were babies, no larger than my thumb. Does God know
they exist? Does the universe care about a frog?! How'd
I do it? These little ones were fast, I tell ya. I trapped
them inside my shoes, opened the door to my screened-in
patio, and set them free.

"Go on little guys ... *live*! Have a great life."

Something there is inside me that cares about a frog.

THE CARDINAL'S PARTNER

I woke up to the sounds of, *tap tap ... pit pat ... thump* coming from my kitchen. They were light soft sounds, nothing like someone breaking in, but a pecking noise.

I asked my husband Drew, "What's that?" He didn't know.

I slipped out bed, almost sleepwalking to the kitchen, and saw a six-inch red cardinal with a long yellow beak perched on one of my hurricane shutters. His song was chirping sweet, but I couldn't understand why he had been smacking himself against the window.

"I'm afraid he'll break his neck!" I told Drew. "How do we stop it?"

I've experimented with every solution, from closing the hurricane shutters, to switching on the two kitchen lights. No effect; the red beautiful cardinal keeps pecking and flailing his body against my window. Walking outside to inspect the sight for a fourth time, I noticed a nest in a tree alongside the window. The nest was hard to see, and situated far inside the tree.

Ah, the cardinal's looking for a mate, I concluded yesterday. He sees his reflection in the window, and he must be looking for a partner! No one inside this house for him.

I went to Home Depot and bought a blind. Hopefully, tomorrow, the blind I install will stop the cardinal from hurting himself while trying to find the perfect mate.

Still, I think everyone has a success story and a failure story at dating and finding true love. Guess what? Even birds do.

PICNIC

I might as well have stepped back into the 1960s today!

After moving to Brevard County almost a year to the day, I attended a church picnic, actually a baptismal church-family gathering. A prosperous and blessed family at the church allowed the congregation to have a celebration at their house and baptize people at their beautiful spacious lake. For me, a friend-shy person, I attended for my son's sake. He's a teenager, trying hard to fit in and find acceptance. Me? I've come to believe that even when people appear cold, apathetic, and snobbish: *Be the Change You Want.* Church folk aren't much different than people you pass by at the mall. I guess we all need God, Jesus, and the Holy Spirit! And only when we reach Heaven will relationships be different.

My husband said he was ill and didn't feel like going to the picnic.

I wanted to just drop our son off with a dessert, but something kept prodding me to attend.

You see, I've been a back-seat church attender for over twelve years. The last church I felt "a part of" was a church in Carlsbad, California. After we moved there and began attending services, right away people included us, like family. "Join the choir," and, "Come to our after services lunches."

I put my heart into the place, helped out in their preschool for free, and cooked meals in the kitchen. A famous clergyman named Henri Nouwen once said: "When we honestly ask ourselves which person in our lives means the most to us, we often find that it is those who, instead of giving advice, solutions, or cures, have chosen rather to share our pain and touch our wounds with a warm and tender hand." People were truly forthcoming, generous, and caring there. I loved being in that church and fellowshipping with the people. They were my authentic brothers and sisters!

After living in Carlsbad for three months, Drew lost his job in San Diego, and we had to move after he began a new job in Hawaii.

We left for Hawaii on October 31, 2001; and ever since, I've been church-fellowship avoidant. But hey! I did get to live in paradise for a little over four years! Some anonymous person once said: Moving on is easy but what you leave behind is what makes it hard.

Years later, after another five moves, the Tornado of All Moves drops us in Melbourne, Florida. The week after the garbage men hauled away all the empty boxes, I exhaled in resignation, telling my husband, "Just pick the nearest church of our usual denomination and let's just start attending there."

Months later, after always walking into the service late because I can't get everyone motivated to arriving on time, I learn about this picnic. My son wants to meet his friends there, so I agree to take him. Gosh I know no one. A quote from Proverbs comes to mind on my way to the picnic. "A friend shows his friendship at all times—it is for adversity that [such] a brother is born" (Proverbs 17:17). The word, *adversity*, means: *difficulties, misfortune, trouble, hardship, distress,* and, *trauma.* Life's tendency comes to my mind. Most times, people walk in the world with Friendship masks on their faces; therefore, it's always easy to be a friend. I think about all the times I say, "Hi, how are you?"

I always receive the reply, "Fine, and how are you?"

"Just great," I add, and then we part ways.

I guess God wants us to know another way to exist in

this place his created where the good and bad collide every day. If we want to be true Biblical brothers and sisters, meet people in their moments of adversity. And if you look real hard around you, it won't take long before you see people experiencing adversities, and become aware of their adverse situations.

So, how can I become a friend? I wondered remembering another quote: "If you want a friend you have to be a friend." Here's my chance at this picnic to try again…

At 4:35 p.m., I parked the car, and my son walked away from me. "Bye Mom." As a teen, he's a bit "ashamed" or "embarrassed" to be seen with "Mom."

Okay, but now I'm alone, so I walk toward a crowd of people who are sitting in lawn chairs around a giant lake that looks like a halo around the moon. I pass by fathers throwing footballs to their children, a clown toss game, and children playing paddle ball. In the distance in front of an estate home is a continuous stream of smoke from a giant cooker. As I slink between lawn chairs and crowds of people who obviously have known one another for years, I approach several long picnic tables that people are stocking up with fluffy desserts and every type of delectable salad imaginable. I inhale and cough from all the smoke though. I must smell like a cigarette smoker right now from all the barbecuing! Tonight, I'm going to have to shower like Niagara.

Meanwhile, people are gathered in front of the lake in close-knit groups. I call them all: Friends Forever Clubs. They are, and they've been in church groups, Bible study circles, small Life groups, and volunteer ensembles for decades … maybe since the church began in the early 1900s. I spot the Elderly 70s and 80s club, various teen groups, new mom's league, toddler mom's fellowships, and deacon and pastors club.

In another part of the bustling landscape is a basketball court filled with young adults; and beyond them by the lake, fishermen (and women) are casting into the water in the hope of catching fish. Have I missed anyone? If so, feel free to fill in the blank with groups from your own imagination because everyone's here, except the people who usually drink too much and get drunk. There's no alcohol at this picnic! Still, from the popular person, to the "robust" lady ... we're all the same, 'cause where Jesus is concerned, the ground where his cross struck the earth was flat and everyone could attend his crucifixion.

Uh-oh, I remember ... I didn't bring a chair. I have to find one, darn it! I see a large barn and ask one of the men I recognize as a pastor: "May I use this chair." I tell him how hurriedly I left home. "But I promise to return it before six."

I then hear the pastor begin a prayer of thanksgiving over the food. After silently praying along, I walk through the food lines, eavesdropping on peoples' conversations. They've done business together, have been involved in their children's' preschools together, or enmeshed in Bible studies.

How the heck do you accumulate years of friendship in a day? You can't. It's called, starting over, and starting over is the price I have to pay for moving around so much, even though I had no control over those "changes." Life...so many paradoxes, wouldn't you agree?

Arriving at another food line, I ladle beans and potato salad on my paper plate, fork a chicken leg, and serve myself a plastic glass of sweet tea. I recognize a batch of cookies I'd made and brought, so I nab one of those too.

Two teenage girls direct me to the ice. "Thanks!"

After standing like a wall flower behind the drink table, I walk back to my spot under a distance oak tree, trying hard to locate my green-and-white frayed lawn chair. *Where the heck are you?* Looking for it is like searching for a best friend at this point 'cause that's what it is, like a security blanket among total strangers.

Finally, I see my chair like Alcatraz above the horizon! So alone it's setting there, under rustling leaves and vibrating boughs beyond the friendly crowds. I pass by the choir director. Gosh, the guy's as loud off the stage as he is when he's performing! Then I realize I'm being judgmental, and change my visual direction. After all, if you judge, you will be judged. *Oo*, ouch, sorry God. Another Bible passage enters my mind: "the measure with which you measure out will be used to measure to you" (Matthew 7:1). I look up into the blue Heaven: "Lord, remove my perfectionism please, 'cause if ya don't, I'm in a bundle o' trouble when I meet ya!"

The breeze is cool on my skin, the sky is crystal blue, and a three-quarter moon is 45° above the eastern horizon. Beautiful, and everyone's laughing, talking, and rearranging tables and chairs to eat. As I eat, I noticed so many little things ... trying to soak in people and their happy moments:

An old man with a blue hat is holding a baby. He must be a grandfather.

Teenagers are in a large group, talking about music and YouTube videos.

One is my son! I move my lawn chair back a bit because I know he'll leave if he sees me. Sometimes, moms and dads just want to observe how their children are getting along in the world. It's a bit of a reflection on yourself, and whether you've taught your child well.

After all, if you *really* want to know yourself, ask the question: What do I do when no one else is around? In this case: What's he doing when I'm not around?

One of my favorite sayings appears in the form of advice from Henry's mom in Stephen Crane's novel, *The Red Badge of Courage*. Henry's mom tells him before he enlists in the army during the Civil War: "I don't want yeh to ever do anything, Henry, that yeh would be 'shamed to let me know about. Jest think as if I was a-watchin' yeh. If yeh keep that in yer mind allus, I guess yeh'll come out about right." My son's doing fine.

I suddenly spot someone I met months ago, but I forget her name. We greet each other. Gosh I hate not being able to remember names! She tells me her name is Debbie, her husband's name is Larry, and their son's name is Jim. I can't believe she's sitting right next to me! Coincidence? I don't think so. Thank goodness I don't have to eat alone with my stomach agitating like a washing machine.

We share general conversation I call "small talk," about her children, my new neighborhood, and an air show that happened earlier in the day. Then she asks: "What made you chose the place you're living in?"

I remember a year ago, almost to the date. "We sold our home in Texas," I replied, my feelings uncomfortable like grating sandpaper. I kept telling myself, *don't say too much, divulge too much because that's what chases people away.* So I try a little harder to step out of my chrysalis of protection. "As soon as we arrived at the apartment we rented, we called to make sure the home we'd been viewing online was still available. It was! We bought it right away. It wasn't the big place we were accustomed to in Texas, but it's just what we need, and we're happy, and blessed."

Then she had to leave. "Baptism are about to begin at the lake."

I walk quickly to join a large crowd gathered around a small shoreline. The pastor is baptizing several people, but one person stands out in the line. She was a little seven-year-old girl with short brown hair and a shy sweet smile.

The pastor asks her before baptizing her, "Why do you want to be baptized, Ella?"

After a little grin, Ella replies, "Because I want everyone to know I love Jesus."

I felt blood stick a little in my skipping heart. She is so pure, honest, and sincere! I pray: "Please, God, keep her this way forever." I remember what Jesus had said about children and how I need to be: "I tell you that whoever does not receive the Kingdom of God like a little child will not enter it at all" (Matthew 18:17)!

I know the reality of this world. Disappointments, troubles, and the bad in some people will leave their stings marks on her. I pray she won't have to suffer too much.

As I walk back to the spindly chair, I see a couple with a little baby. I'm going to be a grandmother in December. I need advice! After exchanging an introductory conversation, I ask, "Would you have wanted *your* mother there with you?"

She didn't want her in the delivery room, which I wouldn't want either, and then she says, "But I was so happy she was there the week after I had the baby so I could sleep, and she cook and do laundry, and dishes."

Just what I wanted to hear! "I'll pray for you," I tell her, and she said she'd pray for me and my daughter. We part ways...and then I meet another young mother of two children. She had one child right after the other!

Wow! I remember my daughter saying she'd like to do have five children, although my son-in-law didn't appear enthused about her suggestion because he gave her a frightened glare. Oh well, that's not for me to butt in and offer advice, but for them to resolve. I recall what someone anonymous said about letting your children make mistakes. "Being a good parent requires knowing when to push and when to back off; when to help and when to let them make mistakes, and then being strong enough to watch them go." I'm going to be there for one birth, and try to be the best support system.

I grab my frayed lawn chair and walk back to return it to the large tool shed. On the way, I see plastic forks, wind-tossed napkins, and plastic wrappers on the grass. I pick 'em all up and toss 'em in the trash. I've gotta be useful and make a little bit of a difference today, right?

I see Debbie again. She and her family are about to leave. "I'll pray for you," I call to her. Shock appears in her wide green eyes. Did I say something wrong? "I'll pray for you … just thinking of you and praying for your days to go well."

Finally she says, "You're so sincere."

Now that shocks me!

"What other way is there to be?" I asked her as I turn and leave to find my son. There he is…walking down a sidewalk between two people. We meet and ride back home.

"Mom, Dad needs to buy life insurance." He's worried we might one day be poor.

"We have everything we need," I tell him. "We don't have what you want, but at least we have what we need."

Hey, I'm grateful! I know other worse off places than we're at, and we could be living under worse conditions. But we're not. We've been blessed. I believe that.

"Life is so fragile and passes so quickly," I tell him. "This morning, I read an obituary of a man my age who died a few days ago."

That shuts him up. When I arrive home, after telling my husband about the picnic and my change in attitude, I take my Bible off the table and open it up just to see how God will surprise me. He does! "For people don't know when their time will come any more than fish taken in the fatal net or birds caught in a snare; similarly, people are snared at an unfortunate time, when suddenly it falls on them" (Ecclesiastes 9:12).

Thank you God for one more day and another chance at this life you gave me. Amen.

MOCKINGBIRD DANCE

Rain is coming, and I've been swinging on my porch swing outside on my backyard patio, waiting for it.

There are three mockingbirds having a peculiar relationship in my backyard. Two are perching on the left fence, while the third keeps lighting on the back fence and wiggling its silver tail feather at the other two. Are they rivals?

I notice one of the birds darting into the magnolia tree.

Ah, my first clue! She must have eggs in the magnolia tree that has large lush green leaves to hide from her foes. The second mockingbird is keeping watch on the fence. He's the daddy, I'm sure. Nearby is a loose plank of wood that rocks whenever it's touched. He keeps jumping from his station to the wood, rocking there a bit, and then hopping back to his safe lookout. He must be the dad, so the other gray bird with his flitting tail *must* be a rival. They do not like each other! I wonder how this competition is going to play out...

Thick blue-gray clouds are about to burst open with gigantic drops of water. It's been drizzling, and drops are hitting the pool cover in tiny ripples. I've seen this type of storm several times. The rain pummels roof tops in hail-sized drops.

I'm worried about the mockingbirds. Are they gonna be alright? Still, if they've survived this far, and lived through all the raccoons, stray cat appetites, and squirrels foraging for food, I'm sure they'll survive another night of thunderous showers.

Probably in a few weeks, I'll see beautiful, mockingbird babies. I can't wait!

MOWING DAY

Unlike Mondays past after I first moved into my new home, my eagerness to mow my lawn is waning. Back a year ago when we bought our house, I'd drop our son off at school, come home, eagerly put on my shorts and old shirt, and then whip out the lawnmower like a kid playing with her hula-hoop. I was so excited not to be living in an apartment anymore. I was so grateful a bank finally approved a home loan. Appreciation flowed in my blood like water in the River Jordan. I remember walking around the house, thanking God and working my hardest to fix all the little annoying things, like hiring a plumber to replace a connector in the tub faucet that wouldn't produce hot water, installing a new toilet in the second bathroom, and replacing lights and a few ceiling fans.

Ah but ... after the settling of Time, there's something about having something new that fades like paint in the scorching sun.

Mowing the lawn is one of those eagerly anticipated chores now tasting like buttermilk. And I've been trying so many things to change my attitude. A friend once told me: Try looking at the problem from a fresh perspective, and then your feelings about the problem will change.

Okay ... hmmm ... when?

So, what positive, enticing, motivational phrases can I think about today, Monday morning, that'll make me wanna stop writing my novel, change clothes, go out into the Florida heat, mow my lawn, and trim my landscape? Here are some of my self-talk attempts to alter my stale attitude:

"You'll burn calories, so you can eat one of those blueberry muffins when you're done."

"You can jump in the pool afterwards and the water'll

feel great!"

"You've been stalled on Book III anyway, so what's another hour?"

"You'll be closer to lunchtime when you're done."

I get out the edger and begin edging grass along the driveway and sideway, humming a tune as I step along the way: "It's a world of laughter a world of tears; it's a world of hopes and a world of tears...."

You know how the song goes. I can sing in perfect step to that or the lyrics to *The Song That Never Ends*. This weekly lawn mowing project has now become—My Lead Booted Chores!

All the while, I see trucks with trailer pass by me. They're landscape services I could call and hire: Larry's Lawn Care, and, Three Gals Landscape. I hear their mowers and blowers—revving and cycling like band saws around my ears. As I stop and watch those workers, I ask myself: How the heck can they mow such expansive lawns in just ten minutes? They do! I've time them!

Heck, my edging, mowing, and weed-whacking takes at least an hour. *Oh*, I realize the answer: They have more than one person doing the work, and they have professional riding mowers, and they're using state-of-the art equipment but leaving the cut grass in the street and on the sidewalks.

I, on the other hand, sweep up my mess, and make sure the chafe doesn't remain in the street to wash down into my other neighbors' driveways and clog the drainage ditch.

Now, I have another question: Why do I have to be so nice and thoughtful and considerate *all* the time? I scratch my head and can only think of one answer: It's just in my nature I guess ... the way I was brought up to be neighborly and helpful in a community where we all have to live among one another and get along.

Well, it's muffin time. I've also been drinking water like a hippo in a river! I notice we have ten muffins. Why the heck did we buy that many in a pack since my husband has diabetes and shouldn't be eating sweets in the first place?

I see my neighbors across the street, so I wipe off the sweat, wrap up a few cinnamon muffins, and take them over to them. I stand and chat with her for a while, and we talk about what we did over the weekend, the upcoming week, and plain talk that people exchanged while swinging on porch swings or walking down roads as in "the Old Day," sometimes, even sipping lemonade.

I'm looking forward to next Monday now.

HAWAIIAN DELUGE

It's early in the morning, the sun is shining, but it's raining. I feel stuck somewhere between the cumulous cloud bulging like coal over the house across the street and the cotton candy cloud on the horizon. The cumulous cloud reminds me of a time when I lived in Hawaii in 2002. The downpour was so heavy. I had to get a shovel and dig trenches.

We had just signed papers on our new house and moved in two weeks later. In August, the rains came to Kapolei. Rain in Hawaii is sporadic. You can be on one side of the street and get soaked, or be on the other side of the street and miss the rain entire, and even see a rainbow!

But that long hard rainy night in August scared me. It was the first time I'd ever experienced Nature in her tropical angry state! I felt like I'd never survive the storm.

The two-story house was on a hill in a new development, Star's Edge, but we didn't get a backyard landscape job when took possession of the keys, that's for sure! No grass, no trees, no fence... You get the picture, just dirt, red volcanic rust-tinted dirt.

Now, in a downpour, dirt turns to mud, and mud fortifies into a sticky flow of paste. I call a flooding of it, "cold-red vanilla-shake." You might have seen something akin to this cold red paste in old *Godzilla* movies, or Jules Verne movies, like *Journey to the Center of the Earth*, starring James Mason, where a volcano gushes forth in a red-tinted vanilla shake of bubbly goop. In a downpour and subsequent flood, this type of Hawaiian rain flow can appear deadly.

On that early rainy evening, I was at the windowsill with my hands under my chin, monitoring the accumulation of muddy goop. *Nano-Inch ... mini-inch ... full inch....*

I dashed from window to patio door, monitoring the rain levels in the backyard that appeared to be sifting off dirt down the steep cliff almost to waterfall intensity. Then I noticed rivulets of mud nudge toward our covered patio. Uh-oh!

"What should we do?" I asked the kids. Why did I even think I could expect a three-year-old and a twelve-year-old to have answers?

I called my husband on his cell phone while our two children, Andrew and Jenny, hunkered down in their rooms. Jenny was talking to a friend at her new school while Andrew was jumping up and down on his bed, wanting to take the outside party to MacDonald's to the bouncy. Jenny left her room once, stepped outside on the second-floor balcony, and danced a little in the rain.

Me? I continued to shake a bit in fear, and my eyes were stinging from watching the rain claw its way up to my house—that's what dirt looks like when it clashes with thick rain drops, claws and more claw marks! And what should I do about the jagged claws foraging tiny rivers toward our house

Drew really didn't have any solutions except for a shovel. But he wasn't home! He was stuck in traffic and wouldn't be home for over an hour because of the rain and ant lines on the freeway.

I would have to muscle up against this storm by myself.

The rain was banging and pinging on the roof like hail balls the size of quarters! Then thunder began rolling through the sky—a bowling ball on God's heavenly alley—with claps of lighting.

Jenny exclaimed, "*Oo*—this is cool!"

Andrew didn't agree with her. "When's Dad coming home? I'm scared!"

While calming him down by setting up more Thomas trains and tracks, I wondered: Is God mad, or are the angels battling a flight of demons up there? I prayed!

After Andrew calmed down, the wind picked up. Something worse was on its way.

Watching the news—on-and-off static through our satellite system—I heard the weather report: winds at 40mph and steady tropical rain through the night. Trouble!

Now, I wasn't the only person sticking my face out the front door like a terrified person checking out the neighborhood for burglars. The neighbor on my left had her house centered behind a storm drain. Mud was accumulating in thick long poles at the curved smile of her driveway. Soon, she'd have a half a driveway full of the red mess—that stains by the way.

Shovel.

The suggestion was Drew's, but I had *two* shovels in the garage. I'd need 'em both to divert the water away from my back patio. Could I though? All by myself?!

Lacing up my beige boots, I grabbed those shovels and trekked to the backyard. I felt as if I was wading knee-high through water! And I believed my boots might yank off my feet! The thick mud and I were wrestling hard.

I dug deep, that shovel *slitting* through the mud. I lifted hard on the handle, and then flung a shovel's worth of the rust-red dirt over the cliff. After ten minutes of arm-draining work along the back of the ridge, Nature began helping me in the form of her gravity as the rain merged with the long trench I had been digging at the side of the house. I ran there! Pushing and pulling mud with my steel shovel toward the street, I gasped in relief when I saw the current of dirt suddenly divert from my backyard, and gush into the street where my poor neighbor was raking her heavy flow of mud into the storm drain like a stoker shoveling coal into an engine.

"I'll help!" I called to her.

Then, my shovel snapped off at the base. The thing was cheap! The saying is true: You get what you pay for. Luckily, I grabbed the other one that has a wooden handle. The wood shaft is attached to the shoulder with iron, not glue.

I help her ... for minutes, with rain pelting our covered heads and shoulders. I was sliding around, trying to grab hold of the wind for balance, like learning to skate on ice! All the while, streams of viscous mud roll down the street. The current appears as an ocean, waves of burnt-red dirt streaming down the street toward another huge drain at the end of our cul-de-sac. There, a giant system transports the run off to a creek that winds around the freeway and eventually drops the rainwater into the ocean.

Finally, we clear a clean pathway to the street drain!

She's an elderly thin woman, and she exhales a dreary gasp. "I'll have to complain to the sales office again about this bad drain!" She gestures towards the model homes, to a quaint idyllic office where we signed away our lives when we brought our homes on this un-landscaped hilly site. Her look is forlorn. The large storm drain in front of her house has become "her property," unwanted by all the other neighbors who are waving to us with fearful expressions. They're the brave ones now, venturing out of their homes and risking their lives to the mud-rippling street as the storm begins to subside.

Just then, Drew pulls in the driveway with a smile on

his face. He should be smiling! I've cleared the driveway of all the red mud, for his tires' sake. Now, I'm drained, like the water *pit patting* in echoes down the storm drain. The dregs of mud lolling into "the system" sound like the last flow of water swirling down a sink.

"Whew—it's over," I say, picking up my broken shovel and waving goodbye to my fatigued elderly neighbor. The next time, we'll most likely have to do this again.

The good news is: several weeks later, we hired a contractor to install a draining system that soaks up all the water around our property and spits it into the street. Then came the sprinkler system, then the grass, and then a stone wall and fence around our backyard.

Rain. It's the same in Hawaii as where I am right now. And it'll be the same until the Earth dries up. I look for only one thing in all the rain … rainbows.

SPARKLE

While living in Hawaii and walking to my car after leaving work one November day, I stopped when I saw a wandering white dog with a splash of beige on her small ear. The little dog appeared agitated and a bit frightened. I called: "Come here! Come here!"

Wagging her puffy white tail, she ran right over to me. Instant friends.

I hadn't ever owned a pet dog before; and if I had, it woulda been a Papillion. This dog looked just like a Papillion, except a bit larger. Immediately, I felt a connection to "it." Hey, I had no idea if she was a girl or a boy! But my husband would know. He had once owned several dogs before we married, and had even trained them for dog-shows.

There was *one* problem with my new-found friend though: she had to be part of someone's family, somewhere. But I didn't want to call the pound, and I didn't want to just let her roam off and hope I'd find her again. The answer? Take her home, and tomorrow return with posters so I could staple them around the neighborhood and school, and hopefully locate her family, although I secretly wished that option would fail.

On the drive home, the more I had "it" the more I wanted to keep "it."

Arriving home late that afternoon, I surprised everyone. My daughter, Jennifer, immediately liked "it" and petted "it." My son, Andrew, ran from "it," and "it" barked at him at firs. But then "it" slowly allowed Andrew close up.

Then I had another problem: when does "it" eat? Off to the store to buy "it" food! Roaming up and down the doggie aisle at Safeway, I finally saw a brand of food advertised on TV: Caesar's. I bought the chicken flavored variety, and a collar and leash. All the while, Jenny and Andrew were playing with "it" in the car. We all felt so happy.

"We have a dog!" they kept saying.

"Not so fast," I cautioned. "I have to type up a poster with a picture of "it" and display the photo around my workplace. If "it" is someone's pet, we need to return "it.""

"*Ahhhh*," I kept hearing, every time I said those dreadful words. But I always believed in Karma: what goes around comes around. If I'd keep something that doesn't belong to me, that's stealing; and someday, someone would do the same thing to me. No thanks!

That evening, my husband arrived home from work. I heard the garage door squeak closed. I was so excited! None of us told him about my find-of-the-day, so I wondered how "it" and "him" would get along.

The dog charged him! What a shock!

I thought "it" would like Drew. Nope, at least not right at that first meeting. Still, after a minute of "it" attacking, but then succumbing to Drew's nice talk and friendly pets, "it" melted alongside Drew after he fed "her" a thick piece of ham.

"Yes, she's a girl," he announced as she gobbled her Caesar's food right down, becoming friends-for-life with Drew. "I think she's about a year-and-a-half old."

The next day, I put up several posters around that neighborhood, and I even went door-to-door looking for the owner. I had no luck finding her family. Had they just dropped her off in a residential neighborhood, hoping the little half-terrier-half-Papillion would find a new family? That's what some people hinted had happened, and workers at the dog pound also told me that no one had phoned in reporting a lost dog fitting "her" description.

Two days later, I named her Sparkle.

Through the years, everyone's called her Sparky, but between her and me … she's my Sparkle. Now, she's about ninety dog-years-old, and she sleeps most times. Every moment with her, I cherish. We might not have her at all one day soon.

Packing Up

Remember the game, *Don't Break the Ice?* How about *Don't Let the Blocks Drop?* The goal of both games is to keep the objects in place as long as possible. Just pack the ice cubes and blocks as tightly together as you can, then knock out ice cubes or pull out blocks one by one without breaking the entire ice deck or knocking over the tower.

Packing up to move from Texas to Florida was about the same experience as compacting those ice cube and blocks. But instead of dealing with unbreakable objects, I was grappling with the question of how to protect all my items in just the right way so as to arrive in Florida, unpack them, and experience relief that they had arrived in one piece. Not an easy task.

I used every hand towel, blanket, pillow, bedspread, mattress pad, and reusable grocery bag I had to cushion all my fragile items. There's the grandfather clock I bought in Munich, the soup tureen I bought in London, and my Depression era glass collection. Then I needed to tape them with special tape—double taping them. All glass pictures, delicate accessories, and knick knacks need triple protection, and to be supported in just the right position among other shielded objects in special boxes.

Oh, and the availability of boxes! Shopping for just the right one is like going to a candy store but leaving without the sugar. There are all sorts of boxes in many sizes and shapes! I found at a shop called ExoBox in Austin, Texas. Then I had to purchase Styrofoam, bubble wrap, box tape, and sheaths of wrapping and packaging paper. A few things we needed right away and couldn't store. UPS packed those things for us, but at a cost. How did all my objects, some priceless, weather the move?

I read the story of Moses several times—studying his historic journey and all the trials and tribulations those people experienced.

After signing closing papers and while on the trek to Florida, my husband and I kept looking at houses over the internet. We had seen a few that we believed we could make into a home, but we were traveling to Florida blind. We didn't have a home anymore, and our special needs son was also experiencing the backlash of moving, after saying goodbye to his friends.

Moses endured all sorts of hardships; and I know I can't compare my circumstances to a journey through the Negev. However, I felt like Moses and his lost people as we wound our way through New Orleans and the Florida panhandle, heading east, staring at maps, watching for signs, often traveling by way of ocean. Where would this all end? How is this going to all end? I remember whispering to my husband, many times.

All we knew is that our lender told us we could secure a home loan if we bought a house in Florida. So, every day we kept waking up, eating breakfast, and driving. Every early morning I kept saying like a parrot: "Florida or bust! Melbourne here we come!"

At times, life is a series of putting one foot in front of the other, and just walking. After exiting at Palm Bay Road, finding our temporary apartment, sighing in relief, and thanking God that we arrived safely in Melbourne; the next day, we found that perfect place for us and put down a deposit on our home.

Then we waited … for the closing. Our first night in our new home, we slept in beds on the floor and had a few cooking utensils. Thank goodness for McDonalds! Then we waited with bated breath for the movers.

Would our things arrive in one piece? I kept ruminating on those precious things that I just couldn't stand to see broken!

Most of what I had packed in Texas arrived to our new home without breaking. Some things were stolen out of a suitcase, one being a coin collection I had since I was ten. In all the rushing, I forgot to put a lock on the suitcase. Bad mistake. Never again!

Then again, I hope I never have to move, because I love Melbourne, and my family and I fit right into our neighborhood as if we'd lived here all our lives.

Rat Lady

I woke up this morning, opened the door to get the paper, but discovered a dead rat on my screened-in front porch. I jumped back and the air left my chest! I called my husband Don for help, but then I spotted a jagged white piece of paper under the rat. After running to the garage and getting the broom so I could move the dead rat off the paper, I quickly poked and prodded it out of a cloud of feeding gnats and read the oily words on the note: *Keep yer rodents in yer own back yard!*

I showed startled Don the note. He grimaced, scratching his early morning stubble. "Who'd do such a thing?" he asked, sweeping up the dead rat into our blue dust pan and then holding it outstretched way in front of him as if it might be emitting the Ebola virus. He opened the garage door, rolled out the can, and then dumped the carcass. The dead rat wasn't releasing a smell, yet, but trash collection wasn't until tomorrow.

If one of the neighbors was angry about something now, surely tonight might be much worse, and a pungent odor inflaming his or her anger. Luckily, Don seemed to be thinking my same thoughts, sprayed a coating of Febreze over the long plump oily beast, and then covered it with a black plastic lawn bag.

Peering out the screen door, I looked to my left. "I don't know who did this," I replied, feeling sad and so puzzled. "Whatever have *we* done? We don't have rats as pets!"

After donning gloves, he picked up the note at the corner while holding it far away from our line of sight. "We've done nothing, see? This says: *keep your rodents in your own back yard.* Someone caught the thing and believes it's our fault for their infestation. Huh! Nuts!"

I huffed and craned my neck farther out the screen door. "But how are *we* supposed to do keep rodents out of someone else's yard?" I felt a bit panicked...and scared. What else might happen in the future? Will the "rat dumping" get worse?

"I don't know," he replied, "and I don't wanna find out! I'll just call the cops if it happens again and file a report." He appeared scared as he whispered: "You know people these days ... they can be crazy and pull a shotgun on ya if ya piss someone off. So let's forget about it." He walked inside. "I'm making coffee ... come on."

"No, Don!" I was never the type to take well to people disliking me. "You make coffee. I'll be inside in a minute." Now I felt like spying. I had to do something!

"Fay! Just forget it! Whoever did that is obviously nuts...and you could make him or her worse if you investigate. Just let it go. The cops 'll handle it if it happens again." Don was buttering toast ... I could smell the breakfast starters. "Don't say I didn't warn ya, Fay."

"Right, right," I whispered, still peeking out the door to my neighbor on the left. I knew the neighbors on our right, Cindy and Dave; but neither Don nor I had never seen met the neighbors on living left of us. As a matter of fact, come to think of it, I've always called them "the neighbors on the left," vowing I'd one day walk over there with some type of goodie in hand and introduce myself. That's so unlike me though!

Then I remembered when we moved in. I saw someone shut the blinds as if the person might be expecting a hurricane! We bought the house three months ago, but no one we had introduced ourselves to had ever said anything about those neighbors on out left, and I'd never asked anyone about them either. Who did live there?

At nights, the house was always dark, except for a little light shining out of a slit in the back window curtains. Once, I peeked over the fence. Curiosity trumped my interest! I never thought I was a snoop, but that one evening I just couldn't help myself. It was so quiet, dark, eerie spooky with all those backyard trees drooping like ghosts, and there was a full moon. What was I thinking? Expecting a werewolf or a vampire to run out of the block house and bite me? Naaaw, I was just inquisitive … like I'm feeling now.

Sneaking into the kitchen so Don wouldn't stop me and ask me what I was about to do, I grabbed a loaf of banana bread I bought last night at Bob Evan's. People like that sort of gourmet treat, right? Surely "the person" on my left would be happy to slice off a piece and eat some while we could exchange cordial greetings of "so nice to meet you finally," or "if you ever need some sugar or an egg, I'm next door." Strangers like that sort of friendly offering, right?

Tiptoeing next door, I passed a little smiling gnome that had a crack in its hat like someone had kicked in anger. Then there was the dead bush that appeared poisoned, then the rake I tripped over…tumbling onto the neighbor's steps. "Ahhh," I shouted, picking myself up. My left knee was scratched and bleeding.

"Whatchya doin' out there?" a gruff voice called. It didn't sound like a man's voice or a woman's voice, but I smelled cigarette smoke, burned toast and strong coffee.

I cleared my throat—my knee stinging. I could feel blood rolling down my shin. "Hi, my name is Fay Stevens, and I moved in—"

"Whatchya want!"

I swallowed hard, my tongue dry on the roof of my mouth. "Like—like I said, my name is Fay, and I live next door, and I—" I saw a toppled fern in a planter, and quickly dashed over to lift it up. "Well, I saw this messed up plant, and I thought I'd be neighborly and pick it up for you...." I still couldn't see a face, only a shadow—an outline about as tall as myself. You ever read the book *To Kill A Mockingbird?* This is a real-life Boo Radley scenario. "Do you mind if I pick this up for you?" Not taking my eye off the cracked open door, I gently and slowly picked up the toppled plant and set it straight up next to the driveway with hair line cracks and in-grown weeds.

After a low grunt, the neighbor replied, "Sure ... ya go right on ahead, and then leave."

"Wait!" I breathed. I had to try and make a connection with this obviously disturbed individual. Still, I recalled what Don had warned: some people are just plain nuts, you can't trust neighbors like you used to, and you could end up regretting helping someone when the person turns on you.

"Whataya want," the gruff voice boomed.

"Did I do something to make you angry? 'Cause if I did, I'd like to say I'm sorry." I held out the half-squished banana bread. As if I might get eaten while still trying to be friendly, I added, "Here, I brought this over for you. I thought you might like it." I laughed a bit and rubbed my chin all the while feeling trickling cold blood from my knee roll down my shin. "Consider this an ice breaker ... just trying to be neighborly. I'm the neighbor on your right."

The door quickly opened, and a hand with age spots and yellow-stained fingernails grabbed the bread. The screen door slammed shut like a lightning clap.

I jumped back. I thought I'd take a chance at bringing up the dead rat. "I'll work harder to make sure rats stay out of your yard." That sounded a bit too accusatory! I stepped back a bit further, almost knocking down another weathered and bleached gnome.

I heard a growl—a human grunt. A woman's voice. "Ma'am?"

"*Aww*/righty," she replied. I heard the cellophane wrapper around the banana bread crinkle, followed by munching noises of someone old, perhaps wearing dentures, and who hadn't eaten in weeks.

"And if you ever need me, I'm next door...like I said, my name is Fay." I stepped back through her circular walkway, nearly tripping on a dislodged stone pavement and disjointed black edging. Someone was mowing the lawn, but not doing any type of repair, trimming or edging. I hadn't ever even heard a lawnmower! She had to be cutting her lawn sometime during the nights.

The screen door clapped shut, followed by the worn wooden storm door. Looking around, I felt a warm breeze waft over me and noticed a hedge of skeleton rose bushes. All the flowers were dead, their round rose hips dotted with white fungus and brown insect bites. She was inside, probably just about as withered and worn out as everything on the outside!

I walked home, looking forward to spending the day with Don, drinking morning coffee, reading the paper, and not once complaining about anything.

THERE'S NO FIGHTING
A HURRICANE

I baked a cake for the church party my family is supposed to attend, but the darn little Florida ants meandered into it while it cooled overnight on the counter. I had to dump all my hard work in the trash.

The party's in three hours! What do I do?

Buy one at Super Walmart ... *that's* the solution.

So we show up at "Sue" and "Martin's" party they're giving for their teen group from church. Our son is in the group, and he's nervous as a jumping bean to make sure we arrive on time, have the sodas cold, and have his swim suit and towel. Having arrived in Florida under a year, we're just new to "the church." Let me tell you, it's so hard fitting in and making friends with people who've known one another for twenty-years-plus! The close friendships they share are awesome. They've long ago moved past the awkward stages of: "how do I look," "mind my manners just right," "don't talk too much," and "don't talk politics."

I'm trying to fit in, without which luck. Ever been there? My nickname should be "Tryin".

Sue and Martin are "the perfect people." They married young, have been in Bible studies with other church members for years, and get along with all the parents in the teen group as if they all met in high school. That's great ... wonderful ... fantastic! I can only sit—twirling my fingers, making light conversation, and watch their closeness. They've obviously all been talking on the phone, or via email, 'cause they know what one another's been up to over the last week let alone ten years. They could shoe share, and clothes swap, no problem.

While the adults are chit-chatting in the kitchen, the kids are swimming, and the TV is playing a sweet Disney movie. I feel like an ant on a high wire, watching share stories, and make themselves at home. My arms feel like rubber, my throat is dry from tenseness, and my eyes feel about ready to tear like Niagara Falls.

What the heck's wrong with you? Snap out of it! I keep telling myself. Doesn't work. I offer to help in the kitchen. Hey, I'm trying, right? I can only do what I've always been told to do: be polite, offer to help, talk about light topics, compliment people, listen, and just be yourself.

Be myself? Yikes.

When I'm sitting alone after I've done all of the above, a bad haunting memory hits me, and I'm drawn into it like a Category-5 hurricane....

"Joycie!" mom calls. "Get in here right now!"

I'm eleven. I'm dressed in a pink dress with a little bow at the neck. I'm waiting for everyone to leave for church. "Coming!" I stand up from watching *Sunday Morning* with Charles Kuralt. The artificial sun is blaring on his introductory page and a light music is playing. When I arrive in the back bedroom, I see the baby crib against the wall and my tiny baby sister lying in it—her legs bicycling in the air.

"Didn't you change the baby?" she her black eyes piercing in anger.

I feel my breath leave my chest and I pee my pants. "No, I didn't know—"

She launches at me. *Smack!*

That back hand of her hurts like hell on my cheek.

"Now get over there and change Fanny!"

"But you never said—"

Smack!

I think my face is beet red as she pushes me against the wall.

Smack! Whack!

Just do what she says, I think, but the room's spinning by the time she's unleashed all her fury. Quickly through shaking fingers and blurry eyes, I change Fanny—again peeing in my pants.

But *I* can't change! They're all leaving for church, and calling mom and me to get into the station wagon. All the way there, I feel burning on my legs...and smell the urine that's fomenting like yeast on my pink dress. It has to be showing behind me like a big stop sign! No one notices...until I arrive in church, and my classmates see me before mass, and confront me like it's ring-around-the-rosy time in the entryway.

"Pink, you stink, Pink!"

I hear laughing, and, "Pee-yew, stink Pink—"

"Fink—"

"Pinkie Stinky...."

I wanna punch the you-know-what out of 'em all. Can't. Just stuff it down and try tuning them out.

My mother yanks me by the arm to our pew, and I sit down, feeling cold on my legs turn hot ... the urine smell wafting like skunk spray all around me. But no one notices. I have a half-brother on the right of me, and my little brother sitting on my left. The priest is praying us all in, and my mom's singing like a holy canary.

Where are the angels? God? And St. Peter? I wonder

I can't sing. My throat's burning, my eyes stinging, and I feel like a drill is carving out my insides, hollowing out the center of my body into a rag doll. Looking at my shaking brother who has sticks for arms and legs, I see he's about ready to pee in his pants too. "Just hold on…our dad 'll take us away someday. He will!" I whisper. Lost in his own fog, he nods.

The kid sitting in the pew across the aisle snickers, and I scowl at her. She's the popular one, and has all the friends. She's also the orchestra leader in my classroom, training everyone on how to perfect the *Stinkie Pinkie Stink Fink Pink Purple* chorus. Tomorrow's Monday, then there's Tuesday, then Thursday…. Death would be better. But my brother needs me.

Back in the present forty-five years later, I gasp, but decide to go on a walk with Sue and her teen group. She lives next to a garden, and I've always loved nature and the beautiful Florida habitat. Lunch is over, and my son appears happy for once. I've got to do my best to try to fit in, be helpful, and make friends, all the while praying to God to intervene and make it happen.

'Cause you know what I've learned?

In those moments when I feel no one is there, and I'm never going to have a friend in the world, I have God. I hold onto those words: "I'll never leave you or forsake you."

What else can a person do to fight a hurricane? Hold onto God until it passes.

COLONIZING MARS SIMPLIFIED

In the early 1900s, my grandparents emigrated from Hungary to America. I can just imagine their long voyage—from leaving a familiar home, to arriving at a strange world with a serious Statue of Liberty to greet them. I'm sure they felt frightened, but also excited! The door to their home had closed behind them at the Pacific Ocean, yet horizons opened in the form of opportunities.

At first sight of the Statue of Liberty, they must had shouted with joy and exhilaration, and most likely trying their best with the broken English they were working so hard to master so they could blend in, make friends, and succeed on their new entry-level jobs. They were sixteen—really kids compared to today's generation— when they left the safety of their homes, with dreams and goals. They also had to have certain elements in place before embarking on that long arduous steamship voyage to the United States. Colonizing Mars basically entails the same process and applying the same principles.

I remember my grandmother telling me, "I had to have a sponsor and a job waiting for me before I arrived in the United States."

My grandpa said, "And I had to be healthy … or the inspector at the terminal wouldn't let me step on American soil."

A sponsor, a job, a place to live, a bill of health, and some cash-in-hand were initial consideration for making their long trip from Hungary, through Germany, and then across the Atlantic. She and my grandfather planned and created backup plans prior to leaving their Hungarian homes. My grandfather had his brother Joseph in New York City. He would room with him, and Joseph procured a job for my grandfather as a copper wire cleaner in a factory. My grandmother had a sister in Jersey City who procured her a job as a governess. They took care of their health, had a calculated strategy in place, and practiced as if they were training for a battle prior to leaving the comfort of their homes, friends, churches, and culture. I'm sure they also had questions: "What's the food going to be like? The clothes? What about stores and shopping?"

They conducted research, sought out mentors, and spoke with people who had settled in America and returned to Hungary to visit. Those people were like traveling story tellers, beacons of possibility to curious Europeans grappling with whether to leave the "Old World" to venture out into the unknown.

Will life be better there than here?" I'm sure they asked themselves.

And, another question: *Can I really survive there?*

Applying this same principle to colonizing Mars, future settlers of the red planet have former astronauts who are current story tellers with vast experiences at their disposal to encourage and help train future astronauts for the 35.8 million mile journey to Mars, at our closest point on July 27, 2018. Those colonists I'm sure are asking themselves that great question while combing their hair in the mirror: Am I the type of person who can leave Earth for years and survive on a world void of flowing water, a magnetic field, Earth-type gravity, bright sunshine, greenery, and fresh spring-time air? The night sky of Mars will be awesome to see, but aren't those the he ultimate questions? Are we built—genetically and environmentally—to handle that Martian terrain for perhaps decades without going nuts or dying out? There is an example of either poor planning or poor location: the Lost Colony of Roanoke, Virginia.

To prepare to colonize Mars, we need to enact the same plan, and backup plans, and even triple contingency plans, because we're sending people to settle Mars, to remain there, and make a small section (in the beginning) home.

What are some preliminary steps we need to have in place before the first people launch to Mars? When my grandparents arrived here, they had luggage. They studied the places they were going to live like a thoughtful tourist creating a step-by-step trip. The process was meticulous, and detailed. They looked for areas where they might have weakness as well as strengths, and they buffered up, muscled up, and prepared mentally and emotionally for the journey across the Atlantic—at that time, the grant expanse. They also had a place waiting for them in the United States, albeit their rooms were extremely small.

On Mars, at first, rooms most likely will be small in accommodations as well! However, ancient cultures survived in cliff dwelling structures, for example, the Manitou Cliff Dwellings in Colorado. Preparing for Martian touchdown, prospective astronauts are training underwater and in conditions replicating the Martian terrain. What also helped my grandparents were the friends they made here after they arrived, and the relationships they fostered in the New World prior to leaving Hungary. They socialized with people who knew Hungarian and English. They had a cultural connection with people who could empathize with their experiences and with whom they could congregate after working hours. My grandparents met at a Hungarian dance in Jersey City, and marriage shortly thereafter.

Odds of survival increase with numbers. Social support, cultural connections, and rest-and-relaxation (entertainment) are positively correlated with living longer and happier lives, studies show. Laughter and group support during sorrowful times will be needed when things might go wrong, or mistakes made. There's a saying: what can go wrong will go wrong. And another saying: The best laid plans of mice and men often go awry. Robert Burns was wise!

But let's not be tricked by pessimism that's perhaps igniting peoples' fears. Colonizing Mars is not a suicide mission, but a goal to attain the possible. The need to explore and discover is in our bones—a hallmark of humanity. On Mars, settlers will need community-based encouragement and survival techniques, as my grandparents once had in place in this expansive, strange alien world they began calling their new home. Step-by-step, they began memorizing the terrain, following a schedule, and seeking out support.

What might this same plan look like as we set our sights on colonizing Mars? Our luggage will be supplies: everything from oxygen, food, tools, living sections (perhaps strong domes), clothes, machines (for drilling and excavating), recycling equipment, technology to recycle waste, to a pet and vegetation (greenery). Creating an extensity water supply, oxygen supply, and food supply are priority! When my grandparents finally bought a farm in Hannah, Indiana, I remember the giant white shed my grandpa and dad built to store the tractor, and the chicken shack my grandma used to house the hens and roosters beyond my little red swing set next to the pine tree wind break.

Going to Mars, we'll need more than forks, knives and spoons … and a little measly tool chest. And the first colonists will have to be survivalists, and a jack-of-all-trades. I remember Abraham Maslow's Hierarchy of

Needs formula. We'll need to consider so many crucial and critical elements as we plan our vault through space to Mars—and accomplish our dream. Neil Armstrong said: "One small step for man, one giant leap for mankind." Well, Neil, women will be stepping on Mars this time.

Thanks Neil and Buzz.

Final Science-Fiction Short Story
(For Now)

The Rip

Peering into the isolated reaches of space, astronomers have discovered 18 planet-like objects far from any sustaining star, where no planets should be. The stars are not alone....

As the final dregs of suspension coating slipped off his torso and soaked into his hibernation pod, Kent Johnson felt the surge of new life race to his limbs. He ran his hands over his chest and heaved in a long draft of oxygen. "Yes, I survived stasis!" He sat up, the dizziness spinning his senses.

"I made it through trillions of miles of space, without communicating with anyone, without my chips and beer, and one virtual game of football." He patted his cheeks, wiped the lingering sleep from his eyes, unfastened his shoulder straps, and regained his focus when he spotted a bright hologram projecting a planet at the center of their U-shaped cockpit. The date and time was yellow blank. "What?! No calendar and timetable?" He had an antique watch under his command chair. After slipping it out of the pocket, he saw the last date and time. "We left Mars June 2, 2665, at 4 p.m., Coordinated Mars Time. You can't tell me the time and date now, Am?" Am was their A.I. quantum-system running, *Amelia*, their starship.

"Not without retracing this starship's flight, Kent," Am replied, appearing in holographic form in front of the celestial image. Before they left Mars, he had programmed her as an Aztec manifestation, a reminder of his own ancestral roots.

"What gives? Why can't you retrace our steps here?" He slipped his watch delicately back into its special location.

"I am activating a tracker right now, Kent," Am replied. "But an unknown blend of forces is interfering with space-time in this location."

"Huh!" he said, drinking out of a bottle of water that popped out the food port beneath their cockpit. "Well, figure out where Earth is please, and then connect the dots through all the space-fold conduits ending here. That should do." He gestured in frustration at the black world with the choppy surface rotating fifty thousand miles beneath them. "I don't see a star, Am." He squinted into the distance while enlarging black space. "Or a solar system ... or galaxy!"

"There is no star for this rogue world, Kent," she said.

"What?" Confusion spread through him, the dizziness he'd just recovered from. "If there's no star, then there's no life, Am."

"The ship detected a signal, Kent, and thereafter I assessed the frequencies as intelligent." Her calming presence always projected self-assuredness with all the base facts and interpretations coursing through her quantum-computing.

He didn't doubt her analysis, and he joined her side to peruse the odd planet drifting through the universe. He scratched his stubble. "Okay, Am, tell me what you heard emanating from this rogue world."

She activated another hologram depicting a communications instrument. "Two days ago, we received a whine." She increased the volume.

"Ouch!" He covered his ears.

"Sorry, Kent, but I needed to show you the pattern because I have directions to exit space-fold flight, and awaken you and Lisa in the event I encounter either an exoplanet, or an alien presence," she said.

As more whining resounded, followed by Am's

assessment of the pattern, he glanced at Lisa Simmons, his Co-commander, still basking in suspended sleep.

Wake her? Let her be?

He needed more facts before decided whether to resuscitate her. If this drop into real-time wasn't important, she'd just have to return to stasis, the process taking a few days to fully engage, and that would be a few days of aging for her, one of the reasons she signed on for deep-space mission voyages with Mission Mars.

"That noise is coming from *that* planet?" he asked, enlarging images of the black world that appeared charred and frozen. "It looks completely dead ... like it encountered a weapon's burst, or something took a bite out of it."

An entire portion of the planet appeared chomped. Yet in spots, a faint steam was lifting off the surface. An atmospheric condition being kissed by some celestial angel?

"Okay, Am," he began. "Discover our location, and give me a date and time." He walked behind his stasis pod to change out of his lose-fitting biometric suit into his standard blue-and-black uniform. "Looks like I gotta revive Lisa!"

He was a commander, and he had a mission to accomplish and tasks to perform. But he didn't have to do them all alone. He had Lisa Simmons, his co-commander along with him. After checking her vitals that their AI starship was depicting as normal readings for a deep stasis slumber, he peered into her face, glistening with stem-cell suspension. "Time to get up, Lisa," he whispered through her artificial atmosphere and stem cell mixtures thin over her hibernating body. "We have *work* to do." He initiated her resuscitation code. "Simmons, 09212065." It was her birthdate, and also the day ten years ago—in real time, not space-fold time—when she took command beside him on *Amelia*, their Lockheed-Martin/Boeing starship, constructed to space-fold through the cosmos in search of habitable exoplanets discovered by astronomers on Earth and Mars.

She'll be awake soon, he thought, and then we can find out the date, time, and location...I hope.

A red light flashed on his armchair indicator as several warning sounds blared through their cockpit.

"Are we under attack?" he asked.

When he leaned into a sleeping scanner, his eyes triggered a response, igniting several holographic displays throughout the cockpit.

"We are receiving no signs of life from the planet, Kent," she replied.

"Then what the hell is happening down there on that dead world?" He began pacing around the catastrophic images that could have been responsible for prematurely startling him and Simmons awake, and perhaps quashing their exploratory mission.

"Something powerful and destructive is out there, but we just can't see it," he told their super-computer AI, powering their starship. "Can't you home in on just one anomaly so we know what we're up against, Am?"

After a *drone* and *hiss*, she reappeared alongside the hologram of the planet. "I am assessing all radioactivity in this location, Kent, and I am picking up an anomaly, but the anomaly is over one-light-year from our ship."

He noticed a blue-shift frequency in the blackness of space...with a little white dot behind the frequency that appeared as a long line. "So this anomaly is heading straight here, right, Am?" He pushed back his sweat-soaked collar.

"Yes, Kent, the anomaly is distorting Space-Time, and

on a trajectory here."

He took a swig of water that an auto-food chute sent to him from below, and then he proceeded to walk around and peruse several holographic images showing possible results of Am's startling readings, including surface science instrumentals, gas chromatophraph reading, Doppler wind instruments, and spectral radiometric readings. Starship *Amelia* had hull sensors, spectrographs, detection instruments, communication equipment and particle collection devices—all at Kent and Lisa's command. He topped at several holographic images of danger. "The anomaly isn't a meteor, an asteroid, a comet, a black hole, or some type of weird gravitational expanse."

More holograms materialized in front of him like fireflies in the dark.

"Could the anomaly be an alien species?"

After another hiss and drone, Am rematerialized alongside him. "No, Kent, but then again, we're dealing with a light-year's distance." She disappeared and then reappeared next to the giant hologram of the rogue planet. Her South American look made her appear goddess-like in her alterable programming. He could change her, but he didn't want to confuse her with Lisa, who also had short dark-brown hair and an athletic physique. He glanced at her vitals beeping and displaying her heart rate and brain wave activity. Soon she'd be awake. *She'll have more insight into the anomaly and why we can't get a solid date and time stamp,* he thought.

"So, Am," he began as he paced around several confusing readings on the planet and the blue-shifting anomaly a light year away. "We *could* potentially be meeting and greeting an alien species soon, if what all these readings are indicating, right?"

"Yes, Kent." She had the planet's dense atmosphere deconstructing in the giant hologram and several instruments working on the hull to accumulate data on the planet's surface.

He sighed from his gut and glanced again at Lisa still heating up with her vitals steadily perking up—animating her back to consciousness. "Before I make a decision whether to leave, and while you back-track our course here, I want to figure out if this place is some type of Cosmic Wonder."

"Cosmic Wonder, Kent?" Am asked, her eyes glowing in the dissonance.

He laughed. "Yeah, like the Wonders of Nature, or the Seven Wonders of the World on Earth," he said.

"Oh yes, Kent, now I understand," she said, activating several holograms imaging famous landscapes on Earth, and Olympus Mons City on Mars. "I can't wait until Lisa wakes up hear her opinion on this situation."

"Me as well, Kent," Am said, walking around the columns of holograms projecting at the center of the cockpit.

He had another thought. "No one from Earth could be out there by that distant anomaly, causing this Space-Time distortion around us, right?"

Am activated her transmission history since Lisa and he had been in suspended sleep.

"No, Kent," she replied.

"And you didn't send a distress signal, right?"

"No, Kent," she said, showing him their last transmission, but with the date and time missing.

"Well, at least send Earth our location, and let them know our status," he said as she activated a com hologram with a beacon signal. Now he was broadcasting through a conduit to where he hoped scientists from

Earth and Mars would hear him. "We've stop to explore an unknown quad in space," he began. "We appeared out of space-fold flight when our AI, Am and our starship intercepted a patterned frequency." He gestured at the com link still playing the message, but on mute. "We're sending you what information we have on our location, a rogue world we've discovered, the weird frequency that Am is still in the process of translating, and a blue-shifted anomaly just over a light-year away from us...but heading towards us."

He turned to Am and gestured quickly at the date-time indicator. "When is the anomaly supposed to arrive here?"

Her eyes scrolled statistics and algorithms—comparing them with rate, time, and the x-factor of distance. She stopped and touched the distant bright-white nail-sized anomaly, still blue shifting with a long contrail in a deep field. "Four hours, twenty minutes, and thirty-two seconds, Kent," she replied.

"You've heard her," he said. "I'll transmit when Lisa Simmons and I find out more about our situation. Out." The com closed, and the beacon *beep*ed, *beep*ed as the space-fold quantum-communication line continued projecting in the direction from which they had traveled.

"I just wanna know what the hell gives here in this place, because what you're showing me inside all these holograms isn't at all what's affecting our starship." He plopped down in his command chair situated next to Beal's empty chair droning into activity as it prepared to accommodate her biometrics.

"I have every inside instrument and hull detector working on the solution, Kent," she replied.

He ground his teeth and drank more water. "Am, we're counting on you to inform us if there's is a threat out there, or something worth exploring on that planet that looks like a rotten black walnut."

"Yes, Kent. I am focusing on the light-year anomaly now, Kent. I detect a connection between it and this planet, Kent." She never took one breath.

He had programmed her to display her oppositional feelings by saying his name three times. "Okay, sorry, Am. It's just that you're the smartest AI Mission Mars NASA ever constructed. If *you* can't determine what's out there in space a light-year away, and approaching fast obviously, Lisa and I shouldn't even be attempt to explore the quadrant, but instead high-tail it outta here fast."

"I understand, Kent," she said returning to the giant hologram and inserting incoming results into from the hull and *Amelia*'s detection devices inside their starship.

He scratched the stubble on his chin, drank some more water, ordered up food, and began conducting an thorough analysis of everything from hull integrity to their inside environmental stats. Their equipment, machinery, robotics, and environmental integrity were fully functioning. Then his neural implant flashed him a memory. "Am, we *were* scheduled to encounter Ori-52 in the Sigma Orionis galaxy. Are we near the place?"

Am activated an image of the galaxy and exoplanet, swiping that hologram next to the one imagine the planet below them. Sigma Orionis was the last image he'd seen before Lisa and he had settled down into their stasis pods.

"I am attempting to get a current location, date and time, Kent."

"Oh my God," he huffed, "this situation we space-folded into ... or that *you* dropped us into, Am, is makin' me crazy! I gotta bad *feeling* ... that's all I can say ... a *really* bad feeling about this place." He glanced at Lisa, her vitals almost stable enough for her to gain consciousness. "Get up, 'cause heaven knows I need you, Lisa."

The dizziness of suspended sleep moved through his mind, turning his sense of logic into sudden confusion. He closed his eyes and whispered a little prayer.

Than the two holograms united at the center of their cockpit as a drone resounded in echoes like a drum beat. It extinguished all other holograms. "Kent, I have a comparison and one re-constructed composition."

"Finally!" He touched the interior of the hologram.

A powerful white line of energy magnified at the center.

The visual zapped the air out of his throat. "My God! I've never seen *anything* like this! The energy...or anomaly as you called it, Am, looks to be expanding ... and growing ... like a gulley full of intense lightning."

"There is oxygen at the core, Kent. I have that spectral signature," she said, her holographic form standing right next to him.

He closed his eyes. "Could this powerful energy, or force, be chomping up the universe?"

"I am still analyzing incoming data, Kent."

"Naw, this can't be!"

"A gravitational phenomenon is inhibiting me from compiling a concise composition, Kent," Am said appearing and disappearing in several locations around the giant hologram of the planet and the white-hot energy line in the distance. Her eyes continued scrolling elements and electromagnetic frequencies.

"This *has* to be all a dream." He breathed, and drank down an analgesic Am had ordered for him from the starship's food pod. "Maybe I'm just sleepwalking!" he said, stumbling back, feeling dizzy. "God, it feels like the universe is about to end."

When he opened his eyes and recovered his balance, he saw the white-hot line of powerful energy stretching as far as the eye could see, just over a light-year.

He repeated the words over in his mind: *What the heck could be capable of unleashing such energy? Where did it come from?*

"Where is the oxygenated gravity-infused phenomenon heading to, Kent? That's what I wanna to know," someone said. The voice wasn't Am's. Yawning, Lisa Simmons stepped off her suspension stage and removed her aspirator while outside their starship, a purple haze of dimensional flight exploded into a show of fine yellow sparks.

The surface of the planet below them was drastically beginning to change.

"Wow, what's going on out there that woke us up and is turning our hull into a Fourth of July party?" she joked facetiously.

A tall strong woman with short black hair and sharp features, Mars Mission NASA chose her as Kent Johnson's co-commander after she sidestepped a four-star general's instructions and defeated an entire army of terrorists in the Negev. Earth and Mars hailed her a hero. In return, she wanted space, and "to leave my past behind me," she said two months before launching from *Station II* orbiting Mars.

Kent tapped lights along a row of life-support panels. "Well, everything inside this starship indicates we're alive and okay. And I want to *keep* us alive, Am," he said in the AI's direction. "So keep analyzing that anomaly."

"Yes, Kent, and Hello, Commander Simmons," she said, appearing next to Lisa and then retreating back to her station alongside the giant hologram of the planet and distant anomaly.

"Hi, Am," Lisa replied, her short dark-brown hair cresting around her face. She pushed her hands through her bangs, and her cheeks flushed with reviving air. Then she blew a huge breath of air out of her puckering lips. "Kent, all I ask right now is that ya let me wake up a little first, okay?"

"You got it, Lisa, but I'm sure happy to see you on deck," he said, chuckling in relief.

Shaking her muscular arms like a swimmer infusing them with energy before a race, she licked her dry lips and pressed her fingertips into her shiny curved forehead. "Ya got a caffeine tab?" She punched the food-pod dispenser, taking her order. "I need an adrenaline boost … and food, now." She looked around her command chair and began searching the crevices of the biometrically activated seat, all lined with lights, waiting for her special touch. "Isn't there *anything* I can get in my hands and swig down right now so I can wake up and help ya make sense of this wacky place?"

"I've got something that's gonna knock your slumber slippers off," he said, tall and proud.

"What's that?" she asked, rubbing her eyes while he grabbed her elbow and guided her to the giant hologram displaying the vibrant glowing anomaly at the center of their cockpit. "*This* thing's out there…and a planet is below us. But this…I don't *what* it is yet, is a light-year-long energy source unlike *anything* Am can deconstruct and recognize."

She grabbed some water and took a gulp. Then she joined him right up close to all the stats, data, and holograms projecting the world below them and the phenomenon in the great expanse of space. "Could it be a singularity from a black hole?"

"No, Lisa, it has a containment field," Am replied.

"So something or someone's controlling it then," Lisa said.

"I'd like to know from where though," Kent interrupted, "'cause we haven't picked up readings of any giant craft, which surely we should be seeing by now considering the length and breadth of that energy stream."

Lisa dashed back to her command chair. Obviously she had some foresight into a way to dismantle the anomaly's rudimentary parts. "Well, let's see if we can help Am figure out that lightning bed's composition."

"I'd sure like that, Lisa ... and so will everyone on Earth if we can disseminate the anomaly into its constituents." He gestured to the time that had activated when Am woke him up: 00:56:05. "We better work fast though. Soon, we're gonna have to decide if that thing's a threat, whether we're equipped to fight it, or whether we should just leave."

"Or whether we *need* to fight it ... but just explore this place for a while," Lisa added, gesturing inquisitively at the changing planet below that now appeared to burst with rays of light from its surface.

"I don't know," Kent said, still pulling apart data results inside the powerful hologram at the center of their cockpit. Every now-and-then, he'd home in on the white-hot line of energetic forces way off in the distance. Slowly, by the minute, it was drifting closer. "If it would be something like a black hole, I'd say it's a thief in our universe. But that energy band looks like it's swallowing *up* the universe. I think it needs to be diffused!"

"A challenge, Kent," Am said, her eyes still scrolling algorithms, elemental codes, and frequencies. Even their starship was engaged in the search for answers, always humming, hissing, and droning as if experiencing growing pains in the attempt to make sense of the anomaly and the changing planet.

"I'm working to find answers to all these big problems as well," Lisa said, eating a food bar that the auto-pod snapped up into her hand. All the while, her green eyes were fixing wildly on the tracking instruments over her command chair. "One thing's for sure, Kent, that energy band is *definitely* on a steady trajectory toward us...and in the past five minutes it's traveled ten thousand miles."

"Commanders," Am suddenly intervened, her holographic form stepping between their command chairs, "I have located an approaching object, orbiting five-thousand miles over the planet."

"What kind of an object?" Kent asked.

"Probe-like in appearance, Kent, but with a field surrounding it, thus not permitting us to penetrate its structure and determine the craft's composition and purpose," Am replied. "The object is maintaining the exact speed as our Stealth 484 starship...and heading in our direction."

Lisa straightened up and glared at Am. "I am receiving titanium signatures, Kent, but nothing carbon based surrounding the object, signifying life forms."

"Commanders," Am suddenly interrupted. "The planet under us is Ori-52."

"That can't be!" Lisa cried, enlarging the giant hologram in front of them. "Where's the rest of the solar system? What about the entire galaxy of Sigma Orionis?" She sat down breathless, and activated maximum hull protection.

"Well if Am says the object is Ori-52, it's gotta be Ori-52, Lisa." He exhaled, trying to decide the next course of action.

"But way our here? How?! And all alone? A *genuine* rogue?!" She gasped for air, but then grabbed the armrests on her chair, obviously the maneuver helping her to cope with her emotions.

"Ori-52 is a rogue planet, Lisa, thrown many millions of years ago out of orbit with its solar system and galaxy," Am said.

Kent raised his hands in an attempt to calm Lisa *and* Am. "Okay, let's recap." He stood up from his command chair and began pacing around the giant hologram of the distant bright-white band of energy, Ori-52, and the alien object orbiting the planet. His titan frame was a muscular reflection in the hologram as he perused several energy signals, with the most disturbing frequency, *unknown*, blaring red. "We have this force about a light-year away that we can't analyze…and a changing planet, and an object that's *orbiting* the planet and will be under us in … how long, Am?"

"Five minutes and twenty-two seconds, Kent," she replied.

He rubbed his eyes, his long nose crinkling in the frustration, but also intrigue. "No one's ever brought back to Mars or Earth solid proof of alien life."

"For sure," Lisa said.

"So this *could* be *our* chance to do just that…and to encounter a *new* phenomenon that might help humanity understand the universe," he added.

"But we also have to stay safe and keep alive, right, Am?" Lisa asked.

"Yes, Lisa," Am replied, the AI's eyes reflecting algorithmic code while also processing with the starship.

"So you just let us know if we're encountering any harmful levels of radioactivity, or if you glean any threat so we can space-fold the hell outta here if necessary, okay?"

"Yes, Kent," Am replied.

"We can't risk our lives," he added, "and we can always live another day to assume another mission."

Lisa had activated a communications hologram, and a green line appeared as their starship began backtracking their space-fold flight. "I'm sending an emergency transmission to Earth, Kent. I'm also using a five-tiered dimensional portal to make sure an alien species can't block or intercept our message."

"Good idea, 'cause we have no idea if Ori-52 is specie free."

The hologram of the outside cosmos showed their approach to a shiny orb twice *Amelia*'s size.

"Is it a pod?" he asked.

"It looks like a giant yellow pool ball," Lisa said, igniting *Amelia*'s laser-weapon matrix.

Kent tossed a hologram that collided with her program, extinguishing it. "Not yet, Lisa. If aliens *are* existing on this rogue planet somewhere, or the orbiting pod under us, we don't want to give away our technological capabilities."

"I know, Kent, I was just activating them, not using them, gee!" she huffed in agitation.

He gestured an apology to her and sighed. "Let's figure out a way to communicate with them first. Then we can evaluate this entire situation and make a plan on how to proceed."

"You know what they say about plans … they always go wrong," she whispered with skepticism. Her eyes warmed with the dregs of yellow-orange particles, the residual effects of the hull recovering from *Amelia*'s space-folding journey.

Then their starship flew over an obscured side of Ori-

52.

Lisa gasped and zoomed in on the surface.

"What the heck happened down there?!" he asked.

Lisa had powerlessness and fear lining on her smooth rosy cheeks. "This rogue planet looks sawed in half! What could have done such a thing?! Am, what's your assessment?"

"Carbon, nitrogen, oxygen, and gold are the composites of Ori-52, Lisa," their yellow-glowing A.I. replied.

Kent finally managed to create an entire hologram in the scope of the rogue world. "You ever see that old movie, *Star Wars*?

"Oh, yes," Lisa replied, leaning in to discern incoming readings of Ori-52.

"This place looks like that Death Star in the movie," he said, a shot of fear rippling through him.

"Yep it sure does, Kent, and that Death Star was a killing machine if I'm not mistaken," she said with a cold chilliness in her voice. "I hope that's not what we're dealing with here on Ori-52!"

Their starship began a fast descent to the black-top shiny surface. From afar, Ori-52 was emitting elements comparable to those on Earth, with a warm iron core, but a hostile cold atmosphere of 170° below zero. The closer their approach to the planet, the more jagged and frosty the terrain appeared, even spindly in small sections. Am was showing them a few petrified forests...and a glistening blue island with a composition of undulating sand.

"But the entire planet appears covered in a fog, Kent...water vapor obviously, but Am is receiving low levels of oxygen and hydrogen that can't possibility be enough to generate this type of fog ... so dense ... like clam chowder soup."

"Except for the glow," he said.

"It's like bright lights are shining under it all...so weird!" She showed him surface readings—microwave and mass spectrometry results.

"I have examined the movie you mentioned, commanders," Am began, "and the planet beneath us is *not* a Death Star."

"Whew, that's good to know at least," Lisa gasped and plopped down in her chair. "Still, look at the dimensions of this rogue planet. It definitely resembles a world that once had a thriving civilization. I'm betting we meet aliens."

Kent's mind went suddenly blank, but he fought off the glitch in his neural implant that was nearly rendering him immobile. Their starship had always directly transmitted special signals to act as analgesics or adrenaline to help them maintain emotional stability. His felt way off now. "Ouch!"

"Kent, what's wrong? You look like you saw a zombie!" Lisa said, suddenly bending down in pain herself.

"Darn— neural implant is— flitching, I think," he grimaced.

"The interference from the *unknown* particle permeating *Amelia* at neutrino-level intensity could have that effect on the human brain, Commanders," Am said, showing them their biometrics, and in particular, their encephalograms. "There is a slight irregularity in your cerebral cortices, Commanders."

"That's just great ... all we need right now," Lisa stomped. "Our neural implants are starting to put us on pins-and-needles one moment and the next moment rendering us agitated. We're gonna be emotional wrecks if this keeps up, Am, so do something." She glanced at her shaking hands, and inhaled deep gulps of air.

"Modifying the dispensing of neural chemicals to a lower level, Commanders," Am said, as a fiber-optic ceiling strand hummed in compliance—the *Amelia*'s interface with Am.

Dabbing off a bit of sweat, he then touched Lisa's hand. "You're not alone in this, Lisa," he said. And when he felt a calmness waft through chest, relieving his anxiety, he exhaled in relief. "That's better!"

"Yes, better for now, but I don't like our situation, Kent," she said with a foreboding expression on her face. "Everything's moving out of sync, and us along with the confusion and uncertainty. You sure we shouldn't reconsider what we're doing, and just leave?"

Suddenly, *Amelia* encountered an atmospheric pocket of disturbance, and their cockpit rattled as *Amelia* fledged left. They had every hull monitor activated, transmitting in their cockpit all the incoming visuals.

He pointed at two holograms with their descent statistics going haywire. "Am, stabilize our speed. We're descending too fast! This rogue's environment is so varied, and its gravitational forces differ in spots." Lunging into his cockpit chair, he peered out a small portal to the frothy atmosphere—red-black, chaotic whipping clouds mixed with white currents of air like the River Styx. "Five hundred miles until surface contact. Lisa. Strap in!"

After following his order, she grimaced at the black-red rogue world enlarging beneath them outside their window. "What do you think we'll find down there, Kent?"

He wished he could tell her something positive, something encouraging. He had always been good at keeping up morale, but this time, there were *two* unknown forces to contend with, both potentially hostile and deadly. This rogue planet, and an even more vicious force in the universe, that bright-white hot zone half-a-light year away from them, and closing. They need to make sure they were always making the right decisions, and the pressure to do just that began weighting him down like the mighty gravity of Ori-52 volleying *Amelia* around a bit in its volatile atmosphere.

"Kent, what do you think we'll find on the surface, based on Am's results on the composition?" she asked again, turning to decipher the statistics. "Five thousand miles to surface contact."

Lights over their command chairs flared every warning signal; monitors on the walls were scrolling stats out of control. Some were stabilizing, some continued warning them—*unknown, unknown, unknown....*

"I'm uncertain, Lisa, but scientists from Earth might have answers. Did you send that message?"

"I sure did" she said, her face red in her every breath. "But it'll take ten days for us to receive a reply."

"Ten days?"

She gestured at the off-kilter space-fold clock not measuring time in the familiar way. A time bar on the central hologram platform flashed a new date.

"That's June 25, 2995, Kent."

"No way!"

"Yes, Kent, 2995," she said firmly, wiping sweat off her forehead.

"But we launched from Mars in June of 2665!"

After a pause of shock, she said, "Kent, we don't really know the date and time, and Am doesn't either obviously because we're lost ... and stuck."

When he tried confirming the date, time, and their

location; everything around that Time bar turned bright red, shakes higher than the frothing red-black clouds between them and the alien world. Then he glanced at the indicator panel at the front end of cockpit. The pod they had seen just minutes before in another orbital position was now approaching them.

Lisa turned away from a blinding flood light. "Gosh that thing is emitting light almost as powerful as our sun! When did it start doing that?"

Am appeared next to her and swept a hologram over to her showing the pod's new capability. "This is the second burst of electromagnetic radiation the pod released in the last two minutes, Lisa."

She glanced at a little landscape on the planet where the fog had parted to reveal a large mound. "Do you detect photosynthesis, Am?"

Am disappeared from her side to materialize alongside the giant hologram of the planet with a picture-in-picture view of the pod, deep space, their backtracking trajectory, and the little ribbon of unknown force heading straight for them in hours. "The pod's radiation is sufficient to produce plant life, Lisa, but I am receiving an insufficient amount of carbon dioxide by-products."

"No planet life them," Tom shrugged, monitoring conditions as the landing shafts opened up on the hull. "We can't abort now." He aligned *Amelia* with the surface to prepare for landing.

The warning lights and holograms that had flared throughout their descent suddenly faded to *off* mode. "Take us in gently for a landing, Am," he called to her, and then she appeared on the other side of the hologram, syncing with *Amelia*'s laser-landing gear propelled by ceiling hardware at that second of their starship. Her goddess figure and wide eyes scrolling code and algorithms were spiritual in her quantum-exchange of information with *Amelia*. "There is the pod again, at the azimuth, Kent," she said, showing them the round sphere 32° on Ori-52's south-south eastern horizon.

Lisa's lips pursed as she squinted. "It's lighting up this place, Tom…I believe heatin' up the planet!" She showed him the outside temperature: 165° subzero.

"Definitely a slight increase," he said, copying the pod's image and sweeping it into the giant hologram where it appeared above the planet so they could receive a holistic composite of the energetic pod, Ori-52, and the distant unknown force. "I bet the pod's probably been monitoring us for quite some time, but it hasn't harmed us."

"I'm sending out a few cloaked UAVs to get close up of the pod," Lisa added, launching them.

"Still, if aliens are around us, and obviously disguising themselves from us, they haven't harmed us yet, and I don't think they'll start now, unless we attack, or they feel we're hostile to 'em," Kent said.

"Perhaps, commanders, they are as inquisitive about us as we are about them," Am began, "or perhaps they need us for a task. After all, those are motivational aspects of *all* intelligent life on Earth."

"True," Lisa said.

"Yes, but our only chance to meet them and begin a dialogue is down there—" He motioned firmly at a small mass of dark land in the middle of the planet. "So drift on over to that land mass fifty miles north, Am, and land there."

"Yes, Kent. I am opening igniting plasma engines to landing mode intensity."

The plasma engines swooshed on, and *Amelia* slowed for a prepared perfect touchdown on Ori-52.

"This landing site we're approaching, with all the white fog, appears as large as Alaska," he surmised.

"Three times larger in surface area, Kent," Am corrected.

"Good that we've got enough space to plant our feet down then for a while," Lisa chuckled.

"But keep in mind that we need to explore fast, get some phenomenal readings for scientists back home, and then high-tail it outta here before that white line of unknown energy arrives and chomps us down," Kent said. "How long do we have, Am?" He activating an outside view of Ori-52 that had glowing fog moving through tall skeletal structures over the several locations around their landing sites."

"This was once a thriving society indeed!" Lisa interrupted.

A hologram appeared in front of their command chairs, showing a low mountainous area in the distance with two rusty monoliths stretching to a red-aurora, shimmering sky.

"We're gonna need Level-5 suits with head gear," Lisa said. "The planet has a containment atmosphere a mile high, but the environment is cold, and the air not at fit for human breathing." She showed him surface readings and atmospheric composition. "Another species *could* live here. But never us…at least the way things are now here."

"I'm wondering if some of them still do, considering that little pod that's orbiting," Kent said.

"I have received no reply to our greeting communication, Commanders," Am said, still standing in their midst, and activating and deactivated essential holograms for their perusal.

Kent enlarged the image of the rogue world drifting

through the universe. Then a sudden chill swept through the cock pit, winding around him like turbulence, piercing his thoughts with doubt. The starship wasn't keeping him focused so well anymore, but anxious and sometimes filling with self-doubt.

We're so far from Earth, on a black wilderness of a planet where autumn, winter, spring and summer had most likely existed, but not now, only wreckage from when gravity unleashed Ori-51 from its solar system, sending this place into the vacuum of space. "We can do this, Lisa, one step at a time."

She gave him a perturbed glance. "Of course we can Kent," she said, putting her hands on the sides of her armchair and sitting up rigidly. "I'm not scared at all," she coughed and then returned to all the details of their landing.

As their plasma engines reversed into a soft touchdown, fog spiraled over *Amelia*, nearly encapsulating it, the hull attacked with hairline ice crystals.

Lisa rounded off all the decimals that Am was projecting in confusing holographic columns. "Will you please just give us the basic composition of the outside environment, Am? I'm showing a mish-mash of elements doing molecular hula-hoops!"

Light in their star ship cycled like a strobe. "Surface temperature one hundred sixty-two degrees below zero. Atmosphere seventy-eight percent nitrogen, twelve percent sulfur, six percent oxygen, one percent helium, one percent *unknown*."

A wisp of steam curled out of Lisa's mouth. "Unknown? I thought the only unknown was the interior of that white-hot energy line in deep space?"

Kent sighed, rubbed his cheek, took a bit out of his food bar, and began staring at the light burning *unknown* into his eyes.

"What are *you* thinking unknown could be?" Lisa asked. "I know that look of yours. You have ideas, Kent. As long as I've known you, you've never like just giving an opinion, but you appear to believe you have an answer."

He was pacing in front of the giant hologram depicting their new environment—outside glowing fog, an orbiting pod flooding the atmosphere with light, and now an unknown element, force, or entity lurking everywhere around them. "Should we just call it quits, right now, Lisa?" He shrugged and threw his food wrapper at the robotic cleaner that picked it up off their floor and instantly recycled it. "The readings we have just aren't adding up and making sense. And I know my idea of gravity and electromagnetism flowing abnormally would most likely destroy the universe if true." He slammed the rim around the hologram stage in frustration.

"That's an understatement you just made," she huffed, making a final inspection of their space suits before stepping out onto the tumultuous mysterious surface.

"We could encounter dangerous territory out there."

"But we have good weapons, and suits that can withstand the conditions," she countered, showing him laser fire power on her wrist devices and ankle devices.

"True, but that *unknown* variable Am's been flashing to us could answer a lot of questions, like why certain stars and planets are gliding through space without any galaxy or solar system. Could another force, other than gravity, be responsible?"

She appeared suddenly excited. "*Hm*, if we could pin-point the force or energy—"

"Or lack of force and energy…or many even some type of new element," he interrupted.

"We could harness what we find, and use it to time

travel, or find another mode of stellar travel, like voyaging through one of the other seven dimensions, besides space-folding," she said.

He laughed and swallowed the last bit of food. "We might become famous. You ready for something like that?"

"Hey, big prize money is awarded for discoveries made in outer space," she said enthusiastically.

He waved his hand at the hologram imaging *unknown*, and it extinguished.

"Still," Lisa began, "everything *unknown* has name, Kent. We just have to discover it and name it." She returned to checking their suits and having Am certify them as perfect. "That's why I might be scared to death, because our neural implants aren't helping us—" She touched her forehead. "But I'm determined to trek the surface, and find out what's making this sawed off rogue planet tick."

After Am gave them their Level-5 suit stats, he compared that analysis hologram to the environmental data of Ori-52. "With these suits set to maximum, a brief exposure to the unknown element, force, or whatever it is, *should* be harmless. This material we'll be wearing will ward off radiation for twenty-four hours, and that's neutron bomb radioactivity."

"Yeah, I think we'll be fine out there on the surface, especially staying close to Am, the ship, and—"

"And close to each other," he said firmly.

"Hey, I'm not walkin' off, dude!" she scoffed jokingly.

"At least our pal and perfect A.I. Am will be synched with us." He tried tapping her encouragingly on the shoulder, but his hand swept right through her. She shrugged. "And you'll be visually available everywhere we wander out there, right?" he asked Am, bouncing on the balls of his feet.

"Yes, Kent," she replied. "And I've powered up the decontamination chambers to accommodate you immediately upon return to the airlock."

Meanwhile, Lisa had been staring out a portal she open while inhaling deep gulps of chilly cockpit air. "That's some atmosphere out there…some harsh terrain under all that fog I bed." Her face glowed in the reflection of shimmering fog lights emanating from under the undulating air.

A green-field hologram flashed on.

"Am adjusted to the surface, Kent, so we have a stable fit to the ground," she then said, her eyes keenly observing all the incoming soil readings. "There's five feet of malleable soil to walk on, Kent, and I'm receiving algae and fungus molecules, although none that have coagulated on the surface." She showed him a hologram of the microwave readings and radio-waved stats several UAVs had brought back and streamed to *Amelia*. The hardware fiber-optics on the cockpit ceiling were coursing with quantum information, *Amelia*'s form of communication, and their lifeline while separated from the starship.

Then a bright light from outside struck the hull.

"What's that?" she asked.

"Am!" Kent shouted.

Am disappeared and then reappeared under the spot where the light had penetrated the hull. "Electromagnetic radiation in the high-frequency zone…converting into visible light energy, Commanders," Am answered.

"What's that mean?" he asked.

A hologram of the space pod they had seen earlier prior to landing had orbited high above them. "Commanders, we are experiencing the effects of artificial sunlight," Am answered.

"So aliens *are* here … somewhere?" Lisa whispered, her brown eyes glancing around the cockpit fearfully. She picked up her suit and swept up her biometrically syncing helmet.

"Yes, Lisa," Am replied. "But as of yet, I have not received any vital signs of alien life other than decomposed hardened layers of carbon fifty-feet below ground."

"So perhaps a species existed here, but then died when their planet was thrown out of its solar system?" Lisa said. "Maybe there's underground technology still on they forgot to turn off … or a war of some kind threw them out into the universe, or—"

"Lisa," he stopped her, helping her breath as he initiated the biometrics on his own helmet. "There's only one way to find out." Her eyes were pools of ice fear until she blinked several times, and a watery calmness appeared to flow through her. "We get out there, and start lookin'."

Then she slapped the side of her head in a gesture of self-correction. "We have camouflage capability!"

"Yes, Lisa," Am said, showing her the 100% transfer power of invisibility cloaking energy between *Amelia* and their suits while spending time on the surface.

"So if that pod that's orbiting as an artificial sun also has the capability to detect and fire on anything *not* of this world, we'll be able to deflect its detection method—"

"Certainly, Lisa," Am interrupted.

"I'm sure that'll give us sufficient time to run back to *Amelia* and launch," he concluded. "See? Piece 'o cake!" he said, blowing a little kiss to her. "Come on, now let's get movin' and get explorin'," he chuckled.

They quickly donned their suits and began making

final adjustments, also synchronizing their instruments and weapons devices. "Am, counter-electromagnetic mode, proceed."

Their starship camouflaged with the frozen dew, red flaming sky, and glowing fog circling around them. Then, they stepped into the airlock that sealed behind them. The countdown began to Ori-51's atmospheric contact.

"We could still return, and leave, Kent," Lisa said, gesturing to the tiny portal behind them.

Am appeared in her holographic brightness next to her. "At any time, Lisa, anyone can turn back."

He checked his watch app that appeared as a time dial hologram over his wrist device. "Am, how long before that white-line of energy becomes a threat?"

They were needing to breathe through their suits, but A.I. Am could walk anywhere suit free while always syncing with them, and next to them.

Am's bright eyes began scrolling down statistics of rate, time, and distance.

"Three hours and forty-two seconds, Kent."

"So if we limit our exploration time to, say, one hour, we'll be fine, right?" he asked.

"All indications suggest you are correct, Kent," Am replied.

"So let's go," Lisa said.

Then Kent stopped her from punching the first airlock release lever. "Lisa, I think we should take the two-seated rover." A giant Jeep-like car unlatched and began lifting from the far side of their airlock.

"Good idea. That monster truck can push through any kind of obstacle known to man," she chuckled, but then she stopped again, and breathed as if she might faint.

Kent realized her hindrance. "The first mission on an exoplanet is always the hardest, Lisa," he said tenderly, glancing out of the portal into Ori-52's flesh-biting air.

"I know," she breathed, "I'm just a bit, well…I don't wanna lost my life, that's all."

"Me neither! So don't you think I'll be looking out for the both of us?" he chuckled, patting her on the shoulder. He pinching a piece of suit material. "Just do what we practiced in all our drills." He gestured for her to watch him, and then he snapped his suit again against his skin. "Full protective mode and invisibility cloak, Am, please."

Am appeared, and her eyes flashed green in compliance. "Done, Commanders."

"I copied you." Lisa pressed a tab on the rim of her visor. When her suit glowed blue, she was ready to step on the surface, and Kent opened the airlock.

Am exited first, floating down into Ori-52's foggy surface in her holographic light to ensure conditions were safe, and the soil solid to explore. All the while Am's eyes were scrolling stats and algorithmic equations of calculating perfection. "You may step down now, Commanders. The surface is safe," she said, inspecting the fog-covered terrain ahead of them with her A.I. special vision syncing with every device on and around *Amelia.*

Lisa hesitated at the thick threshold. "Kent—what if I sink? Or drop? Or that orbiting pod targets us?! I— I don't know if I can do this!"

The thick-skinned Jeep drove into the complicated fog, bellied up, turned upright as if a child was playing with it in gravity, and then settled feet in front of the airlock. Kent had already stepped into the fog—now undulating a bit more than previously—settled there a bit, and then jumped into the Jeep. The Jeep's curved lid was open, and the interior instruments could not be exposed too long to Ori-52's harsh conditions.

He had to get her moving. "Lisa, it's okay! Just step down and then hop into the Jeep," he directed.

"I can't see my feet though if I step down into this mess," she countered.

"Just keep your eye on the vehicle, Lisa," he said, "and you'll be okay because Am certified the surface safe. Besides, I stepped down. I'm okay!" He showed her his arms and patted them.

She continued testing the strange medium with her toe. "But that *unknown* force or charge might be interfering with Am, and scrambling what she's analyzing, giving skewed readings."

"The surface is…modulating fog—" Am stopped suddenly, ten feet in front the Jeep that appeared as an aquatic vehicle half concealed in fog. "I am receiving no threat, Commander…only safe and stable ground readings."

"God—I know what Buzz and Neil musta felt like when they stepped on the moon," Lisa shouted, inching her right foot through the shimmering moving fog.

To the horizon on the left stretching into the dark red sky were the skeletal remains of a city, mangled steel beams and green-copper weathered monolithic towers, obvious religious or cultural structures because they appeared as pyramids, their sides positioned in the same direction akin to the ones in ancient Egypt.

Lisa had them always in her sight, an obvious coping mechanism for dealing with the unknown. "I feel like I'm riding one of those mega rollercoasters, and I'm at the top-most spot, ready to fall," she laughed, then coughed. "Here goes!" When she stepped onto the spongy surface, she reached for Kent's hand. "Help!"

"Gotcha!" he said, grabbing her fingers, lifting her into the Jeep. Gravity appeared to be changing. When he'd lifted a few instruments that had toppled over from the Jeep, they weren't heavy at all, but now Lisa felt her normal 130 pounds. He was about to ask Am about the alteration, until Lisa landed in a thump inside and the Jeep's lid that automatically shut and locked. He exhaled in relief. "We're okay, so let's get started and head to what appears to be a city." A hologram activated with a compass and the distance to the city. Am was hovering outside their vehicle that was rolling a bit catawampus over the rugged terrain. She was maintaining her standard ten-feet scouting position. "Time's valuable and we don't wanna waste it."

Lisa glanced back at their starship, *Amelia*, slowly appearing to sink in the thickening and intensifying fog. "Am," she called to their outside AI guide. "Keep *Amelia* on following close behind us!"

"Yes, Lisa," Am replied, and her hands glowed—a signal that she had accomplished that directional trajectory. "We need the *Amelia* in our sights constantly so we can escape easily and return to her fast."

"Yes, Commanders," Am replied, waving them forward to the skeletal city a mile in front of them.

"I'm detecting ice formations under the Jeep, Kent," Lisa said through her visor while showing him an analysis of the surface.

Ice crystals were slowly forming in hairlines on the Jeep's window, and the atmospheric winds high above them were howling on the monitor, analyzing all the outside environmental conditions. A few screeches and cries resounded.

"What the hell was that!" she asked, tapping her visor to connect to Am.

Kent stopped the Jeep, and Am halted her progress outside.

"I am assessing the change, Commanders," Am said, standing statue-like in front of them, her holographic presence wavering as a slight static ripple.

Kent and Lisa re-checked the outside composition and send *Amelia* a transmission to stabilize Am.

All our instruments indicate Ori-52 is void of life. But what the heck were those screams and shrieks?" Lisa asked. "This place is becoming a frigging fright zone, Kent, and this planet is changing all the time…like something has triggered this place to alter. Maybe us? Or the light-year anomaly?"

"Maybe that's it … the anomaly that's a half-a-light year away from us is causing some type of change to occur in this quadrant in space," he said.

Suddenly, the Jeep lobbed to the right, dipped down, and bounced off the surface like a pebble cascading over water.

"Ah!" Lisa screamed, holding onto her chest harness. "Did something push us?! It sure felt like something pushed us, Kent—damn!" She grabbed his arm and held on tightly as their Jeep scratched across the bumpy surface and then came to an abrupt stop at what their instruments were indicating was a mile-wide mound formation.

"Someone pushed us, Kent! I'm telling ya!" she gasped, looking back at their starship that was half-way amassed with the unusual white-shimmering fog. "We have to get back to our craft—now."

"We can't in this Jeep the way it's tipped over." He tried using the side bars to lift them back on their tires to operational mode. The engine revved, rocking the Jeep, but then it reverted back on its side like a broken robot creaking and clanking before its absolute disconnect. "Am, do you detect any movement out there besides us?"

Am appeared frozen.

"Has someone or something intercepted our AI? Am is dead in this foggy water, Kent," Lisa said, activating holograms that turned fuzzy and unresponsive. She kept poking them, swiping them, but none would connect and give them an answer. "Shoot!"

Kent had already anticipated the next move. He had his visor back down over his smooth chiseled face and his gloves biometrically syncing with him. "Let's move out of this Jeep, Lisa. It's our *only* option."

She gestured outside to the mound and the distance mangled city. The pod was orbiting above them again, shining its artificial light in a giant circle on everything within a one-hundred mile radius. Whatever the light touched, the elements morphed for seconds into complete structures. "Kent! This place is reanimating!"

"That can't be!" he said, igniting more holograms over his wrist device. "Am," he called to the frozen AI outside their rover Jeep.

She was unresponsive, transfixed in a brilliant glow.

"She's changed, Kent," Lisa began, preparing to leave the Jeep for the changing surface. "Can we sever its contact with *Amelia* until it, and Am, can auto re-unite?"

He pulled himself upright and grabbed her hand. "That's our first job, Lisa, to get outta here, get in her face, and see if we can reactivate her ourselves. She's gotta listen to us when we're in 'er face." He motioned at the time. "We have three hours and eighteen minutes before that energy band becomes a threat. So I think our best bet right now is to cut short our investigation into the *unknown* element, or force, try to reconnect with Am, 'cause she's integral to us, and leave Ori-52."

"I'm with ya, Kent!" Lisa said into her visor, syncing her gloves and suit to intensify her biometrics with their starship since Am had disappeared. "Let's go!" She pried out of her seat as Kent popped open the Jeep's lid, exposing them to a new changing atmosphere.

His readings began adjusting in holograms around them as Am, still appeared frozen and shining in the distance, almost like a Statue of Liberty.

"She looks like she's going to supernova, Kent," Lisa said, pulling herself up and then stepping out onto the side of the Jeep.

"I'm trying to re-sync with the ship…and hopefully it will reboot the quantum processor and reel Am back to us," he said.

Meanwhile, Lisa unleashed a survival tether out of the Jeep's tire pocket, wound it around her waist, and threw it to him.

He quickly fastened it to his suit belt.

"Let's make sure this connection is strong, Kent, 'cause we can't get lost now!" she cried.

Her voice came in loud and clear into his visor microphone as he tugged on the tether. "It's perfect," he said, syncing his biometric stats projecting over his wrist device with Lisa's stats always showing in a miniature hologram over her wrist device. "Just keep an eye on the tautness. In this evolving landscape, we can't risk falling."

He jumped off the side of the rickety Jeep and landed waist deep in the eerie shimmering fog.

"Aren't you scared to death yet!" she gasped, her brown eyes wide showing debate.

He touched his forehead, really his visor. "Not with the neural implant that keeps adjusting my limbic system," he chuckled. He felt a raw wind curl up his legs, wind around his arms, and vent heat on his visor. Fearing his helmet might fly off, he pushed down hard on the glass, all the while attending to the harsh sounds of spouting geysers shedding Ori-52's stale surface sleepers. "This place is definitely waking up, Lisa."

Gurgling sounds were emanating in the distance.

"I think a river is forming … or lake out of some dormant water source," she said. "Let's get up to Am, try to re-sync her with *Amelia*, and then leave. I'm for leaving, Kent!"

"Me too, Lisa." Over his wrist device, another hologram activated.

The alien pod had passed over the horizon at 45° latitude, more of the planet awakening.

"The light that pod is giving off is kicking this place into high gear, Lisa."

"And resurrecting the life forms that used to live on this world," she said.

"Or creating them," he added, as screeches, screams, and cracking noises resounded from the re-cementing monoliths and straightening steel beams over a mile in front of them. "I just want to know on what kind of ground we're walking on…'cause this *isn't* what we stepped into at all."

Lisa shifted through the fog, and they both activated directional lights on their suits, camouflaging with the undulating fog. Their ankle devices initiated a weapons app, blue lights on their shins. They possessed the ability to incapacitate any life form; and like an electromagnetic pulse, they had the power to render everything technical in nature, dead in the sea of fog, all at as verbal commands. The two of them appeared as illuminated beacons while they slowly stepped toward brightening Am, her quantum abilities frozen with *Amelia*, its titanium nose one-hundred yards behind them.

"The ground's safe, Lisa, I'm sure," he called, his suit technology scanning the frothing terrain around them.

"This place is warming up though. I'm showing the temperature at 10° above zero now."

"Wow—what an increase in just thirty minutes!" she said, glancing at their time. "We're down to three hours and ten minutes before we have to leave this quadrant in space, Kent."

"I know." He glanced down at his feet. "Hey, Lisa! The visibility's improving!"

She loosened the pull on their tether the closer their approach to stalled bright Am. "Kent! Look beyond that mound where the Jeep crashed."

The surface was rumbling a bit, and white stalagmites were inching upward like fingers into a highly charged fog.

"What the hell?" he exclaimed. "You can't be thinking about exploring that place, are you?" When he saw AI Am drifting up into a tumultuous wilderness of black space, he stopped going after her, and snowflakes began slashing her holographic image to bits. "Am!" he cried. He turned to Lisa, now approaching the mound with her instruments of discovery illuminating in colorful twinkling lights. "Lisa, something, or someone, is acting like a traction beam on Am!" His wrist device launched a counter measure as it droned in an attempt to home in on the threat.

"I'll be there in a sec, Kent!" she replied. "I received that unknown assessment again…and it's just feet beyond the mound…and I'm almost done compiling enough data so we can return to the starship and acquire unknown's composition."

After Am hadn't re-appear in the black-red sky, helplessness curled through him. "Lisa, I believe Am has been kidnapped. But we're still connected to the starship."

"Thank God!" she gasped, making her way up slowly onto the changing mound, her tether to Kent holding. "Just a little more…almost there…"

He opened a com to the ship. "*Amelia*, you know our situation … our A.I., Am, appears to have been kidnapped by an alien around here somewhere, or perhaps that alien that's been orbiting this rogue."

"Yes, Commander, Am has disconnected with the *Amelia*." This A.I.'s voice was low, and he remembered endowing the quantum-system with an opposite of Am so he could always easily distinguish the two, and have a discernible difference should a moment as this occur.

Lisa stopped her trek up the mound. "We can sure use you to guide us as we accumulate data."

"Yes, Commander Simmons," the AI replied.

"Based on the changing Doppler wind instruments, can you initiate a weather manipulation and stabilize our ground current so we can head back easily?" Tom asked. He was about to order Am to do that, but then remembered was gone, and they alone with direct monitoring. He felt another type of frightening disconnect. "The conditions are changing rapidly here, as if this rogue world is waking up from some type of stasis."

Their starship unleashed a spray of fine laser lights into the air. "Depolarization set on maximum efficiency, Commander Johnson," the ship's system said into his visor.

"Call us by our first names, please," Lisa said.

The ship was still engulfed with a fog—its landing lights glowing brightly, giving their ship the appearance of the Nautilus under an undulating foaming sea.

"Yes, Lisa," it replied, "but I cannot appear among Kent and you."

"What type of interference?" Lisa asked. Her breath steaming up her visor, she bounded through a small bank of fog and stopped when a peak of foam rose up in front of her. Then her body suit began coursing with caution lights. "I'm detecting this unknown element and you need to make sure you have the frequency in the ship. It's like … coming from feet below the surface … and right here." She paused, terrified to take another step. "Something, or someone, is beneath us, Kent," she whispered.

"Starship A.I.," Kent said, "begin to determine what's going on subterranean!"

"Yes, Commanders," the ship's AI replied.

Then he noticed Lisa's lose tether, and a ripple of panic spread through to his bones. He waved her toward him. "Lisa, you're way too far displaced with the tether! Come back!"

She was shaking her head vehemently. "We have to discover the identity of unknown, Kent, and I'm reading a force, not an element … an opposite in the universe."

"If it's opposite in the cosmos, then the force must be like antimatter," he said. He began running to her, his breath hot in front of him. "If that's the case, Lisa, and you're receiving an antimatter signature, then we *must* get back to *Amelia*, and leave 'cause the Space-Time around this quadrant in the universe will explode hotter than the brightest supernova!"

"With the power to annihilate the entire universe," the ship's AI added.

"That's why I'm trying to find the best spot in order to detect it where the disturbance is coming from," she said, lifting her hand high into the air. "That's it!" She gasped at the anomaly now like a white streak of lightning in the cosmos. "I show it's a little under two hours and fifty-four minutes away ... and the force is *definitely* tied into this rogue world."

Like the eerie silence before a terrible hurricane, the air stilled.

"Kent!" She had white panic on her white cheeks beneath her visor.

"Just reel yourself back with the auto-clamps, Lisa...and let's split!" he kept waving her toward him.

"If I take one step," she breathed, her body languishing in apprehension, "I might not live," she cried. Then, as a giant curl of fog opened up yards behind her, she screamed, and began staggering down the side of the mound, their tether like a whip, dangerously close to breaking.

Stalagmites beyond the mound began cracking...and quickly shattered and exploding ... revealing a surface below as soft as cotton with the Jeep sinking like a weight in quick sand.

"The fog is really a subterranean atmosphere rising around us like white, sea serpents ready to pounce on us and devour us," she cried, almost reaching his arms.

"Hold on with your life when I grab your hand!" he shouted, clutching her arm while tapping his laser app on his wrist to fire on the moving land creeping toward them.

"What the hell is that spot?"

"I don't know, but let's run now to *Amelia*!" he said, contemplating a possible end result. They could go mad if something abominable should appear because he could see no cave to dash into, no crevice to hide in, and not even an icy crawl space in which to huddle for safety, only *Amelia*, glowing gold through the encapsulating fog.

"We're at the mercy of Ori-51 right now, Kent, until the ship can cut through the interference and launch us the heck outta here," she said.

He pulled out a thin strip of metal from his exploration kit, and elongated it in his trembling hands. "I'm taking soil samples." He burrowed quickly into the cold thawing dirt. "And I'm sending atmospheric samples constantly, hoping everything together will give us an answer as to what the unknown force is that appears to be slowly destroying our universe."

"An intensifying," she added, gesturing to the bright-white string of energy that had doubled in size in space. "I think they're connected, Kent, involved in some type of cosmic dance together."

"We'll see, when we reach *Amelia*," he breathed, his nitrox supply low in his filter system.

Lumbering toward the ship through the fog, she asked almost depleted of air as well, "Is that pod shining the artificial sun still orbiting?" She looked up, and peered into the red-azure sky, and then at a gas chromatograph device attached to her arms. "I can't believe it!"

"What now?" he said, calling *Amelia* to open the airlock in thirty seconds, almost the exact number of steps to the gargantuan hull in front of them.

"This atmosphere now has a high oxygen and nitrogen composition. We could almost take our masks off and breathe it," she replied.

"I wouldn't." He suddenly stopped in his tracks and peered up. "I— I need to rest a sec."

"Me too," she said, bending down and breathing hard, her arms shaking. "We have twenty-five yards to go to *Amelia* ... I wanna arrive in once piece," she laughed, sipping some water that elongated in a tube to her lips.

Waiting for his invisibility program to recover in energy and camouflage him with the color and shape of the fog around them, he could discern only distorted stars, and bands of stars that looked like thin arms of the Milky Way, dissolving. They were really ice clouds forming in space from Ori-52's oxygenation, and the sun-pod re-igniting the rogue world back to life with its mysterious artificial sunlight. Then he saw the threatening energy band that appeared to be like a magnet attracting this rogue. "Two hours and forty minutes...then *kaboom*, Lisa, that's if what you detected back there holds true, and this rogue planet and that energy stripe in space are attracting bodies. I'm wondering why this place is coming back to life all of a sudden when it *should* be a death zone." He tapped his mice—a connection to the ship. "Any clue as to where Am is yet?"

After a pause, the system's voice droned back to activation in his ear. "No, Kent. But I am still sending pulses to attempt a reconnect with the piece missing from me."

"Great!" Lisa interrupted. "Our ship's missing a part of its brain! I wonder what *that* means for us!"

"As soon as we get inside, we're gonna do everything we can to find Am while programming a launch into space-fold time, and leave."

She stopped him. "Kent, think about what you're saying and what we've discovered."

He felt side swiped. "What?"

"If that energy band that's a little less than a half-a-light year away from us is attracting this planet in positive and negative rations, then our entire universe *will* explode, and we'll die. I don't think we can leave, Kent."

He stopped and gasped as he contemplated the magnanimity of her disclosure. "You're right, Lisa. We're looking at a cosmic extinction-level event, right—ah, what should I call you, starship A.I." he asked the new

AI on *Amelia*.

"TIP, Kent ... you can call me TIP," it replied.

"Oh that's right," he said, noticing their suits were cloaking with the environment at 100%. "TIP...that's short for Tele-biometric Intergalactic Processor."

"Yes, Kent," TIP replied.

Suddenly a thick bank of fog swept over and around them.

"Kent!" Lisa called. "I— help!" In just one second she appeared yards away from him.

"Lisa!" He groped around in an atmospheric contest to fight to reach her in the direction from which her voice emanated, the compass showing north, and then south, but then wavering as if magnetism and electrons were battling it out for control of the universe. Then, as quickly as the chaos began, it stopped, but Lisa was nowhere.

"Lisa!" He scanned the terrain. "TIP, search for her!"

"Yes, Kent," and lights from the starship just yards away activated, their floodlights searching the red-blue sky.

"Simmons!"

Only a blustery wind and another piercing scream from the distance calling back to him.

"Lisa!" He felt disoriented, and faltering, like his whacky needled compass. "Answer me!"

Three-hundred feet away, a small geyser unleashed its hot steamy force fifty feet into the sky, the rumbling quake toppling him to the ground.

Crawling to his knees on the slimy bumpy ground, his visor broke; and his lungs filled with the new atmosphere. He heaved and jumped to his feet. Believing someone had taken her, he cracked off his visor. With scorn for the sky, he clenched his fists at the agitating clouds. "Lisa Simmons … give her back, *now.*"

A screech resounded, piercing his ears, the sound much more intense than they had heard in the past. High up, he could see no alien orbiting pod. Then he spotted a long, bright blue ribbon on a mountain range in the distance. "What the hell?" The ship might know the answer. "TIP, home in on the phenomenon." He activated a visual hologram over his wrist device, syncing with the *Amelia.* "I can tell you it wasn't there before, TIP, but it *could* be responsible for taking Lisa. Can you detect her biometrics there? What's its composition? *What* exactly is showing up on your center holographic stage with this entire planet?"

After a static, the *Amelia*'s airlock began hissing open. "I have the image at center stage now with spectral radiometric and every science package analyzing the phenomenon, Kent," TIP said.

As he waited for the airlock to adjust to the outside atmosphere and activate a decontamination spray, questions were spinning in his mind as the blue anomaly turning, approaching, and enlarging by the second. He put his gloved hand on the wall, and felt a shock that pierced him to his chest. "Ouch!" he cried, grimacing at the bright-blue crystal slab. Is it an ocean?"

"I am receiving no oxygen and hydrogen elements, Kent," TIP replied.

"So the phenomenon is *not* an ocean then. How about a structured cloud formation? Or ice from an atmospheric disturbance?" He kept tapping the airlock stats to adjust to his biometric body suit and let him inside. If he couldn't take refuge in *Amelia*, the blue anomaly would be at him in thirty seconds. "But our priority, TIP, is to locate Lisa Simmons, *hopefully* alive."

"Yes, Kent, I have three UAV's launched and searching for her," TIP answered.

Then he found himself feet from the airlock again! "What the hell? It's like some kind of moving walkway is under me, TIP. Send a countermeasure!"

"Yes, Kent." Three floodlights ignited over the airlock and a weather stabilizer beam of radiation flooded the space between his feet and the airlock.

"Keep that airlock ready, TIP, 'cause I'm comin'!" Running to *Amelia*, he felt his legs pumping like rods through water. TIP shot him out another tether, and he grabbed hold of it for dear life. "Shoot! I'm up against some type of force that doesn't want me reunited with my ship!" He gasped. *Amelia*'s airlock was so close to touch, yet felt impossible to reach. "What the heck is happening to reality in this place, TIP?"

"Dimensional patterns, Kent— colliding—"

The air-mix inside his visor suddenly altered, and he felt a hand on his shoulder. With the airlock hissing wide open, he grabbed hold of the steel and turned around to see who was behind him. There she was standing! "Lisa!" Then he felt almost weightless, with his feet lifting off the ground until she grabbed his hand, yanking him back to the surface.

"Am I losing my mind or what?" The bright blue ribbon was enlarging behind them, and they had seconds before contact. Quickly, he clasped her arms and they jumped into the airlock that sealed the outside behind them.

"Where'd you go, Lisa?" He shook her a bit as a decontamination light surrounded them, cleansing them.

"Stop it, Kent!" She stepped back. Her visor was gone, her suit torn in spots, and her brown eyes were wide with shock. "I've been right here. I didn't go anywhere! I've been recording data. Are *you* all right?"

"But you—" He heaved in air, warm and tranquil now in his lungs with a calming effect. "—I turned around to talk to you back there," he gestured to the changing mound, bursting to life with lush green plants and small trees. "But you were gone!"

"Really?" She appeared to have lost minutes and was confused as she rubbed her forehead. "I don't think so," she nodded. "You were talking to me, telling me TIP had discovered the unknown force, and we needed to get back to *Amelia* to ensnare the sun-pod."

"What? I never said that!" He felt a strange panic clawing at his throat, and a delicate whisper in his ear, distortions in Space-Time, also giving him dry mouth. Then he turned her attention to the bright-blue crystal sheet closing in behind her. "We're not dead yet, Lisa, but with that phenomenon closing in on us, we're might die if *Amelia* can't stop it from striking us."

"It *could* be a weapon," she said, glancing at its hologram that she activated inside their decontamination chamber. She recoiled when she saw the giant blue sheet high in the sky. It was turning and tumbling at times, light glistening off its surface. "If it were white, I'd say it was a long cirrus cloud ... if black, I'd say it was a storm cloud. But blue and shiny? The thing looks like a sheet of glass!"

"Scan it with a genetic scanner, TIP," he ordered, and a hull panel opened up with instruments of analysis.

"I have been running a continuous scan on *several* anomalies on Ori-52, Kent," TIP replied.

The decontamination lights extinguished, and they exited the airlock and entered the cockpit. "Thank goodness—home!" he said in relief.

"What are the genetic results of the blue phenomenon,

TIP?"

In the center of their cockpit, the hologram of Ori-5—with the white-hot energy field behind it in the distance of space—was continuing to project, and the starship's instruments were droning and hissing to measure the exact composition and parameter of the bright blue ribbon floating so close to *Amelia*.

Lisa stepped away to change into her standard uniform behind her stasis pod, and she disappeared.

"Lisa!" He ran to the spot that had snatched her out of Space-Time air. "I can't believe this! TIP! Where'd she go?"

"Time— distortion— field, Kent."

"Well un-distort Space-Time and find Lisa, 'cause *no one* just disappears, TIP," he ordered, feeling his eye sockets sore and stinging. "*I'm* here. Why aren't *I* disappearing, TIP?" Then he saw the blue atmospheric disturbance at the center of the cockpit, landing in front of *Amelia*, and closing in at a hundred meters. The fog was dissipating, appearing to welcome its presence.

He drank some water and splashed some drops on his face. Maybe the distortion had whisked her away? "TIP, try locating her outside."

Static and a splash of white noise filled the hologram of Ori-52, and panic rose in goose bumps on his arms as a chill pecked at the quick of his fingernails. "TIP? He remembered some type of dimensional distortion in patters that had been playing on their Space-Time. "TIP! I hope to God the distortion hasn't torn apart half this ship, taking you along with it into another dimension. That must be what's happening ... *another* dimension intruding on *our* Space-Time."

"Yes, Kent," TIP finally answered through images of Ori-52 appearing and disappearing from the cockpit.

"Some of these settings happened before Lisa and I left the starship," he gasped, sitting down in his command chair and realizing he might as well be tuning in and out of existence.

Inside the hologram he had a perfect view of the outside world. Another geyser flared its daggers into space beyond the airlock as a deep fissure opened, unleashing a surge of trapped subterranean water that began bubbling in rivulets toward *Amelia*.

"TIP, double check that you closed all the plasma gear shafts," he quickly ordered, running to inspect a systems' analysis of *Amelia*.

"Yes, Kent, they are sealed."

Lisa suddenly materialized by his side, and he almost smacked into her. "Lisa, damn! My suit's weapon system mighta fired on ya!"

She collapsed on the cold floor, and a robot rolled to her side, unleashing an automatic biometric scan of her body. "Lisa!" He swept her into his arms and carried her to her command chair. "You're back! Thank God."

She wasn't breathing, but a rag doll in his arms.

"TIP, engage with her cerebral interface and revive her," he ordered, grabbing the charging defibrillator from the small robot, and energizing her heart. "Come on, Lisa … come on." After checking the charge on the device, he returned to zap her again. What he saw on her face made him scamper back and gasp in fright. "You're … a skeleton! How? TIP! How can this be?"

"Lisa Simmons is dead, Kent," TIP replied, matter of fact.

Kent rubbed his watery eyes. "I am going crazy!"

Suddenly, a curtain of bright blue light filtered through the cockpit as the hologram of Ori-52 showing the previous chaotic world began displaying a plush green rolling valley with two rainbows on the distant burning blue-green horizon.

"Where the heck are we, 'cause this is *not* Ori-52!" he cried

"We *are* on the surface of Ori-52, Kent," TIP replied.

He turned off the defibrillator and sat dejected, staring into Lisa's shriveled face. He recalled a few micro-dreams he had had when in stasis, that felt like he had been entombed. He touched his arms. Numb. He drank water. Tasteless. "Am I alive? Or dead?"

"You are alive, Commander Johnson," TIP began, and then proceeded to list items on his resume.

"Shut up!" he screamed, his stomach an acid pit. "*I* musta done this to her." He hit the floor and his knuckle bled. "*I'm* responsible somehow." He felt his head ache and throb, and he quickly remembered his psychological situation. His neural connection with *Amelia* had long ago severed, and he was experiencing all his raw emotions. "I'm sorry, Lisa," he said into her mummified face and touching a rip in her suit. "I should have turned back, when ya told me to." He rubbed his stubble, hot from the passion of self-hate steaming around his face. "I should have aborted this mission when we had the chance...the *hell* with scientific discovery and trying to locate secrets in the universe, 'cause now, we're both dead I think. I killed us." He lay down, peering into the cockpit ceiling with *Amelia*'s quantum-computer, fiber optic network coursing information.

"I'm sorry ... *so* sorry."

"You are not dead, Kent Johnson," TIP announced, again.

Kent stood and touched his suited chest. "You coulda fooled me, TIP, but I'm not sure I want to survive if Lisa isn't with me. I'd rather well—" He walked over to his chair and hit it. "—I'd rather just die than return to Earth without her, TIP." Then he noticed the hologram at the center of their cockpit. Inside it was Ori-52, and the giant-shining crystal sheet positioned right in front of *Amelia's* airlock. "What's inside that thing, TIP?" He gently covered Lisa's body with a sheet, and approached the hologram.

"Inside the medium are all of Ori-52's inhabitants, Kent," TIP softly replied. "I am detecting biometrics in nano-microscopic readings."

TIP suddenly began speaking another language as Kent saw tiny faces appear inside the shimmering glass. Their faces were not human—but aquatic and amphibian in structure. At some point in Ori-52's history, birds and sea creatures had combined on to form an advanced species. TIP had connected with them, and they were communicating. Still, nothing on their starship could restore Lisa, not even Tip, because TIP would need resurrection power to bring her from death to life. But perhaps, the species inside Ori-52's blue stasis world *could* revive Lisa.

"TIP!" he called as he peeled the death shroud off her body. He gestured at the aliens slowly emerging inside the blue-crystal medium. "*They* might have the capability to manipulating DNA. Can you ask *them* to revive Lisa?" He waited, his breath thick in his chest.

TIP was still communicating with the Ori-52 aliens in piercing screeches and squeaks.

"Tip, ask them … and give me an answer."

A light hissing sound emanated through the cockpit, and when he glanced outside into the bright blue genetic medium containing millions of aliens, he saw Am at the center. He ran to the portal, pounding on the thick glass. "Can you hear me, Am? Lisa died. I think a dimensional world sucked the life outta her. Can ya help her? Am!"

The aliens were like microscopic lights flowing through the bright-blue crystal medium, and but glancing up at the wide white-hot ribbon heading toward Ori-52. Am was larger at the center of them, her bronze face illuminating like a small sun. She appeared content.

"Am—answer me. Can they help Lisa?" he begged again.

"I *am* receiving Lisa's condition, Kent," he heard, from inside the hologram of their blue world outside *Amelia.* "I am transferring your Space-Time to the Neptunian species so you can communicate with them through *Amelia* and me."

"Neptunian? Is that what they call themselves, Am?"

"Yes, Kent," Am began, her voice coming clear and crisp into the cockpit.

Relief spread over him like a warm shower. "Maybe they can bring ya back, Lisa," he whispered to her, as a little yellow halo appeared over her body—an interaction between her, the quantum-ceiling network, and the Neptunians. Then he felt a stinging inside his head as his neural connection with *Amelia* ignited back to life. Inside his mind, he could sense the population of an entire species trying to activate a calm dialogue. "Please, bring Lisa Simmons back to life."

"Yes, Kent," Am said, her connection into his mind succinct.

From *Amelia's* fiber-optic ceiling, a flow of energy began engulfing Lisa's shriveled body. The light began dancing with images of her while she was on the surface, and her face began rounding in mass and infusing with life.

"Vitals are commencing, Kent," Am said.

"This energy source is like angelic magic!" he

exclaimed. stepping back, but also wanting to touch the power, and her.

Then, a voice—quite an alien voice—boomed to life inside his mind, urging him not to get within a foot of the energy source, or he might trade his life for her life. Then, he collapsed on the floor, next to her.

The alien voice began narrating what had happened to the Neptunians. "Long ago, billions of years ago, our people discovered a way to preserve DNA as living material in stasis form, before Ori-52 unleashed from its solar system, before the fling into the cosmos rendered our planet a lifeless, hostile free-floating rogue in space. We will take TIP, and Am, and return to you Lisa Simmons, Commander Kent Johnson."

When he awoke to consciousness, in the waning particles lifting off of her revitalized body, he saw her arms move, and noticed her stable breathing. "You're alive!" He kissed her cheek softly.

"She opened her eyes and a quirky expression appeared on her face. "Gosh what the heck did I taste when I was outside *Amelia*, because my tongue feels swollen, and I have a sour taste in my mouth," she puckered. "But gee ... I feel so rested." She yawned and quickly smiled.

"You're *definitely* alive, Lisa." He laughed, hugging her. Her face was so young again, more youthful than we she had ... died. But he didn't yet want to let her know what had happened to her that would spoil her joy. "You haven't changed a bit ... always complaining...never just happy that I've done something good for ya."

"Why, what happened?" she asked, sitting up in confusion and wonder. "I was, gone somewhere." She glanced around the cockpit nervously. "But I can't figure out where exactly, except...." She touched her arms and face. "I think I was swimming in this fantastic ocean, with these weird aquatic creatures. They were so playful, and we were just turning around and spinning everywhere in the ocean." She had tears in her eyes. "I felt like I was a kid ... and there wasn't any gravity ... just open air and endless blue sky!" She appeared near hyperventilating as she stood up and peered longingly into the hologram at the center of their cockpit projecting the Neptunians' blue stasis world. She looked prepared to walk right out of the airlock without conducting her normal stat routine.

"Calm down, Lisa," he coaxed. "Breathe slowly."

When she took a few steps, she appeared wobbly, and he set her on her command chair that activated an oxygen vent. Air streamed into her face. "*Ah*, that's better. I can't explain it, but I felt funny."

Peering around the new landscape, he believed he had an answer to one of their questions. "Maybe this rogue world might have also had contact with another alien race, much as what happened when we landed."

"Could be, Kent," she said, eating a food bar. "Gosh this smells great! Like my senses just got shot with new DNA!" she laughed. She was childlike in her exploration of the cockpit, and then she spontaneously kissed Kent on the lips.

"What's that for?"

"Just giving you back what you gave me," she answered, her face glowing with a loving expression. "I think my neural connection to this computer system is gone now, so maybe that's why I'm thinking more clearly and experiencing everything as if I'm seeing it for the first time."

Inside his mind, he heard another voice. "Commander Johnson, you need to capture our sun-pod, that has brought our planet back to life, and propel it into the graviton field." The white-hot energy zone brightening the blackness of deep space suddenly enlarged

"Graviton field?" Kent asked, glancing up at the fiber-optic ceiling.

"Gravity and electromagnetism are blending so quickly, that a Comic Rip in the fabric of Space-Time has opened up, devouring everything in its path. *We* are meant to stop The Rip," the voice inside his head told him.

"Kent! What's wrong? Snap out of it," Lisa said, running her fingers gently over his forehead.

His trance with the Neptunian ended, and he laughed. "You said your neural connection is gone? I don't believe mine is."

"What do you mean?" she asked, sitting down at in chair with holograms activating around her. One was The Rip—the white-hot field of destructive energy due to intercept Ori-52 in what their auto-clock was displaying as one hour and thirty minutes.

He told her what the voice inside his mind had instructed him to do.

"It's them!" she said, gesturing outside *Amelia*'s hull, and then at the hologram in the center of their cockpit, showing tiny lights flickering on-and-off inside their blue crystal world." She tapped her heart. "I believe you … and we should do as they ask because what this hologram reads of their origin, the Neptunian species has been in this universe since the first massive stars. They know it, like we know our solar system."

"How vastly immense we see the universe, but another more advanced species doesn't," he sighed. "Okay, let's open an outside view from out there to in here."

A giant hologram of the bright blue sheet appeared at

the center of their cockpit. The Neptunians then appeared.

"They're little sparkling dots in the millions!" Lisa marveled. "And I know them … I believe I've *been* there with them inside that vast ocean that only looks like a sheet of blue crystal. I don't get how this is possible!"

Then, inside the hologram, one body emerged to stand in front of the crystal containment field, and a voice in high-pitched squeaks resounded through the cockpit as the fiber-optics hardware on the ceiling coursed with power.

Lisa put her hands over her ears, and the sounds decreased to the level of tolerability. "She's using our kidnapped Am to begin a translation, and our minds as conduits, Kent."

"She?" he said. "The voice sounds male to me."

"I am both genders," the Neptunian said. The fiber-optic ceiling began absorbing the entity's high-pitched, musical, screeching sounds in perfect unison with the entity's speech. "Shore is my name, translated in your English language," the Neptunian said.

Lisa fell back in her command chair, her eyes fixed on a mesmerizing sheen of the Neptunians appearing clear in the hologram at the center of their cockpit. "We can't pronounce any of their words, but I understanding *every* word she says."

"Me too, Lisa." Then Kent gestured at the time. "We have ten minutes, Shore, before The Rip as you call it destroys this universe."

More alien voices resounded from the blue crystal containment field.

"That is definitely like an ocean world they're living inside," Lisa said making sure her armchair programs were recording the entire scene at the center of their cockpit. "And I can even smell salt."

"From our subterranean ocean where we have been living for millions of years to preserve our species since gravity flung our planet out of Sigma Orionis," Shore said.

"All the biometric readings I've been using to analyze Shore, Lisa, tell us the Neptunians are mostly aquatic," he said across the aisle to her.

"Shore has the head of a porpoise, but her nose resembles that of our species; and her shiny gray body is that of a porpoise, but she's thinner, and has arms and legs."

"He has gray-blue arms and legs, and definitely is a combination of aquatic and mammalian," Kent added.

"I say her, you say him, so I'm confused whether Shore is female or male," Lisa whispered, obviously trying not to offend Shore.

"We are *both* male and female genders," Shore said.

"Wow—how evolution in the universe has taken some might big turns," Lisa chided.

"Look at us, male and female," Kent chuckled.

"From your knowledge center on this starship, and TIP, and Am," Shore interrupted because time was becoming scarce. "We have learned everything about Homo sapiens and your spirituality and our common connection to our creator," he added, calling TIP and Am out from the bright blue crystal containment field. They appeared as twinkling stars, and then materialized next to Shore. TIP looked like Leonardo Da Vinci's Vitruvian Man, and Am had the body of a bronze-skinned goddess. The Neptunians had given them both real bodies for their A.I. personas, fit perfectly to adapt to the Neptunian alien environment. They waved and then walked backwards, stepping slowly into the blue crystal world they appeared to want to join permanently.

"They're happy," Lisa said.

"But *we* won't be unless we can diffuse that Rip that's coming at us," Kent said, sitting back and letting his mind go blank. "If I just remain calm, my mind becomes a clearer conduit so Shore can communicate more clearly to me."

Lisa did the same. "Okay, Shore, what do we need to do to stop the destructive force ... but also save your species?"

Outside, Ori-52 had become a thriving planet with a habitable atmosphere. "Use the electron tracking beam on the *Amelia* to propel our ancient sun-pod into the graviton rip."

"After that, how will you manage to leave? To take an *entire* planet to safety?" Lisa asked.

In their focused state of concentration on the blue crystal world with Shore standing in holographic form in front of them, Shore's voice sounded old, beyond any ever heard with human ears.

"Lisa is right, Shore. If we propel the pod into The Rip," Kent began, his mind in a trance-like state of connectivity with Shore, "you and your people will surely be engulfed by it. The universe will have been healed, but surely Ori-52 that's just now reviving will be destroyed."

"As the time indicates—"

Shore motioned to the holographic clock.

"—will occur within forty-five minutes," Lisa said, the *Date-Time* hologram continuously projecting the time but still void of a specific date.

Then another holographic projection appeared, and Lisa motioned for it to synchronize with Shore's bright-blue crystal containment field. "Kent, have you ever seen such algorithms ... in 3D and photon particles?" Lisa gasped.

Amelia's ceiling was pulsing with new energy. "This isn't quantum-computer energy, Lisa, but string-theory *dimensional* energy because of the processing speed."

"Connecting with your plasma engine thrusters," Shore interrupted, his gray-blue facial expressions projecting certainty, and his deep-set green pupils showing wisdom. Shore's thin peach-colored lips were moving as if vibrating, the Neptunian language being audible still in fine high-pitched squeaks and dolphin-similar sounds. Shore also had little ears next to his porpoise-shaped head, the ears every so often twitching as if they also functioned as finely-tuned antennae to navigate their blue-crystal reality.

Amelia's engines ignited under the craft, lifting the starship slowly off Ori-52.

"Shore!" Lisa shouted. "I have your sun-pod engaged with *Amelia*'s attraction magnetics, but you still haven't answered the question as to how you and your species—"

"And Ori-52," Kent interrupted.

"Are going to make it out of the incoming Rip alive," Lisa said.

Shore opened up a holographic view under *Amelia*'s cockpit dome. Eternal night and white stars had given way to a powerful energy: the graviton-destroying rip forty minutes from unleashing destruction through the universe.

"One hundred kilometers and rising, Kent," Lisa said. "And we have the sun-pod we're supposed to propel into The Rip directly at our helm."

"I am charging our sun-pod now to act as antimatter, and to explode The Rip on contact with the graviton," Shore said.

"Shore," Kent began, "please give us *some* indication of

what will happen to you and your species. After all, you also have two of our own with you, TIP and Am."

Shore was adding energy to the blue-crystal containment field. The field and all its millions of twinkling Neptunians were extinguishing.

Kent tapped the hologram responsible for controlling propulsion on his armrest as another hologram of space and Ori-52's position in the quadrant appeared in front of them. "I'm launching off Ori-51."

"We have plasma engines at full force, Kent," Lisa began, adjusting fission-fusion to the correct mix and ensuring that the hull and all its bay doors were sealed.

Shore was now small and stepping back into the blue crystal containment field. "I am creating an extra electron-proton energy that *Amelia's* particle accelerator needs to propel Ori-52 out of The Rip's influence."

"Oh, I think I know what Shore's planning," Lisa said.

Kent had initiated the powerful process to use the extra energy to fling the Neptunian sun pod at space-fold speed into The Rip, sealing it. "What's the plan?"

"A dimensional portal," she answered.

"Dimension six to be exact, Kent and Lisa," Shore corrected.

"It sounds like you know a lot about The Rip. It's obviously been in existence since you've been here in the universe, huh?" Kent asked.

Shore had almost disappeared into the bright blue crystal now undulating with a shining energy *Amelia* was displaying as *unknown*.

"In reality, we've discovered that *unknown* is the graviton, neutrino, and dark energy mixing to alter a particular spot in Space-Time into a portal leading into another dimension," Kent said.

"Dimension six to be exact," Shore said, sending the

Amelia the mixture.

Every time the starship received Shore's communication, the ceiling flickered and flashed with jolts and flurries of photon-electron particle energy that re-translated to human understanding.

"You now will have the formulae, to take back to Earth in the future," Shore said.

Kent stood up and approached the blue-shining world of the Neptunians, but then shielded his eyes. "When did you discover this mix?"

Shore was now a twinkling light like a blue dwarf star about to join his species Rip, and our best scientists managed to keep it at bay in this universe. The Rip is seasonal—"

"Like the sun spot cycle of our sun," Lisa said, motioning to a hologram of Earth's solar system.

"The Rip appears through a crack in the universe every one billion years," Shore began. "No one can predict, however, where it will materialize."

"How did you know to revive out of your stasis?" Kent asked.

Shore was now gone and speaking only into their minds, and they were receiving him as images of his former self that had stood among them.

"Your appearance on our rogue world jump-started our resuscitation, and we immediately began an exchange of knowledge about your species and predicament with your starship, and your A.I.s, Am and TIP. Your intentions were to help us."

"So that's why Am froze after we landed," Lisa said.

Shore continued, "The Rip must always be confronted and closed in the Multiverse, or all matter will extinguishes, in what *you* describe as death."

"Kent," Lisa interrupted, "we need to start propelling

their sun-pod into the rip now!" She had a desperate expression as she worked with holograms to assess and analyze The Rip, now closing fast on them.

Meanwhile, Shore had disappeared into the bright-blue containment field, and the hologram of them all faded from their cockpit.

"They're all gone," Kent said. Then he glanced up at the hologram still under the cockpit's ceiling, still coursing with fiber-optic hardware energy. "They're still on Ori-52, but not for long."

Above *Amelia*, the bright-blue crystal containment field was shimmering and soaring through space, leaving Ori-52's atmosphere with a white contrail.

Amelia's core engine ignited.

"I'm strapped in," Kent said, watching their cockpit elongate into a glossy white thread as *Amelia*, their giant starship, spiraled around Ori-52 and whipped the pod into space-fold mode to appear in five minutes inside The Rip.

Lisa had been tracking the Neptunians whose containment field had suddenly disappeared off *Amelia*'s radar. "Now they're gone," she said in a sad voice, and ran her fingers through her hair. "Gone outside ... and my neural connection with them gone."

Kent de-activated the look-out hologram. The Rip had become a blinding force. "They're gone from here, but alive in Dimension six. At least we know they'll be alive...and hopefully their sun-pod will be enough of a graviton force to counter the effects of The Rip."

"Oh, I activated another AI, Kent," she said.

"What's the name of this one?" he laughed.

"Zoe," she replied, initializing the hologram that appeared in the aisle between them. With Asian characteristics and an athletic composition, Zoe began synching with their biometrics and initialized their holographic projections next to the stasis pods in preparation for slumber.

"Countdown to contact between the sun-pod and The Rip, Zoe?" Lisa asked.

"Space-folding now to get us outta here!" Kent exclaimed.

Zoe began, "Five, four, three, two, one…"

Time stopped. Kent felt himself floating above his sparkling body. The cockpit had altered into a multi-prism of rainbows around them—light refractions of Dimension Six dancing everywhere. He tried to speak, but couldn't. Lisa was mouthing words, but he couldn't hear her. Even though his hands and fingers could move through one another, defying Space-Time, although he could feel him; and even though physics dictated no state of existence could *possibly* survive in the universe as they were existing in it now, they were still alive. One long rainbow shone on Lisa's forehead, and the cockpit flared with light, and then faded to blackness.

When the cockpit lights illuminated, they were back to their former state before they had unleashed the Neptunian sun-pod into The Rip.

Lisa was standing motionless in front of her command chair.

"Lisa!"

Then he saw her chest rise and fall in her delicate breaths.

"*Whew.*" Checking out his own condition, he stood up out of his chair, began the reactivation process to re-install Zoe among them, and then returned to fold Lisa's hands peacefully across her laps like a medieval maiden waiting for a kiss.

A wall of cold air suddenly hit him, throwing him into

his stasis tube that shut, automatically locking him in a deep stasis....

As dregs of suspension coating slipped off his numb extremities that felt icy cold and tingly, he woke up. Lisa was almost in his face, screaming, and manipulating reading in a discerning expression on his biometric hologram resuscitator. "Kent, we've been approached by a rogue planet. *Amelia* woke me up first, a half-an-hour ago, and ever since, I've been trying to discover where the galaxy, Sigma Orionis, is situated."

"What?" He yawned. *Something doesn't feel right!* "What's the date and time?"

"I don't know, Kent, this quad in space is showing up weird on all our instruments...as if an unknown force of element is interfering with *Amelia*'s fiber-optic network to our stasis pods," she said angrily.

"*Hm*, ouch! What a helluva headache I've got," he said, realizing stats on his vitals were showing his cerebral cortex more active with emotion.

"It's our neural connection with the starship, Kent...severed I believe due to this unknown interference," she whispered, obviously bothered by every loud noise.

After he stood up groggily from his stasis pod and stepped behind it to change, he noticed he wasn't wearing his usual biometric stasis suit. *How could I remain in a stasis pod without a biometric link to Amelia? Is some type of new or added system up and running in here?* The suit he had on was a Level-2 suit, meant for cockpit interface with *Amelia*, and his was dotted with stains and a few tears. *And I thought this starship had more A.I.'s in its program to assist us. Where are they?* He felt dizzy and disoriented, brain fog clogging his thoughts. "What the hell?"

"Hell what?" Lisa asked irritated. "Just get over here and help me, Kent."

"Sure," he said, quickly changing, sipping some water, and sitting down in his command chair. "Something doesn't feel right, Lisa."

"About...." she waited.

"Just everything," he gestured in frustration. "No A.I.'s, no *Date-Time* signatures under the center hologram that's displaying a lifeless black planet around which we're we about to establish orbit." He peered up to the ceiling coursing with its usual fiber-optic hardware, until his eyes stopped over the center of their U-shaped cockpit. "Something was there ... someone? Gray-blue?"

"We're supposed to explore this place, Kent," she said. "That's why the *Amelia* woke me up. Then she had a look of mystical knowledge waft into her eyes. "But you're right. *Amelia* hasn't received *any* data from our gas chromatograph, or spectral radiometer. Weird. It's like we're in another Space-Time!"

"But that's impossible, Lisa!" He checked the hologram at the center of their cockpit displaying a black shiny world floating through dead space. The world appeared halved, as if some massive alien saw, or asteroid, had bombed out a quarter of the planet. A quick idea popped into his fog-filled brain, and he gasped. "Lisa!" His knees buckled under him.

"Kent, what's wrong?" She ran to him.

Pulling himself up from the hologram stage at the center of their cockpit, he could barely manage to breathe. "What's the date, Lisa ... the date?"

She appeared confused as if the words "date and time" had been sliced out of her vocabulary. "I— I—"

Her hands began shaking and she ran her fingers

through her hair.

"—this neural implant ... ship connection has me a bit confused," she laughed. Suddenly she began staring at him as if an invisible entity had usurped her body. "Time has stopped Kent. There *is* no date and time."

Confusion wound around him like a frost-biting coldness he could feel but not recall. "There's no such thing as *no* time, Lisa." He began enlarging holograms around the cockpit—activating them to trace their steps since they began their mission. "It feels like we left Mars just months ago." Then he saw his hands. A few wrinkles. But that would mean they'd been gone hundreds of years! "Lisa!" He pulled her to their biometric readings next to their stasis pods. "We don't have an exact date and time, but we do have these...and they're telling us we're—"

"Oh my, gosh!" She stepped back with her hands over her mouth. "I'm six hundred and ninety-two years old?" She fainted, and he lifted her up and guided her to her command chair.

Outside their craft the yellow haze of dimensional flight had muted into a purple show of lightening sparks. Visions streamed through his mind. Snow, a skeleton of a landscape, and fog like white water snakes trying to bite them. He began slapping his arms to chase them off.

Regaining consciousness, she grabbed his arm. "Kent, I don't know what happened to us, but for some reason we're here, and we have a job to do." She rubbed her sweaty forehead and drank some water a robotic thrust into her hands. The robot too appeared to have been taken prisoner from an entity wheedling its way within it.

Inside a hologram monitoring the distant cosmos over a light-year-away, a little ribbon of white-hot energy appeared.

They stopped, hypnotized by its distance while intuitively knowing its power and capability.

"I've seen this—"

"We know this!" she exclaimed, pushing her fingers through her bangs.

He paused and glanced around, his biceps hardening into two taut knots. He tried to recall images from Earth and Mars. "I can't remember *anything* about home," he began. "What about you?"

She ignited holograms of Earth and colonies on Mars. "They're all inside *Amelia*, but you're right, Kent. I can't remember *anything* anymore about home." She was shaking, and propped up by her command chair. The instruments and apps on the armrests were glowing stats, shining code, undulating frequencies, and land-based images—all showering the front of her body.

Then he saw his reflection in the giant hologram at the center of their cockpit. In the background was supposed to be situated Ori-52. "Is this Sigma Orionis? I don't know, Lisa. I feel like Space-Time is off, especially since we don't have an A.I. standing around us, and the *Date-Time* rendering isn't working." He hit the wall, and the light source throughout the cockpit illuminated a giant pane of blue that quickly disappeared into the fabric of the fiber-optic ceiling.

"What was that?" she asked.

Pacing the floor while staring frightfully into the vibrant coursing hardware, he gestured for her to stay put. "This isn't our universe, Lisa," he began. "It's just a feeling I have, but we're somewhere else."

"Yeah," she said, wistfully, "you're right, Kent...a gut feeling that's like God's voice inside of me. I hear the voice … loud and strong."

They said in unison: "Seal this universe!"

Suddenly, a hologram activated over Lisa's com-chair arm.

"There's an alien pod orbiting the planet, Kent," she said, swiping up the round pod that looked like a shining star circling the planet.

He checked the incoming readings. "The pod is an artificial sun."

"And we need to begin reviving this place," she added.

They both stopped suddenly, staring deeply into each other's eyes.

"We've done this before, Lisa," he said, knowing he was moving on autopilot. He walked to the airlock and began preparing their Level-5 suits. "How else would I know exactly what to do?"

"The same reason I'm doing what *I'm* doing," she replied, crying and chuckling at the same time. She had already activated two A.I.'s from *Amelia's* database to sync with their biometrics and monitor atmospheric conditions as *Amelia* flew past the sun-pod that had begun spraying the rogue world with resuscitating warmth and light.

When Kent looked out one of the airlock portals as he prepared one of the Jeeps for surface exploration, he believed he saw bronze-skinned woman staring in at him, waving him down to Ori-52. "Ah!" he shouted, careening back inside the safety of their cockpit.

Lisa reached for a tube of water that had rushed up to her from the food station below ship. "Did you see her too?" she whispered, her fingers shaking. "Please tell me yes, because I've been seeing all sorts of things popping in-n-out of existence that's been making me believe I'm crazy!" She laughed, but her every movement was beginning to exude terror beyond belief.

When she sat down, obviously working hard to fend

off her perceived attackers, Kent felt confusion race through his mind. He was cold now, an experience he remembered walking through during an intense exoplanet exploration. He couldn't recall exactly *what* had happened, except that a voice within him was trying to communicate something to him, but he felt too agitated to listen to it.

"Something went wrong, before we landed here, Kent," she suddenly said, gasping.

"I know. I feel that same way too. But let's make sure that whatever went wrong before doesn't go wrong now!" He sat down and began a systematic track of the sun-pod that had already finished two orbits around the rogue world. The yellow inside the hologram had a calming effect on his racing thoughts, and he yielded to the peace, staring hypnotic into the light communicating to his brain. He recalled battling against a terrible trouble—a horrible destructive force in the universe. He suddenly spotted it. "There!"

"Where?" she asked.

He left his chair and raced to the giant hologram at the center of the cockpit. In the distance was shimmering a white-hot line of intense power, enough to annihilate everything. "The Rip."

"We've got to stop it," she added. "Stop the Rip...*yes*, I know now. I remember, I think."

"Again!" he added. Then a peaceful feeling flowed through his mind, a calm he had known but without images to ground him. "This is our job, Lisa."

She touched his hand and tears fell on her cheeks where she swept them away with her fingers. "Not going home to Mars?"

He shrugged. "I don't know ... but as long as there's another universe that needs our help, we have to take on that Rip out there and destroy it." He felt angry. "I don't know why us … or if—"

"We're caught in a palindrome of sorts then!" she yelled. Then she cried, and he held her. "But I want to go home."

He hugged her. "At least we're together … and not dead, but alive."

Her eyes were reflecting The Rip, still tiny like a white painted fingernail over a light-year away from them. "It's coming, Kent …soon."

Their starship activated to life. "Four hours, thirty minutes and twenty-two seconds to detonation, Lisa," *Amelia*'s A.I. articulated.

"What's your name?" Lisa asked.

"Zoe," the tall brown-haired A.I. replied.

Lisa left his side. "You get the suits, Kent." She dried her eyes, took a bite of her food bar, and then donned her wrist devices. "Maybe after we stop The Rip—"

"Again," he interrupted, "and maybe again after this."

Her body sagged in the fatigue of it all. "Okay, again whatever! Then, *Amelia*, you take us home, ya hear?"

"Yes, Lisa. Yes, Kent."

###

Grandma's Call at Dusk

Old gray hunching stubborn barn!
The murk seeped under it—
The floor spaces between boards,
Then mere inches to the ground.
Hail fed you;
Rain, snow, ice,
Tree roots, angry autumn leaves,
Scorching sunshine (and a tornado!),
Moon phases,
Planets passing you overhead,
In the feathery Milky Way,
Thick with stars.
I miss you!

Your hardy foundation is no more.

You're *so* ancient,
Worn well by steps from the past
And steps not taken in the future.
Where will you be in fifty years?
The sun won't splinter you then,
While Earth's precession spins out
Another 26,000 years
As new clouds ripple and thunder over you,
And memories of me in your DNA, buried.

No—not yet. I'm *here*! See me. I'm 9,
Still sitting in your splintered corners,
Where we meet, and I touch your dirt-tossed
boards smelling of the four seasons,
with a hint of fresh rain and cut-grass crispness
   mmmm...

Every boards *creaks, creaks*—
Strings vibrating music on your shiny violin,
Weak delicate strings that any moment might
    snap,
Sending me hurling to the dust underneath
Your exciting, bowed, dirt-woven boards:
The tapestry of your life since Grandpa and
    my dad
Nailed you together in this deep woods.

Now, the tractor grinds in the distance.
Grandpa!
In the vacant corner with slants of light
Streaming in, illuminating tossing particles of
    dust,
I sit,
Listening to flies, and a bee, and a wasp in the
    upper corner,
And a happy cricket
That time is playing on its vocal cords....
What sounds!
Then quiet.

The wind tosses in, and a tiny dust devil dances
At the center of the bumpy knotted floor,
lifting musty hay, a few old black grumbling
    leaves—
survivors of last winter—
And other breeze wheezes through the boards;
Again, a beautiful song.
I can't sing it!
I pull my knees up against my chin,
And cry, in the heat of disappearing daylight.
Then, I breathe.

I could go to sleep, right now, until....

A wasp whirs;
A frog's breast beats: *ribbit, ribbit*....
Movements under boards
As shafts of lowering light
In the dusk peek in, and wake me up
And the tractor, again that grinds...
It's Grandpa, coming in from the field!
With him, a new song is on the horizon, sunset,
In orange through the western boards.
"Ahhh, do I haveta leave?"
"I don't wanna go!"

"Joiiiceee!"
Grandma!
[I thought she and Grandpa were dead?]
Her breath is on the breeze
That just wafted to me through the oak trees
Outside the sad old shoulder-slumping gray shed.
Now look. My name on their breaths is heading
    west!
"Joiiiceee...." she calls, again.
"Drats. I don't wanna go yet."

I stand up to call back to her,
But the tractor grinding and revving in the field
interrupts me. She's always calling.
She'll never let me be. So,
"I'm here! I'm coming!"
It's dinner time now, on the farm. 5:30 sharp.
The cathedral boards
Above, beside, and below me,
And the smudgy window pane on my left,

Are so tall and thick, they make me dizzy,
Like the spinning dust my tennis shoes
Just stirred up.

"*Oooo*," the owl outside just said, high up in a
    pine tree.
Or is the *Oooo Oooo* a dove's voice?
I heard you this morning!
And every summer morning before that!
Outside the creaking stubborn door
That seems to want to keep me in
But has no handle or rubber threshold from
    the hot and cold.
Leaves are now rustling, like foil that
Grandma rips off to protect lunchmeat from
    spoiling.
Another storm is coming;
Soon, the dark.

"Joiiiceee!"
She's still calling me,
Beyond the sad gray barn
Now in total shade inside an eclipse,
Where the tractor's still grinding
And her voice is circling the world
On the wind to my ears *always* hearing.

ABOUT THE AUTHOR

J.P. Osterman is a science fiction author and blogger. She won the prestigious Rupert Hughes Award at the Maui Writers' Conference for her novel, *The Matter Stream*, the only sci-fi book ever to win the award. J.P. is one of five finalists for the 2015 Patrick D. Smith Literary Award. Her one-act play, *The Man Next to Me*, won First Place at the Southern California Writers' Conference. She subsequently transformed the award winning play into the novel *Pete's Crossroad*. Thirty years in the making, she recently compiled and released an anthology of her short stories entitled: *Commuter Collection: Short Stories from the Edge*.

J.P. has written nine novels, primarily science fiction, from exploring Mars in *Cosmic Rift*, to spacefolding to an ancient alien world in *First Communication* (Book I, The Nelta Series,), *Battlefield Matrix* (Book II), and *Astrocity Sagan* (Book III). Her other novels include: *The Screaming Stone*, and, *Corporate Revenge*. She co-wrote a play with Richard Mariani, *Salt and Sand Never Tasted Better*, published in the anthology, *Love and Rockets*. She is also a contributing writer in the anthology, *Gratitude*, published by the Space Coast Writers' Guild. J.P. currently released her devotional, *God Designed: 366 Days of Inspiration*.

She completed her Bachelor's Degree in English (Emphasis in Writing) from the University of San Diego, and received her Master's Degree in Education from Azusa Pacific University. She is a member of Brevard Scribblers and the Space Coast Writers' Guild. You will find a synopsis of each of her books with excerpts on her

website at: www.jposterman.com